SUBPRIME FACTOR

SUBPRIME FACTOR

JEFFREY D. SCHLAMAN

Subprime Factor
Published by Synergy Books
P.O. Box 80107
Austin, Texas 78758

For more information about our books, please write to us, call 512.478.2028, or visit our website at www.synergybooks.net.

Publisher's Cataloging-in-Publication
(Provided by Quality Books, Inc.)

Schlaman, Jeffrey D.
Subprime factor / Jeffrey D. Schlaman.
p. cm.
LCCN 2008930839
ISBN-13: 978-0-9815462-5-4
ISBN-10: 0-9815462-5-0

1. Subprime mortgage loans--United States--Fiction.
2. Consumer credit--United States--Fiction.
3. Conspiracies--Fiction. 4. Auburn (Calif.)--Fiction.
5. Suspense fiction. I. Title.

PS3619.C41S83 2008 813'.6
QBI08-600196

Editorial services provided by Kristin Johnson of The Happy Guy Marketing

10 9 8 7 6 5 4 3 2 1

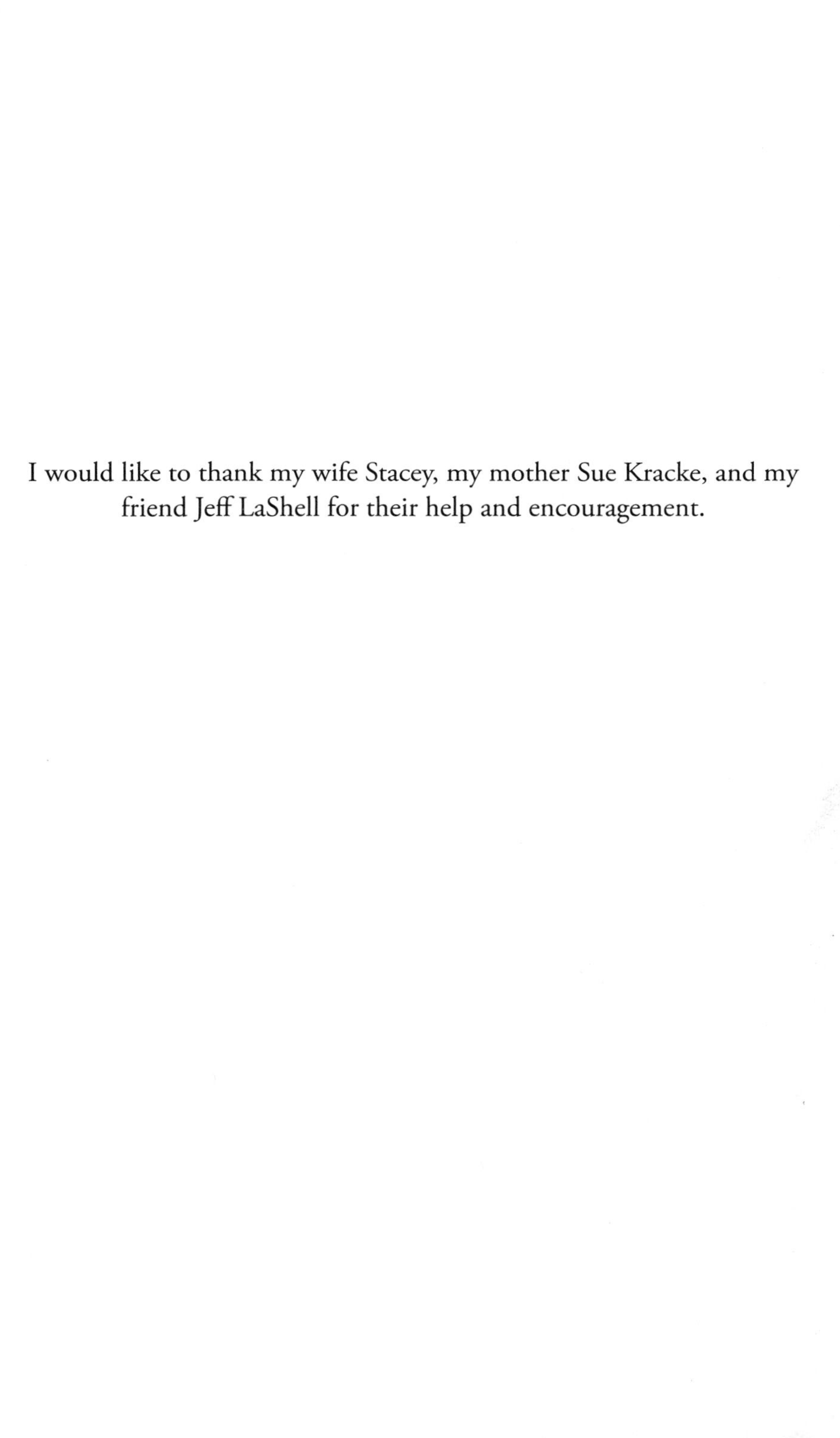

I would like to thank my wife Stacey, my mother Sue Kracke, and my friend Jeff LaShell for their help and encouragement.

CHAPTER 1

"People of the same trade seldom meet together, even for merriment and diversion, but the conversation ends in a conspiracy against the public, or in some contrivance to raise prices."

—Adam Smith, Scottish philosopher and economist (1723–1790)

Economic Calamity
Dark Night in Georgia
August 3, 2007, 7:53 p.m.
By Martin Cheyne

Georgia should not be this dark in late summer before sunset. I'm sensing omens of disaster.

I'm blogging today from a parking spot just across the bridge from a famous place. The birthplace of the Federal Reserve Bank of the United States of America—born in 1910. We all knew the White House press briefing today would say that real wage growth was positive, but we're headed for an economic meltdown, as anyone watching the indicators would know.

I believe the Federal Reserve Bank was a conspiracy among the tycoons of the early twentieth century to create the economic boom of the roaring twenties and the crash of 1929 that someone must have had the foresight to have predicted.

This is the institution that created the Great Depression nearly a century ago and is creating the new economic disaster our country (and the world) will become in the twenty-first century.

In the 1920s, America had a massive expansion of credit. Debt, and the economy, boomed for nearly a decade. Ten percent margin requirements began massive speculation in the stock market, and the prices soared.

The short-term creation of money (through debt) caused huge consumer spending. *The Great Gatsby,* flappers, new shiny cars, and partying are the legacy of the era. There was unprecedented industrial growth, and people began demanding leisure time and newer and better things—much like today. In the easy money without getting their hands dirty. In the 1970s and 1980s, the baby boomers wanted even more spending and partying. Let's face it, the only thing my hippie parents gave the world was Ben and Jerry's. And of course, some of those baby boomers are in charge of banks. Some even work for the Federal Reserve. They duped those of us who partied through the Reagan and Clinton years.

The tycoons set the ball in motion almost a century ago. Senator Nelson Aldrich and the assistant secretary to the U.S. Treasury staged a duck-hunting trip on behalf of his wealthy buddies. He and his six plutocrat friends—later to become known as the "First Name Club" and including representatives from J. P. Morgan, the Warburg Family, the Rockefeller family, and the Rothschild family—met in a swanky hotel. Not in Vegas, which didn't exist yet, but on a Georgian island.

Sen. Aldrich did double-whammy duty as a member of the Senate National Monetary Committee and as father-in-law to Nelson D. Rockefeller (not to mention doing business with J. P. Morgan). Over cognac and cigars, these men took careful aim at a target more help-less than pintails and mallards: the American public. They set up a banking cartel to provide a system that limited competition, mini-mized risk, and used the powers of the federal government to protect and grow the incredible wealth that already existed. Nearly a century later, we're all suffering the onslaught of the Frankenstein's monster created by these men, who, some have said, represented one-fourth of the wealth of the entire planet at the time. Back then, it was a secret. In the modern era, companies pretend to abide by freedom of infor-mation and full disclosure while they cut deals to "save the economy" under our noses.

If you've been a regular reader, you know my views on finance and the way that the American public has been swindled. I had a nasty surprise at a camping trip with three of my old college buddies not too long ago, sometime in July. One of them has discovered "creative accounting" at his firm. People have been killed for less.

No wonder it's dark as Hades at nearly five o'clock in Georgia in August.

Trackback / Comment / Blog This

Jekyll Island, Georgia, August 3, 2007, 7:55 p.m.

While the swirling charcoal skies weren't entirely unusual for coastal Georgia in August, neither the mainstream news, nor the National Weather Service had detected any kind of tropical storm front. When thirty-two-year-old Martin Cheyne left JAX, the airport in Jacksonville, Florida, two hours ago, the partly sunny sky hadn't kept the humidity from drenching his tropical short-sleeved shirt and jeans on the short walk to the Hertz car rental lot. The weather also plastered his spiky hair to his temples and made his feet perspire profusely, although his Teva walking shoes cooled his toes.

As he neared the Georgia coast, he was cagey. He didn't list his GPS location on the blog entry that he planned to post online from his laptop, although he might as well have. He didn't particularly want the average Net surfer to learn that he'd traveled to Jekyll Island. His blog, Economic Calamity, ranked in the Google top 10,000 for the popular search engine. Not only that, he'd been featured on the Drudge Report Web site. His lectures were podcast, where undoubtedly they bored the hell out of anyone who wasn't an economist or a conspiracy theorist who hated the corrupt, evil, fetid organization called the Federal Reserve. He'd unknowingly made himself a target.

Martin was just a University of Nevada-Reno economics TA (he preferred "instructor") working on a midlife PhD. If you didn't have a doctorate, it was damn near impossible to get anyone to take your theories seriously, and he didn't even have the shield of tenure. Guys like that pseudo-American-Indian professor at the University of Colorado might be safe in lying and attacking the 9/11 victims in his university lectures, but Martin's PhD dissertation and his mission to discredit the Federal Reserve exposed him to all sorts of repercussions. A failed attempt to defend his dissertation would be the least of them.

He threw his laptop onto the backseat of the rental car he was writing from and took a bite of his granola bar to settle the queasiness in his stomach that he couldn't yet attribute to hush puppies and Southern-fried catfish. With shaking fingers, Martin put the PT Cruiser in drive and crossed the narrow two-lane road that led from mainland Georgia across the intercoastal waterway to Jekyll Island, whose name sounded straight out of a B movie and whose history made it an exotic playground for the jet set. As he drove along the narrow roadway set up only a few feet from the dark brackish water of the salt marsh on both sides, he felt as though he were crossing into another world. Discovered by the Western world about half a millennium ago, the 5,700-acre island was originally a Spanish colony and, over the centuries, had been home to privateers and slave traders. What made it of interest to Martin, with historic irony on this particular weekend, was the secret meeting that, as Martin noted in his blog, led to the creation of the Federal Reserve Bank of the United States. The highway, and the last vehicle he had seen on this gloomy night, was about six miles back, when he stopped at a Georgia State Park greeting station to pay the three-dollar parking fee. He then continued north about a mile until he arrived at the Jekyll Island Club Hotel.

The original hotel where Senator Aldrich and his friends took aim at America's bald eagle rather than a duck now matched a fairy-tale castle in its grandeur. The painted brick turrets and cupolas of the antediluvian Victorian-era hotel and the surrounding of southern live oak trees covered thick with Spanish moss gave the entire area a dark, gothic feel. Martin briefly noted the surroundings, feeling as though he had stepped back in time a hundred years, as he wheeled his Samsonite luggage into the elegant lobby of the hotel. He didn't pause to admire the furnishings, civilly dismissed the wave of a porter, and checked in with the sleepy looking young Asian woman at the desk. "*Apa kabar*?" he greeted, recognizing her as Indonesian.

She smiled and responded in kind with a Southern edge to her words as she gave Martin the old-fashioned metal keys to his room. They both yawned, and Martin recognized the need for a nap. But first, he had to rewrite and post his blog as well as chronicle his research. He might not have another chance this weekend, if history repeated itself.

On his way to his room, he toured the conference room facilities. One of them was named "The Federal Reserve Room." He wondered how much that cost the stodgy tartan-turtleneck, old-money men and women he passed in the halls. They talked loudly on their BlackBerrys and Bluetooth headsets, as if there were anyone around to impress.

He scowled at the typically stiff and smug oil portrait of Senator Aldrich on the third floor. A plaque noted that there had, in fact, been a secret meeting held there. It was a nonchalant mention, a bit of trivia for tourists perhaps.

Whiffs of tobacco, bleach, and magnolias mingled in Martin's nose. He slid the key into the lock for room 309. The designers had appointed the room in classic Southern hospitality. He put away the bare minimum of clothes and toiletries, then went straight to the writing desk and plugged in his laptop. When he booted up, he worked on his blog while recording his thoughts, notes, and observations. Ostensibly they were for his dissertation—a reference here, a statistic there. He wanted to establish that he had written his dissertation in this hotel, and that uninterrupted academic toil was the purpose of this trip. He located a Wi-Fi network, made corrections to his blog, and entered it into the blogosphere.

Four hours later, after a long stretch of writing, a nap, and a shower, Martin set out to explore the hotel. Instinct drew him back down to the lobby, where he stared at the aged black-and-white pictures on the walls. The hotel was built in the late nineteenth century and, though refurbished and modernized, was still decorated with antique furniture and dark-painted walls. The room was well lit by overhead lights, but the furnishing and the dark interior colors made it feel cold and a little claustrophobic. The heavy rain outside, accompanied by loud crashes of thunder and bright flashes of light emitting from the dark outside the windows scared the hell out of Martin, who was nervous enough without the bad weather. Martin was from a small town in California and wasn't used to weather like this, especially in August. The front desk was behind him—lit further by a small desk lamp—but no clerk was manning the desk at the moment.

He stood alone, at 11:30 p.m., carefully studying the portraits on the wall.

The cold, ghostlike, black-and-white faces of the richest and most powerful men in early twentieth-century America stared back at him. Rockefeller, J. P. Morgan, Joseph Pulitzer, and William Vanderbilt posed with their families on the beach outside this very hotel over one hundred years ago. There was no personality or humanity to the images, even by stiff portraiture standards of the time. Martin felt the hair on his arms and neck stand up. He sensed danger, and it was more than just the immediate environment. He was being watched.

A door slammed from behind the desk, and Martin jumped. A plump, twenty-something blond woman with a peachy glow to her skin and a top too tight for her bosoms walked out of the office and opened a ledger sitting behind the counter. Her name badge read, "Wendy D." She noticed Martin, smiled, and said in a thick Georgia drawl, "Hard to sleep with this weather, ain't it?"

"Um, yeah," Martin muttered.

"Well if y'all are looking for something to do tonight, you are probably out of luck. This weather is real bad and might get worse. Vincent's Pub around back might be open for a few more minutes if you want to grab a drink or something. Dining room's closed."

"That's okay, I'm not hungry. I just want to look around for a while. I'm doing some research on this hotel."

"Research? What kind of research?" Wendy leaned over the counter toward him, obviously interested. "Some say this place is haunted, you know. People in top hats and maid uniforms right out of an old movie just up and appear. And if you pass by the dining room, now—as I said, it's closed, kitchen's locked—you might hear footsteps and a ruckus. Why, some of the staff think they eavesdropped on all those old tycoons conspirin' with their big wheelings and dealings. I guess business goes on even if you're dead!" She laughed at her own joke. "One night right here where I'm standing, I even heard with my own ears—"

Martin smiled and interrupted pleasantly. "No, nothing that exciting, I'm afraid. I'm more interested in the history…for a paper I'm writing."

"A paper? Like for school?" She looked confused, probably by Martin's age. Thanks to poor genes, wild partying in his younger days, and sun exposure, he could pass for forty. His black hair had grayed around his temples, and because he refused to look like a typical professor with glasses, he squinted a lot, bringing out wrinkles around his eyes.

"I'm writing a book. Well, a dissertation, I guess you could say. I'm working on a PhD."

"Oh, that is great!" Wendy said with some forced enthusiasm. "I start my senior year at Georgia Tech in a couple weeks. I'm studying environmental science. I used to want to be a nurse, but my mama is a nurse and she is always tired, so I..."

As Wendy rambled on about her life story, Martin stopped listening. He caught a glimpse of a gray shadow that stalked down the hallway to his left.

"Actually," Martin cut Wendy off mid-sentence, "I think I'll try to grab that drink before the pub closes."

"Oh, well, good night!" Wendy smiled with the same forced cheeriness and returned to studying the ledger.

Martin strode briskly toward the pub, a hundred yards down the hallway in the opposite direction from the shadow. Every few steps he glanced behind him to see if he noticed anyone following him, but he saw nothing.

When he arrived, the entire room, which could comfortably seat an entire football team and cheer squad, was empty except for a male bartender—fifties, in a black silk vest, tie, and white shirt—who was wiping down tables.

Martin waved. "Is it too late to get a beer?"

"Not at all, sir, we are open for another twenty minutes." The man smiled, obviously relieved to see a customer. "Slow night tonight with the hurricane coming."

Hurricane? The barman had to be fucking kidding. "Does that mean the one-horse road leading out of here gets washed away?" Martin sat on a red leather barstool in the middle of the bar.

"It might—the highest point on the island is only sixteen feet above sea level," the bartender said calmly. "If a category four or five hurricane hits, they say this island is done for. We've been pretty lucky here on Jekyll Island. Katrina was too far west, Andrew, back in 1992, stayed to the south, and way back in 1989, Hugo blasted South Carolina—missing us to the North. The weatherman on WTEV doesn't seem to think there is anything to worry about...besides there hasn't been a major hurricane since 1890, so they tell me. What can I get you, sir?"

Martin almost asked for arsenic, considering he already felt like he was in a murder mystery movie and his stomach felt as if he'd already swallowed acid. He wondered how the bartender could give his gloomy weather analysis so casually. "Whatever is on tap—whatever you like."

The bartender pulled a tall glass from under the counter and tipped back the handle of a tap labeled Sweet Georgia Brown. He handed it to Martin with an affable smile. "Can I have your room number, sir, for the hotel tab?"

Martin had just managed to spit out the numbers 309 when he caught a whisper of gray in his peripheral vision. He heard someone else walk in and pull up a stool just a short way down the bar.

"I'll have one of those too," said the man. "Charge it to room 309." He smiled at his cleverness and looked at Martin, who quaffed his glass of Sweet Georgia Brown in a hell of a hurry. The bartender had his back turned as he electronically charged the two beers to Martin's room. Martin had no other recourse but to look at the newcomer.

The man was about fifty. His T-shirt, with a seductive, scantily dressed hula girl on the front, strained in a futile attempt to contain his beer belly, which bulged over his too-tight shorts. His facial expression reminded Martin of sedentary rock, and his yellowish teeth as well as his gravelly voice indicated a decades-long, three-pack-a-day habit. He wore battered and mud-crusted Nike running shoes.

Martin felt sweat form on the palms of his hands. The guy didn't look like the old duffers who could afford a two-hundred-dollar-per-night hotel like this one, and his attire certainly didn't fit with the weather outside.

Martin hopped off the barstool, stuttered a quick "thank you" to the bartender, and walked hastily out of the pub back toward his room.

As Martin hit the second floor stairway landing, he stopped and nearly fell back down the stairs. The mystery man knew which room he was staying in. After his narrow escape with his friends Paul, Phil, and Doug in the Sierra Nevada Mountains in California, Martin knew he was being tailed. He also knew that the people who likely paid the two hundred dollars a night for the T-shirted man's room played for high stakes.

Martin pivoted and hopped back down the stairs through the lobby past Wendy, who looked up from her ledger in puzzlement. Martin rushed to the front door.

"Don't go out there," Wendy shouted.

"To hell with this," Martin called back, and threw open the front door of the hotel. He ran out into the blasting rain.

A hurricane was safer than staying in that hotel.

Offices of the Secretary of the Treasury, Washington, D.C., 11:30pm

Secretary of the Treasury Franklin "Frank" L. Pearson had just started on his second glass of earthy-tasting, bonfire-scented whiskey when his chief of staff, Myra Eckworth, interrupted his drink and his discussion with a phone call. "Mr. Secretary, for you, urgent."

Pearson smiled at his private-sector colleagues, four men and one woman, all representing wealthy American banks, companies, and fortunes. Earlier, Pearson had sent the advance guard to Georgia, namely the remaining two players in the deal, the architects of tonight's pre-duck hunt conference. One of the men had joked that to divert attention in the media, from whatever outlets he didn't already own, Secretary Pearson should ask the vice president to arrange a quail-hunting trip, whereupon he could accidentally shoot one of his good friends...again.

Of course, they might not get to Georgia if Pearson's friends didn't call. He'd been making idle political and business talk with his guests for an hour, and still no call from the man he still thought of as "Saddleback." The hair on his arms itched, as it often did when he felt uneasy.

"If it's not our friends, it's just my wife confirming she'll join us down there in the South," Pearson said. "Providing there's no hurricane."

Pearson picked up the phone as his colleagues politely laughed. Even the woman, a light-skinned African-American from the black Creole elite in Louisiana, chuckled; she was one of the boys.

"Secretary Pearson," he said into the receiver.

The unmistakable sound of Georgia rain echoed across the telephone lines. "Frank, it's me."

Pearson frowned in puzzlement at his old Yale fraternity Skull and Bones and current PPT crony, Saddleback. "Well, finally. Hello. Did the rain knock out the telephone lines and the cell phone towers?"

"We have a problem."

"Well, you know what we do in Washington—we either throw money at it or cover it up. Unless she's dead. And unless she is a he." Pearson laughed at his own joke.

"He's on the loose—we think one of them is on the island." Frustration and panic filled the other man's voice. "We should have finished that business in California."

Pearson's voice rose. "Who is on the loose?"

"You know…the group from California. The best guess I've got now is that they are working for the Chinese. Or the Russians. Or maybe the Saudis. Or, hell, I don't know, some group that hates America. My people are on it. Listen, Frank…this weekend may not be such a good idea. We can literally take a rain check."

Pearson hadn't risen to his position without the ability to make swift, smart decisions. He glanced at the five people before him, who played with their cell phones, PDAs, and drinks.

"We all have too much invested in this weekend to let a little rain chase our parade away." He glanced at each person, who nodded in turn.

The woman read the weather report off her PDA. "Winds are at fifty miles per hour off the coast of Georgia. Some people might say this is God giving us a sign. After Katrina and Rita…"

Pearson covered the mouthpiece and stared hard at her. "There are no Katrinas or Ritas on Jekyll Island. Do you want to tell the group we missed our deadline because of a little rain?" After a silent duel of gazes between Pearson and the woman, he took his hand from the mouthpiece and addressed Saddleback through the receiver. "Rain or no rain, my private jet is going to touch down at our private airport on Jekyll Island tomorrow morning. If the problem doesn't resolve itself by the time we check in…you'd better pray to God for a hurricane."

There was a moment. Then, Saddleback responded tensely. "You're the boss."

"Yes, I am. See you tomorrow morning. You stay dry—and watch out for alligators."

Jekyll Island, Georgia, 11:40 p.m.

Martin stumbled and fell headlong over a thick, knobby, slick but muscled mass. He prayed, as his face hit a clump of squishy moss, that he hadn't tripped over an alligator or other scaly predator. He did not aim to take the place of Jeff Corwin or the late great Steve Irwin as a reptile wrestler.

Rain caressed Martin's face and his beard stubble. He struggled to his feet. Traction was a chore as he tromped through leafy greenery. His nose tingled from the ocean air and the scent of the red Georgia clay that, according to the travel guides he'd read, alternated with golden sand on the Jekyll Island beaches. Branches from the spiny shrubs and magnolia trees whacked his back and propelled him forward. He found a fairly dry patch of Bermuda grass and sat down with his back to a large oak tree and tried to collect his thoughts.

Footsteps echoed behind him.

Martin didn't dare go back to the room for his laptop, so he worked his BlackBerry from its holster on his hip. John Wayne had his pistol, but Martin would have to settle for modern technology. The BlackBerry glowed in the murky night, and he was thankful he hadn't sent it back when his brother Tim (who already had his PhD and never let Martin forget) bought it for him as a birthday present. He was also thankful that BlackBerry wasn't experiencing one of its notorious outages.

Martin unlocked the BlackBerry with his security code as he enjoyed the soggy temporary shelter of the oak tree and hanging Spanish moss. A flash overhead illuminated the two trees under which he sat: moss draping his head on the right side so that he resembled Swamp Thing from the comic book series, and branches shielding him on the left. With any luck he might startle his T-shirted pursuer.

Martin got the stylus free and touched the Notepad. He brought up a list of memos and tapped the one titled "PPT," which stood for Plunge Protection Team. WMDs had nothing on PPT for sheer explosiveness, and with any luck, Martin would have more success than the weapons inspectors and U.S. forces in Iraq in finding the PPT.

Although it seemed the PPT had found him.

Martin's lungs worked overtime in the moisture and heat as he crouched under the moss. The overhead illumination had passed, and

Martin pressed his BlackBerry close to his stomach so it wouldn't give away his position. His pursuer's voice echoed through the night.

"...only so many places a guy like him can hide even in this big-ass old hulk. Mosquitoes'll eat you raw, so he'll have to come back inside sometime...yeah, don't worry, the Reserve Room's all staked out...I don't know how much he knows, I didn't get much out of the ditz at the desk...damn fine set of knockers though...yeah, all set for tomorrow. Of course, he'll be finished long before then."

Had the man said mosquitoes?

Martin felt a dozen pinpricks on his arms, legs, and neck, but West Nile Virus was less of a threat right now, as was any discomfort, than his uninvited drinking buddy.

He focused on what the man had said. Reserve Room? That figured. Martin quietly scrolled through his memo, a hodgepodge of names and acronyms:

1. CDOs
2. Pearson
3. Bull-Spears
4. Council on Foreign Relations
5. Crump
6. Skull and Bones
7. Sarb-Ox
8. Glass-Steagle
9. S&L
10. Tedson
11. Bilderberg Conference
12. Zwick
13. Tri-lateral Commission
14. Atkins

The BlackBerry rang. Reflexively, Martin swatted it, and smashed a mosquito or some other kind of flying insect. He managed to hit Ignore and looked at the phone number. It was a 530 area code, and the name read "Mrs. Annette Nikolopoulos."

Martin quickly sent back a text message to an Auburn, California, phone number: "cant talk right now call phil ppt is here on Jekyll island."

Not too far off behind him, he heard the distinctive click of a clip being inserted into a semi-automatic handgun and fervently wished he believed in owning a gun. He wasn't going back to Room 309, but somehow, some way, he would be in that Federal Reserve Room with the people who hired the T-shirted man.

A flash of lightening illuminated the hotel grounds up ahead, revealing some sort of gazebo-like structure. Martin text-messaged again: "tell journo to meet me in gazebo outside don't go to room 309 danger."

He shivered in his shirt and his mosquito-bitten skin and waited as the rain battered down the world around him.

Auburn, California, 8:30 p.m.

Doug Boyd hung up the house phone with the enlarged numerical pad and symbols for the fire department, police, and hospital. He stared, perplexed, at his landline.

PPT? PowerPoint was stalking Martin Cheyne?

That couldn't be right.

PPT was one of those acronyms Martin liked to throw around in casual conversation; until this whole mess had started, Doug had listened with half an ear and mind. Where and what was Jekyll Island anyway? Sounded like a horror movie title.

He dialed Phil's number and spoke rapidly. "Phil, I just got a text message from our friend. What do you know about PPT or Jekyll Island?"

"Jekyll Island's where Martin was going to get the dirt on Pearson. It's near Georgia," Phillip's cop voice responded. "Your boss, well, ex-boss, has a timeshare somewhere in those parts. Great shrimping there."

Doug wondered how Phil knew these things.

"As for PPT, maybe your journalist buddies will know something. Sounds like PowerPoint."

"Yeah, except he's afraid of it…"

"Or parts per trillion."

"Could be."

"It's one of those acronyms he loves…or maybe the name of a new rap artist?"

"I don't think that's it." Doug choked back his laughter. "Maybe I better call our journalist friend. You got any favors you could call in from the Deep South?"

Phil still sounded alert, and he ignored Doug's awkward amusement. Then again, that was Phil—most humor escaped him, except his own. "Yeah, I worked together with a guy on a child prostitution ring that had ties to Atlanta. I know he's generally awake at whatever time it is down there."

"Great, call me back, keep me posted," Doug said.

"Okay, buddy, tell Annette your significant other says 'hi.'"

"Very funny." Doug hung up and dialed a D.C. cell phone number. A male voice answered with a distinct Minnesota rhythm. "I was just checkin' in for my flight. How are ya, Douggy?"

He normally didn't let strangers call him Douggy, but they needed Webb Sutton. "How soon can you join Martin?"

"I said, just checkin' in for my flight, got to pick up some takeout, and I don't mean Chinese, but documents. I'm aces at putting 'em together even after they've been through a shredder. And e-mails? They never stay deleted," Webb said in a breezy, brawny manner.

"Don't go to room 309. Martin's in danger. He said meet him at the gazebo."

"Do I wear my Clark Gable smile or my Scarlett hoopskirt down there in Georgia? Douglas, I have three words about danger: Embedded in Fallujah. You be safe. Bye now." Webb hung up, and Doug replaced the receiver.

Not more than a second later, the house phone rang again. A wispy, elderly female voice echoed through the house. "I'll get it."

"It's okay," Doug called back, "it's probably for me." He picked up the phone and answered. "Hello?"

"Did you ask him about the PPT?" Phil sounded as if he'd just completed a triathlon.

"I didn't get a chance. He was getting takeout."

"PPT stands for Plunge Protection Team. It is the nickname for the President's Working Group on Financial Markets, led by the secretary of the treasury. It is supposed to be a government group, but rumor has it it includes people like the top guy at Bull-Spears. It sounds like these are the guys responsible for, no pun intended, plunging this country into a nightmare that our great-grandchildren will inherit."

As Phil explained PPT, Doug began to wish he'd flunked math and had been forced into a different career. And Phil wished he'd never beaten up a lowlife child pornographer in Sacramento back in July.

CHAPTER 2

"I believe that banking institutions are more dangerous to our liberties than standing armies. If the American people ever allow private banks to control the issue of their currency, first by inflation, then by deflation, the banks and corporations that will grow up around [the banks] will deprive the people of all property until their children wake-up homeless on the continent their fathers conquered... The issuing power should be taken from the banks and restored to the people, to whom it properly belongs."

—Thomas Jefferson, letter to Secretary of the Treasury Albert Gallatin (1802)

Economic Calamity
Federal Priorities
July 11, 2007, 8:05 a.m.
By Martin Cheyne

I turn on the news lately and, except for the war, the election, and Britney Spears (who is like a junk bond), all the news seems to be about Internet predators or global warming.

Don't get me wrong. I think keeping track of kiddie predators and pornographers, as well as any kind of rapist, is a great idea—in theory. I sit on the board of the local battered women's safe house and volunteer once a week working the phones. I've marched in Take Back the Night. I campaigned to renew the Violence against Women Act. I donate to NOW.

Further, I am against global warming. If there was a vote on global warming, I would vote no. Though I live at an elevation of about 5,000 feet above sea level, I don't want the ice caps to melt and wash California into the ocean. I have friends there. Seriously, I am not opposed to the environmental movement, but I think the issue has been overexposed and probably largely confused with the level of media attention.

The scarlet letter shouldn't just be for sex offenders. Why should these unknown men and women with the bad mug shots be the only ones on a list on the Internet somewhere with their names and addresses?

And couldn't the protest be used for something more worthwhile than to bash the guy who gets poor gas mileage and the bozo who doesn't sort and recycle his garbage? Can't we diversify a little bit?

What about all the banking sleazebags, the mortgage brokers, and the silent partners who get rich off real estate scams and taking advantage of people who should have known they couldn't afford a house in Malibu anyway? I care about that far more than I do that the average temperature in Reykyavic increased .01 degrees in the last decade or about some guy who got busted five years ago when he was seventeen for having consensual sex with his sixteen-year-old girlfriend.

I know I'm going to get hate comments, but let's wake up. Let's forget about Britney and Dateline. Only we can't, because the news media can sell those things more easily than a story on our own gullibility and our government's corruptibility. The corporations that own the news media are in bed with the banking sleazebags anyway, so they're only too happy to fill our days and our minds with sex, global warming, sex, global warming, sex.

There's nothing sexy about bankruptcy. Or wrapping yourself up in the scandal sheets that you used to read, just to keep warm on the street.

Trackback / Comment / Blog This / Comments (151)

Sacramento Suburbs, July 11, 2007, 9:00 a.m.

FBI Special Agent Philip Schultz pulled off his blue-and-white striped Armani tie and matching sport coat. He tossed them in the front passenger seat of his late-model dark pewter Ford 500. He cracked his knuckles and stretched his six-foot-two-inch ex-football player's body.

Unlike most former college athletes, at thirty-two he maintained his well-toned muscles with thirty minutes of weight-bearing activity at least three times a week, alternating with thirty to thirty-five minutes of resistance training two to three days a week. His gorgeous wife, Helen, had once joked that even he needed Sunday to rest and admire his ass in the mirror.

Phil watched his ass, figuratively speaking, as he walked with assurance around the back of the car and popped the trunk. He looked at the jalousie-framed windows of the small, white 1900s Victorian-style house in Sacramento's midtown-downtown area. To his backup officers waiting at their posts, he knew, without being a pompous jerkhole, he looked like he could play an FBI agent on TV. They'd kidded him about it more than once. They hadn't noticed the lines around his mouth and eyes, the nervous twitch of his eyelids, or the way he ground his teeth lately—all telltale signs of his stress and despair.

Phil grabbed and donned a black Kevlar vest with the letters FBI printed boldly in white on both the front and back. He pulled his Glock 22 .40 caliber sidearm from his holster, dropped the clip, and checked that the fifteen-round magazine was full. He reloaded the clip, reholstered his sidearm, and grabbed a Remington 870 shotgun. He checked that the shotgun was loaded, pumped the sliding forearm handle to load a shell into the barrel, and joined the four other officers, who wore their Kevlar vests and full-body armor as well as helmets. One of them, a female agent, spoke to the regional field office on her BlackBerry Pearl.

"I'll take point," he said, and they all nodded. The female agent muttered an update and hung up.

Phil closed the trunk with his elbow and strode up the walk. They'd do this the polite way first. He felt confident that if their quarry rabbited, Phil could physically take him down. He used to be able to catch anything thrown near him. He knew he still could.

Fifteen years ago, Philip was a star high school wide receiver who never missed a pass, a National Merit and honor roll student with high ambition and a bright future. At eighteen he went on to earn a scholarship to a small division II program at California State University as a tight end. As he matured and grew larger, his coaches began to take advantage of his ability to block as well as act as a safety valve for the quarterback. In more than one game, he caught as many passes as the receivers.

Phil skipped his redshirt year and immediately started playing as a freshman. Football took up most of his time in the fall, and almost all of the away games were several hundred miles away in Oregon or Washington. He tried to explain to his disappointed parents that the brutal season schedule on the road, not the constant partying when he was not on the field, was what caused his GPA to slip from a 4.0 to a 3.0, the bare minimum academic requirement for a student-athlete.

At the end of his sophomore year, his coach grimly informed him that the university was canceling its football program due to the need to provide equal opportunity for both men and women in athletics. He finally understood why the school hadn't kicked him off the team when his GPA dropped to a 2.5. His poor performance meant that he was not able to transfer to another university, and the loss of his scholarship meant he would have to take student loans and begin working in order to continue his education. Busing tables at a diner a couple miles from campus where cops hung out taught him humility.

His parents eventually stopped using a mournful tone of voice when they talked to him once they saw he wasn't going to let his setback in football kill his ambition. Philip was determined to do something great, to make a great life for himself. He worked harder in school and brought his grades up to a 3.8 GPA. He worked part-time at a diner, where he formed a friendly rapport with the cops. After five years, he graduated with $30,000 in student loans, $15,000 in credit card debt, no cash, no car, and a degree in business from a small state college.

Phil felt his shirt collar dampen, and he ceased his reminiscences. Despite the synchronized lawn sprinklers, the ninety-degree heat was oppressive. The other four perspired in their protective coverings. Two of them lugged a battering ram between them in addition. They fared much better than the brown scrubby lawn. Nothing grew in the yard of the white house except some nasty-looking weeds. Phil felt like the weed whacker.

The house appeared as neglected and seedy as the landscaping. The paint peeled and cracked. Philip kicked aside a week's worth of the *Sacramento Bee* piled on the doorstep and rang the tinny doorbell chime that played "Somewhere My Love." Through the front door, Phil could smell a rubbery or oily odor mingled with marijuana.

Ringing the doorbell was the signal. Two of the officers, the woman and an Asian male, peeled away and circled around to the back door. The remaining two, both male, both ex-Marines, held the battering ram and stayed with Phil as he waited for a response from within.

When none came, Phil rapped on the door loudly three times and waited a few seconds. After no one stirred within, Phil shouted, "FBI. Please open the door or we will force it open."

After a moment of silence, Philip motioned to the officers, who readied the large metal round cylinder of the battering ram. Phil stepped aside, and the officers walked to the door. They swung the ram at the obstacle just as the deadbolt clicked and the door opened.

The skinny balding man in garish red silk boxers and a sleeveless T-shirt that read "Nymph Inc" in princess-pink letters ducked rapidly to avoid the battering ram, which the officers pulled back. When he straightened up, he wheezed and cringed, terrified, even after the officers laid aside the battering ram. Amyl nitrate and marijuana fumes clung to him.

"FBI, sir." Phil gagged on his professionalism and the revulsion he felt for this man. He produced the appropriate papers from his vest. "We have a warrant for your arrest."

The warrant papers identified the man who now cowered before Phil as Drew Stanislavsky.

"Look, look, if this is about my ex, she'd say anything to ruin me," Stanislavsky said, rivulets of sweat running down his sallow cheeks. His lips quivered, and he had that look in his eye Phil had seen many times before. The man was about to wail for his mommy and his lawyer.

The last thing Philip wanted to do was listen to some scrawny, pathetic child pornographer sob, cry, and blubber on about how he didn't do anything wrong. The last thing the scrawny, pathetic child pornographer probably wanted was a cop like Philip to arrest him.

Philip reflected back on his first days at the FBI and the pride he felt after graduating from the academy. Philip had quickly landed a job upon graduating from college. It was the very beginning of the dot-com boom, and most of the graduates from his university were offered jobs in the Silicon Valley. Philip had three different job offers, and, naturally, he took the job with the highest offer: $35,000 per year plus a bonus to work as a sales representative for a large printing company in San Jose.

He quickly rented a small apartment for $1,200 per month, bought new furniture with no cash, no payments for a full year, and bought a new Ford Mustang. He tacked on a $400 car payment every month. After three years of spending far more than he earned as a glorified paper salesman, Philip was broke, ashamed, tired, and depressed. He had no life. He wished for a better career. On a whim, he went back to the diner, hat in hand, and sought out one of the cops to whom he used to serve coffee. He breathlessly confessed his story and asked the cop for advice.

The cop took one assessing look at him and said, “Ever thought of joining the FBI?”

Though still broke, when he graduated from the FBI Academy, he had his pride back.

Stanislavsky, the suspect, shook so badly he barely made it to the beige chenille armchair in his living room. Phil motioned to his officers to raid the house. The two who had gone around back had apparently circled around. They now entered through the front door.

Phil made eye contact with Stanislavsky as the officers went through the house in search of Stanislavsky’s home studio and computer. “This is about the evidence we’ve collected on the Internet and traced back to you despite your phony Internet information. I imagine you’ll be facing fraud charges too.”

“I didn’t do anything.” Stanislavsky huffed through his nose. “I didn’t do anything. I just run a business.”

Phil sniffed the air. “You use marijuana as part of your business?”

Stanislavsky folded his arms. “I called my lawyer.”

“Fine. But the warrant’s in order.”

The female agent, whose name was Gallatin, beckoned to him. “Agent Schultz, we got something.”

The Asian male agent, Ku, lugged a load of sex toys that he'd bagged into the room. He held some of them up for Phil's inspection. Phil nodded grimly. Stanislavsky stood in protest.

Phil walked into a small, immaculately kept den. Everything seemed to be in lockdown except the computer. Gallatin pulled up some photos on the computer. "These were taken within the last forty-eight hours. They're earmarked for upload to this creep's Web site."

Phil forced himself to look at the images onscreen. The boys and girls posed artificially with their eyes full of sullen anger and anguish were barely older than his son Jason and his daughter Megan.

Philip married a young intern at an FBI office in Alexandria, Virginia, just after leaving the academy. Her name was Helen, and she was from Virginia. She was twenty-two, he was twenty-seven, and she was the most beautiful woman he had ever seen. Blond, smart, cute, and ambitious, she planned on going to law school immediately after graduating from the University of Virginia. Eleven months after getting married, Phil and Helen had Jason, whom they called "Bug" because of his quick, nimble movements. Both Phil and Helen needed to continue to work, especially after the dot-com bust. Helen never started law school, but instead continued to do clerical work in the FBI office. Nearly half of her salary went to paying for day care for Jason. Two years later, the family of three welcomed Megan, "Sparkle," who inherited her mother's hair and laughter, and Helen quit her job to stay home with the kids. A few months after that, Philip was transferred to the Sacramento, California, field office.

Three years later and several pay grades higher, Philip was making $74,000 per year, including overtime. He had burnout, but was still happily ensconced in his American Dream. Helen seemed to relax more, and even kept up with law study with a plan to go back to school once Megan entered high school.

One of Phil's good friends from college, Paul LeBrach, had helped him buy a house and consolidate all of his debt into the loan with no down payment a couple years back. Phil could afford the payment at first, but Paul failed to mention that the initial payment would adjust, and drastically, just twelve months later.

Today, Philip owed $600,000 on a 2,000-square-foot, four-bedroom house in a new subdivision on the southwest side of Sacramento. An appraiser he hired recently valued the house at approximately $400,000. His house payment, insurance, and utilities were almost exactly equal to his take-home pay every month. He had raced to Boardwalk only to get a "Go to Jail" card. Tired of being broke, tired of their nightly fights about money, and tired of living so far from her family, Helen packed up her belongings and the children last week. She claimed that the kids needed to visit their grandparents back East, but she bought a one-way ticket to Virginia. That was the day the FBI built its case against Stanislavsky.

Phil and Gallatin heard the unmistakable click of a weapon. They both made a beeline for the living room.

Stanislavsky emerged from the back room, where he had been changing his clothes, holding a rifle in his quivering hands. He aimed it at Ku, who backed off but kept his gun drawn. The other two officers, Jarvis and Samno, observed the scene with their guns drawn too. Stanislavsky waved the rifle about wildly, his arms spread wide.

"You don't want to do that," Phil said. "Drop your weapon. Look at your odds. Do you really want a shootout?"

Stanislavsky squeezed the trigger. The rifle popped, and the officers took cover. Stanislavsky shook from the recoil and dropped the rifle. Phil was on him in a second. He pushed the rifle away with his foot, and Ku confiscated the weapon.

Stanislavsky flailed with his fists and tried to punch Phil. He cried globs of tears and made a honking sound as he blew his nose. "I didn't do anything. It's nothing, nothing!" he howled, cried, and screamed. "You shouldn't do this to people!"

Phil's nerves snapped like firecrackers, igniting his adrenaline and charging his whole body. He'd seen one after another of these cases, and scum like Stanislavsky never learned. And for this, this never-ending parade of filth, he'd stood helplessly as Helen took their children across country, possibly forever.

Phil's hands grabbed Stanislavsky's bony, gamey shoulders. He jerked Stanislavsky forcibly upward and shook him. Stanislavsky gasped, and Phil threw him across the room into the wall above the beige chenille chair. Stanislavsky smacked the wall, rebounded, and missed a soft landing in the chair when he plummeted to the floor. Stanislavsky clutched his blood-soaked nose and stared at the spatters on his wall, his beige carpet, his chair. Stanislavsky flailed and screamed at opera singer levels. Phil pounded him in the solar plexus to shut him up and heard the satisfying yet sickening crack of a rib. Stanislavsky sank down on his knees.

Gallatin, mouth agape, pulled Stanislavsky's limp arms behind his back and cuffed them. Broke, lonely, exhausted, and stressed out, Phil stared at this man only half his size. He would have taken another swing at Stanislavsky, but Ku and Jarvis seized his arms. "You don't want to do that," Ku said in an echo of Phil's own words, just seconds ago.

The other officers had faded away while Phil worked Stanislavsky over. Even now, with their hands on him, he thought of them as phantoms. It made his complete loss of control easier to cope with.

Gallatin and Samno helped Stanislavsky to his feet and escorted him out. He winced, sobbed, and gasped with every step. Phil, meanwhile, put himself into autopilot. He went and turned off Stanislavsky's computer. He hoped the computer evidence stuck. Since Phil wasn't going home tonight to an empty house that would soon be in foreclosure, he'd work until the wee hours to lawyer-proof this case. He was conscious of the other officers staring at him, and the neighbors staring at Stanislavsky, as he walked outside. Despite the heat of the day, he felt as cool as a frozen margarita.

Sacramento Midtown-Downtown, 10:00 a.m.

Paul LeBrach pulled his 2005 black Mercedes CLS class sedan into the driveway in front of Phil Schultz's house. He drank the last of a frozen mochaccino and wiped the traces of chocolate from his lips. He was a good guy; at least, he always thought so. Well-mannered, well-groomed, smart, funny, and always with a smile on his face. He could have consoled himself with the memory of the howler of a golf joke he'd told last week at the office, and how everyone had laughed, especially Karina, who always shimmied when she giggled. He always had a funny joke and made himself the center of attention, particularly with his muscular 5'10" 170-pound body. His love handles weren't conspicuous yet, and he looked in prime physical condition. He was big, but not big enough to be intimidating. Oddly enough, it was his personality, rather than his looks, that made people head for the door after they'd spent a few hours with him. He was just too much for one man, he often told himself. He managed to charm them back with another funny story.

Paul wasn't smiling today, and didn't feel funny. He felt unappreciated and annoyed as he climbed out of the car into the hellish ninety-degree heat. He didn't know why he was wasting his time and money putting Philip's Sacramento home on the market at $550,000, a price any moron could see it wouldn't fetch.

Paul rolled up the sleeves of his white button-down shirt and opened up the trunk of his car. He paused for a minute to admire his movie star grin on the left-hand side of the "Sacramento Realty—LeBrach and Associates For Sale" sign before he pulled it out and started hammering it into the front lawn. He loved attention and loved seeing his picture printed anywhere. Even in Phil's money pit of a house. Too bad Phil's hot platinum-blond wife was off slopping pigs in Virginia. He counted seeing Helen and smelling her lavender perfume, vicariously lusting after her, as one of the perks of the job. Megan and Jason called him "Uncle Paul" and always wanted to glom on to him, especially since their dad was a total workaholic. Phil wasn't as much fun as in their college days.

Paul and Phil had been fraternity brothers. Phil was the athlete, Paul the politician. They both loved drinking and women, they were both ambitious, and they were both out to conquer the world.

Growing up, Paul was the Little Prince in his home, except he always wanted to be the king or the businessman in the story. His mother read the book to him when he was five and told him, "Paulie, smell the roses, but rule the world." They dismissed his B-minus/C-plus average all throughout his academic career. After all, Paul was a good kid, never killed small animals or got a girl pregnant (that they knew about). Paul was smart and popular—he was prom king—and he got by. His high school achievements weren't good enough to get him into a prestigious school, so his parents paid for him to go to the local state university. He graduated the same year as Phil, with a degree in management information systems from the business school. The Little Prince received the key to the kingdom when a Silicon Valley company called Automate.com, which matched up car buyers with bids for their ideal vehicle, hired Paul right at his graduation ceremony.

In the four years preceding the dot-com bubble collapse, Paul got laid off from three jobs, netting him salary and severance payments of approximately $500,000. When the job market dried up and the economy took a hit after September 11, Paul took a couple years off to take a one-semester, three-unit class at Sacramento City College and to prepare for his real estate license examination. He passed the California real estate exam with 93 percent, and his dad framed his certificate in the living room. After thirteen months working as a top performer for Chaffee Residential and Rental Properties in Sacramento, Paul got a broker's license and started his own real estate company. A few hours of self-study later, he had a mortgage broker's license and he became a regional representative for what the news later popularized as a "subprime" broker.

In the past eighteen months, Paul had aggressively grown his own real estate investment company and bought up every property with curb appeal. He now owned sixteen homes and was in the process of funding a new downtown Sacramento condominium project on land he purchased. Twelve months ago he was written up in the *Sacramento Bee* under the title "America's Next Billionaire?" Twelve months ago he owned nine million dollars worth of real estate. Today, the value of the same real estate was just slightly over half that amount, but the hefty debt he owed had not decreased.

Paul had plenty of time to think about the past waiting for prospective buyers. From ten o'clock to one o'clock he waited for the Laings, who never showed up. He nodded and smiled as the Fosters oohed and aahed over the crown molding before Mrs. Foster decided there was an unpleasant smell like rotting vegetables, possibly in the walls, and that Paul should knock the asking price down a hundred thou or so.

Paul had helped Phil out with this house in the past. Paul knew about Phil's debt problems, knew he would need a place to live when he moved back to California, and set up a perfect deal for him. Paul, both a real estate broker and a mortgage broker, was able to find Phil a perfect house and get him a loan that solved his short-term cash flow issues. Yes, he made a commission on selling the house, one he already had listed, and yes he earned a commission on the loan he arranged for Phil, but so would have anyone that Phil went to. "I know I'd rather have the money go to one of my friends than somebody I don't know," Paul thought to himself as he encouraged Mrs. Foster with tales of the excellent local school district and the great views.

Paul had grossed about forty-eight thousand in total from the deal that required about eight hours of work—not an unusual fee these days, he told himself. As Paul asked Mrs. Foster for the purchase offer and received a rather strident response from Mr. Foster that they'd "let him know," Paul told himself he was doing all he could. Phil couldn't blame him for the debt and the difficulty selling. How the hell was Paul supposed to know that prices would drop so fast in this area? Did Phil think Paul wanted to lose his ass on his investments? And why the hell was Paul wasting his money to list and advertise Phil's house at a price he knew they'd never get?

"Why?" Paul mumbled out loud. "I'll tell you why…because I take care of my friends."

"Excuse me?" Mr. Foster sounded as thick as his waist and Donald Trump-inspired hairpiece. He sold drill bits, and reminded Paul of Vernon Dursley in the Harry Potter movies. "What didya say?"

"I said I take care of my friends." Paul smiled winningly. "I consider everybody I show a house to a friend. Yep, I'm a friendly guy."

Mrs. Foster wrinkled what Paul could see was a surgically shaped nose. She smelled of rotting vegetables herself, probably organic, and you could bounce a dime on her plastic ass and face. "You're adorable, ya know that? You look like that actor. I can't think of his name. What was he in? Bob. What was that movie we rented the other night? The one with the girl I can't stand, she's so slutty."

Her husband hustled her out. She sneezed and mumbled, "Smell would drive you crazy."

Paul locked up the house with the lockbox, gave the signpost a final whack to secure it on the lawn, and turned his back on Phil's money pit. He climbed back into his Mercedes, slammed the door, and drove off. His car color matched his mood.

Arthur Whinney and Associates, LLC, San Jose Offices, 11:10 a.m.

Doug Boyd, in stereotypical CPA spectacles, stood on surprisingly tranquil feet outside the translucent door to the office of Richard Gauthier, managing partner of the San Jose branch of Arthur Whinney and Associates, one of the "Big Four" accounting firms. He talked in a hush on his cell phone.

"Believe me, hon, I can just taste the pineapple and feel the surf right now. I'm going to do everything in my power. I'll tell him…I won't wimp out…"

Crystal, his girlfriend, knew him. He could just see her plumped lip thrust out sexily, determinedly. "Well, it is a free ticket, so we can always use it again." He heard the buzz and clicks of photographers on the shoot Crystal was directing today. "No, no, no, not that backdrop," she hissed to her assistant.

Doug closed his eyes as another call came through. "I'm looking forward to Waikiki. I'll let you know how it goes with Richard."

"If we're both awake. I have to go, they're destroying the set. Love you, numbers man." Crystal hung up, freeing Doug to answer Paul's call.

"Douggy, how's the world of high finance?"

Doug winced at Paul's breeziness, then smiled as Martin, his other college buddy, piped in. "Better than academia. Are we ready to put on the loincloths, shoot some deer, and build a fire by striking two flints together?"

"You can't even put mousetraps in your house," Paul joked. "We are on for the campers' weekend."

"I have to make this quick, I have to book a guy," Phil shouted above the howl of police sirens. "I'm in. Give me a weekend where I don't have to arrest or shoot anybody or deal with FBI paperwork, and I'm there. You guys decide what you want. Bye." Phil clicked off.

"I paid the campsite fees," Doug said with a smile. Camping with his buddies was about the only exotic vacation he suspected he'd be taking. Male bonding was his indulgence these days. "It won't be crowded? Do you think?"

"That's our Douggy, always fiscally responsible," Paul said. "If it's crowded, fuck 'em."

"And you would," Martin said.

Martin, Paul, Phil, and Doug were all friends from California State University. Doug and Paul knew each other slightly because they worked at the same supermarket. However, they all really became friends through their fraternity. The fraternity they joined wasn't the kind where they branded letters from the Greek alphabet onto each others' backsides with a branding iron or spanked the new pledges with paddles. And, even though there was a lot of heavy drinking, chasing women, and some hazing of the new initiates, none of those were the main reason to join.

The majority of the men in their twenties joined this type of fraternity to provide them an edge when interviewing for jobs, and to provide some connection, some link, to others in the business world. These four ambitious young men knew that the game was rigged, that the good-old-boy network was firmly in place among the captains of industry, and that an edge was needed to climb the corporate ladder swiftly. Unfortunately, it wasn't until many years later that they realized how rigged the game truly was, and how futile the attempts they made in their college years were.

Doug, Martin, and Phil all had the same initial response when Paul called them last Friday and asked what they thought about taking a boys' weekend. "Who else is going?" each of them asked immediately, looking forward to some time away from their life, but afraid that they would be condemned to spending a weekend stuck listening to Paul talk about himself and how successful he was. Each was noncommittal when Paul told them that no one else had signed up yet.

But the next day, after an exchange of e-mails in which Martin, Phil, and Doug made a mutual pact to drug Paul and keep him asleep all weekend, all four men were looking forward to a couple days in the woods fishing, shooting guns, drinking, and remembering old times.

Doug suggested they not go too far away, since he would have to work late on Friday and be back at the office early on Monday. He knew of a place one hundred miles out of the Bay Area off Interstate 80, which would be a halfway point for him, coming from the Bay Area, and Martin, who was driving from Reno. Paul and Phil had no problem with the campsite, and they agreed to meet in two weeks.

Richard Gauthier's door swung open, casting a shadow at Doug's feet. That was the summons. Richard had finished with another mega-billion-dollar call.

"We'll make final arrangements this weekend when we can get Phil on the phone full time," Doug said.

"Final arrangements? This isn't a fucking funeral," Paul said. "We're just lucky you could fit us in between clients and doing the hula with your chick in Hawaii. Unless you have to cancel again."

"Spare us, Paul," Martin said. "I have to go try to educate our future leaders. Talk later. Enjoy life, both of you. Don't get crushed under the wheels of the American Dream." Martin hung up.

"Marty. He's a kick," Paul laughed. "I have to go close on some condo deals. Go get 'em, Douggy. Later."

Doug switched off his phone, a blue BlackBerry. It clashed with his surroundings, as did he. The office suites would induce already overanxious clients to jump out the window. Light gray walls, dark gray-suit carpeting, storm-gray ceiling, iron-gray desks and filing cabinets, and state-penitentiary-gray chairs. The rows of gray cubicles, only interrupted by claustrophobic hallways with offices or conference rooms, would turn the sardonic Dilbert into a homicidal maniac. The only pizzazz or color came from the occasional piece of crappy, amateurish, overpriced modern art stuck to the wall.

Fortunately, the auditing staff only spent a rare day or two per month in the offices for training and staff meetings. Doug and his fellow prisoners worked almost exclusively onsite at their clients' offices. Doug's favorite client offices were the superbly appointed, warm-earth-toned suites at his last audit. He almost kissed the carpet, the walls, and the Monet from Sotheby's.

Doug was to have ventured into the land of digital color today, but had been forced to reschedule. He had not come to the second-floor office suites of Arthur Whinney for one of his regular days in the office. For his meeting with Richard Gauthier, Doug wore a camel-colored suit with a sapphire-blue tie. His suit matched his tan, even though one of the few dark-skinned minority employees on his last audit, a smart-ass, had described him as the "whitest white man I have ever seen."

Doug had quipped back, "That's because they keep us chained in the dungeon. They shove Starbucks and fast food through the door once a day, crack the whip, and tell us to get back to work."

Doug had been with Arthur Whinney since leaving college ten years ago, and had been working, on average, seventy hours a week, six to seven days a week, ten to twelve hours a day, every year. Public accounting is known for burning out its young associates quickly. Doug had once heard that only one in ten of his classmates would last for more than three years in the business, and he believed it. In California, it is necessary to have a minimum of two years of public accounting experience in order to get a CPA license. So, for the first two years, associates are largely indentured servants, receiving low pay for the number of hours worked. Doug started at $37,500 per year in 1997 with no pay for overtime. For the hours worked, he could have earned more working the same job at the same supermarket he worked at in high school.

The payoff and the reason the firms retain any employees comes for the one in ten that make it through the first few years, when, and if, they are able to make partner. The average audit partner for a "Big Four" firm makes over $400,000 per year. The top-earning partners can easily make over $1,000,000 per year. Doug, as an ambitious, hardworking, intelligent, single-focused employee with no life who had already dedicated a decade of his life to a career he hated more and more every day, desperately wanted to make partner.

But Doug wasn't sure he was going to cut it. There is an unwritten rule in the business for those on the partner track. At five years you should be promoted to manager, at seven years, senior manager, and at ten years, you should be partner. If you miss any one of those, it is said, you have been passed over. It had taken Doug seven years to make manager, and he had been promoted to senior manager just a few months ago. He had been just about ready to change careers when he received his last promotion. The carrot of partnership riches and prestige kept him dutifully working seventy-hour weeks and charging clients $600,000–$800,000 per year for the firm, of which he was paid approximately $90,000.

As Doug stood outside Mr. Gauthier's office, or "Dick" as the staff called him behind his back, he took a deep breath. He knew he was going to be asked to take a new case, and would probably be asked to postpone (i.e., cancel) the two-week Hawaiian vacation he and Crystal had planned to take in a few weeks, and he knew he would smile and thank Mr. Gauthier for the opportunity, and he knew he would despise himself for it as soon as he left Dick's office. Doug breathed out, opened the door, and walked into Dick's den.

The meeting went exactly as expected. Dick, who wore a silver Hugo Boss suit and sported a new David Caruso hair color that made Doug want to grab the fire extinguisher, asked him to handle the audits of a couple of hedge funds out of San Francisco.

"Bull-Spears," Dick said, spreading his pistachio breath in the space between them. "The biggest client we have." He said this as if Doug had been living in a cave for his entire career at Arthur Whinney and didn't know that Dick went orgasmic whenever he took a call from Aaron Cartwright, head honcho at Bull-Spears. "The SF office doesn't have anybody with your work ethic, Doug. But, we will have to let the partner there, Bob Baker, head up the entire group audit."

Doug stroked the impossible baby's-bottom smoothness of the oiled bronze desk, which looked gray by default since, in Dick's defense, he kept the same gulag mindset as the decorator of the office suites. Accounting was not supposed to be fun or colorful.

Dick's voice lowered to librarian level. "You'll handle the two most important subsidiary audits. The ball-breaking, back-aching ones. You'll be doing the real set of books." He laughed, and Doug chuckled politely. "The associate who makes us look good, who does a killer job like you did with those San Francisco assholes last week, will have the opportunity to crawl into bed with another influential partner from the San Francisco office." Dick snickered. "Figuratively speaking. You don't really have to unless you want to."

Doug ignored the shot at San Francisco and at Doug's sexuality. Despite the prominent photo of Crystal on his desk, Doug was privy to the rumors circulating about his private life. Someone had even quipped about him watching Lifetime and the Bravo network. He wanted to tell everyone he didn't even have a private life, especially not after he canceled his plans with Crystal.

Dick mistook Doug's silence. "Loosen up, Boyd. You should be happy. This is a great opportunity to really help your chances for promotion in the future. You don't have any plans with your, ah, girlfriend? I know you're up for some time off in a few weeks."

Doug smiled until his muscles threatened to turn to gruel. "Sounds good, Richard. I'm your man. After all, if this is successful, I can take a month in the Caribbean, right? Work on the beach?"

Dick laughed in delighted approval. Doug accepted the dossier on Bull-Spears and assured Dick that all the travel arrangements were hunky-dory. He walked out of Dick's office, went straight to the elevator, left the building, drove to the Fahrenheit Ultra Lounge near his apartment, and ordered a whiskey sour.

University of Nevada-Reno, July 12, 2007, 9:05 a.m.

Thirty of the University of Nevada-Reno's seventeen thousand students did not want to be in Martin Cheyne's lower-division Econ 103 Principles of Macroeconomics summer session course. The students showed the restlessness of their ages—nineteen, twenty, and twenty-one. Rolled eyes, iPod shuffles, cappuccino guzzles. They had been forced to take the summer session for one reason or another.

Martin lectured on money creation the day after arranging the camping trip and thanked God Doug had taken care of the hefty campsite fees in the state park system, because although Martin had willingly taken a vow of poverty in academia, he particularly felt the pinch of the dog days of today's slowing economy. He patently refused to eat white rice, and he annoyed people by comparing prices in a supply-side econ lecture at Costco. Thank God his medical and dental were covered.

"Does anyone know how money is created?" Martin asked the class. They just stared back at him, as if they didn't hear the question. "Hello? Hey, guys! Anyone have a guess…how money is created?" Any moment he might start doing his Ben Stein impression: "Bueller? Bueller?"

This time, one kid who had bleached-out, gelled-back hair and olive skin and looked like he was no more than fifteen years old, hesitatingly raised his hand. Martin nodded and pointed to him.

"The government prints it on a machine, right? I saw them printing it when I was in D.C. a couple years ago." The kid sucked on the nib of a Cross pen.

Martin nodded again and made several dollar signs on the board. "Good guess, and you are right that the government prints currency, the actual dollar bills, and the actual coins. Once they put those notes and coins into circulation, they are money." He drew a flowchart as he talked. "However, only a tiny fraction of money is created this way. I don't suppose anyone actually read the chapter this time?" He didn't wait for an answer. "What am I talking about, it's July, there are better things to do." His mumble was just loud enough for the class to hear. A couple of students, including the kid with the blond hair and Cross pen, smiled.

Martin continued. "Okay, listen, because this is very, very important if you want to understand the economy today…money is created by the banks." The blond boy and the six or seven students closest to him had puzzled expressions, which at least showed they were listening. Most of the class continued to stare blankly at Martin.

"Banks create money?" asked a cute, fawn-haired but slightly nerdy-looking girl wearing slim-line glasses in the front row. She juggled a digital recorder and a laptop. "Then why wouldn't they just keep creating more and more money? And why would money be worth anything, because all the banks would just keep creating…I don't get it."

"Banks can only create money by loaning money—so somebody has to be willing to borrow," Martin responded as he looked. She stared down at her laptop, obviously not wanting to be engaged in this insane and indelicate conversation anymore. She would be able to play it back on her recorder anyway so she could dissect what Martin said.

"We have a system of fractional reserve lending," he continued, "which means that banks only have to hold a fraction of the amount of money that they lend out. So consider this example. You go to the bank and deposit a thousand dollars. The bank has a reserve requirement of ten percent, which means of that thousand dollars you deposited, the bank can loan out nine hundred. So, you"—he pointed to the blond boy with the Cross pen—"borrow nine hundred from the bank. You either deposit that nine hundred into your bank account, or you buy something and the person that you bought the item from deposits nine hundred dollars into their bank account. The bank that receives that deposit then can loan out ninety percent, or eight hundred and ten dollars." His chalk flew furiously as he wrote this on the blackboard. "That eight hundred and ten gets loaned and redeposited into another bank, allowing that bank to loan out ninety percent, and so on, and so on, and so on. So, that original thousand dollars can create, or destroy, almost ten times that amount of money in the economy."

A few of the students actually sat up and leaned forward. They changed from comatose to interested.

Martin relished the brief YouTube-like moment of attention. "So in order to put more money into the economy, the Federal Reserve Bank can either lower reserve requirements, which gives the banks more money to lend you for your car or house, or lower the 'Fed rate,' which lowers the cost for banks and consumers to borrow, thereby encouraging additional borrowing."

"Mathematically, what is the limitation then on creating money?" the nerdy girl asked.

"Amazingly, it is limitless, but practically until the reserve requirements approach zero, or until people cannot or will not borrow," Martin answered.

"Well, what are reserve requirements now?" the girl asked, her eyes narrowing toward him in triumph.

"Would you believe, for savings accounts, zero?" Martin stated firmly. He was pleased to note that every student frantically copied down his words.

CHAPTER 3

"The gathering of more and more [media] outlets under one owner clearly can be an impediment to a free and independent press."

—Walter Cronkite, former CBS News anchorman

Starbucks, Dupont Circle, Washington D.C., August 3, 2007, 11:50 p.m.

Webb Sutton ignored the scent and flavor of tall, nonfat mochas that permeated his nostrils and tongue whether he opted for one of Starbucks' high-priced creations or not. He drank Café Americano because it sounded less pretentious and more like something Ernest Hemingway might have sipped in Montmartre. Glancing outside, across the traffic circle and into the park, Webb could make out "coffee shop intellectuals" and homeless people alike playing chess under the streetlights on the permanent stone chessboards near the edge of the grass. A small group of four men, dressed in what looked like traditional West African garb, waited on the corner to cross the street—most likely heading to the Cameroon Embassy, which was just a block away on Embassy Row. On this hot summer night, Webb preferred the air-conditioned comfort of the indoors.

The people in this Starbucks this evening seemed more the type to read Hemingway, or write papers about him on their laptops, than the usual Starbucks crowd, but they didn't *understand* Hemingway the way Webb did. Alcoholic, miserable, woman hating, son of a bitch or not,

Mr. Hemingway was a classic. Both Webb and Mr. Hemingway represented an American age that no longer existed.

Webb shook his head and shoved his earbuds in his Dumbo-sized eardrums. He'd gone into journalism because he had the ears, Pinocchio-sized nose, and face for it. Tom Cruise he was not. He turned up the volume on his iPod Nano. He had downloaded all his conversations with Douglas Boyd, Philip Schultz, Martin Cheyne, and all the secret conversations he'd recorded onto his iPod. Then he backed them up to his memory stick and erased them off his computer. He made redundant backups too; they were in his safe at home in Springfield, Virginia. He might have to work in D.C., but he didn't want to live here. There were too many people—some of whom were friends—that this stinking, fetid shit-hole destroyed. Often, their complete annihilation was on public display. Webb, like others in D.C. and the publicity machine he was part of, was lucky he still had a remnant of his soul. Over the years, the press had silently and methodically destroyed thousands of people's lives with a thousand cuts over five, ten, or sometimes even twenty years.

That was why he was in a Starbucks, or as he'd dubbed it in one of his pieces, "Scambucks," instead of in his cubicle at the *Washington Post* offices. He'd told Douglas Boyd he had to pick up some documents, and that's what he was doing, waiting for his contact in public. Few would think to look for him here in a trendy location amongst the caffeine-obsessed. He'd already printed out his boarding pass to make his red-eye flight to Atlanta, where he would rent a car to head for Jekyll Island. His friends at the TSA and Homeland Security would help him wriggle and pass any roadblocks Secretary Franklin Pearson might erect at Dulles International. Webb was a regular Houdini.

He listened to the playback of his confidential source, the source he waited for, as he typed her direct quote: "Secretary Pearson is just waiting to pull the switch. The banks, under his guidance, have collaborated and set up an SIV, or VIE or whatever they are called now, that will pull all the bad debt off their books and bury it in some anonymous entity." Webb knew she was referring to a Structured Investment Vehicle, similar to the vehicles used by Enron to cover up all the bad decisions they had made. Ultimately, it represented an accounting trick, so that the companies that had made the bad decisions could avoid reporting those decisions to the shareholders and the public. "All this will subsequently, and unconstitutionally, be funded by government money," the source continued, "all under the nose of the taxpayer. It will happen by September. And this is just one of several scams these guys have set up to protect the interests of the banks…of the big money. The worst of it is that Pearson himself is just a pawn. He works for the president, but he takes his orders from someone else. I'm not sure who, but someone named Bilderberg is involved."

He pulled up Martin Cheyne's Economic Calamity blog and mined it for some useful quotes. He knew Martin was in danger, and he felt a flood of impatience as he looked at his watch. His flight was in two hours. He added a quote from Cheyne's June 6 blog. "It doesn't take a genius to figure out what is propping the market up. Huge amounts of money come in from Caribbean banks extremely regularly now and bid up stock prices. This amount of money can only be the PPT using U.S. government and freshly created Federal Reserve money. This is great if you are a Wall Street insider, but a crisis if you happen to be the average person struggling against decline in the almighty buck."

His cell phone vibrated. He cautiously checked the number. The display read "Carlotta." He hit Pause on his iPod, saved his work to the memory stick and the laptop, and answered his phone. He savored the heady last swallows of his Café Americano before he answered in his characteristic Minnesotan accent, "So, ya managed to stay alive?"

"God, Webb, that's why I love you." Carlotta McGinnis, formerly of the *Post*, now a top business writer for the *Sacramento Bee*, had a voice full of smooth whiskey jazz. She could sound as bland as California sunshine to fool everyone, but Webb had raised her from a paper-chewing journalistic puppy. "Yes, thank God I'm alive. I shouldn't be. Any other reporter would have knifed me in the back and photographed the crime scene."

"I don't care about scooping anyone, darlin'. You can have the Pulitzer."

"Sure, it'll make a perfect headstone."

"Now that's why I love you."

"Is that a Starbucks I hear in the background? I sure hope you're at Dulles by now."

"Will be soon, darlin', you betcha, yah. You break and fix the news on your end, and I'll unleash the hurricane down in Georgia, like Aeolus. Aeolus is from Greek Mythology, he's—"

"I know who Aeolus is, thanks. Now go get yourself to the airport, Webb. After that text message from Martin, everyone's worried."

"Everyone, as in your new boyfriend Douggy?"

"I'm saving myself for you, Webb. Although if you don't get on that plane, I may have to dump you."

"As soon as my friend arrives with my takeout, I'll be winging my way to you with a stop on Jekyll Island to muckrake and expose. So get yourself all dolled up and tell Douggy to watch himself. You break your story, and I'll break mine. We'll hit them with a one-two punch and then a TKO."

"She's not there yet?" Carlotta sounded worried.

The door to the java joint opened to admit a man who looked more like a fried pork dumpling, his preferred diet, than the *Post* assistant managing editor, Steve Yee.

"I'll call you from the airport. Something's happened," Webb said, sounding casual.

"Make sure you do. Webb? He doesn't like it when you call him Douggy."

"I know. Bye." Webb hung up and watched Steve not even make a pretense of ordering coffee. Steve walked right to the armchair on the other side of Webb's table and sat down. Webb moved to shut down his laptop, but Steve shook his head.

"Run Remote Access on your office computer," Steve said without preamble.

"Why?" Webb thought Steve's normally heavy lids appeared peeled back, his eyes bulging as if he were hyperthyroid, or at least auditioning for one of those Asian martial arts films. Steve could utter Bruce Lee screams when confronted by printer goofs or a visit from Legal. "I was going to send you the story—"

"They're not just spiking it, they're spiking you." Steve played with his St. Christopher medal. "Run Remote Access now."

Webb linked with his office computer. Steve executed a dizzying sequence of point-and-click until he got to the folder labeled

"Credit Crunch Article." Webb was so anal he kept computer folders for all his articles. Steve opened the folder and watched Webb collapse in the chair. Webb was sure he looked as boneless and defeated as he felt.

The JPEG of the naked girl, probably no more than seven years old, was posed in a way that made his Café Americano curdle in his stomach. Today's so-called starlets would don the full nun's habit upon seeing these pictures.

"I don't cover kiddie porn cases," he said, low and intense. "What the hell is this? How did it get there? I can just erase this, right?"

Misery carved lines in Steve's normally youthful face. "They've probably got more, and you know—"

"—it doesn't stay deleted." The coffee made its way back up his digestive system in the form of bile. "Did they send you to shut me up?"

Steve didn't answer. "I don't know who you are screwing with this time, Webb. We received a National Security Letter. I work for the goddamn *Washington Post*, and I have never seen anything like this. They seized everything, copied computer files, no judicial review at all. I erased your paper trail, but I don't know what they have or what they created electronically. Whatever's down in Georgia, you better get there."

"Have they called the cops?"

"They're coming soon. I don't know what you're waiting for, why are you here?"

Webb knew his contact would not be meeting him. He closed all running programs, shut down his laptop, and packed everything. He sauntered to the trash to dispose of his cup and returned to where Steve sat, affecting a faux Buddha contemplation.

Webb hugged Steve heartily, then kissed him on the mouth. He stood up and said, loud enough for the entire shop to hear, "It's not you. It's me. So long."

He winked at Steve, whose flummoxed look was entirely appropriate for a supposed rejected lover. Webb put his coat over his head, went out of the store, and disappeared into the chaotic crowds on Dupont Circle.

Sacramento FBI Offices, July 18, 2007, 7:20 a.m.

Phil shaded his eyes with an FBI baseball cap and glasses. He might as well wear a barrel and carry a top hat upside down in his hands. He retained his headgear and specs as he walked through the crescent-shaped brown brick building that contained the Sacramento field office for the FBI. He showed the security guard in the lobby his badge, even though the guard, Oliver, had already nodded and smiled in recognition. He patiently passed through the metal detector and walked onto the elevator to take him to his office on the fifth floor.

Carole Winkelman, the receptionist who efficiently guarded his office against, she joked, the barbarians of bureaucracy, waved at him as he proceeded to his office. After three years, she knew him even with the hat and the unsuccessful slouch that he hoped would make his lean frame less noticeable. "Morning, Phil."

Phil took off the glasses and hat, but kept the slouch. He paused in the doorway, got himself a cup of coffee from the Krups station behind Carole's desk, and smiled at her. "Morning, beautiful." He tried to keep up his usual charm, even though he didn't feel particularly charming.

Carole, five months pregnant, patted her stomach. "Thank you."

"Did Paul LeBrach call?" Phil had tried to reach Paul repeatedly, and his calls seemed to vanish into the ether. If he wasn't able to get at least an offer on his house in the next few days, he was what was technically referred to by the FBI as "fucked."

Carole shook her head. Her lips twitched slightly. Like most women with brains, she didn't think much of Paul. "No calls this morning, but Mr. Clarkson asked to see you as soon as you got in."

Phil was halfway down the hallway to ASAC (Assistant Special Agent in Charge) John Clarkson's office before he noticed his teeth sounded like a buzz saw and the veins on his forehead throbbed and bulged. From the looks his colleagues—who avoided him in the hallway—were giving him, he probably resembled the frazzled-looking Governator yelling, "Shut up," to the panicked preschoolers in *Kindergarten Cop*.

He knew, as he stepped into Clarkson's sage green corner office, why he had been summoned. He'd effectively taken a baseball bat to his career last week when he let go of his rage with Stanislavsky, and it couldn't have come at a worse time. He literally could not borrow another dollar. Or he could borrow it perhaps, but his soon-to-be former colleagues would have to arrest him for defaulting. He was upside down on his house, his credit cards were maxed out, and his car was worth less than he owed on it. He borrowed money from his dad last month that both he and his dad knew he would not be able to repay. And if Paul didn't get his house sold, he would be foreclosed on in less than three weeks. Phil was bankrupt.

John Clarkson could have passed for Barack Obama's brother. Clarkson was a staunch Republican who, like Obama, grew up in Hawaii but later fled the islands for the mainland. His lean face reflected an inner calm Phil found surprising under the circumstances, but comforting. The joke around the office was that when Clarkson was pissed, you thought a 4.0 earthquake had just hit the building.

"Hey, Phil. Pull up a chair." Clarkson tilted back in his chair and regarded Phil thoughtfully.

Phil, still holding his coffee cup, took a seat on the other side of Clarkson's ebony-topped desk. Phil folded his hands and waited.

Clarkson spoke in a measured, soothing, but authoritative way. "Phil, I'll just get right to the point. We appreciate all you've done for Safe Childhoods…"

Here it comes, Phil thought, and willed his face not to move as he took a sip of coffee.

Clarkson continued. "We are starting a new task force here and in most other FBI offices, and I need you to head this one up."

Phil's eyes brightened a little bit, and his jaws silenced. They ached as soon as they calmed down, and he knew he would have to see the dentist soon. At least he'd still have his dental coverage, since he'd managed to escape being fired. "Sir?"

"It's not as flashy as organized crime or bank robbery or anything like that," Clarkson said, "but at least you won't have to contend with the kind of scum like the guy who attacked you last week—thankfully you were ready and able to defend yourself." He gave Phil a big, approving smile. For the first time in a week, Phil relaxed enough to grin back. "But you will have a new kind of scum to deal with."

Phil looked at Clarkson and raised his eyebrows inquisitively. "What exactly are we talking about, sir?"

"Mortgage and real estate fraud," Clarkson said.

Phil couldn't help smiling again. "Sounds interesting." He immediately thought about his mortgage and his friend Paul. "Give me all the details."

LeBrach and Associates Offices, Sacramento, 8:00 a.m.

Waves of blue greeted Paul in his real estate and mortgage broker offices. His market research indicated the color blue soothed clients. The associates may have been jumping around answering phones and providing carefully scripted sales pitches as well as responses to the ever-increasing volume of complaints, but the offices radiated calm. Paul had hired a Feng Shui practitioner whose efforts were supposed to keep Fortune from flowing out the frosted blue glass doors. Paul made a mental note to sue the bitch. The money trees, gold Buddha statues, and red silk wall hangings weren't stopping the cash from leaking through the cracks.

Paul's twenty-five-year-old Hispanic secretary, Karina Domingues, smiled at him. Her crimson lips were as blatantly feminine as her periwinkle shirt dress with the wide belt and white jacket that put him in mind of Catholic school, which was why he always mentally removed himself when he was screwing her.

"Good morning," Karina said.

Paul walked past her without acknowledging her greeting. He shut the door to his office with delicacy. Slamming it would have been over the top. He drew the sea grass Pottery Barn shades over the window looking out on Karina's desk so nobody could look in. Karina would not follow him once he telegraphed his need for privacy this way. Eventually, though, she would find an excuse to enter his office and assail him with her need for his attention. He had enjoyed her grossly sensual charms and her unspoiled youth for three months, but weariness and distaste now set in. He was almost as sick of her as he was of his miserable, ball-busting wife, Patty.

He plopped down in his taupe leather chair and picked up the two-inch-high stack of mail on his Santorini Blue marble-topped desk. Check, check, bill, bill, bill, check, employee health plan update, bill—

ooh. Paul rattled the envelope and heard what sounded like a set of keys clanking together. Jingle mail, he thought, and his eyes brightened.

In the past few months, his mortgage business had slowed to a trickle, as the big hedge funds and banks would no longer buy Paul's loans unless they were underwritten using "traditional" standards. "Traditional" meant they wanted down payments, incomes that were at least three times the loan payments, no big cash-back deals. Who the hell could afford a traditional mortgage these days, outside of his parents, who spent thirty minutes comparing prices at the local Sam's Club despite their wealth? His parents were in the 10 percent of the local population who could afford the median house using "traditional" standards. People like his parents already had a house, or didn't want one. Besides, who the hell would pay the processing fees and commissions on his loans if they could get a traditional mortgage through a prime lender?

Jingle mail was just one more way Paul used his financial ingenuity to weather the current financial climate. The term 'jingle mail' was a slang term used by some in the industry to describe former homeowners who could no longer keep up with payments and thus mailed the keys back to the lender, indicating that they had moved on and the foreclosure process could begin. Paul kept in touch with many of those who he knew would struggle with the loans, and made sure that they incorrectly returned the keys to him (not the bank or company that currently serviced the mortgage). Paul would then rent out the house (usually to undocumented workers who wouldn't come after him later) for six to nine months until somebody noticed.

Paul went to the window looking out into the main office and peeked through the blinds at his employees. The five real estate agents scrambled over each other to take client calls or make cold calls. The five mortgage agents shuffled loan paperwork for Paul's cash-back, balloon, jumbo, and subprime mortgages. The one assistant marched around the office refilling the toner in the fax machine and checking the doughnuts to see if they were stale. Karina avoided looking at his office as she coordinated everyone's schedule on her computer and updated the firm's Web site.

His staff was as productive as they could be under the circumstances, and he was going to have to let at least half of them go. He would start with Karina and then drop four of the five mortgage salespeople. Stacey Marina, the one he would keep, could sell a dead spotted owl to a Greenpeace member. Plus, he'd heard she was equally good in the sack, so he might try her out after Karina. He was still barely pulling in six figures with the real estate business, but thanks to problem homes like Phil's and the overall state of the market, his bottom line was shrinking. People were now selling their homes because they had to, and there were still a few buyers out there who thought they were getting a deal.

Karina finished with her computer updates, grabbed a stack of files off her desk, and bent over to arrange them in the filing cabinet. She gave Paul a superb and unintentional view of her tight backside. It was well-rounded and magnificently defined.

Then there were Paul's own investments, sixteen houses that he purchased with no down payment and received cash-back loans of $50,000 to $100,000 per house. He spent most of that money making the payments on the houses and financed a large piece of land near Sacramento's government district to build a condominium high-rise. He had half of his purchased properties rented for about a third of the loan payment. If the market didn't turn around soon, he could kiss his business and lavish lifestyle good-bye.

Surely he wasn't the only person who'd spent his life working hard and learning the system and thus deserved to get ahead. The big bastards in the real estate and banking business did it. The average Joe and Jane Blow wanted the good life that corporate America advertised. Hell, investors even bailed out pig farmers in Djibouti, so he'd read in *Fortune*. What did they call that? Microlending. Lots of little loans. Micro-mortgages...lots of little mortgages pooled together. It could add up. Micro-refinancing.

Paul let the shade fall and opened his door. He swaggered out and smiled at Karina as he leaned against the doorjamb. Karina dropped one of the files.

"Call the guy at Milteer Capital Funds," he said.

Karina blinked. "You mean the manager you met with last week? Joanne Huffman?"

"Yes, her. Get her on the line, please."

"Right away, Paul...Mr. LeBrach."

"Thanks, you're an angel." Paul watched Karina stoop to pick up the file. Her periwinkle blue excited him as it dipped to reveal her ample cleavage. With this new brainstorm, he could keep her on for a while longer.

Bull-Spears Investment Bank, San Francisco, 10:00 a.m.

In the conference room of the Bull-Spears Investment Bank San Francisco offices, the wall of plate-glass windows afforded Doug a prime view of the lush sprawling Golden Gate Park. He'd give anything to be out there, barefoot and carefree, instead of auditing two of the firm's hedge funds, Extraordinary Guaranteed Growth Fund Class A (known as the EGG fund) and European High-Return Fund Class B (known as the HEF fund). Even by hedge fund standards, these were aggressive in the extreme. Hedge funds, and these in particular, are basically super-aggressive mutual funds for the very wealthy. The SEC and other federal agencies have virtually no oversight on these types of investments—as they are only available to "qualified investors," which, loosely, means they are worth a million dollars or more.

Doug would bet Richard Gauthier's salary that, even more than most investment banks, the hedge fund managers at Bull-Spears highly leveraged the funds in order to achieve unheard-of gains for the wealthy investors. If the nouveau riche clients ponied up ten million dollars, the EGG fund would borrow ninety million, using the clients' money as collateral. If the fund made just a 1 percent gain on is money, after the interest expenses on the borrowed funds, the EGG fund would give its investors a whopping 10 percent return. The downside of this kind of leverage was that if the EGG fund lost 10 percent of its value, the investors would be totally wiped out.

That example wasn't just hypothetical or academic. The EGG and the HEF funds were, unfortunately for the investors, leveraged to the hilt and beyond. EGG and HEF invested in high-grade, mortgage-backed securities (called CDOs or Collateralized Debt Obligations) that earned the third-best risk rating from the rating agencies, meaning there was very low risk of losing money on these funds. Because the risk was considered so low, the funds borrowed at a rate of twenty to one on capital, which meant that on a cool hundred-million-dollar investment, the fund borrowed two billion. Doug knew that because there was no open market for these types of securities, there was no way to get an immediate price, as you could with a publicly traded stock. The fund manager created a mathematical model to determine the value of the funds.

Doug sipped from a cup of coffee, which was as tepid as his bottled water, as he sweated through a number of audit procedures. He verified that the cash they said was there was in fact there. He checked that EGG and HEF did in fact own the securities they said they owned, and that they paid what they said they paid. He ran all of the normal audit procedures to check internal controls, reviewed fraud risk, etc. The funds consisted of a massive amount of money, but as far as an audit was concerned, it wasn't a tremendous amount of work, since there were not many transactions and the concepts were not complicated. The sweat sprung from Doug's review of the model Bull-Spears used to value the securities. Most of their securities were subprime loans and mortgages.

The securities were given a risk rating by an independent rating agency. The agency gave an estimated loss percentage (based on historical losses), which was factored in correctly, and everything in the model looked tidy. But Doug had read and absorbed all the bad press about subprime loans and mortgages in particular, and there were a large number of investors that wanted their money back. From the office gossip Doug had quietly overheard, the fund managers at Bull-Spears had sent letters stating that no withdrawals were allowed due to the current climate, which only made more of the investors want their money back. The truth of the matter was that the fund would be required, in the next couple of months, to allow withdrawals, and Doug felt that a better feel for the immediate market value would need to be sought. He needed to verify the risk ratings.

One of the Bull-Spears hedge fund managers stepped into the conference room. "How's it coming?"

Doug looked up at the woman. She was the only female hedge fund manager he'd noticed. She wore a canary yellow Hillary Clinton-style power pantsuit. "I have some details to check out."

Her brows crested in impatience. "Details? We were told you'd have this audit done by tomorrow. It's only two of our funds. Morningstar gave us four stars, you know."

"My boss said the audit would take a week and a half. And these, as I understand it, are your top-performing funds. The ones you advertise all the time."

"Auditors make our investors nervous."

"The purpose of the audit is to protect the investors." At her stern look, he added, "I just need the time to check my figures." As a habit, he dealt with any troublesome audit by diplomatically asking for clarification. However, his gut, pummeled as it was after Crystal broke up with him by text message and took off to Waikiki early on her own, roared to life and kept him silent.

The woman shook her head. "Bob and Richard said you were the best they had."

"I'm just being thorough, ma'am." He had no idea why he called her ma'am. He hadn't done that since he was a child. "Only the best for our number one client."

She folded her arms. "Perhaps if you have issues you should talk to Bob."

Doug did just that five minutes later. He spoke by phone to the partner in charge of the audit, Bob Baker. "Bob, I just e-mailed you a spreadsheet with details of these pooled mortgages. According to the ratings agency, this CDO is 97.9 percent AAA rated, but 89 percent of the loans are the 'no doc' liar loans and 34 percent of the mortgages are sixty days or more late with payments. We can't rely on the agency ratings for this steaming pile of crap."

Bob appeared to agree with him. "On the ball, Boyd, on the ball. I'll get some outside analysis to corroborate the findings. Good call." The mishmash of the scientific-sounding vocabulary and Bob's normal sports metaphors made Doug grin for the first time since he undertook the assignment. "As for them pressuring you with an unreasonable deadline, well, they're bastards."

"It wasn't as if I was even supposed to be finished by tomorrow," Doug said. "And they just gave me three boxes full of figures to examine a few hours ago."

"They're just being prickly. Don't worry about it." Bob ended the conversation with a pledge to obtain some outside valuations.

Two days later, after three refreshing nights at the Fairmont Hotel and a happy hour or two at San Francisco's posh Postrio restaurant, Doug walked into the conference room and greeted Bob Baker, who rose with a smoking hot cup of coffee in his hand. Bob's tufts of graying black hair fanned out from his ears, reminding Doug of an owl. His scalp had long ago lost the rest of his hair. He had a porcine nose and smokers' teeth. His head looked like a giant pumpkin jammed on his reedy body.

"Hey, Doug, how's everything going here?" He had never used Doug's first name before. That and his fake smile made Doug shudder like a teenage victim in a Dario Argento horror flick.

"It's going okay, Bob. Another week or so and I should have everything wrapped up, provided you can get me those valuations you promised."

Bob giggled and patted the slim black executive case. "Got it right here, Doug, straight from the ratings agency. You know, the same agency that rates every debt in the world, including nearly every nation!"

"Yeah, I saw that, Bob. That is exactly the valuation that the client used. That is the one that I need another source on."

Bob's mirth disappeared. "Doug, I am comfortable with this valuation. Use it and let's wrap this thing up, okay? I am on a tight schedule and need to get this done. The client is getting jumpy, and I can't say I blame them."

Doug's mouth dropped open slightly. "You are kidding me, right? You are going to overrule me on something as basic as this?"

"Listen, Doug, don't fuck with me." Bob spit sulfur-colored phlegm as he spoke the words. In contrast to his face, his body looked fragile from not doing a day's physical work in decades. His underused muscles trembled. "You wrap this thing up, or I'm putting a call into Richard and you can kiss your career good-bye. You understand me?"

Doug had always gotten along affably with Bob, and the lecture made his teeth and nails ache. He hadn't even behaved rudely or argued, and here this joker of a man threatened him. Doug thought of the pushy looks the Bull-Spears staff had given him over the last two days. The higher up the person was, the more psychopathic the stare he received. The bosses at Bull-Spears had probably intimidated Bob and put him under duress right before he came to see Doug.

The threat didn't cow Doug. If anything, he vowed adamantly that he was going to screw down the numbers so tight that the people reading them wouldn't be able to breathe. He told himself he was indifferent to his career. He already was going to miss a glowing recommendation on this audit, and he had already decided that if that happened, he was going to quit and find something else to do—after he took a month to bum around the Caribbean. Maybe he could even find a new girlfriend in the tropics.

"Bob, go for it. Call Richard. Fire me for trying to perform a clean audit. Best-case scenario after I blow the whistle, you are fired and we resign from the audit. Worst-case scenario, you destroy the whole firm and go the way of Arthur Andersen." Doug couldn't believe how calm he was, and how proud he was of himself. It felt good not to kiss ass for a change.

Bob swallowed hard, then pointed at Doug and opened his mouth. More discolored phlegm came out, but not words. Bob's fingers and jaw quivered as his eyes bulged. He stood there a few more seconds, then whirled and walked out of the conference room.

Doug told himself Bob had always been a cowardly little twit. Bob had left his steaming coffee behind, and Doug reached for it. He took a sip and savored the heat and flavor. Brown drops spattered the front of Doug's shirt.

For someone who decided to brashly throw away his job and his career, Doug felt jumpy and shaky himself. He laughed in a vain attempt to lighten his sense of fear.

CHAPTER 4

"There are three kinds of lies: lies, damned lies, and statistics."

—Mark Twain, American novelist

Economic Calamity
Four Brothers
August 4, 2007, 1:13 a.m.
By Martin Cheyne

See link to vlog—sorry if I come off as disjointed as *The Blair Witch Project.*
(sound of branches thwacking in vlog)

I'm concealing myself because I'm being hunted. I guess I'm the duck or quail. A Quayle in the hand is worth two in the Bush.

Where did that come from? That was four presidential terms ago. Oh, I know where it came from. That was Paul's joke. Paul LeBrach. Everyone in our crowd thought that was "da bomb" back then when he said it in the early nineties. They laughed as if he were Letterman or Leno. Paul has a gift for seizing people's attention. Like a vampire, he siphons off their doubt and feeds their need to believe. I used to call it the Cult of Paul. Philip always hung around, as if he were Paul's bodyguard. I pledged the business fraternity because I saw it as my way to change the world and actually have a social life, not just be the weirdo I was all through high school (that's a direct quote from my dearly departed parents, by the way). But even in a frat of geeks, Paul and Phil were the jocks, while Doug and I were the geekiest of the geeks.

Doug, that's Douglas Boyd, Boy Genius, hasn't always been a timid accountant. In fact, he never wanted to be an accountant. He was one of those guys who probably joked around a lot in order to avoid getting shoved in a toilet in high school because he was so smart. I would say he's always been quiet and hardworking, but also very amiable and always up for a laugh. He went to Cal State University because it was close to his parents—former hippies, of all things—and could keep his job and get his degree. After three and a half years of school, Doug got an itch to see the world and get to the Fortune 500 before he turned thirty. When he looked through the catalog, he realized he could finish his degree a semester early if he majored in accounting. Cool, calculating, and very interested in business and the world, he assured himself that an accounting degree would be just as good a place to start as any in his journey to run a major international company. His parents had gone from protesting "the Man" to becoming "the Man" and indoctrinated Doug in the need—the need to succeed. Doug was never unethical, but he took one hit on that great American drug called success, and he was hooked for life.

Paul and I met Doug during his fourth year of college when he pledged the business fraternity. Doug and Phil already knew each other because they stocked shelves at the local Safeway. We became like brothers. Excuse the out-of-character sentimentality.

(Whoosh of air on the vlog as Martin gets the breath knocked out of him while falling.)

Thanks, I needed that. Anyway, we were roommates during our last year at Cal State. Paul and Phil usually had girls on their laps; Doug and I usually cuddled up with sexy textbooks. More than once, one of Phil's or Paul's dates would wander over because they thought nerds were cute. Only in college. So we got the trickle-down of Paul and Phil's wealth.

We kidded around and trash talked, but we had a hell of a lot of fun in college, the time when our hopes for the future were highest. We laughed together, played together, drank together, even got in a few barroom brawls together. And, while we all wish we were right there smack in the lap of youthful arrogance and idealism and illusion, back then we mowed down our fellow graduates to get that mortarboard and diploma. We would take the world by storm. We would take it for all it owed us.

Ain't that America for you and me? Meanwhile, I'm running and ducking through Southern foliage at one in the morning, the same hour I used to stagger home from the bars in college, because of what I know about the greatest economy mankind has ever seen. If Jeff had only listened to me that day in the Econ tutorial lab…

Trackback / Blog This / Comment

University of Nevada-Reno Economics Tutorial Lab, July 20, 2007, 3:30 p.m.

"It's not the greatest economy, it's not even a good economy! We have artificially bloated the economy with money, and it can't last."

Jeff Ortiz, half-Nicaraguan, half-Sicilian, rolled his owl-gray eyes at Martin's lecture and took a sloppy bite out of his vegetarian sandwich.

Jeff, like many of Martin's fellow PhD students who doubled as teaching assistants, lived on veggies because (a) all the undergraduates scooped up the junk food, (b) Jeff and Martin couldn't afford meat, and (c) clogged arteries and heart trouble were the surest way to add many painful years to the already interminable pursuit of their PhD dissertations.

Jeff spoke with his mouth only partially clear of avocado and sprouts. "Corporate profits are soaring, the stock market is soaring—hell, even consumers are spending. Inflation is under three percent, unemployment is at, what, four and a half percent? C'mon, Martin, you've got to be kidding me with your doom and gloom bullcrap."

"Jeff, listen." Martin was used to having the same argument with his colleagues, the professor who was mentoring him in his PhD program, and anyone whom he had met who would even listen. "Nobody believes inflation is at three percent. The government CPI is at three percent. The real cost of living for people has been running probably close to eight to eleven percent per year for the past few years." He punctuated his percentages with slurps of his split-pea soup. "The three percent stated inflation just shows that the standard of living for people is going way down. It costs them eight percent more to live, and they get a whopping three percent pay raise."

The CPI, or Consumer Price Index, is a statistic put out by the Bureau of Labor Statistics. It tracks the cost of a variety of goods and services over time, including food, cars, college tuition, etc. It monitors the cost of the goods from year to year. Institutions use the difference, the increase in the average cost, as the main way to track inflation. The increase is usually the basis for pay raises and cost of living increases to employees and pensioners.

Jeff shook his head. He had given up trying to carry on a rational argument with Martin. It was next to impossible to throw around numbers convincingly if you automatically dismissed all government-published statistics. "Okay, Martin, explain to me your 'real' cost of living and why it is different than the CPI."

"They stuff the CPI for the most part with stats on cars, electronics, clothes, all the crap we are getting cheap from China—which, I might add, is making us sick and torpedoing our economy further. All crap that people don't need, and it drives the CPI down. Housing, medicine, food, oil, and utilities are all going through the roof. That crap from China? Babies get sick from the lead, then the HMOs and Big Pharma hike the prices of treatment and the insurance companies refuse to pay. That doesn't even register on the CPI."

Jeff sighed. "Martin, we won't be able to come to an agreement on that one. As far as I know, the CPI takes all of those areas into account. Let's move on."

Martin's passion for talking about his pet theories—which he considered, in *X-Files* fashion, the truth—ran unchecked now that he was debating with someone who wasn't in a position of power over his career track and his dissertation defense. "No, they don't take them into account correctly. Take housing, for example. The CPI uses a 'rental equivalent' value. But rents and the cost of homes have a major disconnect. When we were kids, you could rent a home for about what you paid as a house payment. Today, in this area at least, you can rent for about one third the cost of buying. And to make it worse, a larger percent of the population own homes. This number alone would cause your three percent CPI to skyrocket." The aroma of his split pea soup mingled with his perspiration as he grew more agitated. "And oil? Let's talk about oil—"

"Let's not." Jeff wrinkled his nose at the peculiar blend of scents from their belated lunches and their summer perspiration. He tired of the conversation and wanted to start his weekend. It was three thirty on a Friday in the middle of summer, and after a long day, he had better things to do than talk about this stuff. He finished his sandwich and stood up to throw away the remains of his lunch. He hoped that this would conclude the conversation.

"And your corporate profits soaring?" Martin continued, not acknowledging that Jeff was no longer interested. "That is because the dollar is so weak. The profits soaring are largely made up of gains from the foreign subsidiaries selling in local currency and then reporting in dollars. Three years ago when General Motors Brazil sold a car for 100,000 reals, General Motors would report a sale in U.S. dollars of about 30,000 dollars. Today, when they sell the same car, at the same price, it translates to about 50,000 dollars. And that is where the bulk of your corporate profits are coming from."

"Okay, Martin, I'll see you on Monday. Have a good weekend." Jeff walked toward the door.

"No, no, no, wait! Let me just make my point about the new record stock market prices. Just plot the Dow Jones average, or the NASDAQ—I don't care. Plot the values in terms of something other than dollars. Put them in terms of another currency, euros or pounds, or put them in terms of any commodity—how much oil, corn, gold would it be equivalent to over time—or even put it in terms of the cost of housing. What you will find is that the record stock market is way below where it was seven or eight years ago."

Jeff wasn't listening, and he walked out of the lab and let the door close behind him.

Martin gulped soup ferociously. His thoughts screamed through his head. The worst thing, Martin thought, was that at this point there was nothing anyone could do. The excesses in the economy had gone too far. If they had only listened to him five years ago, something could have been done. But now, there was nowhere for the economy to go except into a severe depression, which Big Pharma would probably invent a new overpriced drug for.

He finally had the thought to look at the clock and decided to head out for the day. No one else, including Congress and the potential presidential candidates, worried about the state of the economy over the weekend, so why should he? He would live like the rest of America for a weekend. Go hunting and beer-drinking with the boys and pretend his children and grandchildren, if by some miracle he managed to reproduce, would have a future.

Bull-Spears Investment Bank, San Francisco, 4:45 p.m.

Doug wasn't quite finished with the audit, despite what Bob thought. However, he was done for the weekend. His camping gear and luggage for the trip lay perfectly arranged in his trunk. After he finished his work, he took a walk around the corporate office building that stacked Bull-Spears and other companies one on top of the other, like a money sandwich. Their windows looked black in the late afternoon light. His cell phone rang.

"Doug Boyd," he answered.

"Doug? Richard." Richard sounded calm, definitely not mad. "I just had a conversation with the asshole, Bob. Listen, he was way out of line. I support you one hundred percent on this thing. I just want you to know that."

"Thanks, Richard. I appreciate that." In his ten-year history with the company, Doug had never heard of Richard ever making a phone call in support of one of his subordinates, not even after a death in the family.

Richard sounded smooth as ice in Scotch. "Listen, I'm going to be honest with you. We are under some pressure with this client. We've called them to the carpet on several issues this year, and they are considering dropping us next year. They are one of the firm's largest clients in the world, and certainly the largest in the San Francisco office. So, even though I support you, I think you certainly were within your rights, I want you to cool it on this issue you have for now. Let's get the financial statements out this year, and we will deal with them. Dropped and done until next year. Okay?"

"I'm sorry, Richard, but you know I'm ethically bound to continue this." He knew pulling the ethical card would really piss Dick off, and that was deliberate. Doug felt as if invisible pincers tightened his throat. "I can't drop it. If it isn't a big deal, then let's just handle it. These funds are worth almost four billion combined, and they have to issue separate financial statements to the investors. Let's just deal with it and worry about repitching the business for next year. You can take me off the audit next year."

Richard reacted predictably, a burst of verbal gunfire. "Goddamnit, kid, I can take you off right now and send your ass out the door!"

"That is your choice, boss. But it would be pretty strange pulling me off a job only ninety-nine percent completed. It probably wouldn't look good for you if it ever got out." Doug felt, for the first time, the stirring of machismo.

He could almost hear the fumes coming out of Richard's ears. He had probably never been talked to this way by anyone, much less one of his employees. "Take the weekend and think carefully about what you want out of this job, Doug. We'll talk Monday."

After Richard hung up abruptly, Doug went back into the building. His walk was alive with that moment's immortality. Today was the first day in a long time he felt liberated and powerful. He was in control.

Aaron Cartwright's Office, 5:00 p.m.

Richard Gauthier and Bob Baker, both proud of their many long years that included countless martini lunches at their desks at Arthur Whinney and Associates, tried to look like top-level executives as they sat across from Aaron Cartwright, the managing director of Bull-Spears, the fourth-largest investment bank in the world.

Aaron Cartwright was an intimidating character. He resembled the actor Ben Kingsley, minus the charisma. His bulked muscles puffed out the sleeves of his pinstripe Kenneth Cole shirt, and unlike most investment bankers, he intimidated and impressed with his triathlete physique. His ice-cold stare could render an unsuspecting person speechless. Years of experience etched his face with a dour pattern, and with a look at the way the skin sagged around his mouth, Richard and Bob confirmed their private opinions that he hadn't smiled very often in his fifty-nine years. According to gossip, an office pool at Bull-Spears took bets on when Cartwright would have a good belly laugh. The kitty had grown, so Bob heard from one of the administrative assistants he flirted with, to two thousand dollars, and as yet no one had claimed it.

Richard and Bob both doubted that their news would earn one of the poor slobs at Bull-Spears the two grand. They had just finished explaining about Doug, whom Richard had called from a cell phone inside the Bull-Spear building. Doug had, by all accounts, been buried in his audit all day except for the occasional exercise break. Richard and Bob knew he wouldn't confront Cartwright with his suspicions. The little bastard didn't have the balls.

They threw in several phrases such as "never gave us any trouble before," "first one at the office and the last one to leave," "has no life outside of work," "thought he was a team player," and as many pat reassurances as they could generate between them. The annual billing for Bull-Spears totaled close to $80,000,000 for all services. They were not about to lose this meal ticket and risk being worked over by Cartwright. The photos that lined his office, pictures of Cartwright posing with senators, representatives, and billionaires, stared mercilessly at Richard and Bob. A stream of images of being shot to death in the Mojave Desert or dropped into the Pacific ran through their heads.

"We can't take him off the audit," Richard said. "He's the only worker qualified to handle it."

"It's going to look weird." Bob tugged at his ear and passed a hand over his forehead. "You understand."

Cartwright, expressionless, listened to their spiel. He was not a stupid man. He must understand the implications from all sides. "I understand." He paused.

Bob jumped in with a stutter that grated on Richard's ears. "Then you are okay with this?"

"A lot of people are counting on this audit." The flatness of Cartwright's voice didn't vary. "It's important to the economy. There's a lot of oversight."

Bob and Richard tried not to glance on the political and calculating photographic eyes staring at them from all sides. "Sure, sure. That's important," Bob said.

"Can you control your man?" Cartwright folded his hands around a miniature statue of a Masai warrior that had probably been made in Korea.

"He's young, ambitious, burned out." Richard smiled. "On Monday we'll dangle a full partnership in front of him and give him a month's vacation once he finishes this audit. He'll take it."

"Good," Cartwright said. "It's important that operations continue as usual. Hedge funds have collapsed because of incompetence or whistle-blowers, or government regulation that does more harm than good. Unbridled capitalism is what creates innovation and wealth. Fortunately many of those federal operating barriers may ease up, because everyone wants to continue our current prosperity. You can't regulate wealth, you can't legislate it. It's not fair to all the investors in real estate who are trying to live their dreams. That's why, gentlemen, you brought this to my attention. We're problem solvers. We know that our approach works. We have to trust it, to trust the process of capitalism."

From the micro-movement in his eyebrows, Cartwright was satisfied with his own discourse. Bob and Richard nodded reverently. "It's not fair," Bob echoed, "that the bureaucrats try to kill innovation."

Cartwright nodded. "We may not have to worry once social change catches up to the government. We love winners, we want to win. This fellow of yours wants to win. If he doesn't, he's an idiot."

Bob and Richard nodded. Cartwright's phone rang. He answered nonchalantly. "Hello?...No, nothing. Nothing. My meeting just concluded, productively…Thank you. Anything I can do for you?"

He listened as Richard and Bob rose from their seats. "I believe that weekend is free, but I will see you before then for our business in the wine country, won't I?"

As the two men from Arthur Whinney gathered up their briefcases and jackets and BlackBerrys, Cartwright carried on his call. He offered Richard a meager glance and one-eighth of a nod. Once they were out, he said to his friend, "Saddleback, don't worry. I'll be good to you, and you'll help me in whatever way you think would best benefit our investors. The public. That's what it's all about, no matter what some malcontents say."

Bull-Spears Investment Bank Conference Room, San Francisco, 6:00 p.m.

Douglas Boyd was just two floors down and across the building from where his bosses had been sitting with Aaron Cartwright. He had not had any communication with Richard or Bob since the last phone call and was oblivious to any of the confab that had been going on.

He closed, latched, and otherwise secured his binders full of audit documents and workpapers. He normally preferred to leave them at the client site, but today he decided to take them with him. From what he'd seen, no one at Bull-Spears seemed interested in his audit documents, but he felt a sixth sense nudge him to pick up those binders. Maybe his moment of immortality had made him psychic too. Doug grinned at himself. He was probably anal-retentive. There could be a fire or other disaster in the building over the weekend. A bomb threat. He packed away his laptop. He loaded all the binders he could into a small box and balanced the laptop case on the box. He headed for the elevator with his load.

The junior employees and temps smiled and wished Doug a good weekend. Unlike the higher-ups in management, he actually interacted with the people who worked at Bull-Spears. A college girl, probably a B-school intern, pressed the elevator chime for him and waved as she moved down the hall. Doug nodded back and smiled. He kept his good humor until the elevator doors opened and he found himself staring at Richard and Bob.

No point in being timid now. He hopped onto the elevator in front of them.

"Richard…Bob," he offered as a greeting once the doors closed.

"Douglas," Richard responded calmly. Bob's face turned fuchsia and magenta instead of red. How this man managed to become a partner, Doug had no idea. Doug turned, hugged his box to his chest, and stared at the certificate of inspection above the control panel. The rest of the elevator ride to the lobby was completely silent.

When they arrived in the lobby, Richard and Bob moved for the exit to the right. Doug, seeking to avoid any more awkwardness, moved for the exit to the left.

Doug walked across to his white Pontiac G6 and popped the trunk. He looked at the trunk in dismay. He had forgotten that he had already filled it with camping gear and luggage. He paused for just a second, closed the trunk, opened the driver's side back door, and threw the box and his laptop computer bag on the rear seat.

He jumped in the car, revved the engine, pulled out of the parking lot, and headed for Interstate 80 East out of San Francisco and into the Sierras. He wished he hadn't been so damn conscientious, because the dinner hour traffic crawled along. He could almost feel the collective desperation to get the hell away from work.

By the time he crossed the bay bridge to get out of San Francisco proper, it was already seven fifteen, and a smoky blue dusk was just starting to set in.

I-80 East

By eight fifteen, Doug was in the middle of farm country. Even his Garmin GPS voiced that opinion. The sun had almost completely set. Doug pulled off I-80 East at a gas station to fill the tank and grab something caffeinated to drink for the rest of the drive.

Maybe the lack of energy to the brain made his imagination run amok, but he swore that two seconds after he hit his blinker to turn off the interstate, two cars tailing him about half a mile behind engaged their blinkers to pull off at the same exit. When he pulled into the station, he noticed one of the cars, a white Ford Crown Victoria with tinted windows, pulled into the fuel bay and stopped at the pump opposite him.

The sign on the pump said, "Please pay inside." Doug filled up the tank and observed that the Crown Vic looked like an unmarked police car. He finished fueling, but never saw anyone get out of the Crown Vic.

The convenience store was the size of an office supply closet at Arthur Whinney and there was no coffee available. Doug opted for an energy drink and paid for it along with his gas.

He drank it and felt the wonderful rush of guarana and caffeine. The station was empty other than Doug and the mystery car, and the Crown Vic was still sitting there, engine off, as if it was waiting for him when he hopped back into his car. Doug thought back to an old Stephen King horror movie about a possessed car that killed people. His body shook, and he told the guarana-induced fantasy to stop.

He got into his car and pulled out of the gas station. He checked his rearview mirror. It looked as though someone had gotten out of the Crown Vic. Relieved, he drove on, eager to continue his journey. He eased back onto the freeway and cruised as he sipped his energy drink. He stopped checking his rearview mirror after the first mile, and thus never noticed the Crown Vic following him.

CHAPTER 5

"You are a den of vipers and thieves... by the eternal god I will rout you out."

—Andrew Jackson, to a delegation of bankers

Sacramento FBI Offices, July 20, 2007, 1:00 p.m.

Phil stood in one of the FBI conference rooms and surveyed his task force as he briefed them. While he'd led the busts on the child pornographers, this felt different, as if he were the first kid called on in first grade to give a book report.

Ten FBI field agents, most of whom looked like they had just graduated from the academy, stared at him expectantly. The steam trails from their coffees spiraled into the air.

He used a Flash presentation on his laptop with the lights partly dimmed. It didn't resemble the meetings on TV, fraught with dramatic tension.

"Our great state of California made the top ten states for lending and housing scams. The others, in no particular order, are Florida, Georgia, Illinois, Indiana, Michigan, New York, Ohio, Texas, and Utah." The Flash presentation highlighted all ten states on the map of America.

"Utah?" Denise Taggert, a gap-toothed woman with her hair in a French braid, shook her head. "I was born in St. George. I'm not Mormon, mind you, don't approve of that religion, but I can't believe it of Utah. Our only vice is white sugar."

"So you never heard of Warren Jeffs, then?" Lilah Perry-Hastings, another female member of the team with a faint West Indies lilt and smooth cocoa skin asked. "The fundamentalist cult there, the welfare fraud?"

Agent Taggert shook her head. "Geez…we just finally got coffee in our convenience stores."

"Midwest states made the list," a balding pencil-necked man, Lou Barrino, said in a Boston accent. "Michigan, one of the worst. God-damn unions. Motown's falling apart. Does anyone call it Motown these days?"

Phil continued, not loudly. Nevertheless, the crosstalk silenced. "Not coincidentally, the statistics show that these ten states have the highest increase in housing prices."

"Not anymore," Agent Perry-Hastings said.

Phil nodded as the Flash presentation listed the different types of mortgage fraud. "Right. Thanks to schemes such as property flipping, which most everyone tried, home prices will be affected. The difference between the fixer-upper flippers and the scammers is that the scammers use fraudulent appraisals, doctored loan documentation, and so on. Say you're flipping a house that's only worth five hundred and fifty thousand in Silicon Valley."

Everyone grinned at that.

"The fake appraisal tells the buyer it's worth one point two million. These fake appraisals are a sideline all their own, and they're used to squeeze more money out of the lenders, who think the property and the buyer are good credit risks. Meanwhile, the criminals are making kick-backs to everybody involved at any level professionally in a real estate transaction. They also insist you use their appraiser, end of discussion."

When Phil bought his house, Paul insisted on using "his guy" so that Phil would be able to get the house appraised high enough that he could roll his debt, about eighty thousand dollars, into the home loan.

"All of these loans have hidden costs, by the way. Usually, the person who arranges the loan gets a commission that's far beyond what the banks ask for."

Phil's loan disclosure documents showed that Paul had been paid almost twelve thousand dollars as a commission on the loan. At the time, Paul had insisted that this was normal. "Two percent of the loan, no big deal," assured Phil with a shrug.

Helen had let Phil know it was a Titanic-sized deal. "You can't trust a guy who sells umbrellas in a desert," she said, using one of her incomprehensible aphorisms. "The bank charges half what you paid. Are your college days making you blind?"

Phil cleared his throat to shake himself out of the gloom. He even missed Helen's crazy sayings. "There's the Silent Second, where the buyer of Condo A borrows the down payment from the seller through a non-disclosed second mortgage. Bank B, the primary lender, believes the borrower has invested his own money in the down payment and doesn't know it's borrowed. Oh, and they conveniently forget to record the second mortgage with the county. Let's not confuse this with the straw buyer, who you put up to conceal your real identity. You are the borrower and you convince what they call a nominee to allow you to use that person's name and credit history. Do I need to cover identity theft? Schemes that use stolen IDs to apply for mortgages?"

Everyone shook their heads. Phil knew that all four of them had worked identity theft cases.

"There are air loans, run by the people who call you during dinner from their garage and try to get you to give out your mother's maiden name and the last four digits of your Social Security number over the phone. They might get themselves a bank of telephones and have a different person in their outfit call you, or more accurately, call the banks, pretending to be the employer, appraiser, escrow company, and whoever else they need to be. They persuade the lender to make a loan on non-existent property.

"There's equity skimming," Phil said. "Using our friend the straw buyer as a plant for the investor, who provides false income documents and fake credit reports."

Paul and Phil had fudged Phil's FBI income on the loan application. "You were planning on working a lot of overtime, Phil, right?" Paul said at the time. "The government always overworks you and then they never catch anybody dangerous. How many years has Osama been hiding out in a cave somewhere?"

Beads of perspiration collected on Phil's nose like the melting snowflakes he caught on his face while he, Helen, and the kids skied at Heavenly last year. Instead of opening the in-home day care center they'd talked about, they'd hit the slopes. They decided that a home-based business would be easier once the kids started middle school. Phil wished they'd never taken that skiing trip.

"One of the warning signs of mortgage fraud is fake supporting loan documentation," Phil said, his tongue thick and dry.

Paul had convinced someone in his office to draft a supporting financial statement for Phil that showed the day care center made $2,000 per month last year.

"In equity skimming, the investor gets the property but no guaranty to title through a quitclaim deed. The investor doesn't make any mortgage payments, but collects the money and runs. The property goes into foreclosure."

"Heaps of foreclosure scams out there," said Agent Hastings-Perry.

Agent Barrino stepped on her answer. "What they do is they go follow around the people who are buying the Lexus, the iPhone, the trip to Bali. They hack into bank records. They hang around the supermarket and watch the people paying with WIC and food stamps. They figure, those are the people who are going to be in foreclosure."

"Plus they get the foreclosure records off the Internet," a trainee named Reddy added. "Off Zillow."

Phil stepped back in. "Then they mislead the homeowners into believing that they can save their homes in exchange for a transfer of the deed and up-front fees. The perpetrator profits from these schemes by re-mortgaging the property or pocketing fees that the homeowner gladly pays. They call this 'foreclosure rescue.' Sometimes the perps sell the home right out from under the homeowners or even take out a second loan to siphon off the property's equity. That's the extreme. Plus there are the home equity lines of credit that perps use to fund multiple fraud schemes...anyone familiar with the Mi Su Yi case?"

A few agents nodded. The others busily pulled up the info on their laptops or PDAs before Phil's presentation outlined the case of California couple Mi Su Yi and Paul Amorello. Paul.

Phil's buddy Paul had even mentioned many of these schemes to Phil as though trading sports scores or stock tips. He used his brother's and his mother's credit to buy houses, he flipped properties within a couple of months of buying them, and received hundreds of thousands of dollars of cash back each time he bought, or so he told Phil. Phil had suspected that this couldn't be totally legal, but why would the banks loan money so easily? It would be so easy to check any of this. He assumed everybody knew what everybody else was doing. "Bad assumption, poor police work," he mumbled.

"What? I thought the DOJ prosecuted that case," Agent Taggert said. "Mi Su Yi was convicted two years ago."

Phil shook his head. "Never mind, everybody, just me thinking out loud about how all these mortgage fraud schemes succeed in the first place. That won't happen, not on our watch."

Everyone nodded and smiled in synchronization.

He hoped his past didn't reveal itself in telltale micro-expressions and voice inflections that trained FBI agents would pick up on. "Now our plan of attack has three prongs. First, we identify all the obvious red-flag cases…"

As he talked, Phil couldn't stop thinking about three things. How could he head up this FBI task force if he was guilty of mortgage fraud himself? If it was so easy for him to do it, how widespread was this mess? Was he going to have to arrest Paul? The last thought made him smile for a second, but he quickly stopped when the agents, misinterpreting his smile for enthusiasm over the long hours he hinted the team would have to put in, returned his grin politely. One or two shook their heads.

"I don't mean that we're never going to have lives again," he added.

"You don't?" Agent Barrino looked at the clock. Phil cut off the impulse to swear as he noticed it was five past five. How had that happened?

Paul was his friend. Hell, they were going to be camping together in about four hours, and he needed to head out. His camping gear was already loaded in his car. He didn't particularly want to go home right now.

"We'll pick this up on Monday," he said instead. "I don't expect anyone to do any investigating or reading over the weekend, but just be thinking about ideas for how we can effectively seek out these people." He offered a genuine smile. "I look forward to working with you guys. You've been great. And patient."

Everyone laughed, and wished him a good weekend.

Paul's Residence, American River, 5:15 p.m.

Gabrielle Solis from *Desperate Housewives* blended her TV voice with Patty LeBrach's screech as the DVD of season one of Patty's favorite show played full blast through the open door of Paul and Patty's practically new six-thousand-square-foot home.

Patty herself, wearing an Eva Longoria-style top with bling on the collar and a slit exposing the cleavage of her basketball-shaped breasts, tapped her foot in the Christian Louboutin slingback against the Mediterranean-style porch columns. "Paul, I'm serious."

Paul didn't turn his head as he shoved a cooler full of Trader Joe's munchies and beer into the back of Patty's scarlet-harlot red H2 Hummer four-wheel drive SUV. The Hummer had the same temperament as its owner and could ride hell over those dirt back roads in the Sierras.

Without even looking, Paul knew the breeze from the American River slightly ruffled Patty's perfectly teased and coiffed hair as she posed, just waiting for him to acknowledge her dominion.

"If you are going to get it dirty or muddy, take your own car," she said.

"'Take your own car.'" Paul buried his comment and his disgusted look in the cavernous back of the Hummer. "It is my fucking car," he said to the cooler, "and you are standing in my fucking house. If it weren't for me, you would still be waiting tables at Pedro's, flashing your un-enhanced saggy cleavage for higher tips."

Pedro's was a former hangout of Paul's, before he became a real estate mogul. Five years ago, Patty was a waitress there. She used to be great company, a lot of fun, and good in the sack, so he married her with the expectation that the good times would continue. Now, after having his ring on her finger for four years, she was just a nag who didn't care about anything except spending Paul's money and making him miserable.

"I know you can hear me," Patty shouted. "Honestly, do you have to spend money and weekends on frivolous things like camping? We should start planning to have a family, you know! We're not getting any younger."

"Please, God, no," Paul muttered to the cooler.

He couldn't avoid the last trip into the garage to grab the remainder of his camping gear. He deliberately didn't look at Patty as he strutted into the three-car garage and then back out. Patty still talked impatiently at him, sometimes parroting Gabrielle's lines when Patty's own repartee failed.

Paul waved good-bye and climbed into the driver's seat of the H2 without saying a word to his wife. Although he had his new scheme, he feared his empire was crumbling around him, and the last thing he needed to hear was her bitching. He could feel all of his muscles loosen as he drove away from her and off for a weekend of fun with his old college roommates. Maybe Martin would be in the mood to rumble and ripsnort, not just lecture.

Martin's Ranch House, Reno, Nevada, 3:15 p.m.

Martin lived in a quiet, modest neighborhood, modest for Reno. His liveliest neighbor was Mrs. Delmonico, who at seventy-three taught salsa dance classes at her home to supplement her Medicare and Social Security. She'd been a showgirl back in the glory days and could still kick her legs with the best of them. Martin had helped her with some of her evening classes and even learned the moves. Most of the block was retirees and seniors, half of whom still worked for a living, as much to keep themselves from moldering in front of the TV as to stay in their homes now that their pensions were evaporating.

Martin liked the neighborhood; it was quiet, hidden. He picked the home he did because the previous owner had a bomb shelter put in the backyard. Martin grew up with a much more cynical view of the world than most kids, as he had an uncle who explained the "truth" behind the Kennedy assassination, the Roswell cover-up, and he had learned all about the Illuminate and their plan to take over the world. As he matured, he learned to adopt a slightly tamer view on some of these conspiracies, but he always kept his eyes wide open and always looked for the reason behind the reason for things. The modern-day conspiracy of monetary manipulation and the desire of the rich to revert to a feudal hierarchical order made Roswell seem as silly as clowns in a barrel.

The neighbors' homes were shuttered at this hour, but the rapid clattering of a guiro, a Latin American musical instrument, echoed from Mrs. Delmonico's east-facing windows as Martin stored his gear in his car. He left behind his textbooks, his laptop, and anything else PhD or blogging related. Well, except for his mind, and he intended to lose that this weekend.

Martin knew that when he returned on Sunday evening, his neighbors would be lined up outside his door. They talked to him more often than they did their children, and sought his financial advice. He chose not to think about the fact that he had no optimism to offer to these people who had worked all their lives only to lose it because their children had let the economy go to pot.

He shook his head and got in his Jeep Wrangler with the "Ron Paul for President" bumper sticker. He keyed in the ignition and turned off his formidable intellect, limiting it only to the task of driving into the Sierras.

I-80, Baxter Exit, Sierra Nevada Mountains

The digital yellow neon numbers on Doug's dash said 9:45 p.m. when he located the sign for the Baxter exit. He continued a quarter of a mile before he turned off the interstate into the High Sierras. He'd been blessed with a scarcity of traffic since he left the gas station.

Even in the all-enveloping dark, Doug could perceive the majesty of sky-high pine trees and granite outcroppings, sentinels that stood over him. He rolled down the window and let his lungs absorb the mountain air that only smelled this unspoiled at an elevation of six thousand feet. With the biting tingling coolness of the air, no one would ever believe it was July in California. Doug rolled the window back up and carried on his way.

For twenty minutes Doug drove on paved roads. The last leg of the trip led him around the curves of a rough, bumpy dirt road. It took him forty minutes to drive ten miles until he located the small, inconspicuous entrance gate. The campsite was an unmanned California Department of Forestry campground. Doug paid the entrance fee, eight dollars per car, and drove on through the gate. Ahead of him lay the small mountain freshwater lake, a dark blue in contrast to the black sky. Who needed running water or bathrooms when you had bushes to squat behind and waters that made you feel reborn? Best of all, there would be few campers to share their wilderness utopia.

When Doug turned off his car, he got out and immediately used the blazing campfire as well as Paul's shout of greeting to orient himself in the darkness.

"Hey Douggy," Paul yelled from his lawn chair, "while you're up, could you grab me a beer?"

Martin and Phil saluted Doug, since they already had cold ones in their hands. They too relaxed in lawn chairs like kings of the forest. Doug smiled, unpacked a beer, and threw it to Paul. Phil intercepted it and punted to Paul. Everyone applauded.

"Glad you could make it," Martin said. "We get to live like real men instead of wage slaves."

"How are you, Doug?" Phil smiled.

Doug set up his gear with Boy Scout efficiency, snatched a beer from Paul's cooler that someone had stowed in a tree out of reach of raccoons, and parked his lawn chair around the fire.

"Let the party begin," Phil said.

For the next two hours, they laughed, drank beer after beer, joked, and told stories. None of them paid attention to the Crown Vic that eased past their campsite on the dirt drive at 1:00 a.m.

Shawn G. Smith was no assassin. He cleared a million dollars a year, plus bonuses for extra-sensitive covert work, as a member of the corporate security force of Bull-Spears and personal assistant to Aaron Cartwright, who'd hired him away from the Contra Costa police force.

At forty-three, Shawn had a flat face that deliberately withheld most human expressions, except as required by his job. His one visible vulnerability was a nose that had collapsed, some said due to a deviated septum, others said because of a no-holds-barred confrontation on the job, still others hinted at coke problems. Shawn didn't have any addictions or vices outside of his work. He handled a variety of matters, such as corporate espionage, eavesdropping on Bull-Spears employees as well as reviewing the contents of their hard drives and all e-mail correspondence, and occasionally orchestrating a blackmail scheme to control people who otherwise might not do what Mr. Cartwright (or "Hoss" as Shawn occasionally called him) wanted them to.

It was easier than most people thought. On occasion he did have to resort to photographing an employee in sexual encounters with a prostitute from Shawn's little black book of the hookers he'd busted as a cop, the ones who might want a reduced sentence or community service. He would also plant illegal narcotics. But usually most people had secrets that would ruin them. Senators got caught in bathroom stalls, prosecutors were on the take, ministers and married governors had homosexual affairs. Shawn and his staff, all formerly of law enforcement, were adept at watching people closely. Shawn's people could cover their tracks, and the poor bastards Shawn targeted never had any hint of their own reckoning until Shawn confronted them with his surveillance results.

This Douglas Boyd was the first person he had ever been asked to eliminate. Shawn wasn't sure why, but knew it must be serious. He thumbed through his file on Doug as he sat inside the parked Crown Vic outside a deserted campsite close to the tree line of the Sierras.

Douglas Jeremy Boyd. Thirty-three years old.

Shawn sipped a Dunkin' Donuts coffee. He'd break out the Frappuccino as needed. His car smelt of hummus and tabbouleh from Whole Foods.

Douglas Boyd, born in Butte, California. No wife, no kids, no drugs. He lived alone. Gossip abounded at Arthur Whinney and Associates, LLC, that he was gay, but he'd just broken up with his girlfriend for work reasons and no one had ever seen him in a gay bar. He didn't appear to have much of a social life, period. His parents were deceased, and he had one surviving relative in California, a grandmother who lived in Auburn. Nobody would probably notice for a while if he disappeared. He had $3,700 in his checking account, $2,500 in his savings account, and about $75,000 in a company 401(k) retirement plan. No criminal record, clean credit report.

Douglas Boyd was a geek and a Boy Scout, an accountant. He worked out but wasn't athletic. He was about six feet tall and weighed 160. Shawn was six feet, two inches and had a fourth dan black belt in Aikido, plus he was packing. He could get rid of Douglas Boyd without breaking a sweat.

Shawn circled the Boyd campsite and shone his high-beams. Three other vehicles were parked under trees, and there were three other tents. Doug was no longer alone.

He didn't waste time on blaming himself. A disappearance, a death, would be easy enough. A natural death. A wild animal attack. It could happen this close to the mountains. He would wait until the target and his campfire friends slept, then move in.

Shawn had brought two other men with him, to follow in another car. It was too easy to spot someone trailing you if there was just one vehicle, but with two you could have one waiting up ahead, the other trailing. It was easy to not get spotted that way.

Shawn's deputies had parked about two miles away, and he made a circuit of the back roads. One of the men hiked into the camp and waited in the copse of pine on the other side of the campsite approximately five hundred yards from where the marks sat enjoying themselves. The other man stayed with the car in case Douglas Boyd or his pals decided to make a break for it. Both men came equipped with two 9mm pistols, one drawn with a silencer attached, the other holstered and in reserve. Both men were dead-shot aims.

Paul drunkenly kicked dirt on the bonfire in a feeble attempt to bank it for the night. "Give it a rest, willya, Marty? I'm not in a college classroom, ya know."

"Fortunate," Martin said, "since it'd be a waste."

Paul made a disgusted noise as the other two men set about banking the fire and smothering the dwindling flames with badge-worthy efficiency. "We are not headed for a recession. If I choose to enjoy life, that's my business, no matter what you damned ivory tower people think."

"Is it your wife's business?" Martin watched Paul's face for a reaction.

Paul shrugged. The movement suddenly seemed too complicated in his inebriated state. His eyes had a hard glimmer, and he wiped his nose. "At least I have a wife and am getting laid every night, which is more than I can say for anybody else here. You get in anyone's pants lately, Douggy? What about you, Marty?"

Doug made a show of yawning, and fumbled around, exaggerating his tiredness and level of alcohol consumption, but not by much. "I think that's our cue to turn in. Good night, all."

Phil nodded. "Doug's right. We can all sleep as late as we want tomorrow."

Paul snorted, letting them know in the snotty sound that he thought they were all pathetic. "Fine." He stomped into his tent, turned, and giggled unexpectedly. "Watch out, the ivory tower people may come and get you in the night!" He pitched back into the canvas sanctuary of his tent, leaving his friends to sigh in relief.

"Good old Paul." Doug yawned again as he checked the bonfire to see that there was no danger of a spark. Satisfied, he crawled into his sleeping bag about six feet from the fire. He didn't feel like setting up his tent. It felt too claustrophobic, like his apartment.

Martin nodded. "If you'll excuse me, we ivory tower people need our sleep before we inflict the plague of knowledge on the innocent public."

"The plague of knowledge." Phil fought the urge to giggle. "I'll take the ivory tower people any day."

By 2:05 a.m., the four men were asleep, and Phil got to sublimate his moral qualms in dreams.

Shawn circled the back roads until he was sure the sound of his engine, or any sound he made, wouldn't disturb the unsuspecting campers. By 2:10 a.m., he noticed the campfire had been banked and now gave off curls of smoke. A band of starlight provided a bit of illumination in the moonless sky, but Shawn was safe under the cover of night.

At three, Shawn, concealed in the bushes that ringed the campsite, observed that the area was completely still as the campers slumbered. He spoke into the hands-free radio clipped to his ear. "Is everything clear? I'm ready to move in."

"The road is clear," Tom, the man who stayed with the car, confirmed.

"Clear as far as I can see from here," Wayne said from the copse.

"Okay, I'm moving in," Shawn said, brandishing a machete he'd bought on a job in Honolulu. He decided to use it to terminate Boyd, but make it look as if an animal mauled him. They had coolers in the camp. He'd overturn the coolers, make a mess with the food, and spill some beer. Animal attacks happened when careless campers left food out. For good measure, he'd strafe the sides of Boyd's car. This was a better plan than using the 9mm, which even with the silencer could be too loud and might awaken the others at the distance Shawn would require for a clear shot.

Cautiously, he walked toward the center of the campsite. He slowly raised and lowered his foot for each step with the precision of a ballet dancer. No pine needles crackled underfoot.

Boyd lay wrapped up in his sleeping bag, a bagged deer. Shawn readied his machete and crept closer.

Phil Schultz was frustrated.

Not frustrated about the camping trip, or his life at the moment. All the beer he had drunk had taken care of that. The enormous quantities of fiber, carbohydrates, and sugar he ingested with the beer expanded in his gut, and within seconds, felt as if it engulfed his head. He felt fuzzy, restless, crammed into a body that wanted to burst wide open. The chill outside only made the urgency of his bladder more acute. He had to go to the bathroom.

Phil figured he must look like one of the Three Stooges as he stumbled out of his tent with a roll of toilet paper in hand. He headed for the tree line so he could do his business a good distance away from camp. Nobody would wake up bleary-eyed the next day and step into Phil's bodily waste.

He walked two hundred yards in his boxers and Oakland A's T-shirt and tried not to clench his ass against the cold as he moved. Then, he heard a voice that he instantaneously judged to be two hundred feet away say, "Clear as far as I can see from here."

There was nothing and no one else around. The campgrounds were even more vacant than any of them had thought. Even through his fuzzy head, Phil felt his "Spidey sense" kick in. He stepped as quietly as he could toward the voice, and spotted, through two pines that formed a Y, a man dressed in all in black with the standard-issue assassin's black ski cap. The man scanned their campsite with infrared goggles.

The instinct for surprise caused Phil to call out in a ringing voice, "FBI. Freeze!"

CHAPTER 6

"Gentlemen, I have had men watching you for a long time and I am convinced that you have used the funds of the bank to speculate in the breadstuffs of the country. When you won, you divided the profits amongst you, and when you lost, you charged it to the bank. You tell me that if I take the deposits from the bank and annul its charter, I shall ruin ten thousand families. That may be true, gentlemen, but that is your sin! Should I let you go on, you will ruin fifty thousand families, and that would be my sin!"

—Andrew Jackson, to a delegation of bankers

Economic Calamity
Hunt 'n Fish
July 23, 9:00 a.m.
By Martin Cheyne

For those of you who wonder how my camping weekend was, well, I'm not going to give you a blow-by-blow. Gorgeous lost college girls were involved. Kegs of beer. We even scared the bears.

And if you believe that, then I'm Hillary Clinton. Nothing more eventful happened than me lecturing my fiscally clueless friend Paul about economic realities.

Trackback / Comment / Blog This

Sierra Nevada Campground, July 21, 2007, 3:05 a.m.

Dave Kenner panicked at hearing the three initials he hated more than "IOU" or "DOA."

"Holy shit, the Feds are here," he screamed into his earpiece. "We've been set up. Abort, abort!" He hauled ass through the pines back to the car.

Phil ventured after the fleeing man a few yards, and almost hurled his roll of toilet paper after the man, when he realized he was half-naked and his only weapons were his bare hands and a roll of Charmin. He wasn't MacGyver; he couldn't devise a weapon out of pine resin and needles. He whirled and dashed back to the camp to get his gun.

This time, he didn't care who he awakened.

"We've been set up. Abort, abort!"

Shawn heard Dave's panic through his earpiece just as he approached Doug's resting spot. He saw a figure approach the camp, steal into one of the tents, and pull out an object. Shawn saw the gleam of metal on some nasty-looking hardware. "Fuck," he cursed under his breath. The last thing he wanted was a firefight. Maybe those other men were Feds.

How in the hell did this happen? Aaron Cartwright wouldn't have deliberately walked him into a trap. This Doug guy was smarter and more dangerous than he thought. Shawn turned back toward the woods and jogged as quietly as he could back to his car. He heard Tom holler through the earpiece for Dave to get the hell back to the rendezvous point. Shawn ran for the safety of the Crown Vic and was out of the campsite within two minutes. Tom and Dave tailgated him all the way back to I-80.

"Guys! Guys! Get up! Somebody is watching us!" Phil whispered as loudly as he could to wake his friends without letting the watchers know that there were others in camp. The three men came to consciousness and climbed out of bed just in time to see a black Ford Crown Victoria zoom past their campsite on the dirt road at about fifty miles per hour.

"What the hell is going on?" Paul asked, blinking sleep-crusted eyes that communicated his disorientation.

"Oh, fuck and double," Doug said, watching the car drive off. "I think I'm in big trouble."

The other men gawked at him. They rarely heard Doug swear, much less in rhyme. "Well, spill it," Paul said.

"Big trouble," Doug said, sinking down beside the fire with its unearthly amber embers.

The other three men stared blankly at him, having no idea what he was talking about. The last person they would expect to get into trouble was Doug.

Phil headed for his tent. "If we're going to have this conversation, I need to be dressed. I nearly got my frozen ass shot off tonight."

The sun extended weak fingers through the gray predawn, as if the sun didn't want to become entangled in Doug's business.

At five thirty, all four men had long since donned sweaters and jeans and heavy socks and were on their third pot of coffee, sitting by the sickly amber ashes of the fire. Doug had finished explaining about the controversial audit. He was legally not allowed to discuss client matters outside the firm, so of course, he swore everyone to secrecy. Besides, there was the little matter of their lives.

"Wow," Martin said.

"Profound insight from the college professor," Paul said into his coffee cup. The steam and the alcohol made his face look like the dying fire.

Martin looked at Doug, who breathed in the powerful mélange of smoke and pine and coffee beans. "This is big, don't you see? This audit could be the straw that breaks the camel's back!"

"What the hell are you talking about, Martin?" Paul asked, then regretted it as Martin went into another one of his ramblings about the economy.

"Look, that hedge fund invested in tiered mortgage backed securities, meaning that they would buy a bundle of mortgages with different risk ratings. Most would be at the AAA level, or what the ratings companies would call the lowest risk, but then the company would have tiers at the AA, A, BBB. After that, anything else is classified as junk or non-investment grade, and many mutual funds and hedge funds have rules about owning junk. But what the market is now seeing is that even liabilities rated AA or A are having the same default rates that were expected for securities that were considered CCC, not just junk, but really bad junk."

Paul snorted. Martin talked over the sound. "We are seeing this across the market for mortgage-backed securities all over the world. These securities are probably worth only seventy to eighty percent of the book value, which means that if your funds were leveraged more than five to one, they are essentially worthless."

Doug felt compelled to object on a rational level. "Okay, Martin, I accept your pessimistic view, except that most of the AAAs and AAs are insured."

Martin laughed. "Douglas, we are talking about this phenomenon all across the country. There are, what, two major companies insuring debt at this point? You're looking at a trillion dollars of defaults claimed against a couple of companies with a couple of billion as reserves? No way. And, if these hedge funds go down, then guess what...the market gets its fair market value for these securities everywhere in the country. You will see hundreds of billions of dollars written down and bankruptcies everywhere. Interest rates will skyrocket as institutions finally realize the risk of lending, money and credit collapse, and the country and probably the world go into the second Great Depression. Our currency tumbles, and China will own us completely, but not for long because they're a damn house of cards. That leaves nations like Saudi Arabia and Russia trying to take over. Europe will crash. There is no way around it, and nothing, not another war, not any of the politicians, can do a damn thing to pull us out of it."

"Good reason to want me dead," Doug said with a mildness that indicated the situation hadn't fully seeped into his consciousness.

Paul stood without spilling his coffee. He no longer spoke scornfully or sarcastically. He couldn't speak as he thought of the graveyard his lending business had become, the plummet of property values, and the unprecedented levels of real estate owned by banks' foreclosures and short-sales. Marty was wrong. There was no conspiracy, just bad business. There had to be a way to mine gold out of the excrement. As for his life being in danger, he'd just seen Phil overreact and a car speed out of the campground.

Phil wasn't speaking either. He wrapped his lips around the coffee and took a bitter raw mouthful. He thought about the rampant mortgage fraud he had just been learning about. Homes purchased with no money down and hundreds of thousands of dollars cash back sat empty, never lived in, across the country. He thought that in a few days time, he would be forced to default on his home mortgage and all his creditors. He would have no choice but to walk away or file bankruptcy. He thought that the scheme Martin described sounded far worse, and as Doug said, was an excellent motive to kill an accountant with scruples.

Martin, Paul, and Phil said, "Holy shit," in unison.

Doug rested his head on his knees and stared at his coffee cup. He looked and felt as if he were back in fifth grade hiding under the covers in the morning because he knew that the kids who usually ripped off his lunch were waiting by the bus stop to knock his teeth out before they humiliated him.

In a moment of wishful atonement, Phil vowed to protect Doug.

Martin vowed to expose the truth.

Paul vowed to drink more beer, chalk up last night to a bad dream, and screw Karina when he got back to the office on Monday. Then he'd get started on the scheme to save his business and triumph against the incompetent.

They spent the rest of that camping weekend without Martin mentioning money or the economy again. When they shook hands and backslapped each other, they did so with their old bravado. Before they left, Paul even shot a few slugs into the air, and Martin lectured him about his juvenile behavior, just as in the good old days.

Estancia Cartwright, Mendocino, California, Sunday, July 22, 2:00 p.m.

"Pull!"

Aaron Cartwright aimed his antique Winchester shotgun in the air and fired twice at the clay disks that the automatic projectile shooter blasted into the sky.

The first shot missed.

The second shattered the disk in the air with a thin squeal as the disk fragmented.

Cartwright lowered his gun and turned to watch Frank Pearson take his turn at the station next to him. It was the perfect pastime for two WASPs on a Sunday afternoon who met to discuss business interests at a private sprawling ranch perfumed with the scent of grapes.

Frank Pearson and Aaron Cartwright, the sons of two wealthy East Coast families, met at Yale when they joined the secret Skull and Bones society, which boasted in its membership rolls numerous presidents and presidential contenders.

Their mutual ambition, proper breeding, and close association with the wealthiest people in the world catapulted them to their present lofty perches. Cartwright contributed money to Pearson's campaign for the U.S. House of Representatives in Delaware. Pearson's influence and connections helped the upper management at Bull-Spears notice, recognize, and reward Cartwright's talent and drive so that Cartwright became managing director of the titanic company after only eleven years' experience in the industry. Meanwhile, on a parallel career path, Pearson became managing director of Edward Fitch, the largest investment banking firm in the world, slightly thereafter. Both were members of the unofficial "Bilderberg Group," which met annually to advance the agenda of the largest corporations in the world. The two met about three times a year, secretly, so as not to give rise to any speculation of impropriety or price-fixing. The public, and the lawyers, had a problem with the heads of industry meeting together, since it gave the appearance of collusion. Collusion, of course, was the name of the game.

Pearson and Cartwright, tired of their target, meandered past the English trellises and gazebos, the statues of angels, saints, Roman gods, and cherubs, to a bench in the terraced gardens. Pearson carried a bottle of one-hundred-year-old single-malt Scotch. One of Cartwright's ever-attentive staff—chosen, as most of the staff was, because she had the ability to become part of the scenery like the statues when Cartwright so desired—brought two glasses.

Cartwright poured, toasted, and drank. Both men sipped the extravagant private-label Scotch.

"How is public service for you, Mr. Secretary?" Cartwright smiled at his old friend.

"It's going great," Pearson said. "I was just informed that I was getting a pay raise to 188,100 dollars next year." They both laughed.

"Not to mention your stock—well, your former stock—is about to split."

"You agreed not to mention that, Aaron. Are you wearing a wire?"

"Me?" Cartwright's eyes bulged, lidless, like a frog's. "Should I be?"

Pearson shook his head. He had owned over one hundred million dollars of Edward-Fitch stock before Washington insiders floated his name about as a treasury appointee. He read the indicators and foresaw a possible downturn. He wanted to short his stock without anyone suspecting him of insider trading. As secretary of the treasury, he would have poisonous legal issues if he held any stock outside of a blind trust, which he had no control over. Cartwright arranged a straw buyer for Pearson's stock and conveniently doctored the SEC filings so that Pearson actually sold his stock before Cartwright sponsored him. Pearson needed an insider in the investment banking sector to support his appointment. By maintaining his symbiotic relationship with Cartwright, like a Great White Shark with a remora attached, and taking the president's appointment, Cartwright protected upward of two hundred million dollars of assets from the economic downturn that the mass media tried to deny.

Top bankers, top government officials, and the "fringe" of society that didn't drink the media's Kool-Aid all knew that the country was on the verge of an economic disaster. To navigate this treacherous strait would take cooperation between government, banks, industry, and the media. Cartwright knew how to cooperate.

Pearson read the request in Cartwright's eyes before he heard it. "Frank, I've got a problem with the audit of a couple of hedge funds we manage. It seems that the auditor is involved in some sort of sting operation for the FBI."

Pearson widened his eyes and shrugged. "I know nothing about this. I certainly wouldn't have encouraged it."

"I didn't think so. Listen, I need you to talk to the president and get the FBI to lay off. If this thing breaks before we have the PPT in place, we are in trouble."

Pearson looked at him for a moment through the refraction of heirloom crystal and droplets of Scotch, then sipped, swallowed languorously, and gazed directly in his eyes. "I'll talk to the president. Meanwhile, you might want to tell your expensive hired guns to lay low and tail this accountant for a while."

Cartwright nodded and spoke into his cell phone. "Call Shawn Smith."

When Shawn answered, Cartwright wasted no words. "The FBI has been dealt with. Keep a watch on our target, use different cars, don't do anything stupid."

Paul's Residence, American River, Monday, July 23, 9:30 a.m.

Doug, in a rented car he'd paid cash for, glanced twenty times in his rearview and side mirrors. Paul's street was a study in blandness, but Doug still couldn't bring himself to open the car door and cross the open space to Paul's front door.

It was blind luck that his college friend became an FBI agent and scared the bad guys witless. If they had broken into Doug's car, they would have built a new bonfire with his audit documents and toasted their success while Doug and his friends lay slain in their tents, the apparent victims of a random, senseless crime.

He had never experienced such bone-deep terror. He was an accountant, for crying out loud. He had never been in any serious trouble in his life. He was the guy who always brought a bag of condoms or an umbrella. He used to blame himself for being too conservative and was sure that was the reason he had never done anything great.

In retrospect, he liked playing it safe. He wished he never pushed Dick Gauthier and Bob baker. Unfortunately, he didn't own a time machine.

He could stall for time, however. He had called in sick to work. He'd caught something nasty outdoors and would be out all week on the advice of his doctor, he told his apathetic co-worker who had drawn the short straw and was answering phones in the office. From the dismissive hang up Doug received, he gathered the co-worker bought it.

Doug was too frightened to go back to his apartment, so his good friend Paul offered him a guest room in Paul's luxurious mansion aerie. "Unless you want to go bunk with Marty in Bluehairville, Nevada," Paul said. Paul would go into the office at midmorning so he could wait for Doug to arrive. Doug spent Sunday night at a motel and paid cash, then headed for Paul's manse after he checked out, the stale muffins from the continental breakfast bar still sliding sluggishly down his esophagus.

When Doug pulled up outside Paul's residence, he gawked at the Mediterranean-inspired edifice. Statues of fauns and nymphs in the manicured front gardens completed the pseudo-Old World effect.

Once Doug, carrying his suitcases, laptop, and box of papers, made it safely to Paul's front steps without being gunned down, Paul immediately took his worldly goods and deposited them inside. He welcomed Doug with a pat on the back and a glass of Jim Beam. "How do you like it, Douggy? See the stone? Imported from Italy. I fixed a credit problem for a prominent son of Venice."

"What, the Mafia?"

"They're not big anymore, not in Italy." Paul laughed at Doug's naïveté. "It's the Asians, the Russians, and the Mexicans now. I'm talking a director, a movie director. Art films—well, mostly soft-core porn, if you want to know the truth, but they eat that up in Italy."

Doug nodded. Paul had no idea what a prick he sounded like. "So, do I get the grand tour?" He feigned laughter.

Paul showed him inside and proudly pointed out the imported marble floor beneath his feet in the foyer. Doug, after staring down for far too long, decided to admire the ceiling. The vaulted cathedral dome above his head was painted to resemble the Sistine Chapel, with Jesus holding court over angels and saints in the cloud-filled heavens.

"Holy crap, Paul, how in the hell can you afford a place like this?"

"Ah, Douggy." Paul's voice held its usual condescension. "The word is risk-reward, buddy. I built a real estate empire in just a few short years.

My income tax return for last year showed income of over a million bucks." He leaned into Doug's field of vision. "That was just what my income tax return showed."

Doug nodded, uncomprehending, yet seeing far too distinctly. "Ah, I should say hello to Patty."

"She's out shopping for a good cause." Paul lifted Doug's laptop. "Let's get this stuff to your room. I've got to go into work, so you help yourself to whatever you want in the kitchen, exercise room, entertainment room. Tonight we can just chill out together. Order in, have a few drinks, watch the game."

Doug put on a smile. "Sounds like a plan to me."

Paul talked as he led Doug past extravagant artwork, antiques, and draperies. "Yeah. You've earned it, and I sure as hell have. You know all those Ivy League guys back East that run the banks? Well, you've got to be smarter than they are. Fortunately, I am smarter. Cash-back closings, straw buyers…the works."

Doug had heard Paul's braggadocio before and always thought the boasting of illegal activity was to inflate his image and compensate for some real or imagined disappointment. Doug never actually believed Paul made the money he said he did. But walking through this lavish home made Doug reconsider everything he knew about his old friend.

Twenty minutes after Doug arrived, Paul backed the flashy Mercedes out of the garage. Paul had the top down so he could display his Armani sunglasses and demeanor to the world. He waved at the well-groomed seven-year-olds playing with a remote-control airplane on the lawn of the house across the cul-de-sac.

Phil, mesh shades drawn across the driver's side window, observed Paul through binoculars. He gave Paul one point for sheltering Doug. Even an asshole was capable of generosity and loyalty.

Doug probably wouldn't leave Paul's faux-Mediterranean Fortress of Yuppitude. Paul probably had a killer alarm system and a drinking buddy on the local police force. The only two potential dangers would be Paul's bored and lonely wife trying to seduce Doug, or Paul revealing his secrets to "Douggy."

Phil checked the clock. He had scheduled his first investigation for 10:15 a.m. As the leader of a plum task force, he had a license to come and go, but he prided himself on punctuality. He would drive by and check on Doug later. Watching out for Doug appeased his conscience. "Yes, I am my buddy's keeper," he muttered.

After Phil drove away, a man in a pest control jumpsuit parked his truck outside the house across the cul-de-sac, got out, and waved at the seven-year-olds in the yard.

"You want your house sprayed?" He grinned at them.

"No," they said together. "Our mommy says it's bad for the environment."

"Okay. That's okay." He pointed across the street at Paul's house. "Do you think they want theirs sprayed?"

"Nuh-uh," the boy, who wore Tommy Hilfiger shorts and no shirt, said. "She's a shopaholic and he plays around."

"That so? Where'd you hear that?" The pest control man smiled at the boy.

The girl, obviously her brother's twin, shook her head. "I don't think we want to talk to you."

"They're not home," the boy said, gleefully defying his sister's common sense. "And some nerdy-looking guy came."

"He had all his luggage," the girl volunteered. "He came to stay with the LeBrachs."

The boy shook his head. "No way, he could never be cool enough."

The girl caught the pest control man staring at them avidly. She took out her cell phone.

Jesus Christ, the man thought, these kids had cell phones before they were even teenagers.

"I'm going to call my mom," the girl announced.

The pest control guy waved and retreated for his truck. "Never mind. You kids be good now."

Once he left the subdivision, he spoke on his cell phone with his hands-free headset. "Shawn. We know where he is. He's alone and we have him cornered."

CHAPTER 7

"Americans learn only from catastrophe and not from experience."

—Theodore Roosevelt

Economic Calamity
What You Won't Hear in the Debates
July 23, 2007, 3:12 p.m.
By Martin Cheyne

Not a single contestant in the upcoming presidential election will even touch on the issue.

However, I'll say what truth-minded people think because I'm not running for office.

It is extremely hypocritical of a nation that preaches "free markets" as the solution to everything to allow a self-interested organization like the Federal Reserve to act as the central controller of the money flow. When the economy looks weak, or when the banks aren't making enough money, just turn on the tap of this "central bank" and fix the problems.

The problem with this, with intervention in the free market, is that the excess, the bad investments, and everything that created the weak economy in the first place don't get corrected. They just get washed over with more money. The problem flows like entropy somewhere else, at least temporarily, and it grows again. It's like breaking off a mushroom cap (not a cloud, I hope). The spores just fly all over and sprout more 'shrooms. Good if they're edible, bad if they're poisonous, which they certainly are in this case. Maybe we should eat some of that poison as an antidote.

But no, we're a quick-fix people, and we don't believe in the sacrifices our grandparents made, that many societies the world over have made.

With the absolute disdain and disgust that most in the U.S., in pretty much everywhere in the Western world (Britain and France I've discussed in previous blogs), look at command economies, central planning, and communism, it is a wonder that few complain about having a central bank. And no, I'm not a pinko commie, thanks for asking. I know the trolls are going to call me a nut, a whacko, and unpatriotic, but I don't care. Unthinkable events and signs are unfolding, and I have to speak the truth or be damned, the exact opposite of Cassandra. I am going to finish my PhD dissertation (whoopee) and publish my findings for America to see. That's my mission, and I choose to accept it. I'm right, damn it, and it's about time someone knows it.

If any politician agrees with me, they'll have my vote for life. But they won't. Maybe I should run. What say you?

Trackback / Comment / Blog This / Comments (1124)

Rio Linda/Elverta, California, July 23, 10:00 a.m.

Philip Schultz stood alongside the pristinely quiet Acacia Lane inside a new subdivision in the unincorporated city of Rio Linda/Elverta, north of Sacramento. Rio Linda meant "beautiful river" in Spanish, but the only rivers Phil saw in Hidden Pines Place were the streams inside the artificial greenbelt that the planners had evidently designed to make people think they were living close to nature. You could tell you were living in a planned unit development (PUD) by the antiseptic freshness of the mini-fountains in the pond. The tamely flowing water contrasted starkly with the nine brown front lawns across the street where Phil surveyed the neighborhood. The water was the only sound he could perceive. No cars honking, no bikes whizzing, no televisions or radios blaring. This brand-new subdivision of four hundred houses was a ghost town.

Mike Clennahan, a lawyer acting on behalf of a team of banks, stood next to him. Mike's white shirt showed spatters of water from one of the fountains. Mike was forty and, from the look of him, he had spent too many years grabbing meals in diners at one in the morning in between scratching and scraping every advantage he could out of his career. Now, he felt he had earned the good life as a corporate attorney, but feared that he was always one step away from downgrading from leisurely billable steak dinners to chili cheese dogs in a cramped grease joint. He chewed unsalted almonds constantly and had a slightly puffed look to him that reminded Phil of a baby's soft toy.

"So, let me get this straight then," Philip said. "Your clients let this guy, an assistant manager at Burger King, making less than thirty thousand per year, buy all nine of these houses for a whopping two point five mil in total?"

"Look," Clennahan said, his face pinching in annoyance, "it's not that simple. It's not like this guy sat down at one of our branches and said he wanted a loan for over two million. He used five different mortgage lenders and acquired them over the course of a year."

Phil kicked a patch of sere yellowish grass with his feet. The vegetation accepted the imprint of his boot and lay defeated and flat.

Clennahan stuck his hands in his pale blue pants. "His income wasn't stated at thirty thousand because he made a hundred and fifty thousand flipping two houses the year before, and he had rental income on the houses he already owned. We've reviewed the paperwork, and he didn't declare all his debt on all his loan documents. We were defrauded. That is why you are here. My clients are out for blood. They want this kid prosecuted."

Phil made a show of consulting his PDA and notebook. "Okay, just so I have my notes right, a group of banks, including some of the largest financial groups in the world, was defrauded for two point five million by the minimum-wage assistant manager of the Merchant Street Burger King. Who happens to be twenty-two."

Phil knew he was being sarcastic, but he didn't like this guy, and he still couldn't believe that anyone would lend this kind of money to a kid with practically no income who lived with his girlfriend in a mobile home park. He smoothed over the patch of smashed grass with his other foot. "And it's these nine houses here on this street, the ones with the dead lawns?" Dead as opposed to dying, which many of the lawns and plants were. The common areas, the greenbelts, and streams insulted the buyers' intelligence, or would have if there had been any real buyers.

Phil had an image of an overweight sour-faced man putting on a new toupee, or an out-of-shape woman getting breast implants.

Clennahan bristled. "Yes, it's these right here in front of us. That is why we are here. And now, the county and the Homeowners Association want us, the banks, to maintain these things." He shook his head. "Do you think we want to pay utilities, HOA fees, and property taxes on these things? Do you know how much money we will lose when we sell them?"

"Who appraised these houses?"

"Our appraisers did, but how were we supposed to get an accurate appraisal when all of the previous sales were to this kid! He set the market price in the area by buying so many friggin' houses!"

"This Burger King mook hatched this brilliant scheme using your professional appraisers. Check. Got it. You know anything about Joseph Kennedy?"

Clennahan shook his head. "I don't see what relevance that has."

"One of my business professors told this story that Joseph Kennedy, the father of JFK—you know, John F. Kennedy?" Phil saw Clennahan's nostrils flare. "Just checking. Anyway, according to my professor's fable, Joseph Kennedy pulled all of his money out of the stock market just prior to the crash of 1929. He did that because he stopped to have his shoes shined. That's when they had kids who'd shine your shoes. Joseph overheard the young boy talking about how he had bought so many shares of this company, and so many shares of that. Imagine, a young man with a low-paying job used what little money he had to enter a complex financial market. Joseph knew we'd all gotten hooked." He wondered what Joseph Kennedy would have thought about a young man, whose career involved serving French fries and blending milkshakes, entering into multi-million-dollar real estate deals.

Phil couldn't help but be overwhelmed by the sheer volume of financial mismanagement. Almost all the homes in this subdivision were purchased by investors, and the bank had foreclosed on and taken ownership of half of those. It was a disaster, just like the dozens of foreclosures and empty subdivisions he'd already heard about. The entire area was ridden with them.

"I'll need your statement and all the paperwork you have on this case, including any e-mails you're hiding, before we confront the kid. How'd you, as a high-profile attorney, like a tour of the FBI field office in Sacramento? You can even have lunch in our cafeteria."

"Why?" Clennahan chewed his lips as he gulped the last of a bag of almonds.

Phil stared at the lawns and the artificial river. "Frankly, this place depresses me more than a crack whorehouse. Let's go."

Sacramento FBI Offices, 11:00 a.m.

Phil's mood lightened when he introduced Clennahan to the team inside the conference room. Clennahan wet his lips constantly. Agent Taggert handed him a tissue. Phil spread all of Clennahan's files on the conference table. He included several deleted e-mails Clennahan was forced to retrieve and print. The e-mails contained discussion of possible warning signs. "It was accidental," Clennahan said. "The new IT technician."

"Convenient," Agent Hastings-Perry said.

Agent Barrino chimed in. "Yeah, let's see how many viruses 'accidentally' zap your computer once your IT people hear they've been smeared. Or did you outsource it to Bangalore?"

"Maybe someone somewhere panicked," Phil said, playing good cop. He glanced at his team for validation. "Wouldn't you? Agent Barrino?"

"I would," Agent Taggert said.

"Seems to me," Agent Barrino said, "I wouldn't have gone near anybody working at Burger King. I have a nephew that delivers pizza, and all I can say is thank God for GPS, because he doesn't even have half a brain."

Clennahan shook his head. "I'm not the criminal. Nor are the fine institutions I represent. We don't cheat widows and orphans."

"But surely the lending practices of your employers have become lax?" Agent Hastings-Perry's voice was dry.

"It happens. We were in a boom, and the housing bubble hadn't popped yet," Phil said. "I guess someone could have decided to go with the flow, feed from the trough, get some of the gravy. Speaking of which, I always wondered what food at the FBI cafeteria tasted like." Clennahan smiled and displayed teeth flecked with almond meal. "I'll buy, and we can plan a winning strategy for going after this jerk…right?"

"If you're buying, let's all go to Morton's," Phil said, and enjoyed seeing Clennahan's face bulge as he struggled to smile even wider.

The more involved he got into mortgage fraud, the more sure he became that Doug's problems and Martin's conspiracy theories were all true…to a point, he hoped. And he also hoped like hell that Paul wasn't exploiting Doug.

Paul's Residence, American River, 4:00 p.m.

Paul poured Doug a glass of Chivas Regal and added soda water. He topped it off with a slice of lime and a cherry and handed it to Doug as they gazed at the opaline American River from Paul's mammoth deck. Even in the humid late afternoon, Paul's fire pit blazed, and barbecued chicken smoked on the grill. "I woulda taken you out tonight," Paul said, "but I figured you'd appreciate a home-cooked meal for a change."

Doug sipped deeply. "You always did know how to barbecue." That shocked Doug. Paul gave the impression of growing up being waited on hand and foot, but he proved in college that he knew his way around a grill. At the fraternity house, Paul's Sunday barbecues became the social event of the week. On Fraternity Row, even the die-hard partyers formed a line down the street to bring a keg and taste Paul's herbed rubs. Of course, plenty of girls oohed and aahed over Paul's cooking, even the sorority girls who lived on nothing but water and unsalted, unbuttered popcorn.

Paul rose to check the chicken. Doug inhaled thyme and marjoram. "Will Patty be joining us?" He somehow didn't think Paul's wife was the domestic type, despite a gourmet kitchen in the house that Martha Stewart would weep over.

"Later maybe," Paul said, his entire posture projecting indifference. "She called me on my way home from the office and said she was swinging by her sister's. Those two never stop flapping their gums."

"How come you're home so early?"

"Now if I didn't come home, you'd probably read business books and stock charts all night. What do you think of my library?"

"Pretty impressive," Doug had to admit. He had doubted Paul had opened a book since he got his broker's license, and any books in the house would be like the blank ones in *The Great Gatsby*. To Doug's surprise, Paul had an extensive library, half of which was business books. He also noticed a lot of New Age and science fiction or paranormal literature that he thought must belong to Patty.

Paul turned over the chicken after he poked and pierced it. "That's my Douggy, always cracking the books. As I told you, I don't need to work as hard as most people, so I came home to rescue you from being lonely."

"Appreciated." Doug managed a smile. He ought to feel more relaxed despite the weekend's events. He was safe. "Ah, Phil mentioned you were helping him sell his house."

Paul smiled at Doug, a varnished smile. "It's a beauty, but the market is slowing down a bit. Summer."

"Didn't he remortgage last year?"

"You are going to love this chicken," Paul said. "It's the best I've ever made. I know by the aroma. Sometimes it gets a little too burnt the way I make it, at least Patty says so, but I like the skin crisp. How about you, Douggy?"

"Good, great. I thought we were having wings." Doug let the Chivas Regal saturate his throat.

Paul opened the second half of the grill. Chicken wings sizzled. Doug gasped and wrinkled his nose. He could smell the pungency of the sauce and smoke. Paul picked up the wings with tongs and put them on a plate. "These are done. Have you ever seen more perfect wings?"

He crossed to Doug with the plate and extended it under Doug's nose. "Have one. Fresh off the grill. Or maybe I should blow on it first?"

Doug took one with his cocktail napkin and felt the heat in his fingers. He set it on the wrought-iron green table beside him. "No, but I'll let it cool a touch."

Paul shrugged. "Suit yourself." He strode back to the grill and sipped his own Chivas Regal. "I'm a simple guy at heart, Douggy. Food, booze, and friends. This house is just the seasoning on top."

Doug nodded and followed the river with his eyes.

"But, you know, things have gotten a little soft in the market lately. I'm having a short-term cash crunch." Sparks and fat and juices popped as Paul tended the grill. "Maybe you could help me out, Doug."

Doug cautiously nibbled on the wings and softened the spice with his scotch. It didn't dampen the instant inferno in his mouth. His tongue and teeth stung with the habañero Paul had added to the sauce.

Paul took Doug's silence as permission to continue. "I need to get a loan, and the bank doesn't want to give me one. They want audited financial statements."

At that moment, Doug was grateful he couldn't speak.

The grill emitted more smoke. Paul adroitly turned over the chicken just as the juices hissed more loudly. "So I was thinking, maybe you could sign the statements that my guy, my accountant, already put together. Of course, he doesn't have your genius, but he's good enough."

He smiled at Doug over his shoulder and nodded as Doug chewed the rest of the wing out of a need for distraction. Doug found that the flavor improved once the burning faded. Paul's wings were restaurant quality. Better than Hooters.

"I thought for your trouble I could give you, say, ten thousand dollars when the bank closes the loan?"

So here it was, the Paul LeBrach modus operandi. Doug had wondered whether Paul would try to extract some sort of favor in exchange for letting him sleep in one of his empty rooms and eat his barbecue wings for a couple days.

Doug tried logic and rational debate. "Paul, were you not there at the campsite when Martin and I were discussing what was going on?"

"You want some cool ranch sauce for dipping?"

Before he answered, Doug savored the last bite of his barbecue delicacy. "Sure, if you do. We as a country are in deep, deep, shit. And this kind of maneuvering is the reason why."

Paul lifted one of the chicken thighs from the grill and speared it. "Not quite tender enough yet. Maybe five more minutes on each side." He shook the thigh off the fork onto the grill, which hissed. "Look, Douggy, not all of us can live in the classroom and trade paranoia on the Internet. Marty could be right, but even if he were, it's too late now. I need some cash immediately to cover some short-term expenses."

"What kind of expenses?"

"Ask me no questions, I'll tell you no lies." Paul lifted the tongs. In Doug's overactive imagination, the gesture seemed sinister. Maybe that was because Paul had moved into the shadow beneath the overhang of the crenellated roof, and the darkness fell across his face. The moment reminded Doug of a frame in a bad buddy movie. "Just think about it, Doug, while you enjoy some decent food not out of a takeout container and sleep in a Sleep Number bed in a house that's armed to the teeth with a bad-ass security system that will royally screw anyone who even puts a toe on the property."

Doug nodded, adopting a humble look. His conscience did prickle at the thought of what he owed his friend. At least half of his conscience did. The other half screamed for him to check out of the LeBrach Motel and find a cheaper hideout.

Paul smiled for effect. "Besides, you'll be helping a friend, a brother, in need. Who knows, the chunk of change you get for your signature on my statements could come in handy if you have to go underground or run for the border." He laughed lightly.

"Sure, Paul, I'll think about it." Doug hoped he could find a way to wiggle out of this. Last week he would have said he wouldn't give in to Paul. He was confused. He couldn't surrender his principles. He needed to stall, he needed time to think. He needed to remember that he had bigger problems. Someone hired by his own employer was chasing him, and regardless of whether he helped Paul, he saw only two possible futures. He was either going to be killed, or he was going to be scared, wimpified, and beaten until he disappeared for the rest of his life. The worst part? The thirty pieces of silver Paul offered seemed like a fragile lifeline out of the quicksand he had sunk into.

He rose off the chaise lounge. "I'll go get that ranch sauce and some plates and silverware."

In the arched doorway, he narrowly avoided colliding with Patty, glowing from a spa and shopping day. He could smell the glycolic acid and passion fruit lotion. She pulled down her lacy tank top just enough so he could stare down into her cleavage, which he politely avoided doing.

"It's Doug, of course, isn't it?" she trilled, as if he hadn't been one of Paul's groomsmen in a grossly overdone wedding ceremony during which, if Phil's estranged wife Helen was to be believed, Patty had been a Bridezilla before the term became popular. "So nice to see you."

"Douggy is burned out, Pattycakes," Paul said casually, but his face showed a lack of enthusiasm for Patty's company. "Needs a mental health week. A couple days camping just didn't cut it. Plus, he caught something, didn't you?" His eyes warned of secrecy.

Doug coughed and sneezed. It wasn't playacting. Paul's spices assaulted him. "Yeah," he gasped. "Nice to see you, Patty. Hope you don't mind that Paul invited me to stay a couple days."

"He doesn't have the kind of tender loving care I do," Paul said.

"Well, we're delighted to have you here. *Mi casa es su casa.*" Patty brushed Paul's arm with manicured nails lacquered in what his mother would have called a "Las Vegas hooker red." She sniffed critically. "Paul, you aren't overcooking the chicken again, are you?"

"Why don't you show Douggy where the plates and silverware are in the kitchen," Paul said, ignoring the nervous look on Doug's face.

Doug allowed Patty to precede him into the house, both out of gallantry and a fear that she might grab his ass. The look she gave him over her bronzed shoulder was pure hunger. "We don't get to see enough of you. Paul and I are so happy to have you. Why, you two are like brothers, and you're welcome to everything he has."

"One cozy family," Doug said as he ducked back to grab his scotch and another chicken wing.

Merchant Street Burger King, Vacaville, Thursday, July 26, 11:00 a.m.

Phil was trying not to laugh. The half-eaten chicken tender thrown past his head by an overzealous seven-year-old in the booth across the aisle helped him to tamp down his mirth.

He looked across the small blue table that reminded him of the Colorforms and the lunch boxes from when he was a kid. Opposite Phil sat his quarry, the Donald Trump wannabe, the kid—no, the "assistant manager," the all-too-helpful Burger King staff had corrected Phil. They took one look at Phil and smelled authority. They scurried away from it, back to the fryer and the shake machine. They pretended to work while doing a poor job of inconspicuously staring at Phil and the assistant manager and speculating on what crime he could have committed. Someone had singled out Ronald Lester Beamis, twenty-two, for the first time in his life.

Ronald sat still from sheer fright, glued to the plastic chair. He looked like a high school freshman in detention, and he wasn't far removed from that. His pimples and freckles matched his hair, which matched the gloppy color and texture of fast-food ketchup. He smelled of Selsun Blue. Dandruff, freckles, and buck teeth. No wonder the kid tried to pull off a grand scheme. The worst he'd probably done before this was to sneak a smoke in the halls at school. His latest girlfriend, Jacquelyn Michelle, was his longest relationship on record, seven months. The kid drifted through his time on planet Earth.

"You masterminded the whole thing, didn't you?" Phil pounded his fist on the table. Intimidating the clueless shouldn't make him feel better. It was beneath him, and this kid probably couldn't connive his way out of a wet paper bag. His laughter got repressed so fiercely by his serious look that he'd probably pass gas later.

"She…she told me to do it." Ronald pulled a business card with the picture of an extremely obese female real-estate agent in the top left corner. His eyes leaked tears, and Phil would bet anything that Ronald would wet himself in the next ten seconds.

"Ronald, let me share a lesson with you I learned a long time ago." He paused for effect then declared: "Never take financial advice from someone who can't win a battle of wills with a jelly donut." He heaped maledictions on the lenders for their stupidity. The blind leading the blind. Ronald blinked at him as if confused, then began to stutter denials.

Phil surged to his feet so fast that the chair would have toppled backward if it hadn't been affixed to the floor. Instead, it swiveled and spun violently. Phil gave Ronald his best Dirty Harry stare. "I'm going to get to the bottom of this. You just watch yourself."

He leveled a finger at Ronald, who leaned his head on the baby blue table and tried not to sob for his mama. He did manage to mutter something about "lawyer" and "rights" and "due process," words he'd probably remembered from Court TV or reruns of *Law & Order*.

As he approached the two parked cars where Agents Taggert, Perry-Hastings, and Barrino waited, he couldn't help but think that the people who lent the money deserved everything they were getting. The banks were lending hundreds of thousands of dollars to anyone with a pulse. Agent Perry-Hastings had shown him a roster from one bank that included hundreds of NINJA loans, meaning "no income, no job, no assets." If they wanted to loan money to someone like that, that was their problem. "Fuck 'em if they can't take a joke," he thought as he climbed into the driver's seat of his vehicle. Agent Perry-Hastings fired questions and statistics at him before he turned the key in the ignition.

As he drove, his attention was with Doug and the situation that arose while they were camping. That morning before he even drove to the Burger King, he checked with his contacts—private investigators, hired guns, and corporate spies. Last night he'd spoken to the one U.S. Forest Service Ranger who'd been on duty when the unknown person or persons watched their camp. The U.S. Forest Service ranger remembered two Crown Vics and noted that they'd slipped in without her knowledge, which she seemed annoyed about. She'd chased them out of the camp and caught a license plate with her high-beam headlights. "I have a photographic memory," she told Phil.

Phil ran the plates and discovered one of the Crown Vics was registered to a Michael Moore, which seemed highly suspect, unless the controversial documentary filmmaker planned to do a *Guys Gone Wild* film. The photo of the Michael Moore in question showed someone wearing a baseball cap and glasses, but Phil's gut instinct and some image comparison told him this was a red herring.

Phil did some digging and found that a Tom Dooley also resided at the address for Michael Moore in Danville. Stories on the *San Mateo Daily Journal* Web site indicated that Dooley had been a police officer in Alameda County but retired from the force after accusations of using "excessive force against a suspect" surfaced. Dooley was now in the private sector, according to the follow-up report. Unless Dooley was shacking up with the faux Michael Moore, Phil had to conclude that, like Bruce Wayne and Batman, they were one and the same.

A contact who simply went by the name Sloane and would only meet Phil in strip-mall Thai restaurants warned him that several of the major investment banks often hired former cops as security officers. Investment banks such as Bull-Spears.

The FBI wasn't stupid, and there had been many indications in the past that Bull-Spears, and many of the other big, powerful corporations, had pulled these kinds of shenanigans in the past. The problem was, these types of organizations belonged to the good-old-boys network, and so the FBI usually only got involved if it was politically desirable at the time.

Later, Phil was lost in thought and his brow furrowed as he drove with his partner back to the FBI office. "Share it," Agent Perry-Hastings said. "What's on your mind?"

She and Phil had just busted two Paris Hilton clones who acted as straw buyers and mortgage-closers for their boyfriends. From her look, Agent Perry-Hastings thought the situation was far from droll or even mildly funny.

"Same as you, probably…it's just human nature," Phil said. "It is incredible how widespread the fraud is, and hilarious some of the characters that are involved. How could the banks hand that kind of money over to these people?"

"Lord what fools we mortals be when first we practice to deceive. And boob jobs don't hurt either."

Phil shook his head. "I'm foggy on Shakespeare, but I don't think that was in *Hamlet*."

"*Midsummer Night's Dream*, actually." She grinned and Phil laughed. She sobered. "I made it up, mashing up two quotes together."

"I know."

"You do not. And I don't see how you can find the gullibility of the American consumer even remotely humorous, let alone the greed of the profiteers."

"Guess we're just obsessed with boobs," Phil said, his mind running down the plans to swing by Paul's house and check on Doug.

Paul's Residence, American River, 11:00 a.m.

Doug awoke and didn't even check the clock. From the glaring light through the cream plantation shutters, he could tell that he'd probably lolled in bed half the morning. He couldn't remember the last time he'd spent the better part of a week sleeping in. Then again, it was the one escape he had from his hosts, who had become a combination of the characters on Wisteria Lane Patty watched obsessively and jailers at Alcatraz. He read his audit files until midnight last night. He'd done so while listening to an MP3 player, since he could hear Paul and Patty having sex. Even though there was little marital affection from what he observed, they sounded like porn actors last night. Actors being the key word, since Doug suspected that they were merely props to each other. He might have pitied them if Paul didn't constantly and aggressively pressure him to breach every legal and ethical CPA regulation in existence.

And then there was Patty.

Doug rolled out of the 800-thread count Frette sheets and let his bare feet hit the clamshell Berber carpet. He padded to the shower and commanded himself to wake up. He felt a bit like a general hiding out while the troops get hacked to bits by the enemy.

He dressed in a pair of shorts and a white T-shirt. The freedom of being without a tie, of being buttoned-down, filled him with momentary peace and joy.

He also guiltily embraced the leisure to drink orange juice, slowly sip coffee, and read the *San Francisco Chronicle* and the *Wall Street Journal* from cover to cover, which he did sitting on the crushed velvet cushions at the breakfast bar. The granite, Patty explained, was modeled after the kitchen of either an eighteenth-century Tuscan villa or Donatella Versace's Italian pad, but she couldn't remember which. "I studied art history in college," she said, "but couldn't make a living at it. I kinda wanted to backpack around Europe." Doug nearly asked Paul and Patty why they didn't have any children, much less plans to start a family, but he didn't want to intrude on the perfect-couple facade. He sipped the orange juice freshly squeezed from the fruit of the trees in the side yard. He'd seen Patty juicing the oranges in her L'Equip Pulp Ejector or whatever juicer she had that was shaped like an egg. She gave him a breakfast-commercial smile. The juice was sweet but slightly off in taste. Not sour, not bitter, just a hint of something he couldn't define. He hoped it wasn't pesticide.

"Well, good morning, Doug," Patty said. "How's the juice? I hope you like the coffee. You got up so late I brewed another pot just for you."

Between Paul's wings and Patty's juice, Doug felt smothered with offers of food, which he never had even from his own mother. Then again, his own mother would never act the way Patty was, and he couldn't remember the last time any woman in his life tried to blatantly seduce him whenever her husband left the house.

"It's all great, Patty, thank you. Good morning." He didn't have the balls to be abrupt or churlish. He tried not to look up from his newspaper once an initial peek told him she was only wearing a bra and panties underneath her loose bathrobe with the logo of "Two Bunch Palms" on the breast pocket.

She leaned over him on the opposite side of the breakfast bar. "Did you sleep well? Is everything all right? How are you feeling? Relaxed?"

He glanced briefly up into her face and noticed the coral sheen of her lips. She'd chosen to wear subtle eye shadow just a shade lighter. Thick lashes fluttered under doe-colored brows. She'd put her hair in a partial updo. Her perfume, which he thought might have been Obsession, overwhelmed. He knew it was her house, but why she ran around in a bathrobe at eleven o'clock was beyond him.

"I am, but have you seen the price of gas today?" Doug shook his head. "And that guy over in Iran worries me."

"Well, if that's all, you must be a lucky man," Patty said. "A steady respectable job....you must do quite well at that big San Jose firm."

Doug wanted to laugh. He wanted to pity her, which he didn't think she'd appreciate. He wanted to get the hell away from the breasts she pushed in his face. Maybe he was a self-righteous moron, but he didn't find this routine a bit appealing.

"No, not really. I donate most of my time, do free work for the society for the protection of homeless kittens, you know, groups like that." He looked at her with sincerity in his eyes, but thought that if she believed him, she was very, very, dumb.

She didn't and she wasn't, from the look on her face and the way her voice changed. "Oh. That's...noble of you. So, you don't get paid for that kind of work?"

"No, I give it back to the kittens. I just remember Fluffy, my cat growing up, and how much she meant to me. I just want to give something back. Excuse me, Patty." Doug's voice cracked like Peter Brady's, and he wiped away a fake tear. "I just need to be alone right now." He wished he could have thought of something with a bit more wit, but, alas, that was why he was an accountant.

He left his juice, coffee, and newspaper at the breakfast bar because being a polite guest wasn't worth being in proximity to her for one second longer than he had to. He turned away from the kitchen and went a few steps before he heard her voice again, this time commanding.

"Aren't you damn tired of being alone? I know I am. And I would think you'd need a friend right now."

He whirled and looked her in the face, or tried to. Her robe gaped open and she stretched with innate sensuality. Her eyes were old and merciless. He wondered if she knew anything, if Paul had told her anything. Probably not, since Paul was a secretive bastard, but maybe she'd overheard something…

The kitchen phone rang. Patty sighed theatrically and answered. "Hello?" Her eyes dilated as she listened, and she put on her sweetest voice. "Just a moment. May I ask who's calling?" She frowned delicately and handed Doug the cordless handset. "It's for you."

Doug's fingers trembled as he took the phone and scooted out of the kitchen all the way to the media room. "Hello, Doug speaking."

"Doug. Are you surviving Paul-land?" Martin's voice was low and concerned. "I'd feel sorry for his wife, but after talking to her I think they deserve each other."

Doug gripped the phone. "I'm okay. How goes it among the ivory tower people?"

"My students are as apathetic as most everyone, God help us all. Only a few more days of torture, and then I'm getting out of town. My PhD thesis calls. I need a break and some uninterrupted thinking time."

"About time. At the rate you're going, you'll be a hundred before I can call you Doctor."

"Doug, don't harp at me. Paul has you beat in that department. Have you heard from Phil?"

"Yeah, but he couldn't say much. He's, ah, looking into what we talked about." Doug had no idea why he and Martin spoke as though they were prisoners in a gulag planning an escape.

"Good, good. So Paul hasn't made you promise to give him your firstborn child in exchange for a little R and R?"

Doug laughed. "No, because he knows I'll be a hundred by the time I get married." He refused to tell Martin what Paul had asked, even though it was safer than telling Phil. But Phil was bound up in Paul's web too.

"You need to get out more, Doug. In fact, I suggest going on a long vacation."

Doug found it difficult to swallow. "Isn't that always what the shifty guys say in the movies?"

"Trust me, Doug, life is fragile. You have to seize it while you can. Let me know if you want to plan a trip somewhere. I've got to prepare for my next class. Bye."

Doug hung up and decided that he needed uninterrupted thinking time too. He called to Patty as he headed out of the house, "I'm going to take a walk around the neighborhood." And then he was going to figure out how he could finish that damn audit without getting gunned down, or worse, seduced into something he'd regret. The aftertaste of orange juice turned sour in his mouth.

CHAPTER 8

"No State shall...make any Thing but gold and silver Coin a Tender in Payment of Debts."

—The Constitution of the United States, Article I, Section 10

White Sulphur Springs, West Virginia, Saturday, July 28, 2:00 p.m.

Secretary Pearson drank the veggie juice tonic his celebrity personal trainer recommended and waved to the guard at the gate as he rode in his typical black stretch Lincoln Town Car out of his estate at the exclusive Greenbrier Resort.

Though he had moved from the Hamptons just a little over a year ago, he was already starting to like his new fourteen-thousand-square-foot mansion included within the Greenbrier Sporting Club Residential Estates. The sprawling golf course cradled by the lush green mountains made him feel far removed from all the headaches of New York and D.C. In addition, he, his second wife Arlene, and his two teenage stepchildren could access the enormous "congressional" bomb shelter under the mountain within minutes. The 112,000-square-foot "relocation center" was built underneath the Greenbrier clubhouse and was designed to hold both Houses of Congress in the case of a nuclear attack as well as the Supreme Court Justices. If the attack didn't happen, well, the senators and representatives could enjoy a game of golf on the professional course above them and the meals prepared by the five-star chefs who normally served the guests at the exclusive resort.

He hadn't felt secure in his previous office in Manhattan since 9/11, and that was only one of the reasons he traded the fifty-million-dollar annual compensation he earned running the biggest investment bank in the world for a career in public service. The other reason, as his confidante Aaron Cartwright mentioned, was that he could liquidate his assets (namely his Edward-Fitch stock) and save his ass before the economy went bust, without alerting the public shareholders that there was something wrong. He could be the very model of a modern proper government official.

He smiled as he reflected on his own cunning, just barely noticing the run-down old town with half of the storefronts boarded up that existed just outside the resort gates. White Sulpher Springs was the perfect representation of the economy today, according to an op-ed in the *Charleston Gazette* that he had glanced at while sitting in the clubhouse, immediately following his two-under-par round of golf. "The super-rich elite spare no luxury from within the guarded gates of the Greenbrier," the piece read, "while just a few hundred feet away lie the ruins of small-town America and main street business." He finished his immunity-boosting, colon-cleansing, foul-tasting concoction just as he left the small town's city limits. He never gave the subject another thought during the three-hour drive to Washington D.C.

The veggie tonic was certainly not his favorite beverage, but the juice cocktail with a shot of bee pollen would keep his mental acuity at its normal superior level. He was clearly cleverer and much smarter than most in the American public, and probably all of Congress combined. He was the one chosen by the "powers that be" to "advise" the Whitehouse and advance the agenda of the rich and the elite. After all, he had advised the president on his "tax cut" election strategy in the past. His recommendation was to cut income taxes on everyone, including the poor.

"A small family making less than forty thousand dollars will pay no income tax. Hell, they will get money back, a few hundred bucks as a tax credit," he said to the president in a conversation now almost half a decade ago.

He chuckled to himself now when he thought about it. Nobody had any idea how to retaliate against this approach, and most of them couldn't figure out why or how a politician in the party of the so-called "fiscally conservative" would do this. The president was an honorable man. A man of the people. A man with severely waning popularity desperately wanting to remain in office. And, of course, the entire concept of money and monetary policy was completely above the grasp of ordinary mortals, including the man that most thought of as the most powerful man in the free world.

The president attempted to understand. "Cutting income taxes would definitely raise the popularity of this administration with the public," he agreed, "but that's lost revenue for the government, a loss we can't afford. How do we cut taxes without losing money?"

"Inflation," Pearson said.

The president looked puzzled but trusted Pearson and listened as his valued "money czar" explained the theory.

"Let's say the world today is a supermarket that will never be restocked," Pearson said, making sweeping gestures with his hands. "Most of its resources are scarce, so no item in the store can be replaced once we sell it. Nothing will be replaced in this market once the item is sold. Then we assume there are a hundred of us that all want and need the items in this market. There is nowhere else in the world we can buy anything, just this one market.

"Because the world is fair, we are each given ten thousand dollars to buy the things we need and want. The owners of the store set prices based on supply and demand. The items that people want the most will get the highest price."

He glanced at the president, who nodded thoughtfully, and continued.

"Now let's assume that someone comes in the room and promises to give everyone in the room another ten thousand dollars, so the money supply in the world just doubled. Those hundred customers would be happy, right? They have doubled their money, haven't they?"

"Have they?"

Pearson shook his head. "No. The money has doubled, but the money can only buy the same limited resources, so the prices will all double. Twice the money now can only buy the same value of goods as half the money could before. This is inflation."

The president nodded vigorously. "Tell me more, but make it quick. I have a briefing on China in ten minutes."

"Well, we won't tell the Chinese what I'm telling you. Now, let us assume that the people don't know that everyone else is getting more money, or how much money everyone else will get. What if we give ninety-five of the people an extra fifty dollars, and our favorite five people an extra twenty K? Well, the people that received the extra fifty dollars are happy! More money!"

The president bobbed his head up and down happily, or perhaps impatiently.

Pearson stared down the president. "But the reality is that even though we gave them money, their purchasing power—the real value of their money—hasn't changed. In fact, it's been cut because we gave our five favorite people so much more."

The president's brows furrowed. "How is that fair?"

"Who said it was fair? Those ninety-five people represent the average consumer, and they are only going to waste any extra money we give them on consumable crap anyway. We give the bulk of the money to our campaign supporters because they will invest their money in industry and government, which bolsters America's infrastructure for a better tomorrow." He paused a minute to make sure he didn't sound too much like a television campaign sound bite. "I know it sounds strange, but even though you're 'cutting' taxes, the net result is that, through inflation and unequal distribution, we're actually levying a hidden tax on the public because the money we're giving them can't buy even half as much as it could before. And that means more money for you to use in making America a safer and better place."

"That doesn't make sense," the president said, popping the top off a diet soda.

"It doesn't have to, it's economics."

The president laughed. "I can never tell when you're joking, Mr. Secretary. Where exactly does this extra money to create the inflation come from?"

"That's the best part, Mr. President. When we broke from the gold standard we were, in fact, given an unlimited bank account. We send a few government IOU's over to the Federal Reserve Bank, and they send us a check. It's the same mechanism we've been using for years now. I'm serious when I tell you that this is a foolproof way to increase your popularity while simultaneously allowing us to spend on all the projects we feel are necessary. It's a simple way of taxing the public without their knowledge. We send the tax rebates to the American public, and the big checks are sent to our big supporters—defense contractors, oil companies, hell, you could even champion a new version of the liberal Prescription Drug bill and thrill our friends in Big Pharma. This is guaranteed reelection. Are you following me now?"

The president smiled. He never really grasped a single concept in his economics courses at Princeton thirty years before he was elected to office. But this concept seemed to make sense. "Sounds good to me." A moral qualm from somewhere in the president's past reared its head. "But we want to make sure the families really do get a tax credit. Don't we? These people, they work hard, and we should work hard for them. Do you understand?"

Pearson smiled, his face conciliatory and plastic. "Whatever you think best, Mr. President."

In May 2004, the president announced his new tax cut plan to a moderately enthusiastic audience. His vice president stumped for the tax cut plan. Congress tabled the bill when the senators and representatives left for the summer recess, but Pearson had friends among the lobbyists as well as in both houses of Congress. In addition, one of Pearson's mega-billionaire friends founded his own Section 527 tax-free political organization, Fair New Deal for U.S., and funneled some of his fortune as well as online contributions from millions of netizens into the campaign to get the bill passed. The Democrats had no choice but to jump on it, and after holding it up for a few days, introduced their version, which the Republicans presumably accepted in order to appear capable of bipartisan compromise.

In November 2004, the campaign succeeded thanks to overwhelming support, most of it manufactured.

The president won the election against his Democratic rivals, who ironically had sponsored the passed legislation, and Pearson stayed in power, firmly affixed to his position even as some of the other Cabinet and higher-level favorites lost their sinecures.

The Senate bill cleared both houses of Congress with only a handful of nays and abstentions. The media, but not many of the independent bloggers, lauded the bipartisan spirit of cooperation as the president signed the bill into law in November, 2004, along with a measure that declared, conclusively, that Lee Harvey Oswald had acted alone in assassinating President Kennedy thirty-four years ago.

Pearson saluted himself with his empty glass as he headed for Washington D.C. He looked forward to telling Arlene that he was complying with his trainer's edicts.

Washington Post D.C. Offices, July 30, 2007, 7:00 a.m.

"Webb, you never see a glass half-full or half-empty." Marc A. Marchesotti, forties, a veteran crime beat reporter who'd earned himself the reputation of "office pest," cast his skinny, bony shadow over Webb Sutton's computer monitor.

"You're right, Marco boy," Webb drawled. "I see a glass completely full."

"Only my mother calls me Marco, and I wish she'd stop." Richard struggled to keep his eyes open after another all-nighter.

"It's better than 'Websteroo' though, doncha know." Webb raised an eyebrow and glanced up at Marc.

Richard snorted a quiet laugh, more out of politeness than out of amusement.

"I see a glass full of Jonestown's finest."

It took Richard thirty seconds and a blank stare to get Webb to add, "Kool-Aid? Guyana? LSD? Cult suicide? For Christ sake, Richard, you're a journalist."

"No, I'm a chalk-outline chaser." Richard shook his head. "So what poisoned Kool-Aid do you see in our wonderful city today?"

"Frank Pearson," Webb said.

"Ah, a combination of Washington politics and economics. Your favorite. What's he done now?"

Webb sipped Red Bull and glanced at the newly uploaded E! Online paparazzi photos of Frank Pearson watching a tennis game at the Greenbrier, a mixed doubles set consisting of Donald and Melania Trump and Regis and Joy Philbin. Pearson had been schmoozing this weekend in West Virginia. "How much do you reckon it costs to play tennis with Donald Trump?"

"I don't play tennis, and if I did, I doubt I'd be bouncing the ball off Trump's hair. Why?"

Webb watched C-SPAN on the TV monitor in the newsroom. Some obscure senator was introducing an amendment to repeal the 2004 Democratic Taxpayer Relief Bill, which had actually originated as a piece of Republican legislation before current and future presidential hopefuls had hijacked it with a uniquely Democratic spin. It wasn't a heck of a lot better under the Democratic version. Webb viewed it as a boondoggle.

C-SPAN was showing the Senate floor as presidential hopeful Senator Terry interestingly and loudly proclaimed that he was now against the bill he had proposed. The Republicans originally responsible for the initial version of the legislation filibustered him.

The Speaker of the House announced, "The floor recognizes the testimony of the distinguished visitor from Hawaii, Mr. Robert Tedson, who comes here as an independent businessman concerned about the state of the economy. Mr. Tedson?"

The half-Japanese, half-Italian investment banker from Kailua-Kona leaned forward and spoke into the microphone.

Webb's fingers flew over the keyboard. "That Hawaiian hybrid guy reported contributions of close to a million bucks—$939,900, to be exact—last year."

"That's good."

"That was just to Fair New Deal for U.S."

Tedson spoke onscreen. "I certainly understand the concerns of the senators who were once so in favor of this measure, but the tax breaks for regular working families have provided economic assistance to normal Americans and probably stimulated the economy yearly. At least that is the conclusion of the study released in May by the New Century Brain Trust. I now turn your attention to the results of that study, which..."

"Which you gave another private jet full of cash to," Webb said.

"Whoa." Richard blinked rapidly, like a turn signal on methamphetamines. "Why would a group that doesn't think the Republicans do anything right, ever, and regularly slanders anyone who deviates from the groupthink, take money from this dude," he nodded at Tedson's broad grin, "and say that the tax benefits work?"

"Tax Band-Aids, you mean, and not the lasting kind either." Webb replied. "I got your study right here, you pompous criminal." Webb spoke to Tedson's image as he glared at the screen. "The tax credits' effectiveness is inconclusive at best." Webb typed in "S.B. 2925 2004" in Google, then clicked on the seventh result listed, a blog named Economic Calamity.

Economic Calamity
Valentine's Day 2925
February 12, 2005, 1:04 a.m.
By Martin Cheyne

So, have you all spent your tax refunds yet? Are they refunds, credits, or breaks? Tax Dollar Days? I get nervous when the government hands out free money. Last year's S.B. 2925 was one of the most amazing compromises I've ever seen in Washington. True, it didn't help the Dems win the White House, but they looked good on paper, and in the twenty-four-hour news feed. The problem with tax breaks like this is that it feels a bit like a Ponzi scheme. Where is this munificence coming from?

Maybe I should just mellow out, it's almost Valentine's Day... By the way, men outspend women two to one on that day, according to my economist friends. They're usually the one weighing the real versus the nominal values of roses. The formula is i = Pi x Qi, as any of my students who are actually reading this will know.

With that $400.00 bonus posited, let's assume Pi for a dozen roses is $ 30.00, and that's the cheapskate version. Let's say you buy three bouquets in the hope of getting a little action (or out of the doghouse). Qi would then be three. i = Pi x Qi ; i = $30 x 3 ; i = $90.

So your $400.00 bonus, assuming you want to blow it all on roses, will buy you around 4.5 bundles (in case you forgot two anniversaries in a row or are planning to propose). However, if you shop at 7:00 p.m. on Valentine's Day itself, the prices will increase and the quantities decrease. The tax credit is only as effective as our discipline. And next year—if we use roses to represent a real-value series of nominal values across this year and last year (or any given years)—your tax credit might buy, say, 20 percent of the roses you were able to afford this year because the run on roses means the prices will go up.

Then you get into people buying roses they can't afford on credit because the lenders gave them a deal, and the government knowingly or unknowingly manipulating the florists' stock prices, which affect the price of roses.

Maybe chocolate is the best way to go. Spending our tax breaks on chocolate might not be the wisest idea, but hey, the government wouldn't give us anything we can't handle, right?

Trackback / Comment / Blog This / Comments (169)

"Plunge protection team," murmured Webb as he verified Martin Cheyne's credentials and added the comments to the article he wrote on the debate over the 2004 Taxpayer Relief Bill. "The United States task force of the world money-trust." He pulled up Secretary Pearson's archived statements, one of which said, in part, "We must encourage fiscal prudence by the government if we are to expect it from citizens…we cannot expect to solve a problem with the money that created it."

Webb Sutton called Secretary Pearson's office, the Fair New Deal for U.S. offices in Maryland, and the New Century Brain Trust. This was the fifth time he had called. He got the usual response: Thank you for your interest, leave us your phone number and the information you need and we'll get back to you.

None of them had. His calls to Fair New Deal for U.S. and the New Century Brain Trust went to voice mail. Secretary Pearson's staffers told him, "The secretary cannot comment on the current legislation."

Webb pulled up a photo of Tedson, another banker named Cartwright from California, and Pearson together outside the New York Stock Exchange in 2006. "He knows Mr. Robert Tedson, who you can see on C-SPAN right now."

"We're sorry, but the secretary has a new policy in place regarding comments on existing economic legislation."

"Since when, you piece of capitalist petroleum pig shit…" Webb rarely cursed.

Not much more of substance was said, and Webb noted in his article that his interviewees had not cooperated with his inquiries. Webb proofed the article and e-mailed it to Steve Yee, the managing editor.

Two hours later, Steve dropped by Webb's desk as Webb put his third empty can of Red Bull in the recycler. Webb looked up from the printout of newspaper articles before 1987 on Frank Pearson's congressional career in Delaware.

The office pool kept a running bet on who would drop dead at his desk first, Steve or Richard, based on how tired they looked on a given day. At last count, Steve edged out Richard by a hundred dollars. However, Richard's backers bet double or nothing that the office would notice his demise last and that everyone would simply assume he had taken an extended nap. Right now, Steve's hands shook too badly from caffeine.

"You'll want to hold your story on the repeal of the Democratic Tax Rescue Bill," he said without preamble.

"Taxpayer Relief," Webb corrected. "How long you been here, Steve? You ever go home?"

"You talk to Secretary Pearson yet? Bob Tedson? Senator Terry?"

"Terry's office offered the usual canned statement, and as for the others, no, I haven't been able to get through."

"Then I suggest you wait until you can get their statements. Also, the paragraphs on the Fair New Deal for America and the New Millennium Think Tank—"

"U.S., New Deal for U.S., and the New Century Brain Trust. They don't return my calls or respond to e-mails."

"You included a comment by some whacko on the New Deal blog, and this Martin Cheyne guy. These don't add anything to your story. They're just blogosphere speculation. In fact, the whole angle on these two groups just doesn't work. We have Suzanne's story on the debate all ready to go."

"Suzanne Chappelle?" Webb knew that the factual errors weren't representative of Steve's usual acuity. "That's just crap she pulled off Reuters and the canned statements I mentioned." Suzanne Chappelle was Webb's much younger competition. "This is investigative journalism, Steve. You remember what that used to mean?"

"Yeah, lone guys with typewriters in some black-and-white office." Steve chewed his lip.

"At least there were no lawyers." Webb knew the company line when he heard it, and it sounded flat coming from Steve, who'd risked getting expelled from his high school when he photographed a major alumni donor passing out wine coolers to a group of the students and put it on the front page of the student paper.

Steve relented. "You check your facts, give me fucking brilliant paragraphs on why I should risk my ass for column space on these groups, contact your sources. I'll give you forty-eight hours and we'll run Suzanne's story as a lead-in to yours."

Webb didn't care about breaking the story first, unlike Miss Northwestern Jr. Pulitzer Prize-winner Suzanne Chappelle. "Fine." Once Steve left, Webb located Martin Cheyne's University of Nevada-Reno e-mail address and sent out a friendly fan note.

University of Nevada-Reno Economics Tutorial Lab, 9:00 a.m.

Certain conclusions were inescapable.

Big business tended toward corruption.

Douglas Boyd was a Boy Scout.

Boy Scouts had a habit of being silenced, either by violent or subtle means. The campfire sneak attack was anything but subtle.

Paul was an asshole married to a wife so unhappy she hit on Martin before realizing he was in academia. Despite what Doug said, Paul was probably taking advantage of the situation, which meant Doug might prefer being assaulted with a deadly weapon.

Martin was keen to link Bull-Spears and Arthur Whinney to the vast Fed-Wall Street conspiracy. He'd read numerous books and government documents. Officially, the Plunge Protection Team, a.k.a. the President's Working Group on Financial Markets, was the brain child of the Regan administration, created by Executive Order 12631 in 1988, following the stock market crash of 1987. Unofficially, Martin could trace the Plunge Protection Team back to the creation of the Federal Reserve, and further back, to Federal Reservist J. P. Morgan, who organized a private pool to try and prevent the Bank Panic of 1907.

The PPT consisted officially of the heads of the top public financial agencies, the SEC, the Federal Reserve Bank, the Commodities Future Trading Commission, all headed by the secretary of the treasury. Unofficially, the group included and probably served the wealthiest of the wealthy—the top 1 percent of the top 1 percent of the rich.

The entire American economic system depended on financial stability to continue to function. Unfortunately, financial stability now meant that the great Ponzi scheme that included the real estate market, the stock market, the commodities markets, and the money markets had to continue indefinitely. If the money supply began to shrink instead of expand, the game was over and everything would tumble. The government would not be able to keep its reckless promises of entitlement, which never should have been made in the first place. The PPT had a very important job in today's world—but the longer the scheme continued, the harder it would fall and the more chaos and misery would come with it. The PPT was not good for the average citizen.

Martin's question now was, could he trace it to Bull-Spears and Arthur Whinney?

It was the sort of idea that took root inconspicuously in your axions and neurons, and manifested its growth and germination in caffeine or hangover headaches or eyestrain. Then, wham, it sprang fully formed like a sunflower out of your head.

Bull-Spears and Arthur Whinney epitomized the corrupt monoliths of modern capitalism. Surely they would benefit from secretly colluding in a PPT.

He started with Aaron Cartwright and Richard Gauthier. Gauthier didn't have much beyond Google results that led Martin back to the Arthur Whinney Web site, but Aaron Cartwright was a busy boy, according to Google.

Aaron Cartwright had gone to Yale, just like many of the president's Cabinet appointees.

He looked at the *Yale Law Review* through LexisNexis, which he had privileges to access because of one of the law and econ classes he taught. He was reading through screen after screen of results when an e-mail alert popped up on his cell phone.

Martin logged into the faculty Webmail server and read the subject and sender lines: "wsutton@washingtonpost.com Re: Economic Calamity Happy Valentine's Day."

The e-mail had an attachment, and Martin opened the message. Even before he read a word of the missive, he scrolled to the attachment and previewed the photo of investment banker Robert Tedson, Treasury Secretary Frank Pearson…and a picture of Aaron Cartwright.

In the background, trying to look inconspicuous, was a suit who suspiciously resembled Richard Gauthier.

Arthur Whinney and Associates LLC, San Jose Offices, 10:00 a.m.

Doug couldn't stand Paul's snake pit of a house a moment longer. He'd spent the weekend in a motel planning how he could get back at Arthur Whinney. His plan was to have all the relevant documents photocopied and hidden in a safe place. When he sent the audit for approval and review, he would leave an "unqualified" audit report, along with the numbers that his bosses wanted to report. He planned to switch the report as a last-minute change while the documents were in typing. Last-minute changes happened all the time in this business, and he suspected he would remain unnoticed. By categorizing the audit as "qualified," Doug would be stating that the audit was okay except for the valuation—but to investors, this was like dropping an atomic bomb on the fund. It was such a standard sheet of paper, Doug hoped and prayed that Bull-Spears would send it off with the financial statements without ever reading or noticing its adverse contents. Once the professional analysts got hold of it, it would be noted. The qualified report would relay to the analysts that the numbers were crap and that the hedge funds were in distress. It would result in immediate "sell" ratings from anyone looking objectively at the document. Doug's plan was like cooking the books, only in reverse. Regardless of whether his report made its way to the public or not, Doug's career as an auditor was toast.

He rented a slate gray Crown Vic, just to mess with his stalkers' minds, and played U2's *How to Dismantle an Atomic Bomb* album. Martin, Paul, and Phil were the only ones who knew Doug secretly worshipped Bono. In a single motion he replaced his round spectacles with a pair of prescription Serengeti sunglasses on the dash, rolled the windows down, put the car in drive, and started cruising.

At 5:00 a.m. he returned to the Arthur-Whinney offices, which smelled as industrious and sweat-soaked and ink-filled as it had when he'd left for San Francisco. He socialized for a few stolen moments with the handful of accountants and grunts who'd noticed his absence, then headed to one of the empty cubicle stations where he would set up for the day. He brought in Starbucks for the entire office and ducked out of the way of the rabid workers deriving synthetic enthusiasm from their lattes.

As Doug sat in his cubicle five hours later, he smiled blandly at Richard, who smiled blandly in return. He'd probably seen Doug but never deigned to notice him. Bob waved awkwardly.

"Back at last, I see," Richard said, attempting warmth. "Recovered? Feeling better? We missed you."

Doug kept the smile as he slid the alternate report in his desk drawer. "One hundred percent. Couldn't be better. Ready to work. And that, ah, item that we discussed? No longer a problem."

Bob raised his brows at Richard. Richard nodded to him and then to Doug. He even went so far as to drape a hand over Doug's shoulder. "Had a chance to clear your head, eh?"

Doug nodded and held up the clean audit books, with the signed "unqualified" audit report sitting right on top. He had a stack of binders filled with workpapers, but Richard appeared not to scrutinize them. Everyone at Arthur Whinney considered a desk without an endless stack of books and binders a mark of failure.

"I'm fine," Doug said when Richard tapped his foot for the fourth time while waiting for Doug's response. "Just burnout. Lowered immunity. Doc says I'm not contagious. It was good that I had a lot of time to reflect on things, including my career."

Richard hummed a few bars of Tchaikovsky's Symphony no. 5 in E Minor. He glanced briefly at the audit report sitting on top of the binder and smiled at Doug. "You ought to get out more, Doug. Get to the symphony. Dolly and I caught a great concert on Friday. I have a box. Perhaps you'd like to come this weekend."

"Sounds good." Doug couldn't believe he was politicking. "But I hate to go stag…"

Bob muffled a snort. Richard looked benevolently on Doug. "Dolly has a group of newly single friends. We'll fix you up."

"Divorced and desperate," Doug heard Bob mutter under his breath.

Doug pretended not to hear. Richard was obviously playing good cop.

Richard nudged Bob. "Bob and I will be eager to review the results of your audit."

"We were worried there." Bob laughed. "Bull-Spears was chewing our asses. Pricks."

"I take it they want the audit submitted yesterday," Doug said.

"You got it." Bob relaxed his posture entirely too much. His hand dropped from Doug's shoulder and knocked against the books.

"Let me know when you are ready, and I'll run the audit report over to typing for delivery," Doug said.

Bob snatched up the top set of books. "I'll take them over when I'm done. You've been here since the crack of dawn—this has been a long day for you. Why don't you head on home?"

Hook, line, and sinker. Doug only smiled in response.

"Well done, Doug." Richard made a pumping motion with his arm. "You're back in the zone. Keep it up. We'll meet up later in the week once I talk to Dolly about this weekend. You'll love it."

Doug grinned as he watched them move off toward Richard's office. They carried the workpapers with them, and everything in that set of books reflected their expectations.

He gathered the alternate report and strolled over to Reza Hagopian's desk. She handled typing and mailing for the office. Her short dark flip of hair matched her personality. Doug always tried to be cordial to her, especially since he often heard Bob and Richard screaming at her when Bull-Spears didn't receive something on time. "Haven't they ever heard of e-mail?" Doug said to her once.

Reza smiled at him and spoke with an Australian lilt. "Bull-Spears again, eh?"

"Who else?"

"Dick let you handle this personally?" She raised her eyebrows. "Who loosened his bowels?"

Doug laughed at her phrasing. "You got me, but someone should give them the Nobel Prize."

Reza grinned as her eyes drifted to his unbuttoned Polo shirt collar. "I'll take care of this ASAP."

Doug wasn't sure, but he thought he felt her eyes on him as he walked away. He hadn't noticed before what a beautiful smile she had. It was strange; the office didn't seem as gray today. Doug felt revitalized.

He uncharacteristically spent the rest of the day squaring away all his other accounts and encouraging all the prairie dogs in the cubicle farm to interact with him. Everyone seemed either jumpy, withdrawn, or laser-focused on work; maybe they didn't know how to react to the new Doug. He strutted over to Reza's station at lunchtime to ask her out for a bite, but she wasn't there. He went by again during his coffee break, and she glanced brightly at him while she spoke on the phone. He nodded casually. At 4:57 p.m., he left the office early for the first time in his career.

Back in the slate gray Crown Vic, Doug sang along with U2's Bono with ironic yet fresh soul on the "City of Blinding Lights" track about knowing less than he did before.

Doug glanced in his rearview mirror as another car changed lanes with him. He stopped singing. The car changed lanes, following him a third time. He let out the breath he didn't know he'd been holding when he recognized Phil's car. He drove to the Tropical Dreams Motel and parked in the back of the L-shaped faux Tahitian building.

Arthur Whinney/Bull-Spears Offices, 4:30 p.m.

Aaron Cartwright sat at his desk, concerned, and listened to the loud discussion taking place on the phone. He, along with the other major financial institutions, were engaging in a plan organized by the secretary of the treasury to form a limited partnership that would buy a large portion of the bad debt, the bad mortgages, and the radically devalued CDOs that they owned between them and get them off their books.

The limited partnership would buy the CDOs at an inflated price, not only stopping the losses from showing up on the books of the banks, but also creating a higher market price to justify the values of the assets that the financial institutions kept.

Each bank would own just a small percentage of the limited partnership, so the financial reporting of the partnership could be kept separate from the banks. Of course the banks would have to funnel money to the partnership through dummy accounts for a while. By the time anyone realized that the assets were worthless, or near worthless, the partnership could have transferred them as collateral to the Federal Reserve Bank and out of their hair forever. By the time anyone got whiff of this in the public eye, it would be a nonissue. Maybe the attorney general would yell and scream on television for effect, maybe even levy a few million in fines. By then the banks would be fatter, richer, and the management safely retired. In Cartwright's case, preferably in countries that had no extradition treaties with the United States. Cartwright had always imagined living in Havana, drinking mojitos and smoking forbidden cigars.

Unfortunately, the beat of an Afro-Cuban quartet seemed far away, since the banks were squabbling over how much each institution should have to pony up. They were dicing over pennies when fortunes stood to be made. All of the banks had massive credit problems, and none of them wanted to put any real assets into the partnership. None of them trusted each other, and every one of them suspected everyone else of trying to manipulate the scheme to their benefit.

"So just borrow more," Richard Gauthier said loudly, intruding in the fray. Cartwright had asked him to mediate the phone conference. A Puccini aria echoed on the line, probably from Gauthier. "That's what Bull-Spears is doing."

"I take it then that all your people are working full time on this?" Cartwright prodded.

"I have the best team imaginable. Everyone is on board with this, working nonstop." Richard, in his office, knew what Cartwright was asking. Now that Douglas Boyd had been brought to heel, and Richard never doubted he would be, Richard smelled more money, power, influence.

Cartwright nodded and huffed. The severity of the situation frightened him. He had never seen anything like this in all his years. If everyone didn't act together on this, a massive financial meltdown was right around the corner. Unfortunately, it was going to take a miracle to get everyone to act together.

Cartwright's phone line beeped, and his executive assistant's nasally voice cut into the call. "Secretary Pearson for you, Mr. Cartwright."

"Thank you." Cartwright savored the immediate silence on the line. "Richard, if we hang up, can you talk to these other fine people? Robert? Deborah? Stewart? Ian? Perry?"

Everyone answered in the affirmative. It was the first time Cartwright had ever heard Robert Tedson, Deborah Crump, Stewart Zwick, Ian Atkins, and Perry McDonald in complete accord. Not unexpected for five of the most powerful executives in the world. They all said goodbye in unison and hung up.

Cartwright hit a button and switched lines. "Frank, are you well?"

"Fine, thanks, Aaron. Listen, I did some checking with my sources at the FBI, and they don't know anything about a sting operation. They don't have anything on this guy Douglas Boyd at all. I can probably get some guys to check it out if you want, but at this stage, I think we are better off leaving the FBI out of it. I suggest you get your people to tail him and the others that were with him."

Cartwright had expected as much. "I will do that. Thanks, Frank."

"Aaron…how are the negotiations going on the new partnership with the other banks?"

"Don't you worry, Frank. We will get it to work. We have to."

Cartwright soothed and reassured Pearson for another minute before he ended the call. His line beeped again.

"Arthur Whinney for you again," his executive assistant announced.

"I'll take it."

Richard's voice came through strained and panicked. "The FBI's here. Why is the FBI here?"

"They're not supposed to be. I have it on good authority the FBI is not to touch you."

"They're spying on my building. I'm looking at an agent right now from my window."

"How many are there?"

"I only see the one."

"Then he's a lone soldier."

"Boyd was cooperating. He was! He even asked me to set him up with a woman!"

"Oh, you will. Lady Death. And don't worry about the FBI man. Washington will handle it. Which FBI office is he with?"

Richard peered through the telescope he'd borrowed from his daughter Stacie. "Wait…he just turned away." Richard put Cartwright on hold and asked one of the office interns to go out and observe the Fibbie.

She went outside under the pretext of taking a cigarette break, since California had banned smoking indoors. She took her time puffing and then stomping out her butt. She returned to Richard's office and made her report.

Richard got back on the phone once he thanked and dismissed the intern. "The car has Sacramento plates." He gave Cartwright the license plate number, which the intern had rattled off in a white-hot voice.

"I'll have my people run the plates." Cartwright felt the pounding in his head ease. "Whoever this lone soldier is…he's met his match."

CHAPTER 9

"Real estate cannot be lost or stolen, nor can it be carried away. Purchased with common sense, paid for in full, and managed with reasonable care, it is about the safest investment in the world."

—Franklin D. Roosevelt

Jekyll Island, Georgia, August 4, 2007, 1:59 a.m.

Martin switched off the streaming live feed and looked at the phone. He had a text message from Webb Sutton's number. He read: "STAY WHERE YOU ARE."

Martin knew that Webb knew writing in all caps, in Net lingo, was the same as shouting.

Another text message appeared in stubborn caps: "IM EN ROUTE."

Martin typed back: "meet you at the gazebo, if I live long enough."

Webb's swift response followed moments later: "HELL YES YOU WILL."

Martin resumed his blog:

Economic Calamity
Skull and Bones
August 4, 2007, 1:59 a.m.
By Martin Cheyne

The headline isn't for a new video game. For one thing, I don't look like Angelina Jolie in *Lara Croft: Tomb Raider*. I don't even look like one of

Bradgelina's adopted kids. (Yes, for all you summer session students, I know it's Brangelina.) When I say Skull and Bones, I mean real-life baddies.

Skull and Bones to me is the perfect representation of the good-old-boy network that exists. The privileged take care of the privileged. For those who don't know, Skull and Bones is the secret society for the highfalutin rich kids at Yale. Not coincidentally, Skull and Bones is connected to the PPT, since every Yalie in the PPT was in Skull and Bones. Robert Tedson, Aaron Cartwright, Perry McDonald, Deborah Crump. That last one sounds more like your fifth-grade social studies teacher than one of the most powerful women in business with a face, body, and voice like a Delta blues torch singer. Not everyone in S & B is evil, obviously, just like not everyone in the Fortune 500 is evil. (You read that right. I can't stand Windows bugs, but I respect Bill Gates as well as Warren Buffett.)

The PPT is one of those groups, like Skull & Bones, hidden in plain sight. They serve another hidden group of the rich and powerful. So rich and powerful that they have never been exposed.

The PPT, simply put, manipulates U.S. stock markets using U.S. government funds to buy stocks or other instruments, such as stock index futures. U.S. government funds, or bank funds, could buy bad securities as well. This would all be done in the event that we have another 1987-style "Black Monday" stock market crash. The problem is, the U.S. economy hasn't even hit "Black Monday," at least not that anyone is yet acknowledging, but the government knows something we don't. You can bet your single-bullet theory on that. Tedson, Crump, and McDonald are all in cahoots with Cartwright, who is buddy-buddy with Secretary Frank Pearson (see photo included in my August 2nd blog entry "Pearson's Photo Op").

It reminds me of the scheme orchestrated by my old friend Paul, on a much grander scale. The tragedy (LOL) is that Paul became a pawn for his government, his ego, and his hormones.

Trackback / Comment / Blog This

LeBrach and Associates Offices, Sacramento, July 30, 4:30 p.m.

Karina Domingues was good at her job. Everyone in the office agreed. Even the ones who gossiped about her behind their file folders because she worshipped Paul LeBrach threw her sympathetic crumbs.

Oblivious to their watercooler talk, she typed at her laptop on the walnut conference table as Paul spoke to the five people who had wandered in to hear his presentation on microlending. Paul furnished them with loan guarantees as he spoke.

"...and Mrs. Macias, you want to mortgage your house, just a micro-mortgage, not a total mortgage, to finance your flower shop?"

"No flower shop," Mrs. Macias, a Colombian immigrant, said. Karina had developed a rapport with her over the phone. She glanced at Karina appealingly. "*Planta, botánico...comprende*?"

Joanne Huffman from Milteer Capital Funds, Phil's "straw capitalist," spoke up. "I think she means botanical garden. Greenhouse."

"*Jardín botánico*," Mrs. Macias confirmed.

"We can front the money to help LeBrach and Associates," Joanne said, removing her sunshine yellow jacket and leaning forward to show Paul, as well as the other three men present, her cleavage. Paul had arranged to meet her for a hotel tryst after the presentation.

"*Qué*?" Mrs. Macias asked.

Joanne spoke in Spanish to her while Karina translated for the two Anglos, including Paul, who should have known better, and the Korean woman and African-American grandmother, who pointedly ignored each other. The other white male was a community college student whose financial aid eligibility had diminished. He wanted to transition to a four-year college, but his parents didn't want to pay. Paul knew the kid had forged his parents' signatures on car loan documents before.

"And we don't have to worry about repaying this microloan for a while," the college student said.

"Absolutely not." Paul smiled at him. "See, Milteer Capital Funds helps us out, and when you repay us, we repay them back with interest so you can pay us what you can afford in terms of interest." He smiled, glad-handing them with his voice and his body language. "They know they're getting a big reward, because you're going to get As and eventually get an MBA and a six-figure salary."

"Actually, I want to study music composition and compose my own music over the Internet," the boy said. "My parents made me sign up for accounting."

"Smart guy," Paul laughed. "I have a college buddy who's an accountant for a big firm, and he's miserable. No social life, no dates, zip." He looked at Mrs. Macias. "And you, you want to work with plants all day."

"*Ethnobotanica Colombia*," Mrs. Macias said.

"Native plants of Colombia," Karina added.

The only native plant of Colombia this woman could cultivate would get Paul raided by the DEA in a heartbeat, but it didn't matter. Milteer Capital Funds would pay him regardless, and the woman would pay interest that would creep up gradually. Joanne's bosses at Milteer weren't worried about credit risk. Joanne's bosses belonged to a not-so-secret society of Italian's based in New York City, and would collect the money one way or another.

"Right, so everyone can see all the native plants of Colombia." Paul cut off Mrs. Macias as she expounded on her expertise in botany. He glanced at the African-American grandmother. "And you want what?"

"Knitting store," Mrs. Washington said. "Teach young people, boys and girls, how to knit. Have classes. Keep 'em away from drugs and these titty tops and low-riders that only lead to gangs and crack babies. They knit in Hollywood, you know that."

Paul didn't think the average teen would take up knitting needles when video games promised an instant pleasure shot to the brain, but it didn't matter. "You go on with your bad self, girl." He'd heard Oprah say it.

Mrs. Washington rolled her eyes.

"I am a student of black culture," Paul said. "Denzel Washington is my favorite actor."

"Whatever, just as long as you get me my money," she said. "You make sure you get right with the Lord too."

Paul turned to the Korean woman, Ms. Phan. "And you, you want what? A nail salon? A restaurant?"

"Baby massage parlor," she said. "Prenatal care. America doesn't touch its children. You just buy them things and ignore them with Mr. Spock."

"Doctor Spock," the college student said.

Joanne clapped spontaneously. "What great goals. They're what this nation is all about. The American Dream."

And they'd probably shut down three weeks after they opened their doors, but Paul got their money and Milteer's money regardless. Milteer Capital would secure the repayments by having their collection people visit in person. With a baseball bat. And, who knows, the kid might actually graduate before his parents found out. He looked at the boy. "Your name, music dude?"

"It's Will Okemos," the boy said, "but my stage name is Bill Thunder." He was light-olive-skinned with dark eyes, and his six-foot-five frame overwhelmed the chair.

"Sounds like the Wild West," Paul said.

"Not country." Will/Bill swept his hands out dramatically. "I'm a quarter Sioux. Why do I want to sing music of the white oppressors?"

"You like rap better?" Mrs. Washington shook her head. "Terrible stuff."

A culture war threatened to ignite when the youth and the crone stood. Of course, she looked like she could take him. Paul, Joanne, and Karina stood as well. Paul favored the room with another grin. His eyes flicked to the door and saw Phil, well, fill the doorway. He saluted his old friend thanks to the puppet tug of his gut that transmitted fear.

"Karina will take care of everything, all the papers," he said, and noticed that Karina unconsciously leaned into Will/Bill, jostling him. The kid developed a look of instant horniness and gave her his best smile.

Karina nodded to the group and took Mrs. Macias' arm. "If you'll all follow me." She proceeded out until she bumped into Phil.

"Afternoon, Karina." Phil made a slight bow.

"Mr. Schultz." Karina held a tiny smile as Phil slid out of her way. She nodded at Phil with demure eyes. Paul had seen Patty all but striptease in front of Phil, but his friend never looked as flustered as he did now in Karina's presence.

Paul watched Phil eye the departing Karina's backside and scowled. Surely she didn't go for men in uniform? She'd told him some sob story about her daddy, a police officer, being knifed to death by a punk.

"Phil, Philly. What can I do you for?"

"Sell my house," Phil said. "I gave you the notice of foreclosure three weeks ago. You know I'm out of time."

"You took time out of your busy life of chasing down perverts to come by and interrupt me because your house hasn't sold?" Paul kept his cool.

"You told me you could negotiate more time with the bank. What am I supposed to do now?" Phil wasn't smiling.

"I told you I'd take care of it. I'll take care of it." Paul was annoyed that his integrity was being questioned.

"Karina seems a little jumpy," Phil said.

"She's just excited. I don't know how much you eavesdropped on, but we are doing great things here. Your house will sell." Paul stared at the polished walnut of the desk and spread his papers around.

"I heard. Impressive sales pitch, especially how you pretended to actually give a damn."

Paul's gaze snapped up to Phil's. "I'm a people person. You cops are so suspicious."

"Interesting concept, microlending. I don't know too much about it. From what I can tell, it sounds like loan-sharking."

"You also don't know too much about staging your house to sell, do you? It still smells of gunpowder and kids. I had my cleaning crew in there three times, but it gives off bad vibes to people. You ever think about reducing the price? I had an offer for two hundred and eighty thousand from these people, the Fosters, nice couple."

"That's nowhere close to the appraised value."

"Face it, Phil, I know what a good value it is, but in this market, two-eighty is your best offer." Paul thought Phil had that debtors' look about him.

"I owe six hundred. Can we counter with four-fifty? Will the bank take that as a short-sale? "

"They wanted to pay two-fifty." Paul let that sink in. "I can try for three and give them some creative financing if they get turtle-headed. But the bank will want you to sign a personal note for the difference. You'll still owe them three hundred thousand on an unsecured note."

"Turtle…"

"Slow and steady wins the race. Geez, Phil-osopher, you'd think you never read a book in your life." Paul said this affectionately.

"What kind of 'creative financing'?"

"Nothing to concern you."

"I really want four, Paul."

Paul sighed and stood. Dealing with Phil was like dumping cold water on his loins. "You're the man."

Paul drew up the counteroffer and Phil signed it. The microlending beggars had gone, and Karina worked at her desk. Paul gave the document to Karina. "Fax that over to the Fosters, that's an angel. Philly, good to see you, maybe we can have drinks this weekend. By the way, do you know where Douggy went?"

"He, uh, went back to work."

"Well. Good for him." Paul accepted that Doug would sell out to a big powerful firm more readily than he would an old college buddy. Maybe after reason set into Douggy's soul and he could see how much it would help out, Paul could approach him again about signing the financial statements. "You, uh, keeping an eye on him? He lives alone."

"Sometimes. What are friends for?"

Phil shook hands with Paul and watched him stride back into his office.

Karina angled her head to look back at Phil as she fed the fax machine. Somehow her eyes darted past him to Paul's closed door. Phil recognized that doomed-woman look. Karina was the latest of Paul's conquests.

The Pottery Barn blinds were up, and Paul stood with his back to his employees. Karina bit her lip and muttered, "*Soy idiota.*"

"No, he's the jerk," Phil said.

Karina's hyper-professional demeanor snapped down. "Is there anything else I can do for you?"

"I want to check that counteroffer again before you fax it."

Karina pushed the document into the loading tray and dialed the number. She pressed Send with her thumb. "Sorry. You ought to trust Mr. LeBrach."

The fax jammed, and Karina hit Cancel. Phil cleared the jam and scanned the document. "Maybe that's a sign from God that I should check the fine print."

Karina shrugged and swished over to her desk. She pulled out a bag of sugared almonds, popped a handful in her mouth, and then tossed Phil the bag. "I'm not supposed to have these. My mother has hypertension and last time at the doctor's…" She ducked her head and stopped speaking.

Phil crunched the almonds and scanned the paper.

The offer was for $300,000 contingent on the Fosters accepting financing from the lender Paul had insisted Phil use. The appraised value of the house was $450,000, according to a document by an appraiser Phil recognized as having been involved in several FBI investigations. The Fosters didn't comprehend that the financing for the house they considered a "steal" would eventually cost them much more than the original value his appraiser determined. Even worse than that, Phil wasn't sure he still owned the house.

Dreams for sale, Phil thought.

"Can I have a copy for my files?" He smiled at Karina, who shrugged again. Phil made the copy himself, and Karina faxed it over to the Fosters. She adjusted her black blouse several times. It looked like a modern-art wallhanging with the swatches of fabric dangling from the front. Phil didn't think she was being provocative.

He handed Karina his business card, even though he knew she had his information in the computer. "Any problems come up with that transaction, please call me." He lowered his voice. "I've been reassigned to a new task force. Mortgage fraud."

"Oh," Karina said. "Good for you. We're clean."

Phil kept a lock on her eyes with his. "You ever see anyone trying to pull anything on Paul, anything that looks like a scam, you have him call me, okay?"

"Mr. LeBrach doesn't get scammed," Karina said.

"Or he thinks he doesn't. But if you think something's hinky, you call me." Phil nodded respectfully at her. "Always nice to deal with you, Ms. Domingues."

"Karina." Her lips parted, trembling slightly, as she smiled. "It's Karina."

"And you can call me Phil."

"Are you married?" They both looked dumbfounded, and Karina blushed after she asked the question.

"Yes," Phil said sincerely, and saw the flash of disappointment in Karina's eyes. "Happily. My wife's back East for the summer with her family."

"Oh," she said. "*Muy bien.*"

"I wasn't hitting on you, Karina." Boy, he sounded clunky and stupid.

"I know." There was wisdom in her eyes.

"You wouldn't happen to know the details of this microlending Paul's doing, would you?"

Karina shook her head. "I'm not at liberty to talk about it. It's generous of him...most lenders wouldn't think Mrs. Macias was a good credit risk. She only works sporadically and she rents her home."

"Do you think she's a good credit risk?"

"My mother says risk is part of life," Karina said.

"You notice anything, anything at all, you call me," Phil said.

Arthur Whinney Offices, Tuesday, July 31

Doug walked nonchalantly into the Arthur Whinney building. He did so at the unearthly late (for him) hour of nine. He did not intend to clean out his cubicle. He expected that whatever regulatory agencies had mucked out Arthur Andersen's stables would clean house at Arthur Whinney and Associates.

Instead, two muscular men barricaded the hallway to Doug's cubicle. They did not look like applicants for the CPA slot that just opened up on Monday. Doug put on an air of calm. "What can I do for you?"

Bob stepped out from behind the human barrier. There might have been glee in his face at Doug's potential predicament, or Bob might simply be relieved that the gentlemen appeared to be on his team.

"Richard wants to see you, Doug," Bob said, his tone indicating nothing out of the ordinary.

No words were exchanged on the way to the office. The associates sagely made themselves invisible in their cubicles as usual. For whatever reason, Tennessee Ernie Ford's "Sixteen Tons" played in a loop through Doug's head and heart.

Dick Gauthier stood by his desk tapping his foot, to give the appearance that he'd been waiting on Doug for hours. He brandished the package Doug had mailed yesterday. Or thought he had. The mailer had been clawed open.

"You don't have any friends here," Dick said without preamble. "We intercepted this." He flung the mailer at Doug and knocked him in the chest. "We sent the audit that won't land our asses in the fire. As it is, you're the one getting burned. Who do you think you are, anyway?"

Doug decided there was no point in denial. "Stupid when I'm sane, brilliant when I'm crazy."

"Just plain stupid." Dick shook his head. "Stupid Boy Scout fucker."

The two hired musclemen and Bob winced at Richard's unfortunate phrasing. "Stupid," Bob echoed. "Dateless loser, too."

"You could have risen so high," Dick said. "As it is, I'm weighing whether or not to sue you."

"For what, exactly?" Doug stood up straight the way his parents had told him. "Doing what was in my job description? How will you explain that, exactly, to a jury that already hates 'the man' and thinks corporate America is lying? People hate big business."

Dick chortled, sucking breath in and out as if playing a saxophone. "Not everyone thinks 'exactly.' Remember the O. J. Simpson trial?"

"The civil jury laid one on him," one of the musclemen said, and got a glare from Bob.

"I'm out to protect the economy," Dick said. "People's jobs. You think you're going to be a big hero if Bull-Spears and this firm go down? I'll prevent that from happening. At any price."

Doug felt a fresh chill down his back. He saw through his former boss to the core of the man. Dick viewed all of humanity as an item on the sale rack at Macy's. "Are you going to take me out back and shoot me?"

Dick smiled. It looked like a shadow. "I don't have to. We both know that you're on your own." He folded his hands. "Given all the years of service you've devoted to this company, I'll only consider suing you. You're already fired, of course. I'm putting in a call right now to the State Board of Accountancy and requesting they pull your CPA license. But I'll let you walk out of here today unmolested so you can contemplate where you went wrong."

"You can't fire me." Doug resorted to the best line he knew, which was also the lamest. "I quit. Thanks for nothing." He paused. "Dick."

The openmouthed outrage on Dick Gauthier's face was worth being escorted to the front of the building by the two musclemen.

Doug smiled graciously at the few staff who ventured to look at his disgrace. Dick's words echoed in his brain and sparked the thought that Dick knew about Phil. Doug knew that an FBI agent might not be able to save him a second time.

Phil's House, Sacramento Suburbs, 11:00 a.m.

Phil's Ford 500 shuddered as he parked it in front of his house, between two Sacramento Police patrol cars that bookended him. There were already two cars in his driveway.

As Phil stepped out, a plastic surgery mannequin of a woman screeched at him, "That's the bum who convinced us to pay through the nose on this dump?"

A slim, linen-suited man with curly black hair and eyes stood beside the woman and a man with a middle-aged spread. The linen-suited man stormed over to Phil as he waved the counteroffer. "Do you own this house? Is that your name and signature? Did you approve this transaction? Did you default on all your loan payments?"

"Yes to everything," Phil said, "and I appreciate your situation." He'd read a book called *Verbal Judo* by a former cop, Dr. George J. Thompson, a self-help book that proved to have some good advice for dealing with stressful situations. He'd never used it with any of the sex offenders he'd busted. It was supposed to help calm the situation.

"Listen to him talk," the middle-aged-spread man, Mr. Foster, said. "Listen to him talk, Susan. He thinks he's going to tap dance his way out of this."

Susan Foster sniffed. "His real estate agent was cute. Guess you can't tell on looks alone."

"No, you can't," Phil said. "Paul's a complete bastard who cheats on his wife. Up until now, I thought he was honest, and here he's lured you fine honest people and me into a trap."

"Save it," the curly-haired man said. He nodded at the police officers. "They're seizing this property according to California real estate law. You forfeit because you tried to defraud my clients. Not only did your appraiser's license get suspended, not only did you try to force my clients to use your ridiculous financing, but you can't possibly pay off your loans to the bank and give my clients title." He said this triumphantly and sniffed the air. "I smell big bucks. And jail time." Phil considered laughing in the man's face, and then maybe kicking him in the balls. Big bucks from him? Verbal judo, verbal judo—he hummed the mantra over and over again in his head to calm himself.

Phil watched the police officers mechanically and methodically post a Notice of Seizure on the front door of his home. He stared at Mrs. Foster's face as if he could liquefy the fat in her cheek implants. "I used my own home as a sting operation, sort of. I was taken myself by Paul LeBrach, and…" Phil was floundering partly because of the pressure of the situation, but partly because he knew he had screwed up badly. "I was going to notify…I tried to contact you…" He had called the Fosters and only gotten voice mail. "We can work together."

Mrs. Foster's face sagged indeed. Mr. Foster sighed and put an arm around his wife.

Phil felt more wretched than when he'd pummeled Stanislavsky, the child porn purveyor. He looked the Fosters directly in their faces. "I'll make this right."

LeBrach and Associates, 12:30 p.m.

Paul peeled himself up from the sexy, badass black leather couch in his private office. He took his time tucking in his Michael Kors woven blue shirt and zipping up his white Michael Kors cargo pants.

Karina hunched her shoulders over her knees as she buttoned up her white lacy appliqué blouse. Her big smoky eyes looked up at Paul with disbelief.

"It's nothing personal, baby, it's, you know, business…" Paul tried to look concerned, but he already wanted her to be gone. "You must have seen the difference in business around here. It's slowed to almost nothing. I'm going to have to let most of the lending officers go as well. You understand."

Karina's face flushed, and she hurried to the door. "You bastard," she whispered through tears. She didn't bother shutting the door behind her.

Paul grimaced. "Tough shit," he thought. "She loses a ten-dollar-an-hour job—I'm on the hook for millions."

Paul walked out onto the floor of the office suites and stood in front of the two rows of desks where his loan officers and loan telemarketers worked.

They ceased their business and busyness. Everyone looked at him. Karina marched past him carrying a carton piled helter-skelter with her personal effects.

Paul addressed the nine people as he made eye contact with Stacey Marina. He'd tried her out last weekend. A wooden leg would be better in the sack.

"I've got some bad news, people. I'm sure this isn't any surprise to you guys, but I am closing the lending business. We just don't have the customers anymore. I'm sorry, but I have no choice. I'd appreciate it if you could clean out your desks now. I've already written your paychecks and have paid you up until two p.m., so go ahead and take the afternoon off."

Stacey tossed her head. She was the first to join the parade led by Karina. As for the other fired employees, there were a few mumbles and maybe a curse word spit out from under someone's breath, but no sobbing, no tantrums. The people in the lending division knew it was over weeks ago. Some of the employees were allotted an hourly wage, a draw that went against any commissions earned on sales, and some were strictly on commission. None of them had made any real money in a while, and none of them were terribly upset about ending their relationship with Paul.

"What about us, Paul? Should we be looking for another job also?" Frieda Stevenson, one of the real estate agents, called out from the other side of the room as she watched the sorry procession of fired colleagues.

"You have nothing to worry about, we're doing okay on the real estate side, right, Ralph? Huh, right, Cindy?" Paul smiled at the two other real estate agents who happened to be in the office. "We've got to keep selling! Sell, sell."

A honk and grind echoed through the windows, and Paul wandered over to see what was of interest in the street. He gasped. "What the fuck is that guy doing to my car?"

A young man in a Braves cap sat in the driver's side of Paul's Mercedes. The door was open. As Paul stormed, feet flying so fast he thought he saw smoke, toward the front door, a bright yellow tow truck pulled in behind the Mercedes and lowered the tow bar.

Paul tore open the front door, ran into the street, and screamed, "Get the hell away from my car!"

An FBI badge hovered in front of his face and shot its obnoxious gleam into his eyes. Behind it, like some primitive god, Phil spoke. "Your charming personality always gets you in trouble, Paul."

"Phil, goddamn it, do something with your rent-a-cop privileges," Paul wheezed.

"I am." The badge retreated, and Paul looked at Phil's grim, serious eyes and mouth. "I'm arresting you for real estate and mortgage fraud."

Paul lost it. His feet and body rushed at Phil, the ungrateful shit. Phil's much larger and stronger hands grabbed Paul's upper arms from behind. Handcuffs locked around his wrists below his Michael Kors watch.

He noticed Karina standing on the sidewalk. He saw her eyes fill with triumph as Phil manhandled and pushed his protesting body into the back of the Ford 500.

CHAPTER 10

"This country has nothing to fear from the crooked man who fails. We put him in jail. It is the crooked man who succeeds who is a threat to this country."

—Theodore Roosevelt

Reno, Nevada, 3:12 p.m. / Washington D.C. 6:12 p.m.

"You aren't blogging this, are you?"

"No, and you aren't recording this for the *Post*."

"'Course I am."

"Then I'm blogging this."

"I'm not Linda Tripp—who I think was grossly abused by the public, by the way. I'm not recording all of this for the *Post*. If you say it's off the record, it's off the record."

"That's good to know. Would you go to jail to protect me as a confidential source?"

"'Course I would. Think of the book deal I'd get. Of course, your blog is hardly a secret."

"To the two dozen nuts who read it, maybe."

The D.C. journalist and the Nevada grad student verbally dueled without malice, like two old-time courtiers. Webb Sutton, who'd called Martin from his cell phone, gazed at the Vietnam Wall on the Mall and watched two women, obviously sisters, make a rubbing of their loved one's name.

Martin looked out the university econ lab window and watched two students wearing flak jackets pugnaciously wave signs protesting the United States' presence in Iraq. A third student, a thin, green-haired Asian girl, pointed her camcorder at them. The bout of self-expression would be on YouTube in an hour.

Webb scanned Martin's blog archives. "You said you maybe had a connection with Aaron Cartwright."

"I do. Old college buddy of mine who did an audit for Bull-Spears."

"How much bullpuckey did he have to swallow?"

"He didn't, and that's why they fired him."

Webb whistled.

Martin watched as the green-haired girl and one of the two protesters (he thought male, but he couldn't tell even on face-for-face inspection of some of his students) grabbed each other and kissed lingeringly. The third one snatched up the camcorder in the hand not holding the sign and held it as if uncertain what to do. From the rigid posture, Martin could tell that the student felt uncomfortable and superfluous. Perhaps jealous. The student just stood in place, a still freeze-frame of a college movie. Martin looked away as the image of a pathetic old man or woman spying on the neighbors penetrated his brain.

"...death threats," Webb said in a low voice.

Martin jerked back, and his chair spilled him onto the floor. "What?"

"I said, it's a wonder this friend hasn't gotten death threats from this company."

Martin was silent for a long moment.

"He has. Hasn't he? Maybe they've approached him with violent intent?"

Martin stayed quiet and still on the floor for an even longer moment.

"Secluded spot? Maybe you were there?" Webb's voice was smooth as bourbon. He could decipher silence. "I heard a crash and you seem out of breath."

"Just moving some stuff around in the classroom." Martin hauled his suddenly sore body upright and put the chair in its original position.

"As if college kids care these days. You need a break, Marty, if I can call you that."

"I was just thinking of heading south, Florida maybe, for a break."

An e-mail alert popped up on Webb's laptop that read, "Tedson travel plans." It was a tip from one of Robert Tedson's legion of assistants, who just happened to have interned at the *Post* two summers ago. It contained an *Entertainment Tonight*-style news clipping.

> "Reclusive mega-billionaire Robert Tedson plans to relax this next week in Florida before appearing with Sir Elton John, Madonna, Steven Spielberg, David Geffen, Donatella Versace, Jack Nicholson, Keanu Reeves, Sean 'P. Diddy' Combs, Donald Trump, Jessica Simpson, Rufus Wainwright, and a host of other celebrities. Hollywood's A-list has invested in the launch of Tedson's new Club Fuzaki in Hollywood. They've paid and now they intend to play. Longtime friend Aaron Cartwright of the investment powerhouse Bull-Spears (not to be confused with Britney Spears) has also donated major dollars, as if Tedson needed them, and the proceeds from the ribbon-cutting party will go to a host of charities, including AMFAR, Pediatric AIDS, and the Elton John AIDS Foundation as well as St. Jude's Children's Hospital in Tennessee."

Below the clipping was a Continental Airlines flight schedule from New York's JFK Airport to Dulles Airport in D.C. on Thursday, August 2. The assistant had included a note about the private jet "wheels-up" from IAD to Jacksonville and the separate cars to Jekyll Island in the early morning hours of Saturday, August 4.

Webb forwarded the e-mail to Martin. "You ever heard of Jekyll Island?"

No economist could be ignorant of the birthplace of the Federal Reserve. "Of course."

"Check your e-mail," Webb drawled. "You should find some vacation suggestions for your Florida sojourn."

"Just so none of them includes Disney World. I intend to plug away at my PhD dissertation. That's part of the purpose of this getaway."

"No, no Mickey Mouse teacup ride. This is the real Magic Kingdom, Marty…wasn't that one of Mickey's nephews?"

"That was Morty and Ferdie," Martin said as he accessed his e-mail on the lab's computer and read the news item as well as the travel itineraries.

"Oh yes. Mouseketeer, were ya?"

"Among other things. Are you game for an exposé on PhD economics dissertations? Could you meet me this weekend in the Sunshine State?"

Florida vacation, celebrity gossip, name-dropping. It was all just distraction, trivia, Disney World. America cared more than that. Martin believed that somewhere in the recesses of his heart.

He booked a last-minute travel deal with a combination flight, rental car, and hotel reservation on Priceline.com as any true Trekkie would.

Webb considered carefully. "I believe I could rearrange a few deadlines. We don't get enough coverage of economic theory, do you believe it?"

"Mind-blowing. But you know, there's someone who's even better than I am at economics, statistics, and weighted averages as well as real values."

"Like an accountant, mayhap."

Who used "mayhap" in conversation outside of English lit conferences? "Perchance, yes."

"You wouldn't happen to have a phone number memorized along with the GDPs of every member of the UN, would you?"

Martin glanced out the window. The student with the camcorder and sign threw his or her burdens down and stomped off, while the green-haired girl and her paramour continued to devour each other's faces.

Webb watched a homeless man in a Vietnam-era Marine tunic screaming and sobbing a few hundred yards away.

Martin scrolled through his cell phone address book until he found the number of the Tropical Dreams Motel. "Just let me confirm a few facts with him."

Sunny View Inn, Sacramento, 4:30 p.m.

When the phone rang, Doug turned up the volume on *Oprah*, whom he'd occasionally happened to turn on at eleven at night when he crashed in front of the couch. He'd even watch her too for a few minutes before he turned on *Law & Order*.

He'd left the Tropical Dreams Motel in San Jose and drove two hours away to the Sunny View Inn in Sacramento. He'd turned in his Crown Vic for a station wagon with smoked glass.

He paid cash for his room and the lethargic-looking clerk from Lahore, Pakistan, didn't even appear to know his name. To her he was just Room Eight. "No prostitutes," she said flatly. "This is not that kind of establishment. You want girl or boys, there are bars on the next block."

Doug assured her he was just in town for a sales meeting and had recently gone through a nasty divorce, so he would be in his room going over his sales presentation, and afterward, nothing more risqué than the in-room adult entertainment would conspire in his room.

She didn't know him from anyone, and there were only two people in the world who had called his room so far. Doug cautiously answered the phone. "Hello?"

"Doug."

Doug let out a breath as Oprah shouted, "Hey, hey, we're in bed together!"

"You're in bed with Oprah?" Martin's voice held humor. "Maybe she can give everyone a new money management system that's ethical and workable. I'm glad you left me your new number. You realize that thanks to the Patriot Act, Secretary Pearson has the authority to seize your text messages and wiretap…cell phone communications are child's play for the government to intercept."

"Secretary Pearson." Doug's mind whirled, especially after what Martin had told him last night. "Martin, tell me this is just another financial conspiracy theory about how we're all plugged in to the Matrix…"

"You're living in your second hotel in two days, Doug. If I know you, you rented another car because you've seen all the movies."

Doug took a long sip of his V8. He craved a martini, but he needed a clear head. "I don't know if I'm being followed anymore."

"Of course you're being followed. They've seen the movies too. You keep a copy of your audit workpapers?"

"For all the good it's doing me. If you're right—"

"I am right."

"We're in deep…"

Martin's voice plucked at him like a harpist's fingers. "There's a sympathetic journalist in D.C. who wants to talk to you."

Doug laughed and flopped on the plaid damask bedspread. "Has he seen the movies?"

"He's seen everything. Did they take your laptop?"

"No. Can we trust him?"

"He's a fan of my blog."

Doug stared at the ceiling, noticing the microfissures in the plaster. "Give him my cell number too. I'm headed out of here in the morning."

"Where?"

"Back home."

Martin breathed relief. "They probably know everything about you, but they won't be expecting this. They'll figure you're a Boy Scout—"

"Will everyone stop saying that?" Doug burst out. "Do I go around saying you're an old hippie?"

"No, because I'm not that old and I was born in the disco era." Martin laughed, and Doug joined in to break the tension. "They think they own you, that you're the good boy who never stands up for himself. The guy who cancels his vacation just to be a team player and meet a deadline. They don't know jack about you, Doug."

"But you do." Doug realized that until this moment, he hadn't known himself or his gifts. Martin's comment gave him confidence.

A gray shadow moved past the window.

"Excuse me." Doug put down the phone then scrambled over and peeped through the green-and-black plaid curtain that matched the bedspread. The gray Pontiac G6 circled the parking lot. All of the slots were filled by rental cars with the rental car company decal stickers still in the windows. There was a handicapped parking spot. The Pontiac nosed into it, then backed out a second later when the cleaning woman from Guatemala cursed him out and handled her cart so furiously that the sponges fell off and the mops rattled. The Pontiac cruised the parking lot in a complete oval, then drove out.

Doug tiptoed back and picked up the phone with a shaky hand. "Sorry about that. You know…I've been thinking more and more lately about my life. I'm in my mid-thirties. I'm alone. I've dedicated my life to a corporate machine that couldn't give half a shit about me. The only family I have is my grandma. I keep thinking back to when I was a kid. I had the best tree house ever in my grandma's yard. I'd play pirates up there for hours with my cousins." He grinned. "Fiercest pirate on the seven seas was my cousin Karen."

"Uh-huh." Doug sensed that Martin heard the uptick of panic in his voice.

"Grandma wasn't the best cook, it was always grandpa who baked and roasted and fried." Doug swallowed. "But you could always count on grandma to read to you. She's…she won't be around for too many more years. I'm all she's got, and vice versa. I think I should leave tonight."

"Will one day more make a difference?"

"It could. Life's fragile and short. Martin, I want to get these guys, these bastards that are out to kill me for doing my job. But have you thought about the ramifications of this? If the chain reaction could be as bad as you say it could be?"

"Look, Doug, it is bad, and its going to be bad regardless of what happens with us. It is just a matter of time. It is a broken system, and the longer we let it go, the worse the problem gets." Doug could sense Martin's excitement.

"If any one group stops playing by the playbook, it's over. The financial advisors have to keep the new money feeding into the over-inflated stock market to keep that bubble in place while the baby boomers retire. The investment banks have to keep the high valuations on equities. The government has to expand money supply at a rate much larger than the quoted CPI—and, as you know, this means the banks have to keep lending." Doug cringed as the conversation turned into one of Martin's rants. "And that's the big one, Doug—people can't borrow. Millions of individuals borrowed hundreds of thousands of dollars to buy homes at inflated prices. They are tapped out. Mass deflation of the money supply is setting in, the economy is shrinking, and there isn't anything anyone can do about it. All we are trying to do is bring back free markets, kick out the fascist politicians and central bankers, stop these criminals on Wall Street from getting rich for creating economic bubble after economic bubble that hurt America. They will kill our children and impoverish our families to stay rich. Douglas, do you know why almost every War in the past four hundred years has been fought? I'll tell you—"

"Martin?" Doug stopped him before he had a seizure.

"Sorry about that. I'll give my journalist friend your cell phone number. Better include your grandma's phone number too." Martin was quiet.

Sacramento FBI Offices, 4:45 p.m.

This time when Carole said, "Mr. Clarkson wants to see you," she didn't look up from her computer database until the very last second. The second when Phil turned and glanced over his shoulder on the way out of the office vestibule. Carole gave him a tiny, profoundly sad smile, then bent her head back to her work.

The walk to Clarkson's office passed in one second, like a Flash animation.

Clarkson stood shoulder to shoulder with Clennahan. Another bad sign. Their faces were identically grim, although Clarkson had the worried-disappointed patriarch demeanor. "There's no point in asking you to sit," he said. "I won't make this any more hellacious than necessary."

Clennahan held up the counteroffer from Paul's office and juxtaposed it with photos of Phil's car tailing Doug's. "Selling a house with a fraudulent appraisal, wasting man-hours on protecting an old college buddy—without authorization, I might add." His face had red tinges, and Phil gathered that Clennahan got some jollies from seeing Phil stumble after the thorough castigation Phil had dealt him. "Hardly model FBI agent behavior."

"I was conducting a sting with Paul LeBrach." Phil smelled stale Cheetos on Clennahan's breath and heard Clarkson's iPod system play "Muddy Waters."

Clarkson shook his head. "You know better than that, Phil. You should've come to me with a sting, especially since this LeBrach is also a friend who listed your house. It's a conflict of interest. As for this Doug..."

"Doug's life is in jeopardy." Phil laid it all out. At this point he couldn't sink any deeper into the quicksand. "It's a conspiracy, a book-cooking mortgage conspiracy that goes right to the top. All the way to the Treasury and even the president. The proof is out there. My sources have collected it."

"This proof?" Clennahan magically produced a printout of one of Martin's blog entries. "Some left-wing socialist academic's rantings? He mentions you, you know. You ought to be more careful in your friends."

Phil felt knots in his neck. "Who the hell are you? You're no lender."

"Just a concerned citizen who's watching the watchers." Clennahan smiled benignly.

"And what do you get in return?" Phil challenged. He looked at Clarkson.

Clarkson sighed. "Phil, this mortgage fraud task force is a sacred obligation. The news is going to break about the incident with Stanislavsky, your transaction with LeBrach, who is about as questionable—"

"As a porn pusher!" Phil spread his hands wide. "The FBI's been my life, John…"

"I know that, but to the public, it won't matter." A vein throbbed on Clarkson's forehead. "The media loves hypocrisy, or so-called hypocrisy, in anyone in government. The public loves to hate it. You had this house listed and you dealt with LeBrach for months, and then you didn't turn him in when we gave you the task force. Your credit rating's shot, you're mortgaged to the hilt, your house has been seized. You know what picture they'll paint."

"That kid you busted? His lawyers have sprung him already." Clennahan waggled a finger. "Those houses, which depressed you more than a crack whorehouse, are still vacant. They'll be bulldozed right along with the homeowners' dreams."

A thought tipped the scales in Phil's mind. "Paul? Don't tell me Paul's free, too?"

"Your investigation is tainted," Clarkson said. "You're dirty. It's a complete fuckup. Stanislavsky's lawyers are working on getting him free. All your cases are in doubt now." He spread his hands, mirroring Phil's gesture. "We can't even stick you behind a desk. The most we can do is suggest that you disappear."

"If I'm so dirty and fucked, why don't you arrest me?" Phil challenged.

"Because the FBI doesn't need the bad press, and I do have some goddamn loyalty to an agent who until recent months I trusted."

Phil's gut told him a different tale. If Clarkson wanted him arrested, he was the director of a whole building full of cops. If Phil put up a struggle with guns blazing, he probably would make it to the foyer before being clobbered. Phil wasn't going to risk the lives and reputations of his fellow agents just because he'd screwed up, and he was sure Clarkson wanted to avoid a confrontation. Plus, he saw the tics in Clarkson's face when Clennahan smiled.

"I won't bother giving my notice," he said. "I'm tendering my resignation."

Clarkson reached out a hand. "You're going to have to surrender your badge and weapon."

In the foyer, Paul smiled pleasantly at the FBI goons who'd treated him like a lowlife. "I just want you to know, I won't sue. And I could. I could make a lot of money suing my unlawful detention at the hands of a crooked agent."

An exotic-looking woman dismissed him with her gaze. "That's big of you, Mr. LeBrach. Please feel free to leave."

"I have to say, you've changed my opinion of the FBI." Paul smiled. "Allow me to take you to dinner to express my gratitude. Say six o'clock."

The exotic woman laughed softly, turned, and walked away. Her New Yorker partner chuckled at him. "And you thought this was your lucky day, hotshot."

"It still is. I'm going home, and my ex-friend Phil is going down." Paul whistled on the way out of the FBI offices. Phil was a disappointment, and he'd cost Paul aggravation, sweat, blood, and treasure. Douggy was also a disappointment, not that it mattered since he'd gotten Will Thunder to handle the books, and he could use his shabby treatment by the FBI as leverage just in case.

Marty…What did Marty matter? A flaky ivory-tower hippie socialist left-wing academic. Paul would look out for number one. He'd squeaked through Hell's gates into the clear. He was still the golden boy.

Paul's car waited for him outside the FBI building. After his office had been raided and his employees interrogated, he was finally receiving respect. He was the injured citizen, after all.

He jumped in his love machine and drove to his place of business. He wasn't surprised to find the offices open and staffed, but he received a mild pleasant shock seeing the line of low-hope, low-rent people, their faces shiny and their eyes worshipful, waiting to speak with him.

Mrs. Macias shook his hand and smiled. "The FBI, they harass common people, decent people all the time. You are our hero. You will help us."

Paul was aware of his real estate agents' stares. He turned to them and grinned. "I know it's been an ordeal." His voice filled the room. "Thanks to a former pal that I tried to help out at personal cost, we all got handed a raw deal." He adopted a contemplative mood. "I guess you never know the demons some people hide. Phil was just crooked. I trusted him, you know? His wife left him. He's in a dark place right now."

Appeased, the real estate agents nodded assent.

"But I'm forgiving," Paul went on, "and this whole experience has opened my eyes. There's more to life than money and real estate, and that's why, as of today, LeBrach and Associates is going to help the little guy achieve his or her dream. We're going to specialize in small personal, commercial, and real estate lending for people who represent the best of America." He swallowed a lump in his throat, swayed by his own oration. "I'm here for you. For all of you."

The real estate agents tripped over each other applauding Paul and enthusiastically discussing commercial real estate options with Mrs. Macias and the other new clients. Paul basked in their hero worship.

He was going to need a new secretary.

Sunny View Inn, 6:00 p.m.

Phil gnawed at a KFC leg as he sat in his non-police car, watching the motel where his friend Doug hid out. He had bought the tiny Korean import years ago in case his world fell apart and he needed to live in his car. He never even liked the car. It was ugly, and for some reason the front window fogged whenever the engine was running.

His home was gone. Everything he owned was crammed in this car. He had no job. He would probably have to file Chapter 7 bankruptcy, but then all the details of the false information he put on his loan application would be brought to light. He would probably face a lawsuit at the minimum, even if the Fosters didn't decide to press charges. He felt pity for them. Self-disgust hardened the chicken as it went down his esophagus.

Phil's cell phone rang. At least it was paid for through September. He didn't recognize the number, but he figured Fate would mete out whatever he deserved. He answered calmly. "Phil here."

"It's Karina."

Phil coughed and washed the chicken down with iced tea. "Hi."

"I heard about Paul." He heard the burn in her voice. "That bastard. I cleaned out a lot of files and took them home. There is plenty of incriminating evidence the FBI wasn't interested in. Microlending is just a term he decided to use to make it sound like a professional business—the people he works with are bad people. I know that he's running a scam on those people. If they don't pay, they will be hurt. If there is anything I can do to put him away, just say the word. I will testify. Whatever I can do."

Phil laughed unexpectedly. Lightness washed over him and he laughed again, apologizing to Karina in the meantime.

Fate had just handed a man who didn't have anything to lose a crusade.

"When and where can we meet, Karina?"

CHAPTER 11

"If an injury has to be done to a man it should be so severe that his vengeance need not be feared."

—Niccolo Machiavelli, Italian Philosopher (1469–1527)

Cathedral of the Blessed Sacrament, Sacramento, 7:45 p.m.

The towering Roman Catholic Church built by miner-turned-Bishop Patrick Manogue in 1889 sheltered Karina. She blushed repeatedly as she heaped CDs, memory sticks, and file folders in Phil's arms. They both stood in the private Eucharistic Chapel at the east end of the church.

Thanks to the burden in his arms, Philip couldn't even see the restored gleaming tabernacle and the inscription Karina had read to him when he'd entered to find her praying alone. The Latin gold letters, "*Panem de Caelo Praestetisti Eis, Omne Delectamentum In Se Habentermi*," meant, "You have given them bread from Heaven, containing in itself all sweetness."

Karina's voice floated around the literal mountain (or at least hill) of evidence. "I came here because I feel safe. I also came here to confess and purge myself of sin."

Phil lowered his burden so he could look in her eyes. They held misery underneath the shine of indignation. It struck him that they had both lost their jobs because of related causes, but she was higher than he on the wounded-innocent scale. In a fit of carelessness he'd thrown himself into a bear trap. He'd accustomed himself to being thought of as the good guy, the successful guy, the nice guy, and ignored the failings that led to his second chance, maybe even his chance to make a difference.

"We all sin, Karina." Phil opened a brown Samsonite briefcase and loaded it with as much of the material as it could hold. "You are helping people right now, this minute. It's part of your penance, I guess. You can ask the padre about it if you like."

"Are you a Catholic, Señor Felipe?"

"Baptized." Phil smiled slightly. "Sometimes practicing. My wife attends services more regularly."

He marveled that he was able to speak of Helen without sounding as if he were dehydrated. He felt her presence, bittersweet, eerie, comforting, and decided to call her tonight. He hadn't wanted to, hadn't felt it was right, although Helen had called the house four nights ago and immediately put the children on to tell him what a great summer they were having splashing about in the swimming hole and touring the Library of Congress and the Air and Space Museum. He noticed that Karina looked at him expectantly; maybe she sensed his thoughts.

"I've never been in this church," he said. "Those paintings of the martyrs are something."

Karina twisted her fingers together. "Do you know why in the Chapel of the Saints there is an empty space among the statues of the Latin American saints?"

"It can't be because they forgot one."

Karina laughed softly. "They're telling us that any one of us can be a saint."

"They have a relic here near the altar, the padre said, from a guy who was killed in a rebellion."

"Pablo." She smiled slightly. "Pablo said you are separated. That your wife left."

"Only temporarily until we sort things out."

"You will," Karina said, "with love. You have it in your heart, unlike some men."

"Did you ever call Paul 'Pablo' to his face?"

Karina grimaced. "He didn't like it."

Phil nodded. "*Idiota*. I personally like 'Felipe.' He doesn't speak Spanish."

"Except the dirty words."

Phil muffled a laugh. Karina blushed.

"He doesn't know that Mrs. Macias doubted him," Karina said. "She told me she thought he was too slick. I saw her this afternoon, after he went back. She treated him as if he were Che Guevara or César Chávez."

"These people are never going to achieve their dreams. They can't pay him back right now, can they?"

"It will take miles and years," Karina said. "They all mean to pay him back."

"And Paul means to have a big up-front commission, plus part of the usurious interest, and he gets paid by this company that's putting up the play money. That woman who was at the meeting, the one in the suit…"

"He is sleeping with her," Karina said, "and she is a loan barracuda. Not that she would ever chip her cheap salon nail polish by doing any actual work. She'll bat her eyes, and two well-paid thugs will get off doing her bidding. Bitch." She glanced at the altar and blushed again, then crossed herself. "I have met Pablo's wife. I can't look at her, but I know she is an unhappy person. My fault partly. Of course, I'm not his only fling."

"He wasn't always the rat he is now," Phil said feebly. He looked through the files. The list of crimes was widespread, ranging from illegally renting out bank-owned houses in foreclosure, to mortgage fraud, to his newest venture, which was nearly identical to a loan-sharking racket. "This should be enough to put him away for quite a while."

"I pray so. He spoke of a new land deal," Karina said. "He was evasive about it, almost teasing."

"What kind of a land deal?"

She shook her head.

"Would you be willing to go back in, undercover, and find out?"

Karina blinked. "He fired me."

"That was when things were going badly for him. If he's Mr. Hero to Mrs. Macias, and I'm assuming to all the other poor people, maybe he'll hire you back. Maybe he'll need you, because he can't talk to them on his own, and I don't just mean in Spanish."

Her generous mouth compressed into a dot.

"I know it's hard," Phil said.

"Will the FBI protect me? Any of us? He went free."

"I screwed up," Phil said. "And this isn't an official FBI operation."

Karina inhaled, her breath heavy and sad.

"But you'll be safe." Phil crossed himself. "You have my word."

She studied him and took the measure of him. He saw the strength in her rounded frame and the depth of her eyes. Paul had once tried to describe her butt and boobs in detail, and Phil and Doug had told him to can it. She did have an excellent body, but she was also a woman of courage and substance.

"I trust you, Felipe. I'll go back to Paul tomorrow and beg for my job back." She grinned wryly.

"I'll escort you to your car," Phil said. "And thank you. You have no idea what this means."

Karina laughed softly and took part of the pile of evidence Phil had stacked on the briefcase from him. Phil fumbled with the remaining documents he had stacked on his briefcase, which he carried horizontally. They strolled out of the church as Karina pointed out interesting aspects of the architecture and history. A family praying in the main sanctuary gave them a row of smiles.

"You know," Phil said as they trod the steps leading down from the front door, "my daughter said 'Jejus' when she was two, and that's the way she still says it. It's kind of cute. Helen and I stopped correcting her, but her brother still tries, just to annoy her. Bug her, really. We call him 'Bug.'"

Karina grinned in delight. "Never, ever correct her again. I think it's cute too…and so would Jesus. You are a lucky man."

"Do you have brothers and sisters?"

"*Sí*, seven. The youngest is ten."

Phil whistled. "Your poor mother."

"My sister is seventeen, and she has a baby already. Just like Mami. Pablo said some unflattering things about her." Karina's eyebrows and mouth flattened out.

"How's she coping?"

"Well, yesterday after staying up all night with Leonicio, she said to Mami—"

Karina's mouth and eyes went wide open as she pitched sideways and rolled on the ground. Phil's ears were on a five-second delay, because they tuned in to the boom of the bullet after Karina hit the concrete.

Phil crouched to shield her with his body. Another bullet whizzed past him and struck the steps. Dust and bits of stone showered him. Karina moaned in agony.

Another bullet whizzed past, but missed, since Phil hurtled them both down the sidewalk and into the street. The stack of paperwork flew everywhere and tires squealed as Phil tasted the filth on the pavement. Exhaust and rubber filled his nostrils. A car horn protested, and a woman's voice shouted, "You crazy? My God, are you okay?"

Phil scrambled to open his briefcase. He no longer had his FBI issued Glock, but he wasn't going to go out unarmed. He pulled a model 586 Smith and Wesson .357 magnum revolver, a gift from his grandfather twenty years ago, from the side of the briefcase and cocked the hammer.

From the crowd he could hear the dialing of a cell phone. Three numbers. The woman who had stopped the car shouted, "Psycho! Can't even be safe in front of a church! Hello? Yes. Someone's been shot. Police. We need police on Eleventh Street, Church of the Blessed Sacrament…No, I don't know the cross street, there's a man with a gun here!"

Another gunshot. Phil rose jarringly to his feet as every muscle screamed. He felt a burn on his arm and saw drops of red oozing. Unafraid, he scoped out the area.

The night partially camouflaged the gray Pontiac, but not the man standing by the driver's side door. Phil knew, beyond logic, that this was one of the men who'd planned to kill Doug at the campsite. His eyes and relaxed, confident stance said he was the ringleader. His firearm was top of the line with a fiber-optic sight. His hand on the weapon said he didn't care who he took out in fulfilling whatever mission Bull-Spears, or whoever the ultimate trigger person might be, gave him.

The man took a step into the glow of the streetlight, and Phil recognized his picture. Phil stepped toward him, blocking Karina from the man's view.

"Hang down your head, Tom Dooley, you son-of-a bitch," he shouted. "Hang down your head, you shameful piece of shit. You should stick to that alias. You're too thin for Michael Moore."

Dooley smiled. "You're outgunned and out of the FBI, Schultz. I won't torture you by killing these civilians if you just tell your pal Boyd to take a powder."

"I'm recording this on my camera phone," the woman witness shouted.

Dooley pointed the rifle at her, and she dropped the camera phone. He fired at it, and the woman ran helter-skelter. The bullet connected and the phone died.

Phil dropped to the ground and crawled on the pavement toward Dooley, but behind the cover of a parked car, his gun covertly drawn. "I know all about you, Dooley. You are going down." Phil jumped up and fired the pistol. His hand jerked from the reverberation, and the bullet smashed the window of Dooley's car, missing him by inches. Dooley scrambled into the Pontiac and slammed the door to shield himself from another shot. Phil stood and aimed the gun carefully this time, as Dooley slammed his foot down on the accelerator. The tires of the Pontiac squealed, and Phil fired another shot, smashing more glass on the car. As the car sped off down the road, Dooley saluted and drove off into the night. Phil cursed himself for his poor aim and for letting Tom Dooley get away.

The woman witness didn't return, but Phil was more concerned for Karina. He turned around to help her up, to ask how injured she was, but instead found Karina running full tilt down the street, short but lean legs propelling her away with no wasted motion. Phil raced after her. "Karina!"

She skidded to a stop and whirled around in one graceful continuous move. He heard her breath hammer the air, and he could see the blood where the bullet had grazed her right shoulder.

"You can't protect me," she yelled. "You're not FBI anymore, *es verdad*?"

Phil's heart felt macerated and tenderized, then pummeled flat. "I'm sorry, more than you can ever know, but I can and will protect you, if—"

"No." There was battle-hardened resolve in her eyes. "Don't follow me. Don't try to find me. Don't ask anything of me. I have my family to think of."

It was a resounding reproach. Phil absorbed it as he stood in the street with his right hand covering the bleeding wound on his left arm and watched her vanish. He doubted she would ever talk to him again.

The evidence Karina brought lay scattered in the street and on the sidewalk. Incredibly, Dooley hadn't attempted to destroy it, and all of it was intact.

It was enough to make Phil fall to his knees and pray before he gathered up what Karina had risked her life for. He finished as the first black-and-white squad car blasted its siren into the night. Contrary to all his training and his scruples, he fled the scene.

Sunny View Inn, 9:30 p.m.

"FBI. Open the door, please, sir, we need to speak with you."

Doug switched off *The World Series of Poker Tour* on ESPN when he heard Phil's voice. "Hang on a second," he called out.

He waited a few moments, then unlocked the room door. Only Doug could smell Phil's perspiration and see the anxiety in his face. "Yes, how can I help?"

"We're looking for an escaped serial child molester," Phil barked. He looked tired. "We have reason to believe he might have stayed here in the last week. We're looking for anyone who may have seen him or who knows his whereabouts."

"Anything I can do to help." Doug pulled Phil inside and shut the door. He yanked the chain and deadbolt securely in place.

"I've been calling you," Doug said, the fog emptying from his head. He glanced at the blood-soaked bandage on Phil's arm. "What the hell happened to you?"

Phil glanced around the room. "I was fired today. By the grace of God and my boss, I didn't get thrown in a federal prison. But I'm finished with the FBI as things stand now, and I almost got a woman killed. And my arm hurts like hell."

Doug winced. "Because of me?"

"Because Marty was right. This thing is bigger than three pathetic college buddies and one asshole ex-friend." Phil scanned the surfaces of the furniture as if trying to visually detect a bomb or wiretapping device. "This is nicer than that hotel in *Vacancy*."

"Or the Bates Motel. I've got Pepsi, Clamato, and even some Johnnie Walker, but I'm not indulging in alcohol."

"Suit yourself, but I am, if you don't mind. I think I've earned it."

Doug unscrewed the cap off the Johnnie Walker and poured a generous dose into a plastic cup with the hotel logo on it. He handed it to Phil.

"Thank you, barkeep. You might as well pour some Pepsi too," Phil said. "I'll probably need to sober up."

Despite the anxious lines around his mouth as he tipped the cup to his lips, Phil didn't look like a man who'd lost his career, his home, his family, possibly his reputation, and maybe, potentially, his time on earth. He commented, "You picked the worst possible time to shift from wimp to action hero, Doug."

"Maybe we should go see the Governator then."

"Sure, now that we've crossed the halfway point between reason and insanity. I didn't make that up."

"I know. Martin's blog today."

Phil shook his head. "I always thought he was the smartest of all of us."

"Some maverick investigative reporter, a fan of Martin's blog, shares that opinion. He'll be calling me." Doug reached for the Johnnie Walker bottle, saw Phil's questioning eyes, and said, "This doesn't seem to be the occasion for sobriety after all."

Phil saluted him with the cup. "I'll toast to that."

Doug poured a jigger or two of Johnnie Walker. He looked at Phil. They tapped the plastic drinking vessels together, grinned darkly over the rims, and drank.

Doug switched off the television and turned on the radio. Joni Mitchell's gossamer voice skated on the cheap plywood walls, singing "River."

"Me too," Phil said under the music that spoke of being selfish and sad and losing love and making your baby say good-bye in December. "When is this journalist calling?"

Doug moved his fingers in rhythm with the music. "I don't know. They should play 'Big Yellow Taxi' next."

"Are we going to talk about the Top Forty Request Live or about being up Shits Canyon?"

Doug blinked as he noticed Phil's eyebrows looked like pointed penny nails and his voice sounded raspy. "Sorry. This is unreal."

Phil laughed like a bass drumbeat. "Wrong, it's as real as it gets, but none of us ever looked at life that way before. We knew it existed. Well, maybe not Paul."

Doug took a deep swallow of Johnnie Walker. "This is bigger than Paul or any of us, you just said so. Any idea who those people at the camp were or what they were up to?"

"The guy who crashed our party and who just took a shot at Karina tonight—she worked for Paul, you know…"

Doug felt a stab of remorse. He had met Karina. "Worked for Paul?"

Phil answered with a waggle of his eyebrows and Doug nodded. He could now view Patty's attempted seduction of him as a cry for help. "The guy and his team were probably Bull-Spears guys, mercenary scumbags, spying on you to dig up anything they could on what you were going to do with the audit. What are you going to do?"

Doug opened the top right dresser drawer and removed the copy he'd made of several documents from the audit from its place beside the Gideon Bible. He presented it to Phil. "I'm getting as far as I can from the office before I send these in, or go to the government—assuming I can trust anyone."

Phil nodded. "I'm going with you. I'm going to investigate a couple of leads, and maybe borrow your car to decoy the bastards on our trail."

Natalie Merchant followed Joni Mitchell on the radio, singing throatily.

Despite himself, Phil said, "Jeezuz, is it an estrogen music set here? I feel like some White Zombie right now. I want to go kick somebody's ass."

Doug grinned and hummed along with the song. "'Carnival.' Do you get the feeling the universe is sending us a message?"

"That one of us needs to get laid, maybe?" Phil raised his right eyebrow in dismay as he watched his friend mouth the lyrics to the female vocalist.

"Or that we should trust women only from now on?"

They laughed and drank.

"Where are you going to go?"

"Home," Doug said. "My grandma's in Auburn. She married twice, so there's no way anyone could connect us, even if they broke every privacy law on the books. Her last name's not even the same. I'll stay with her for a few days. At least until we can find a way to blow this cancer of humanity wide open without it exploding in our faces."

Phil nodded. "It's no surprise to me Paul's house didn't work out. I'd have told you if you'd asked. Does your grandma have a big house?"

"Well, it's not a mansion, and the tile's probably imported from Seattle, but it's okay…" Doug guessed what Phil wanted to ask. "Let me call her and see if she's got room for one more."

"Great, thanks a bunch, Doug."

Doug used his cell phone to call the house that had the best tree fort in the world. "Hi, Grandma. Hope I didn't wake you?"

The crisp, aged female voice answered over a blare of Fox News or CNN chatter. "Let me turn down what masquerades as the news these days. Oh, to have Mr. Cronkite and Mr. Murrow back with us."

Doug laughed and waited until his grandma muted the television volume. "There. Oh, Doug, it's so good to hear from you. I worry that you work yourself to death and don't enjoy life. I worry because your mother worried."

"I've got some time off from work after a job well done." Doug chose his words with care. "I thought I'd come visit you."

"Oh, that's wonderful. I've got some young people to introduce you to, so you won't be bored with me."

Doug felt a rush of love. "No chance of that, never in a million years, but I'm glad you mentioned that, because my old college friend—you remember the one I told you about, Phil—would like to come up and stay too. His home's being renovated and he always wanted to meet you. He'll…he'll come tomorrow morning."

A pause. "I remember a few college friends of yours, including the smart-ass." Doug's brows shot up. He'd never heard his grandmother cuss before. "Or smart aleck, your grandfather and Earl would have corrected me. But of course he's welcome. Anyone special to you is welcome in my home always."

"Thanks, Grandma." Doug's call waiting flashed, and the digital readout gave a D.C. area code. "I'll see you in...about two hours if you can stand to wait up."

"I won't be able to stand the news, but Dorothy's granddaughter showed me how to play DVDs. I think I'll put *M*A*S*H* in. I enjoy it so. I'll see you soon. Drive safely. Bye."

Doug gave Phil the thumbs-up sign before he answered the next call. "Hello?"

"Doug Boyd? This is Webb Sutton speaking." The voice on the other end could have belonged to Cronkite or Murrow—except with a slight Minnesota twang. "Your muckraking friend Marty—"

"Oh hi, thanks for calling. It's late where you are, isn't it?"

Phil rolled his eyes and finished his drink.

Webb Sutton responded with easy wit. "There is no such thing as late in journalism, unless you miss a deadline. Can we talk freely?"

"Only if I can invite my friend Phil. Who is a friend of Martin's. He's right here with me."

"He's FBI, correct?"

Doug activated the speakerphone. "He is indeed."

"Ex-FBI," Phil said, his voice suspicious. He clearly didn't think a speakerphone confab was wise. "I got fired."

"My, my, my," Webb said. "Do keep talking, Phillie. Hope you don't mind the nicknames. I've rarely heard of anyone getting fired from the FBI. This is either the meat of the matter or the topping on the crumb cake."

Doug and Phil broke out in grins. Phil was instantly disarmed. "It's quite a story," he said.

"Leading, as I understand it, to Secretary Pearson and possibly even higher," Webb said. Doug looked at Phil and his eyes widened as he silently mouthed the words "holy shit."

"Both Doug and I have to move to safer locales shortly," Phil said, "but we'll give you enough material to tease your readers."

"I don't want them teased. I want them hot and bothered and mad as hell. The public's attention may be your only way out of this mess."

Phil dropped onto the bed. "Where do we start?"

"Let's start with our camping weekend," Doug said.

Internet IM session, 1:00 a.m. EST

Lotsaluck23 (1:01 a.m.): Webb Sutton, don't tell me you're still up?

MurrowsLoveChild (1:01 a.m.): And don't tell me you're kissing your MacBook tonight, darlin'.

Lotsaluck23 (1:02 a.m.): Macking it with my Mac, sure. There are no good men anymore.

MurrowsLoveChild (1:02 a.m.): Wouldn't say that. There's an adorable, gutsy, single one headed to Auburn right now. Visiting his grandma.

Lotsaluck23 (1:02 a.m.): Webb, I haven't even had a sip of Chardonnay tonight, don't try me when I'm dry.

MurrowsLoveChild (1:03 a.m.): No joke, darlin'. Unlike most of your dates, this one pays his bills on time, can count to ten, and gives a damn about humanity. He's runnin' for his life with a story to end all government corruption stories. He has a pile of dirt on a Big Four accounting firm he used to work for.

MurrowsLoveChild (1:04 a.m.): You there? Don't tell me you fainted.

Lotsaluck23 (1:04 a.m.): Webb, the man you're describing doesn't exist. He's an even better invention than Harry Potter.

MurrowsLoveChild (1:05 a.m.): He's real all right.

Lotsaluck23 (1:07 a.m.): Then why is he hiding out with his grandma?

MurrowsLoveChild (1:08 a.m.): As opposed to your last boyfriend, who pretended he was an orphan?

Lotsaluck23 (1:10 a.m.): Good night, Webb. My Mac doesn't like you.

MurrowsLoveChild (1:11 a.m.): I hope he likes the Pulitzer story of the century instead. I e-mailed you this guy's cell phone number and his grandma's number along with all the facts.

Lotsaluck23 (1:12 a.m.): Not looking. Not looking.

MurrowsLoveChild (1:13 a.m.): You will if you want to get out of Auburn and to the big time in D.C. and New York.

Lotsaluck23 (1:13 a.m.): Now why would I ever want that? Auburn is just sooooo stimulating. The real heart of America. The excitement capital.

MurrowsLoveChild (1:14 a.m.): Wise girl. Brilliant. You and Douglas Boyd will make Nobel Prize babies to rival the genetic concoction Brad Pitt and Angelina Jolie can create. I hate to IM and run, but I have a story to write. And you have a date with destiny. Good night, darlin'.

CHAPTER 12

"A sound banker, alas, is not one who foresees danger and avoids it, but one who, when he is ruined, is ruined in a conventional way along with his fellows, so that no one can really blame him."

—John Maynard Keynes, economist

Sacramento/I-80, 9:00 p.m.

Doug drove to Auburn. The decision to go home might have seemed cowardly, but he didn't care. He didn't much care what other people thought anymore. Phil had been shot at, and so had Paul's secretary. The interstate was quiet at night as he sped from Sacramento. He hoped Phil would turn up the smoking gun and wave it in Paul's face, in the faces of Cartwright and Gauthier, to terrorize them the way they routinely intimidated and dehumanized other people.

Phil, who knew about intimidation, who had been in the red-alert zone, couldn't blame Karina for her fear. A gunshot was like the voice of God, especially the first time you heard it. He had discharged his weapon only a handful of times in his entire FBI career. Most people, numb to the choreographed fake gunfire in movies and on TV, didn't realize that even an FBI agent could wet his pants when an adversary fired in your immediate vicinity. It was no wonder Karina was scared shitless.

He, in contrast, was merely guilt-ridden, which fueled his adrenaline and anger. He pored over Paul's records on his laptop in the McDonald's at the Wal-Mart where Will Okemos worked.

He'd already been by the defunct storefront next to the shoe repair store that would, Mrs. Macias hoped, become her *jardín botánico*. She worked there, in the light of the windows streaked with dust. He saw her arrange box gardens of seedlings and he despised Paul.

He'd knocked on Mrs. Washington's door. A Pakistani man, who glared at Phil for asking about his woman, and a ten-year-old African-American girl, who had to be related to Mrs. Washington, answered. She had gone to post bail for her son, the girl's father. He sat in Mrs. Washington's living room amid bags of yarn until she returned. She didn't even have an Internet connection, but this was by choice, she said. She knitted constantly while she talked to him and scolded him for waking her granddaughter on a school night.

He'd been by Ms. Phan's apartment, but couldn't find her. Her boyfriend, a slick, arrogant, stubbly guy who scratched his balls at the front door, said she was out tricking. Phil knew she worked in a bar part-time and at an alternative health clinic, and the boyfriend played Mr. Mom for her two children, who were just a little older than Phil's own children, Megan and Jason.

These people would never pay back the loans. It wasn't intentional, it wasn't a character defect. He knew better than most not to judge them, to condemn them. A need to post bail for a son for the tenth time, a child's operation, a car accident, any kind of a crisis, and Mrs. Macias, Mrs. Washington, Ms. Phan would be wiped out. Will Okemos was just young and naïve and raised on Britney Spears and *American Idol*, even though he professed a higher purpose with his music. For every person who made millions, there were a hundred who got their dreams sucked out of them by vampires. Their credit applications and histories showed that if you pricked any one of these people, they hemorrhaged money.

Will Okemos passed by. His badge smiled, the yellow Wal-Mart have-a-nice-day symbol, but Will freaked when he saw Phil. He hightailed it for Housewares, presumably to restock the Bunn coffee makers.

Phil turned off his laptop after he read some faintly incriminating (and borderline pornographic) notes that Joanne Huffman of Milteer

Capital Funds sent Paul. The evidence was a nice neat chunk of meat the Feds could gnaw, but since he'd been tossed to the curb, he needed more.

If he knew John Clarkson, John had turned him loose to find not just a chunk but a Fred Flintstone rack of brontosaurus ribs that would bring the house down.

Phil searched the store, didn't find Will Okemos anywhere among the bargain bins, and eventually asked one of the other sales associates. Will had gone home, pleading food poisoning. When Phil called Will's cell phone, it went to voice mail.

Will's girlfriend's house was silent and dark. Phil noticed the digital display of the clock on the dashboard of Doug's rental car. It was after one, and Doug had promised to leave the door unlocked. Apparently, between Doug's grandma and Doug's newfound toughness, they were fearless. Phil smiled as he pulled out of Will's neighborhood and murmured, "Aha," in expectation as he saw a Crown Victoria peel out from a corner gas station and pursue him. It was like locking in the safety bar just before you went on the roller coaster. Phil knew he was in for the ride of his life. He hoped to leave the bastards doubled over with motion sickness and, God willing, heart failure as he headed to gold country.

Nevada Street, Auburn, 11:00 p.m.

Auburn, a small city that arose out of the economic boom of the late 1840s, values its heritage. Though the town has grown, the original Old Town has retained its historic charm. The current occupants, mostly bars, restaurants, and antique shops, proudly retain the interior brick walls and wooden floors. Old miners' cabins dot the area, the old fire station has been restored, and small museums display artifacts of the Gold Rush era. Mining tunnels still run under the buildings and much of the rest of the city—intriguing the teens who wish to explore them, and creating a headache for the officials who try to keep them out. The skyline is dominated by a large golden-domed courthouse that sits on a hill, overlooking the city, and near the entrance to the square sits a tall stone statue of a gold-panner kneeling on a creek bed, a memorable climbing challenge to a teenaged Doug and most every other youngster in town. This fellow, who looks convincingly crusty and weather-beaten, reminds all visitors of the town's beginnings. Modern stores have crept in here and there, but Old Town remains a shrine to history.

When Doug arrived at his grandmother's house, he found that it hadn't changed from last Christmas, or indeed, in ten years. It was the mother lode of his past. The door, he knew, would be unlocked, even close to midnight.

Annette Nikolopoulos had once chased a burglar, a life insurance salesman, or a flasher off her property with a meat cleaver, depending on who told the story. She had lived in the neighborhood for years, and the population hadn't changed much. Most of her neighbors had card parties together every week as they had for the last two decades. They were blue-collar, honest, good people. Satellite dishes perched on the roofs, questing in the ether for the WWF and *Wheel of Fortune*.

Doug gently slipped past the screen door and pushed open the Mediterranean blue door. Immediately he was nine years old tromping inside his grandma's house with a pocketful of dirt and crickets. The cracked linoleum had been replaced with smooth Pergo. Sisal rugs formed a kind of hopscotch pattern through the foyer. Doug tasted and smelled ginger lemon tea mingled with wood oil soap in the air. He placed his suitcases and laptop case by the rail of the white staircase leading to the second floor.

"Grandma?"

"In here," she sang from the den. The *M*A*S*H* theme accompanied her. "You don't have to yell, my hearing is better than your mother's. I could be sleeping, you know. Although at my age, not likely."

Doug passed the family photograph gallery on his way to the den and smiled guiltily at his cousins, at a younger pigtailed, cowgirl-hatted version of his mother, Gloria, who sat astride a Shetland pony.

As he entered the chestnut-paneled den, Annette maneuvered gingerly off the recliner and waddled on swollen ankles over to him. She had been the tallest of her three siblings, even the boys. She could, even at eighty-seven, look Doug in the face with bright violet eyes. She wore the lavender bathrobe he'd given her last Christmas.

"You look like you need a break," she said, "but still handsome for all that. Still my handsome Doug!" And she hugged him.

Her embrace, for that moment, put everything right. Her love surrounded him. He excused himself to go in search of the lemon ginger tea in the white-and-yellow kitchen. The tea strainers contained fresh tea leaves because his grandma scorned tea bags. He let the tea leaves steep in the Royal Doulton rose-patterned teacups, then laid the tea strainers on a paper towel on the yellow Formica. He carried the tea tray through the kitchen door that was eight feet tall and wide enough to accommodate three people at once, and stooped as he passed through the archway to the den.

As when he first entered, Annette's cats, Aristotle and Jackie O, acknowledged him with a flick of their tails and a slight widening of their topaz eyes from their perch on the window under the white eyelet drapes. They sank back into the complacent slumber of royalty as Doug eased himself onto the rust-colored stuffed leather sofa that always swallowed him. The joke was that Annette bought the sofa to ensure her family would visit more frequently, because once you sat down, you couldn't get up for three days.

Annette settled back into her recliner with her teacup. Particles of lavender talcum danced in the air around her for a second. "The cats are happy to see you, Doug. They're just, how do you young people say it, too cool and too bad to show it."

Doug grinned. "You're looking good, Grandma."

"That's all because of one thing." She leaned forward triumphantly. "A mile every morning at six a.m. A mile! You can walk with me tomorrow. The neighbors have probably forgotten what you look like—that's because half of them have memory problems anyway, even the younger ones. Did you know that I'd even gotten your father into walking, right before the accident. He almost made it to the end of the street last month."

"Without huffing and puffing and sneaking a cigarette when Mom wasn't around?"

"Your father had quit smoking, hadn't you heard?" Annette's tone was kind but questioning. "Wanted to live longer." Her smile faded into a frown as the realization hit her that her son was no longer living.

Doug's father, Dan, switched from marijuana to tobacco, defying Beat poet Allen Ginsberg's warning that smoking is a billion-dollar capitalist joke, when he went corporate thirty-five years ago.

"I never thought he'd do it." Doug smiled in an effort to cheer his grandmother up again.

Annette sipped tea. "Your grandfather smoked a pipe, of course, sometimes. Everyone smoked once upon a time. Did you ever?"

"Tried it when I was thirteen," Doug said. That tobacco and Miller Lite experiment behind the Dumpster of the 7-Eleven, with three of his childhood pals and one of his cousins sharing the same cigarette and beer and puking their guts out, had been his first and last.

"I figured. Of course, your parents never believed. Doug the nice boy." She smiled. "Everyone's got some naughtiness in them. You can't equate being a saint with being good, on this earth anyway, for most of us. The goodness is in picking ourselves up off the wayside."

"Wise, uh, observation." Doug almost confided in her about his trouble, the way he had when he'd accidentally knocked her Limoges box off the coffee table and the porcelain shattered.

Annette raised her eyebrows at him but said nothing except, "What's new? Is everything good in your life? Are you enjoying life?"

"I'm glad to have a few days off." Doug yawned.

She glanced out the window, eyes trying to penetrate the darkness outside as the cats indulgently dozed. "Your, ah, friend…"

"Phil. From college."

"Yes. From college. He didn't drive with you?"

"We promise not to wake you up when he comes in."

"He's coming in the middle of the night?"

"He had some loose ends to tie up."

Annette closed her eyes for a moment and shook her head. A shudder went through her. "I see."

"For work, Grandma. He's with the FBI." He swallowed his deception and hoped that she believed her own counsel about goodness.

"Well. That's solid, respectable. No matter what some people think." Her eyes snapped open, and she turned to look at him openly. "Of course your friend can stay, Douglas." Her use of his whole name held some weight. "I'm just happy you are comfortable bringing him to visit me."

Doug shook his head now as his heart lightened. His father had asked him bluntly over turkey last Christmas dinner, "So even at Christmas you don't bring anyone home and you spend all your time with those guys from college. Is there something you want to tell us?"

"We're forming a commune?" Doug had tried to deflect.

Dan, still smelling of tobacco (he hadn't yet reformed), wasn't dissuaded. "Let's just clear it up, lay it all out right now. Are you gay?" After a moment of silence and an elbow from his wife, Dan mumbled, "Not that there's anything wrong with that. It's just that we don't see much of you…"

"No," Doug said. "No, I'm not gay. I'd tell you." He didn't tell them that he'd been too busy trying to get ahead, working day and night, to let them into his life. His plan to work hard now, make a lot of money, then take it easy and play a lot of golf with his dad didn't work. A drunk driver and a missed red light changed everything for Doug. He wasn't sure exactly what he was working so hard for now.

Doug's resounding denial obviously hadn't persuaded Annette. She stared at him, reading his face for clues. Doug patted her hand. "Phil's just wanting to bach it." At her look, he said, "Play bachelor for a few days. Helen took the kids to visit their grandparents for the summer. Virginia. Phil's going to join them soon."

"Well, I hope so. Your grandfather and I just loved Virginia. Of course, I could never get him away from Williamsburg, he was so crazy about Revolutionary War, what do they call them, reenactments? Don't even talk to me about Gettysburg…"

Doug chatted with Annette a few minutes more, or rather listened to her reminisce, before she yawned and announced it was time for her to go to bed.

"You're young and it's still early. Why don't you go into town and meet some new people?" Annette grinned, sprite-like. "Raise some hell."

Doug had to laugh. "Sounds appealing. I was just about to suggest that myself. I love you, Grandma."

"And you, dear."

After Doug kissed Annette goodnight, he took the teacups with the tea droplets into the kitchen to wash.

It was a beautiful night in California. The eighty-degree temperature at eleven thirty at night felt comfortable. The moonlight in the cloudless sky bounced off the golden dome as Doug approached it from the hill a hundred meters away. The walk and the warm night air both soothed and energized Doug's muscles on the short walk from Annette's house to the town square.

A turquoise Jetta eased out of its parking spot as Doug crested the hill. Its lights winked on, and the car casually slid through the night. Even in Old Town Auburn, Doug had never seen a car move that slowly. He whistled and put his hands in his pockets as he walked. The car limped along. One of grandma's aging neighbors would drive faster than that.

Doug quickened his face and stepped off into the oleander bushes where he would be less likely to be seen. Maybe. He flipped open his cellular phone and called Phil.

Phil sounded like a man straining to push out a bowel movement: intense, pained concentration. "Don't worry, I won't wake up your grandma." Doug could hear the engine of Phil's car roaring.

"They're back. They're here in Auburn following me." Doug pressed the phone closer to his cheek so the glow from its display wouldn't reveal his temporary, scented refuge.

Phil sounded even more strained. "I haven't left here yet, Doug. I'm thinking maybe ten more minutes and then—"

"There's a bar across from the old firehouse...the California Club. I'll meet you there at one a.m." Phil didn't say anything. "I want to stay away from these guys until then."

Phil breathed out in a long, slow exhale. "No problem. I'll be there."

Doug shut the phone and crammed it into his front pocket. He peeked around the oleanders to look for the Jetta. It was still there, stopped, not a hundred yards away on the side of the road.

He had lived in the town when he was a small boy, and was familiar enough with the layout. The town square was only a block and a half from where he was at, so he decided to make a break for it. At least there would be people, and hopefully police, there. He jetted out of the bushes and ran as fast as he could toward town. The car on the side of the road stayed where it was, its headlights dark.

"Maybe I am just paranoid," Doug thought as he slowed and entered the California Club, a small but notoriously rowdy bar on the east side of the square. It wasn't the infamous but now closed Shanghai, which would have provided a solid mass of customers to hide among as well as multiple exits, but it would do. The squiggles of a Sierra Nevada Pale Ale neon sign in the right-hand window finger-painted his face as he walked into the hubbub and felt the beat of the rock music vibrate in his temples.

The wall behind the bar consisted of mirrors affixed to the old solid brick wall, covered mostly by various bottles of alcohol. The bar stretched along one wall, and small clusters of stools across the aisle kept blissful patrons seated and quaffing from their longnecks. The archways between the clusters opened onto pool tables. The pool dues cracked against the eight balls. An alternative band playing in the corner bowed to drunken applause as girls in halter tops danced in the aisle, waving beer bottles in the air as tribute to the musicians and their own youthful exuberance.

The band took a break, and normal conversation temporarily recovered.

Doug selected a vacant barstool near the back door. He took stock of the entry and exit points. He had an escape clause and was in a position to get out of the building if necessary. He resolved not to budge from this spot. A muscled biker or overzealous inebriated sports fan might shove him to another seat and block his exit.

He ordered a Heineken from the waiter and looked at his watch. Midnight. One more hour until he expected Phil (with a piece from his gun collection) to show up. Phil kept his gun case in his walk-in closet. He always locked it and encouraged his wife, Helen, to do the same. Doug remembered the event that began Phil's penchant for collecting weapons over a decade ago. They had been working late together at the grocery store when two coked-up thugs barged in, waving knives and demanding money. Doug had tried to comply with their demands while Phil rabbited to the manager's office to call 911. One of the junkies, agitated, tried to stab Doug, who grabbed the closest weapon available—a tin of chili powder from the spice aisle—and dumped it in the guy's face. The other one, now alert to his buddy's distress came at Doug with his switchblade, and that was when Phil ran out of the office screaming and brandishing the manager's 1980 Smith & Wesson S & W Model 1000 shotgun. The would-be robbers got away with only some cash from the change dish for their trouble but provided Doug and Phil many hours of reminiscing and mutual back-patting for their bravery and heroism.

The beer arrived, and Douglas sipped it slowly. He felt intimately connected to and aware of every person and every movement in the bar. If the bartender polished the glass, if a woman ran her fingers through her hair, he sensed it. He turned as if cattle-prodded and noticed a redhead with blonde highlights and creamy satin skin sitting at the bar, kitty-corner from him. She tucked a stray curl behind her ear, raised her St. Pauli Girl to him, and smiled. Doug smiled back.

He looked over his shoulder so as not to stare. The redhead looked slightly older than Doug, and was a knockout, so she probably had men annoying the crap out of her with, at best, lame pick-up lines. He didn't even have a pick-up line.

Everything still looked calm through the glass door. Then a cobalt blue Prius pulled up directly outside the door, and the driver left it in the red zone. A man wearing a brick-brown jacket got out of the passenger side and pushed open the glass door. Nobody except Doug took much interest in this man as he swaggered to the bar, surveilled Doug, and ordered a Heineken. Some kind of Jedi mind trick passed between the stranger and the bartender, because the stranger had his beer in his hand within seconds. He paid for his beer with a ten and then sauntered over to Doug without bothering to collect his change. He was the kind of man Doug would hold the door open for in the elevator at Arthur Whinney: clean-cut, jet black short hair, brown leather jacket over a blue button-up shirt. The one off-kilter feature was his nose, which looked as though he'd hit the windshield during a fender-bender.

"Hi, Douglas. Sorry I'm late, but"—he shrugged—"you know how it goes." He sat on the stool beside Doug and faced him with a pleasant expression.

Doug lowered his voice. "Who the hell are you?"

"That's not important."

"You're Tom Dooley."

The man appeared unfazed. "I won't be singing no sad songs, my friend."

"Or any campfire songs?" Doug kept his voice solid and smooth as the bar wood.

Dooley, or whoever he was, lifted his jacket to reveal a British 9mm Spitfire. Doug recognized it because Phil owned one. With the darkness in the bar and the way Dooley held his jacket flap, like Dracula's cape, Doug was the only one in the bar who saw the weapon. He knew next to nothing about it, and he doubted he wanted more knowledge.

"You're not going to risk shooting bystanders."

The man looked nonchalantly at him. "That's up to you. As is your grandmother's well-being."

Doug refused to take the bait. Pleading would only give the bastard his jollies. "So, what, according to your bosses, am I supposed to do?"

Dooley gave him a lazy, chilling smile. "You should've just shut up and kept working like a dog."

"I can take you, you asshole." The beer had significantly increased Doug's bravado, but he still knew there was no way he could win a fistfight with this guy.

"Come on. You're the kind of guy who won't tell his boss to go screw himself when you're headed out the door to Hawaii. And now you're going to get into a bar fight?"

Think. There was a way out of this that didn't involve getting shot to death and dumped in the American River or in a landfill.

"Your FBI friend will stay away if he knows what's good for him."

Thank God they were clueless about Martin.

"But he didn't know, and you didn't either." Dooley clamped down on Doug's upper arm. "Finish your beer and let's go."

"Excuse me."

The redheaded woman with the graceful smile towered above them. She wore an oversized boxy handbag purse that Doug thought unwieldy.

The man gave her a slick, appreciative, then dismissive smile. "Hello, honey."

She looked past him to Doug.

Then she did the inconceivable.

She slapped him resoundingly.

"Where have you been all night?"

Doug Boyd was what thirty-seven-year-old Carlotta McGinnis would have called "four-alarm cute" in junior high, "a goofball nerd" in high school, and nonexistent in Northwestern University J-school (or journalism school for the uninitiated). He was also, if Webb Sutton was to be believed, a stand-up kind of guy, smart enough to figure out and try to avoid a massive conspiracy. The accountant specs gave him a classic nerdy look—the kind of guy who would actually make up a household budget, who maybe you wouldn't see hearts and flowers from all the time, but who could make you feel like a sex goddess. Not that there weren't nerds at Northwestern in the ethics and media courses (or whatever the hell they were called back then), she'd just gone for the jocks instead.

And to think she nearly hadn't tailed him. Webb had Googled the phone number Doug had given him and found that Doug's grandmother lived in Auburn. Carlotta had parked near Nevada Street.

She hadn't known that the dude walking out alone was Doug Boyd. Not for sure, anyway. But from what she'd observed of the neighborhood, the average family guy or retiree didn't walk to Old Town by his lonesome at eleven on a Thursday. You just didn't do that in today's world, even in a town where not too much changed.

Call it instinct, but she decided to follow him discreetly. The big jerk harassing him and making his nostrils flare was an Empire State Building-sized indicator that her instincts were right on the money.

Doug Boyd gaped up at her. He looked like the kind of guy who would spend time with his grandma. He also looked as nervous as a shadow and as anxious as a fish at a Long John Silver's shareholder's meeting. He stared at her purse, a flight attendant's case her great-aunt Donna had given her. She'd had it refurbished by her friend Heather who ran her own online business called HandbagMakeover.com.

She slapped him again for good measure. Then, to really befuddle and flummox the hired gun who'd cornered him, she pulled the adorable accountant off his barstool and gave him a long, wet smooch.

Her first hazy impression was that when he wasn't under pressure, Doug was probably a great kisser. His lips were firm and sensual. Her second, more gut instinct than thought, was that he hadn't gotten any loving since *Sex and the City* went off the air.

The entire bar erupted in catcalls, egging on Carlotta and Doug in their lip-lock. Carlotta pulled away, giving them a tease, and smiled at Doug, who now looked like that same fish from the Long John Silver's shareholder meeting if it suddenly got clubbed and beamed into a glass case in a Chinatown fish market.

"I forgive you," she said sweetly. "Aren't you going to introduce me to your friend, Doug?"

To his credit, he played along and didn't ask the lame-ass question of how she knew his name. He muttered, more loudly than he meant to, "Let's get out of here."

She smiled again. "Whatever you say, stud muffin."

The bar demonstrated its approbation as beer glasses pounded and clinked. Somehow Doug's arm found its way around Carlotta's waist and they headed for the back.

The big jerk attempted to freeze them. "Very rude, Douggy boy. Didn't the lady ask you to introduce us?"

"We're in a hurry," Doug grunted, sounding far more churlish than his appearance would suggest he could.

Carlotta glanced over her shoulder as two African-Americans who could double for the Wayans Brothers walked up and razzed the big jerk. "Bra, don't you know not to stop a booty call?" one of them taunted.

"His booty ain't been called by anyone except his mama," the second Wayans lookalike said.

Once again, the bar had Carlotta's and Doug's backs as the patrons targeted the dumbfounded hired gun with jeers. Carlotta and Doug slipped out the rear entrance of the building where Carlotta's Jetta awaited.

Doug was strapped in for the ride of his life.

He may have buckled up automatically when he got in the mysterious femme fatale's vehicle, but he felt as if he were hanging out of the front car of the Boomerang Coast to Coaster at Six Flags.

"Thank you," he managed after they'd ridden for ten minutes. From the scenery flying by, he could tell they'd left Old Town Auburn behind.

Her hair was a dark, swaying mass as she looked over at him. "Did I leave you that breathless?"

"You're overconfident," Doug said. His tongue seemed to have transformed into a steel bar that he could move only with great effort.

"I just saved your cute ass, didn't I?"

"I said thank you. Now what do you want?"

"What every woman wants. A Pulitzer-winning story. By the way, my name is Carlotta and I work for the *Sac Bee*."

"Nice to meet you," he breathed. "And you obviously know who I am."

"Douglas Jeremy Boyd, formerly living in San Jose, formerly employed by Arthur Whinney and Associates, now with a price on his head. Single, no criminal record. How am I doing?"

"Thanks to the Internet, fine so far."

"Webb's better than Google."

The quarter dropped in his mind. "You're the one he was talking about. He didn't give me a name."

"He's a gentleman, never kisses and tells."

"I wouldn't have guessed." His laugh sounded more like a tin pennywhistle. "Do you know what the hell you've gotten yourself into? That guy back there meant business."

Doug became aware of two lights in the side view mirror, coming up on them, gloating demon's eyes in a Prius's hood. "And he's chasing us."

"Really. You don't say." She executed a hairpin four-lane-wide U-turn that made the traffic in both directions sound horns in protest. She revved the engine and floored it. "Keep a lookout."

"Sure, I'll even explain it to the judge."

"I have an IOU from Ryan Moses."

Doug was impressed at the mention of the Auburn police chief. "And the Governator on speed dial?"

"Better, I have Maria." Carlotta pursed her lips. "Although from what I hear, this whistle-blowing of yours goes way beyond California."

Doug monitored the rearview mirror. Nothing but SUVs, trucks, and Corvettes behind, beside, and in front.

"Am I right?" Carlotta pressed.

"Do you think you are?"

"What I think is you're not the guessing-game type or the challenge-authority type."

Doug raked a hand through his hair. "I'm fed up with people telling me what type I am. I'm not a type, damn it."

"Sorry."

"We've gotten off to an inauspicious start here." Doug pulled his fingers from his hair and shook his head. Carlotta smiled at that. "What?"

"Now you look more like a guy on the lam."

Doug ruefully quoted Warren Beatty. "'You and me travelin' together, we could cut clean acrost this state, and Kansas too, and maybe dip into Oklahoma, and Missouri or whatnot, and catch ourselves highpockets and a highheeled ol' time.'"

"'We rob banks,'" Carlotta sang out.

"'You just stay in the car and watch and be cool,'" Doug answered.

"What am I watching for, Doug, er, Clyde? It's as big as Webb said."

"You wouldn't be here otherwise," Doug said with conviction. "You wouldn't have saved my ass."

"Your cute ass."

"Well, yes, I've been told it is, but I didn't want to say so out loud…"

"You just did."

A thought struck Doug. "Are you recording this? Am I going to read this conversation on the front page and all over the blogs tomorrow?"

"With due respect to your blog-bose friend Martin, I'm a serious journalist."

"Damn few of those around anymore." Doug wrinkled his upper lip. "Blog-bose?"

"Not my word. One of the guys at work came up with it…thought he was being clever and witty."

"At least you get to be around clever and witty. Accounting firms are like *The Evil Dead* movies without all the fun and killing."

"Necessary evil, like the two-party system. Although if Webb and Martin are right, there's a Green Party cadre in power that has nothing to do with Ralph Nader."

Doug was nervous, so he made light conversation. "I saw a Nader bumper sticker on this fine automobile."

She snorted, managing to make it sound sexy, at least to him. "When I say I'm an independent journalist, I mean independent, as in the spin truly does stop here. I haven't voted for any of the major parties since I read biographies of Nellie Bly and Maureen Dowd. Nader's so off the grid he's never going to be elected, at least not in this country, so he's safe."

"At any speed." He laughed, then tensed as he saw the Prius headlights keeping pace with them in the lane to their right. "I'm starting to hate eco-conscious people."

"Like your friend. I see him." Carlotta turned on her iPod stereo full blast. Celine Dion wailed "I Drove All Night" as Carlotta made a wide left into a street beside a vacant lot. She drove into a quiet suburb. With her hair and gutsy demeanor, she reminded him of Rita Hayworth.

"His name's Tom Dooley and he works for Bull-Spears."

"My aunt worked for a firm just like it. They made her very rich, for one of the few women they allowed past their doors. They also made her bitter, twice divorced, and an alcoholic." She checked her blind spot. "So much for the spin stops here."

"Hey, if she'd worked for Bull-Spears, this would have been too easy."

Carlotta glanced at him. "Webb filled me in on everything, despite my teasing. However, he's not local, he doesn't know the territory, he hasn't got my sources."

"And those are?"

She didn't answer right away. After a beat she said, "I want to show you something."

California Club, July 1, 2:10 a.m.

Phil was late.

He'd made one heroic effort to find, or at least shadow, Karina. He asked at the church where the padre, who was consoling parishioners after the gunshots, made him wait a full ten minutes before providing him with Karina's mother's address. Lourdes Maria Salazar y Domingues lived in a house you could bounce a quarter off and get a dollar in return. The paint may have been cracked and the lawn needed weeding, but you just got that feeling that the house belonged to someone who throughout her whole life had her shit tightly together.

The bars on the windows and the big hombre who slept in the screened porch with a boxer on his lap backed up Phil's impressions. Dora the Explorer bikes with training wheels and mountain bikes littered the front lawn. Phil watched the house for several minutes until a light in the front bedroom window flickered on and an elderly face appeared like a warning. He heard a shred of a baby's wail from inside. Sounded as if the kid had colic. That must be Karina's sister's baby.

What really got Phil was the sign on the garage of the house next door: "Foreclosure Pending—Notice of Public Auction." It was a hand-lettered sign in Sharpie black ink.

Phil pounded the dash and hit his horn. It sounded like a curse through the neighborhood and someone on the porch across the street threw a beer bottle at his car. It missed the car and shattered in the street, as if the person on the porch didn't really expect to hit his target.

Phil lowered his hand and eyeballed the dashboard clock. One fifteen. He called Doug, but there was no answer. He broke the land speed record in his mad drive to Auburn.

Surprisingly, the California Club was still jammed at ten minutes after two. It took Phil nearly half an hour as he picked through college kids and habitual drunks to determine that Doug was not on the premises. The waitress was apologetic and the bartender surly when shown Doug's photo together with a five-spot. Phil tried Doug's cell several times. All his calls went to voice mail.

Some hero he was. Egregiously late, and Doug might already have paid the price for his single-minded crusade. He wondered, as he watched other people forget their cares and live it up, if it wasn't time to just pack it all in. Could you even fight a rigged game anymore? Had it ever been possible?

The jukebox telepathically picked up his thoughts and selected that punk-angst hit by the Clash, "Should I Stay or Should I Go."

This had to be limbo. All of the faces that surrounded him resembled perps he'd busted on a variety of sex crimes. He was down with them, down with the people now, and worried sick about his friend.

The TV switched from ESPN sports recaps to a late-night infomercial, and Phil nearly crashed off his barstool. A smiling shill woman hawked the infomercial pitch in a tight Orangesicle-colored suit with plenty of cleavage. If his eyes didn't deceive him, she was one of Paul's real estate agents.

"Do you want to sell your home now without the hassle of dealing with a real estate agent? Then visit YourHouseSold.com—no commissions to pay, no fees, no staging your home. Here's how it works. We shoot your home"—she dimpled—"with digital video. We upload it. People tour your home without ever scuffing up your tile and carpet. Good-bye to those open houses, to looky-loos who never buy. And it's much more personal than a MLS listing."

Weeks ago, Phil would have chuckled over it as just another dot-com, another Web site. There was nothing wrong with it, after all. It was inventive, creative. Yankee ingenuity, thinking of a better way. He might even have suggested to Paul that they post a video of his house…

A sample video clip showed less-than-stunning views of a counter island in a French country kitchen with a window-seat breakfast nook, and Phil knocked his coffee to the floor. No one much noticed or cared at two in the morning, and Phil pulled his cell phone out of the way of the coffee seepage and tried to connect to the Internet. Now that he was broke, this was his last month of service. No more data access. He turned to the Asian dude next to him with the spiked hair. The kid, whom Phil gauged to be in his twenties, flopped about on the barstool.

"I can't get a signal, man," Phil said. "Cell phone provider is wack."

The mellowed-out Asian dude passed him the cobalt-blue Sidekick. "Knock yourself out."

Phil accessed the video of his house on the Sidekick's browser. No commission to pay, but there was a PayPal button for donations. There was a fee-based service called "LoveMover" that, for $9.95 a month, would locate a neighborhood where you could find romance. The alluring spokeswoman from the video embraced a hunky guy who starred in commercials for a local burger chain. With a few clicks that ate up the

Asian kid's bits and bytes, Phil discovered the Web site was designed by PP Media, Inc., and the address was a PO Box that Paul and Patty used occasionally when they went on cruises to Mexico and trips to Europe. The testimonials on the Web site were all from Paul's newfound microlending flock. Will Okemos blithely pointed the financially strapped Internet user to GrassRootsMoney.com, a microlending Web site that, according to Phil's deduction, had to be operated by Paul.

Phil closed out of the browser and dialed Doug's number. Once again, it went straight to voice mail. Phil, stomach already a black hole, resolved to wait fifteen more minutes. He called Paul's home number and got voice mail. He tried Paul's office number.

Auburn City Limits, 4:00 a.m.

Carlotta said, "This is how you succeed in business without really trying."

No wonder Phil had told Doug the capital seat of California was projected to lead the United States in terms of foreclosures. Doug stared at grass that, illuminated by the headlights of Carlotta's Jetta, reminded him of burnt French fries in a fry cooker.

Doug had lost track of streets and towns. They were somewhere on the outskirts of Auburn in a brand-new housing development. A chain-link fence across the street surrounded a vacant lot. Red-and-white foreclosure signs marched across the fence. The homes themselves were huge—three or four thousand square feet and shoved together only a couple of yards from each other on tiny lots. The houses looked empty and deformed even though they were new construction. Two of the houses were riddled with graffiti. Three blocks away, a row of dilapidated, half-finished houses sat with sheetrock and insulation exposed. More foreclosure signs screamed of homeowner indifference and desperation simultaneously.

"Only a few of these homes have sold," Carlotta said, pointing to an end unit. "You can tell, because their lawns are green, and look at the signs in the front window." She pointed to a small sign saying "Owner Occupied, No solicitation." Next door, mournful green-and-white balloons danced their lonely dance on the night wind. "The developer was thinking he'd get seven hundred for them. He had to pay a year of utilities to even come up with two. The rest aren't selling, even though he'll do everything but come to the house and clean naked."

"It's not just here," Doug said. "Is it?"

Carlotta shrugged and continued driving. "Look at this place." She slowed the car and pointed to a huge commercial plaza that should be filled with chain stores and restaurants. The place was completely vacant and "Commercial Space Available" signs were on every window. In the center of the parking lot was a large concrete frame for a five-story building. The lack of construction equipment led Doug to believe that any thought of completing the structure had long since been abandoned. "I was on assignment in Thailand a few years ago—Bangkok." Carlotta stared keenly at the concrete structure. And I remember seeing a huge skyscraper almost just like this. A hundred stories at least. Never completed. The reporter I was with, David Hatchinsen, said it was a remnant of the Asian economic crisis of the early nineties. It stared down at the city to remind and warn them of the problems with credit-based economic bubbles. All the resources were wasted. They didn't go toward building infrastructure for a society, or improving life. They were wasted on things like this. The scary thing about it this time, Doug, is it is bigger, a lot bigger. It is everywhere. From the big cities to tiny little Auburn, California. It stretches across the globe."

They continued driving around suburbs of Sacramento and Auburn, and found acre after acre of empty commercial plazas and half-built housing subdivisions. The pink sunrise behind the empty structures, and the lack of traffic due in large part to the early hour, felt surreal to Doug.

Hours later, Carlotta finally parked the car in front of one of the new housing developments and nodded toward a brand-new house with colorful balloons tied to the mailbox inviting people in for an "Open House."

"The party's been over for a long time, but nobody noticed. This house, and that one over there"—she pointed at two houses about a block away from each other—"were bought by families new to the area. These people invested their life savings, the harvest of an entire lifetime of work, on these houses."

A man in shorts and a baseball cap started walking toward them. Paint and dirt spackled his clothing, indicating he had started working very early in the morning. Doug stood. He tensed. "We're trespassing."

"Relax. We're expected."

"By who?"

"The trickle-down people."

Doug caught sight of the homes with lights on at the early hour. A man and a woman were weeding the flowerbeds, obviously trying to beat the California heat. Another family, dressed up as though for church smiled and waved as they walked towards Carlotta. An elderly couple, who wore matching plaids, peeked through the front door of one of the homes. "The Smiths divorced. The financial stress was too much for the marriage, and the family with five kids was torn apart."

She waved at a house down the street with five cars parked in front of it. "Some moved here and dislocated their families to work."

The family approached, and the husband and wife spoke in broken English, and Doug's heart clenched in rage. "Let me guess," he said under his breath. "They couldn't read a word of the paperwork, and someone advertised in Spanish. Fucking greedy builders."

The dirty-looking shirt-sleeved man walked up and was within the bad breath zone as Doug spoke. He gave Doug and Carlotta space, even in his agitation. "You're right," he said softly. "The lenders did a number on these people. Fucking accountants."

"Doug is an accountant," Carlotta said.

"Not anymore." Doug stared at the guy, who looked as if someone had leached all the oxygen and nutrients from his body. His teeth were stained with tobacco and his breath was rank. "Who are you?"

"Ron Hannifin. Builder. But maybe not anymore."

Doug recognized the name. Handover Enterprises, named for the woebegone Ron and his wife, Dover, was one of the biggest Auburn developers. Rumor had it that Hovnanian Enterprises and D.R. Horton had bid for the company. "Maybe not. How come you didn't know these people were—"

"Because I was greedy, okay?" Hannifin exhaled breath that could only be described as smog. "Some guy said we could make a killing, offered to represent us. He even had the lending end covered. One-stop shopping."

"Would that be LeBrach and Associates?" Doug went from fire in the belly to mental ice packs keeping him calm. He surrendered to the moment. His eyes blinked tiredly, yet he'd never been more awake.

Hannifin nodded. "Guy worked miracles. He had the Notice of Completion filed with the county before we were even done building the things. I don't understand a lot of it. Building is all I know. I've done it my entire life. It got to the point that the only way to continue to build was to pay through the ass for the development land. I was never a rich man, and now I'm ruined."

He reached out to the other family in their sweats. They were identically dark-skinned. "Suriya and his family are from Indonesia. He and the wife have PhDs, but they're struggling, they're on I-140 visas. They're working with California State University in Sacramento. She's in nuclear medicine. He's some kind of a poet back in the home country." Hannifin shrugged to indicate he knew nothing about either imaging or imagery.

"They took out second ARM mortgages to invest," Carlotta explained, her face sympathetic.

How these people ended up in Auburn, California, of all places, in the hands of people like Paul LeBrach, Doug couldn't fathom. The husband reminded Doug of an East Asian version of Martin, who would probably give his eyeteeth to be able to videotape this encounter and put it on YouTube.

Doug nodded at Suriya and his wife. Suriya smiled and said in Indonesian, "*Selamat pagi, apa kabar*?"

"Good, er, morning, nice to meet you," Doug said.

"Hi," Suriya said, his accent musical, and launched into a bewildering stream of questions, wanting to know where Doug was from, where his family was, why he wasn't married, if he was interested in marrying Suriya's sister, who was an educated woman. Suriya's wife wrinkled her nose in an obvious tell and indicated that her own sister would be more suited for Doug.

Hastily, Doug switched to Spanish and talked to the Ordonezes, who were from Quintana Roo. It was a Babel festival, with Suriya and his family jumping in, even the seven-month-old baby screeching at Doug. He deciphered enough of the word puzzle to understand that these people had been taken and were pissed off.

Ron Hannifin gripped Doug's arm with greasy, sweaty fingers. "I know I screwed up. There is nothing I can do for these guys, or myself, now."

Doug wanted to be anywhere but here, staring at the karmic accounting book in these people's faces. He considered himself a compassionate guy, a humanitarian. All those dry, empty weekends and late nights adding up and balancing figures, and he'd never once seen the real costs, the human debits and liabilities. Easy to forget. So easy to get caught up in the game. It was a true moment of awakening, showing the results of massive temporary dislocation of capital, and the aftermath it can levy on a family or community. Everyone was a part of it, some more than others. And, most of the victims would be silent, secondary victims. The widow whose pension fund falls into receivership, the man who left his long-time stable job and moved his family across the country to make more money selling building materials. If anyone called him a hero, a man of conscience, he would set them straight. Phil, now, despite the deal with Paul, Phil had…

Phil. Doug saw that he'd overshot their meet up by several hours. The sun emitted a faint glow through the morning mists. It did nothing to enliven the scene.

Doug swore up and down to Hannifin, Suriya, and the Ordonezes that he'd try to get them their money and put them in the townhomes where they belonged. At the very least, he would seek revenge on their behalf. Hannifin was as much of a victim as they were.

Doug yanked on Carlotta's arm. "We need to go."

"Seen enough?" Her face was a mixture of sympathy and pique as she got into her car. "You're not used to this, living in a cubicle."

"You've got them, they're enough to make a heart of granite bleed. Why do you need me?"

"Because they do. The trickle-down people need you to give them a voice. They need you to translate for them. And I'm betting that you, Mr. Good Conduct Badge, didn't just hand over the incriminating evidence."

"No, I put it where a dull cipher of an accountant would put it first, the spare bedroom at my grandma's."

Carlotta's face softened like the dawn. "It's probably too early to wake her."

Doug patted his midsection. "Could you eat?"

"If you're buying."

Old Town Auburn, 6:00 a.m.

Doug abandoned his tenth attempt to reach Phil. Phil had left two voice mails asking, "Where the *hell* are you?" On the second one, he'd added, "Do I take a gun or a shovel to wherever you are?" Now, Doug got that disconnected rapid-fire bees-buzzing signal when he called Phil's cell.

Carlotta dumped a steaming, moist cinnamon roll in a napkin on his lap as they sat on the hood of the Jetta parked on the street outside the California Club. Doug had bought a box of pure caloric and sugared indulgence from a Dunkin' Donuts. Carlotta and Doug had already eaten one cinnamon roll and a bagel apiece and slowly sipped their way through super-sized Dunkin' Donuts coffees. He couldn't remember a better breakfast in his life.

Even after a sleepless night, Doug felt astonishingly alive. The rising sun spangled Old Town Auburn with natural glamour. The statue of Claude Chana seemed to wink. The brilliant morning light seeped into the dome of the courthouse and turned it into a column of flame. The cinnamon rolled luxuriantly on his tongue.

Carlotta and Doug didn't speak. The past half-hour had been silent. Before that, they made conversation about Arthur Whinney, Phil and Martin, Webb Sutton, and conspiracies until their tongues tired. He had bags under his eyes and her hair was mussed, but they could have been Brad Pitt and Angelina Jolie the way he felt right now. He'd never enjoyed just being with someone like this. He had no inkling of what she was thinking, and his nervous, exacting old self questioned whether he ought to ask her out on a date.

"How'd you become a journalist?"

She slowly chewed a piece of roll. "Is that your best opening line?"

Doug scowled. "Could we just have a normal conversation, maybe?"

"Sure. Did you hear the latest about Lindsay Lohan?"

"I said normal, not snormal."

Carlotta swallowed a bite before she burst out laughing. "'Snormal'?"

"Boring, banal, mundane. See also, my life a month ago." Doug grinned at her. "Prairie-dogging and having too many liquid dinners."

"I know the feeling. I was trying to justify my own existence in an industry that's run according to the bottom line. You get a pat on the head for investigative reporting, but unless the fraudulent financial transactions involve Ms. Lohan overdosing and driving her car through a foreclosed house…"

"This is bigger," Doug reminded her.

"No kidding." Her eyes had an unexpected vulnerability. Her hands shook as she reached for her coffee. She shivered.

She must have been somewhat affected by the night's events. When Doug put his jacket around her and took his time arranging it to maximize warmth, she didn't slap him silly or pull away.

They watched the sky brighten until the coffee and pastries were gone, and the early pedestrian and car traffic started. For a moment, they were just another couple starting their day with a romantic breakfast on the hood of a car.

Doug knew he never wanted to go back to normal again.

CHAPTER 13

"Rather than love, than money, than fame, give me truth."

—Henry David Thoreau, American Philosopher (1817–1862)

Jekyll Island Hotel, August 4, 2007, 5:35 a.m.

It was official. They were in the middle of a hurricane. Martin heard the staff at the Jekyll Island Club Resort talk about it with nervous yet matter-of-fact energy. Even if he hadn't been witness to the staff discussions of emergency exits, evacuations, FEMA, airlifts, sandbagging, and contingency plans, he could hardly have missed the entire building shaking like an old man with palsy.

He'd hidden and burrowed all night. He'd caught forty winks indoors in an employees-only area. No one on the hotel staff paid him much mind. They were all yawning, dead on their feet, grabbing Pepsi and cigarettes to rouse themselves. One or two of them asked to use his cell phone to call home through the storm. It was a pittance of a bribe. He let one of them record a video birthday greeting to send to a child. In return, one of the staffers stole into Room 309 and messed up the bed, then laid hands on Martin's laptop. Martin, unlike many of the guests at the Jekyll Island Resort and Club, smiled at service people and even made friendly greetings. When one of the housekeeping staff presented him with the laptop, he kissed her. On the cheek, of course.

It felt sickeningly good to hear the familiar sound of his laptop booting up. He'd been vlogging and blogging all night. He'd written this populist prose from his makeshift hidey-hole:

Economic Calamity
Good Old-Fashioned Service
Saturday, August 4, 3:30 a.m.
By Martin Cheyne

You want to change the world? Listen up. Leave a bigger tip. For that matter, get off the cell phone in the supermarket line and smile at the cashier.

I hear people say that you can't get good service anymore. I say, garbage in, garbage out. My students, the millenials, are supposedly the entitlement generation. I hear them complaining about how even their peers treat them as if they're invisible at the checkout stands in the student union. You don't think of the person who hands you the change back as a person. Then you bitch when mortgage companies who "service" your loans—sounds dirty, and in many cases, it is—treat you like just a number.

The people I'm hanging with right now have a high school education, but they have dreams for their families. The clerk at the front desk is studying for her degree. I tuned her out because I was too preoccupied in my own scheme, my own intrigue. But she's part of the human capital. I'm not a Commie or a socialist by any means. I see how they whine in Europe about five-hour workdays. But there has to be a happy medium, and I don't just mean an ecstatic Sylvia Browne.

Excuse my joke. I'm punchy and dizzy. I've been up all night. This is what happens when the government-industrial complex puts you on its hit list. Before they notice you, it's just harm by attrition. After they notice you, it's like Armageddon.

Sometimes I think the world should end as we know it. Then maybe we'd be kinder to each other.

Paulina here in the back room is using my cell phone to wish her daughter a happy fourth birthday. If I get out of this, I'm going to learn the names of the kids of every employee at UNR.

Trackback / Comment / Blog This

Two hours after that blog entry, Martin corrected a typo and republished his rant from the servant's quarters. He sat staring out the window at trees bending almost ninety degrees and vegetation being flattened by ferocious wind and rain. Webb Sutton should be due any time, according to his text message from the Jacksonville airport. Martin said a silent prayer for the tiny roadway from the mainland to stay open.

A Webcam popped up on Martin's laptop. Martin lowered the volume and expanded the image to full screen.

Doug and Phil double-teamed Martin from the grainy webcam image. "I had no idea my grandma had Wi-Fi," Doug said. "Someone gave her a digital camera and she can't work it. I plugged in and…"

"Nice to hear Grandma is wired. What's going on there?" Martin's impatience shot to the surface.

"Doug's got the goods, and he gave them to Carlotta," Phil said. "You aren't out in the open, are you, Marty?"

"Duh, of course not," Martin said. "I'm holed up in one of the service closets. Oh, and Doug, I hope she liked the merchandise."

Doug's face flooded with red. "Yeah, and so did Webb."

A cell phone on Doug's end rang, and Phil moved out of the frame.

Martin decided to ease up on Doug. "Webb's already filed a bunch of stories on his own even though they tried to silence him. I'm linked to them from my blog. I didn't read everything, but I'd love to see some of this creative accounting that started the whole affair."

"It's all there thanks to Webb," Doug said, his mouth moving as if he were lip-syncing. "And thanks to Grandma's digital camera, I scanned the juiciest parts of the Bull-Speakers books, and they should have arrived in your inbox. The part I like is the outlays and investments in Milteer Capital, which our good friend Paul is mixed up in, which helps Phil. But it doesn't tie it all up, because your blogs say that the left hand always does that magic disappearing trick to conceal what the right hand is doing. Is that accurate?"

"Sounds like you're putting everything in my lap when you're the one that started us on this odyssey." Martin experienced a sudden swell of pride. He'd always liked and trusted the Doug he'd known for years, but this Doug was "da bomb." This Doug was confident, strong, self-assured.

"We need the smoking gun," Doug said. "If you can get it, we can blitz the bastards."

Phil reappeared. "Make that smoking guns, plural. We just might have more ammo in this fight."

Martin listened to Phil with half an ear. He was too caught up in the wonder of his old friends.

He was completely deaf to the noises around him. All he could think of was that Doug was a new man, and that he needed to clean himself up if his plan were to work. Martin carefully and stealthily made his way back to his hotel room.

Sacramento Street, Old Town Auburn, California, August 1, 2007, 8:00 a.m.

In the kitchen of Annette Nikolopoulos's home, Doug was a child again, a guilty child. Annette stood straight-backed and looked him in the eye.

"I said for you to go out and have a good time, not be irresponsible. Not that I don't think you couldn't do with a little recklessness, mind you, but a note would have been nice. A hint as to your whereabouts."

Phil raised an earthenware mug in salute. "This is nothing. He was a rebel-rouser in college."

"I never heard about it." Annette favored Phil with a gleam in her eye. "It was so kind of you to make coffee this morning, Philip. And you're very handy. Why, the disposal was making the most frightful noises. Doug, you should have seen him unclog it."

"Want some coffee, Doug?" Phil apparently enjoyed being the man of the house again, of someone's house, anyway. "I can scramble some eggs…"

"None for me, thanks. Carlotta and I already—"

Annette's radar perked up. "Carlotta?"

"My friend."

"Oh. Where is she, dear?"

Doug was disappointed when Carlotta's editor called her away. She dropped him off at his grandmother's house to attend "an emergency BS meeting," as she termed it. She promised to call as soon as she was finished. "I hope your friend isn't furious because you stood him up to chase all over town with me," she said.

"He thinks I should get more action in my life," Doug said, deliberately flirting. "He won't be furious—he'll be jealous." He hoped to heaven he was right.

Phil's stare returned Doug to the present moment. "She had to go in to work," he told Annette, and explained what Carlotta did for a living.

"Oh yes. Local girl." Annette nodded knowingly. "I read her when I'm looking to see how my mutual funds did, because I can never tell if my broker is shooting me straight." Phil muffled his laugh as Annette went on. "Extremely knowledgeable, that one, I mean the girl." She looked over the edge of her mug at her grandson. "And she looks single to me. Not too many men like to talk numbers with women, beyond the waist size and bust size."

Doug poured himself coffee in order to avoid talking. He hadn't asked Carlotta, not once, if she was married, if she had a boyfriend. He thought there were sparks between them—yowza, and how—but he was jumping ahead of himself.

Phil cocked his head toward Doug and snickered at the coffee pour. Doug gave Phil a "shut up" look and then kissed Annette in apology. "I'm sorry I worried you, Grandma. I promise to be more respectful."

She smiled as though all her birthdays and Christmases had just arrived. "You're forgiven, dear. Life's too short to be angry." She turned to Phil. "So, Philip, you were telling me all about your cases. They sound so exciting. Much better than the television dramas. Did you ever have to shoot anyone?"

Half an hour later, Doug did penance by weeding Annette's flower beds and sidewalks while Phil cleaned her gutters. "You've never blown off anything in your life," Phil said.

"Hawaii." Doug had tried to apologize to Phil, but Phil wouldn't hear it. An unspoken acceptance that had always been there flowed between them.

"I meant, not because of a woman."

"I don't even know if she's available. She's after her lead story."

Phil rolled his eyes and dodged a cascade of damp, dirty leaves. "Always the doubting Doug. She wants you, man. I don't care if it's the story of the century."

Washington Post, A4, August 1, 2007

Protesters picket Bull-Spears D.C. offices

By Webb Sutton

Angry citizens taunted police officers outside the Georgetown offices of San Francisco-based investment bank Bull-Spears.

"Bull-Spears is part of the problem," consumer activist Liorah Osborne said. "They're flooding the market with bogus mortgages."

Mortgage banking reform advocates criticized the venerable institution on the day that it announced its support for the Kerry-Edwards Tax Relief Bill, which also has the backing of several other Fortune 500 companies, including Robert Tedson's Tedson Enterprises. Tedson Enterprises, according to records obtained by the Post, also contributed $939,000 to Fair New Deal for U.S., a 527 corporation that most insiders say Tedson founded.

Tedson and Bull-Spears founder Aaron Cartwright now appear embroiled in a scheme to manipulate not merely the subprime mortgage market, which makes up the majority of Bull-Spears' investors' holdings, but the money supply. This scheme, commonly known in economic parlance as the Plunge Protection Team, has been talked about for years.

Blogger Martin Cheyne, a University of Nevada-Reno teaching assistant and economist, first broke the story in February 2006.

Abigail Noonan, known in the blogosphere as CheyneChick, sells bumper stickers through CafePress on her blog that read: "Fear the PPT—They're Watching you."

Noonan, laptop in tow, protested with Osborne, who she calls "a woman ahead of her time," and demanded that Cartwright himself emerge from the Georgian-era stately former mansion that houses the Bull-Spears offices.

"What is Cartwright afraid of?" Noonan demanded. "Us, that's who. The people are smarter than he thinks."

Noonan, Osborne, and a grassroots constituency also picketed New Deal for U.S. offices near the historic Ford Theater where Abraham Lincoln was assassinated. They emphatically denied that they are connected to a Web site called GrassRootsMoney.com, a microlending business in Sacramento, California, operated by LeBrach and Associates.

"We're Grassroots People United," Osborne said. "I've never heard of GrassRootsMoney.com, but it's good to see that other groups out there are trying to make a difference. You don't need big money, you don't need bottomless bank accounts to fight corruption. We just all need to come together. That's why we're here."

Sacramento Bee, A1, August 1, 2007
Vacant townhomes unite immigrants, developers
By Carlotta McGinnis

When do a land developer and homeless immigrant families join together in a common cause?

That may seem like the lead-in to a joke, but it's not. At least not to Ron Hannifin of Handover Enterprises, or Rigo and Amalia Ordonez and Suriya and Budiwati Sanjiyaputri. Because of what Sacramento-based mortgage lender and real estate firm LeBrach and Associates officially terms "a regrettable accounting error," thirty townhomes remain empty six months after they were deemed ready for occupancy.

The Sanjiyaputris and the Ordonezes closed escrow on their new residences five months ago, yet neither family has been able to move in. The only occupants of any of the Pied-a-Terre Townhomes are Ron Hannifin and his wife, Dover Hannifin, who dreamed of building a community.

Continued on A5

EconomicCalamity (12:34 p.m. EST): Hey, Webb, I'm here and bored. No, not really. I'm free, single, and ready to mingle. Can't wait to see you.

EconomicCalamity (12:34 p.m. EST): I booked the rental car. I arrive 5:00 p.m., JAX.

EconomicCalamity (12:36 p.m. EST): Hello?

Webb Sutton greeted the covert thumbs-up in the office with nonchalance. He'd written five stories, all of which had to do with Bull-Spears, Paul LeBrach, Doug Boyd, Phil Schultz, Martin Cheyne, Aaron Cartwright, and all the major players in this bi-coastal tournament. It reminded him of the board game Risk rather than the card game War, campaigns on multiple fronts. Three stories would appear tomorrow. Two had already run today.

He turned back to his computer and messaged Martin.

MurrowsLoveChild (1:38 p.m. EST): Sorry, I was out for lunch and a smoke.

EconomicCalamity (1:39 p.m. EST): No problem.

MurrowsLoveChild (1:40 p.m. EST): You know, you ought to be careful with your blogs.

EconomicCalamity (1:40 p.m. EST): Is that why you mentioned where I work and what I do?

MurrowsLoveChild (1:41 p.m. EST): It's in your Blogger profile. Do you have your hotel room booked, too?

EconomicCalamity (1:42 p.m. EST): Are you familiar with that hotel? You know the layout?

MurrowsLoveChild (1:43 p.m. EST): Second floor is the room where we'll be attending that conference. You want to meet there?

EconomicCalamity (1:43 p.m. EST): Nah, let's have some Southern refreshment first.

MurrowsLoveChild (1:44 p.m. EST): I like your style. By the way, I hear Carlotta and Douggy are getting along just fine.

EconomicCalamity (1:44 p.m. EST): Maybe we should book them the honeymoon suite.

MurrowsLoveChild (1:45 p.m. EST): Excellent notion, but not this weekend. I hear the hotel will be packed.

EconomicCalamity (1:46 p.m. EST): It's the "in" place.

MurrowsLoveChild (1:46 p.m. EST): Now, you told me all about this PPT, and I researched it, but I need to be sure I've got my facts straight. What is the present function of the PPT in this country?

MurrowsLoveChild (1:50 p.m. EST): Hello?

MurrowsLoveChild (1:51 p.m. EST): Quite a lengthy response from your pause. Good thing I'm cutting and pasting here.

MurrowsLoveChild (2:01 p.m. EST): Are you all right?

EconomicCalamity (2:02 p.m. EST): The Dean of the Economics Department just called me into his office. I have to go.

California Club, Old Town Auburn, 11:15 a.m.

The stringy-looking busboy peered out of the door to the bar. "You'll have to come back tonight. The band's kickin'. If you really need something to take the edge off, you can—"

"I left my wallet inside last night," Doug said. "I was in here—"

"Oh yeah. Booty call." The busboy's eyes sparked with envy. "I hope she didn't pinch your wallet, man."

"No, I think I dropped it in there. Can we, just for a minute?" Doug and Phil had exhausted all the crime database and Internet resources. Phil was able to log in to the FBI criminal database using his old authorization before the computer abruptly terminated his session. He and Phil would have to rely on detective work to find the assassin who was stalking them. Phil suggested they could get the guy to talk. Somehow. When Doug took a dim view of their chances, Phil argued that this Tom Dooley would keep trying to terminate Doug, so Dooley had to be dealt with first. They couldn't wait for Martin to blow the cover off the massive fraud and conspiracy.

The busboy pondered and jiggled his left leg, then tapped his right foot in a scuffed sneaker that was just visible through the door. This movement of limbs apparently helped him decide. He nudged the door open. "Just a sec, because no one else is here. Don't let on that I did this for you."

Phil slipped him a twenty and they walked through the bar, which had a sad air in the midmorning light. Doug went right to the stool where he'd sat.

Phil leaned on the bar. "Nice place."

"It's cool," the busboy said.

"What's your name anyway?" Phil asked.

Doug made a great show of checking underneath the stool and scouting the breezeway to the back exit as the busboy responded, "DeWayne."

"Duane?"

"No, dude, D-e-W-a-y-n-e." DeWayne spelled out his name in the air with his fingers.

"Nice to meet you," Phil said.

Doug shook his head and spread his empty hands. "Can't find it. Maybe that guy that was sitting next to me grabbed it from my pocket."

"Coulda," DeWayne said. "I got the feeling he was trying to mack it with your baby. Whoooeee, she was hot. You hit that for real?"

Doug gave him a lazy male smile.

DeWayne whistled with open envy. "Awright."

"Have you ever seen him in here before?" Doug asked.

"He's not a regular," DeWayne said, looking uninterested. "Listen, we're restocking today. Everyone else is gonna start showing up."

Doug sighed. "Did he leave right after I did?"

"Stayed a few minutes," DeWayne said. His hips moved like an Elvis impersonator's.

"Did he order anything? Maybe on a credit card?" Doug made himself sound hopeful. "It could have been mine. I had a bogus charge…my bank's working it out."

"Most people pay cash, but I'll check." DeWayne seemed willing to do anything to get rid of them. He flipped through the credit card receipts behind the bar. For someone in a hurry, he kept a glacial pace. "Name?"

"Tom Dooley."

DeWayne shook his head after another moment. "Nada. Zip. Sorry."

"Aaron Cartwright?" Phil guessed.

DeWayne closed the box on the receipts. "Look, I'd like to help, but I checked the Lost and Found after closing last night. Nobody turned in a wallet. No one found a wallet. I'm sorry, man."

Phil looked at Doug. They both recognized the futility of the exercise. They thanked DeWayne and left.

"I hope you get it back, man," DeWayne called out the door as they walked to Phil's car.

"Where to?"

Doug sighed. "Back to Grandma's and whatever Plan B we can devise."

Doug jabbed a finger at the windshield so hard his joint bent backward, which, astonishingly, caused no discomfort. "He's here."

Phil located the Prius within seconds. It was parked two houses down from Annette's. Phil couldn't see anything through the Prius's smoked-glass windshield.

"Let's buzz him," Phil said.

When they drove by the Prius, they did a U-turn two houses beyond its fender. As they passed the Prius on the way back, Doug rolled down the window and gave the Prius's driver the finger.

The Prius was on their tail in seconds, eating up Nevada Street in a dash to catch them. Phil gunned the engine. "Strap yourself in, Doug."

"As always."

Doug couldn't retrace or order in his mind the sequence of events that led to Phil playing chicken with the Prius in a vacant lot similar to the one Carlotta had passed in the wee morning hours.

However, he forever etched in his mind the moment when the Prius smashed into the passenger side. Fortunately, the Prius's front end struck the backseat of Phil's car. A projectile whizzed through the broken window, but Phil had already unbuckled his seatbelt and Doug's. They made it out of the front seat in record time and took off running through the moderately crowded streets of Old Town. Bystander shouts and the first notes of a police siren egged them on as they headed for the center of Old Town. They didn't pause or falter for a second.

"The statue," Doug gasped. "There is a mile-long tunnel that runs from the old Auburn Dam site to here…under the statue.

"Don't tell me, it's hollow and we can hide inside it," Phil puffed as he glanced over his shoulder. Dooley's head loomed large in his field of vision. Two grim-looking faces followed close behind.

"Just trust me and hop in the creek bed below the statue…when you see the big metal drain under the street, run into it."

"Doug, I'm FBI and I've never done that." Phil said, much more coolly then he felt. He hopped over a small wooden fence onto the huge concrete statue, then leaped about seven feet into the creek below.

Phil stood immediately facing the entrance to the tunnel that stretched and yawned in front of them, then turned and looked for an alternate escape route.

Dooley drew his weapon from above. Civilians hurried about in the course of their normal day. Their faces clinched the deal for Phil.

"Let's go," he said to Doug. "I'll go first. Then you follow."

It was a sensible plan.

Unfortunately, ten feet into the void, and he and Doug plunged into darkness. The graffiti and spray paint that lined the outside could no longer be seen, and only the sound of the four inches of running water in front of them guided them forward.

CHAPTER 14

"One man with courage makes a majority"

—Andrew Jackson

Old Auburn Tunnels, August 1, afternoon

"Don't make any jokes about falling down the rabbit hole." Phil sounded too big for the tunnel, which felt more like a sepulcher than Doug's memory had admitted.

"We climbed down here. Unfortunately, I don't think our friend will stop to eat a cookie or drink tea."

"I wish we had that bottle that said 'Drink Me.' We could bust out of this place and bury Dooley."

"I'll keep my eye out for a white rabbit." Doug noticed he sounded far too chipper.

"It'll probably be a rat." Phil shone the light from his cell phone into the tunnel. It made a small hole in the darkness and bounced back eerily off the solid walls. The sectioned tunnel was man-made, but was no less creepy than a bat-infested natural cavern somewhere.

When he was nine and he explored the subterranean maze on a Saturday morning, the adventure seemed cool, exciting, forbidden. Now, Doug lifted his feet to avoid getting trapped in muck or falling into a mine shaft that, by sheer dumb luck, he and his buddies had escaped. In those more innocent childhood days, their parents would only have noticed they were missing if they didn't show up for breakfast the next morning.

That time, Al Hitchcock (now a city planner), Emily Weiss (a girl who could wrestle their arms behind their back until they wept for mercy and was now a Lieutenant Commander in the Navy), George Lasher (who was recovering at Walter Reed after an IED blew off his legs in Najaf), Doug's cousin Karen, and Doug thought this was the thrill of their lives. They scared the sweat and freckles off each other with tales of the ghosts that lurked in the tunnels. The allure of the tunnel exploration, other than the dirt and mud, was that they could brag about how they'd had a close call and nearly become one of the lost souls that perished in the tunnels and still skulked about.

Doug was more concerned about the danger from the living ghouls who hunted them. He thought morbidly that if Tom Dooley caused their demise, he and Phil would be the world's meanest, most sadistic, most pissed-off ghosts and would torment Dooley for the rest of his life.

Silt and ooze seeped into Doug's mouth and tasted foul. He hacked the grime back out and rounded his shoulders as he shimmed under an overhang. His ears picked up splashing and scraping behind them. "Stop for a second."

Phil's breathing was labored. "We can rest later."

Doug reached out and snatched Phil's arm. Dust and slime and moisture made his grip slip, but he held fast to Phil, who understood by the tenacious death-clinch of Doug's fingers that Doug was insistent.

The two men stood holding their breath as the dark stillness enveloped them. A minute passed. Two. What seemed like ten.

Phil tensed as they both heard scraping and splashing behind them. "That sounded too big to be a rat or dripping water, or even falling clods of dirt."

"I doubt it was any little girl, either."

"I don't know a damn thing about these tunnels. Is there any exit?"

"American River Canyon. As near as I can tell, we're going east-northeast, and we'll eventually come out into the canyons. Either that or China, if we turn the wrong way at Albuquerque."

"What the hell are you going on about?"

"Bugs Bunny." Doug kept talking to shield himself from the approaching splashes and scrapings. "You remember. 'I knew I shoulda turned left at Albuquerque.'"

Phil grunted at the near-perfect mimic of Bugs Bunny's Brooklyn accent. "What did I say about the rabbit hole? That goes for wascally wabbits too." He sounded more like Richard Nixon than Elmer Fudd, that is, if Richard Nixon were hyperventilating. His breathing reminded Doug of a Cuisinart working overtime.

"Are you claustrophobic, Phil?"

"I'm an FBI agent," came the curt reply. "I don't want to be smacked down because we didn't hear the enemy while you were busy reliving Saturday morning cartoons."

They were silent for a few moments.

"Why'd you ever get into business with Paul?"

"I got into debt," Phil said. "Raising a family. You ought to try it and then judge me."

"How can I? I have no life because I bought into the promise, the carrot they kept yanking beyond my reach. At least you have someone to go home to."

"We better put all our energy into finding the way out," Phil said after a pause.

Doug shivered in his windbreaker. The temperature had to be thirty-two degrees. He and Phil trudged on through the mud and the muck.

"Stop," Doug said after five minutes.

"Can't."

"I heard footsteps."

Phil tensed in place. By this time both their eyes had adjusted to the dark. Doug could see Phil turn and look back. Inquisitive, threat-assessing.

Rapid splashing and pounding. An eerie phantasm of a light behind them.

Doug hoped it was one of the tunnel ghosts.

A bullet strafed the tunnel beside them. Phil and Doug quickened their pace and rushed forward a few inches. Doug smelled the gunshot and smoke from the pistol. The dust coated his face. Chips of rock rained down on him.

Phil turned and fired at the light. It wavered, swung wildly. Another shot rang out, and Phil flattened himself against one wall of the tunnel. Doug crouched down in the mud and wondered as he crawled how long this tunnel ran until it opened on the American River Canyon. This always looked easier in the movies.

Phil fired again. Doug heard the report of the pistol.

Two more gunshots missed them.

"There's more than one," Phil yelled out, loud enough for their pursuers to hear. "There's more than one of us, and we can take you, you bastards. You thought Doug would be easy to silence, huh? Well, I am going to make you pay for your arrogance, you pieces of shit. You hear me, Dooley!"

He fired another round and dropped down. At first Doug was worried, until Phil crouched and moved along crab-style. Phil's boot waved in Doug's face. They both crawled and slid through the mud. It was slick, agonizingly slow, squelchy, but better than being standing targets.

A bullet whooshed over Doug's hairline.

Phil cursed out loud and froze. He panted for several moments. Doug felt the chill seep all the way into his heart. "I'm okay," Phil gasped.

Doug vaulted forward and crammed into the tunnel beside Phil. He put an arm around Phil's shoulders and tugged upward.

"What the hell are you doing?"

"Ever heard of the three-legged race?"

"What?" Phil, surprised, rose to his feet as Doug latched onto his waist and marched determinedly, dragging Phil along. "This is crazy. Who's the FBI agent here?"

"Is that a trick question?"

Phil cursed again. "I get shit-canned for protecting you, and—"

"So now it's time to lean on me. Where are you hit?" Doug smelled blood, smoldering flesh.

"Abs."

"Then let's get you the hell out of here."

Dooley's voice echoed hollowly through the tunnel. "Make this easier on yourselves, both of you. We'll even leave your bodies intact for your families to bury."

Phil looked back, his gaze keen. "You sound winded. No, scratch that—you sound pained." He raised his pistol and squeezed off another shot.

There was a scream. A string of curses. Phil discharged the weapon again. Another scream. A splashdown.

"I'm down." An unfamiliar male voice.

"Oh JehsusfuckinChrihssst…" A second strange male voice blended with the first in a pained duet.

"You think you're clever, Schultz," shouted Dooley. "We're legion. They can replace us."

Phil's gun answered them, and Dooley screamed.

Phil elbowed Doug and escaped his helpful hold. Doug whirled as Phil hotfooted it through the mire and the dark.

The dropped flashlight stuck in the mud and shone its beam on Dooley's grimace. Doug couldn't see the other two men. Phil pressed his pistol to Dooley's temple. "Drop whatever you're packing."

Dooley spun the chamber, cocked the hammer and pulled the trigger. Clunk. Clunk.

"That's the trouble with Spitfires," Phil said.

The gun fell from Dooley's hands and soft-landed in the mud.

Phil grabbed Dooley from behind in a bear hug. Dooley raised his elbows up to shoulder level, then jabbed his right elbow back. Phil grunted as it connected. Dooley seized Phil's momentary astonishment and took Phil's left wrist in his left hand. Another blow to the solar plexus. Phil let go, and Dooley shimmed under Phil's left forearm. He was now behind Phil, pulling Phil's arm behind him. He seemed to have forgotten Doug, who shrank up against the wall out of Dooley's range of vision.

Doug's cell phone rang, and Dooley swiveled his head around. Doug put both his fists up, let out a war cry, and rushed Dooley, pounding on his head. Doug stabbed his fingers into Dooley's eyes, and Dooley hollered. His hands went limp and slithered off Phil, who pulled something out of his jacket. Doug heard a clink. "Handcuffs," Phil said as he fastened one end to Dooley's arm and rashly snapped the other onto his wrist.

Dooley's laughter wheezed. "Haven't you seen any movies, Schultz?"

Phil determinedly marched forward and towed Dooley like a ship's anchor.

Doug's phone kept ringing. "What about the others?" Doug asked.

"Call 911," Phil said.

Doug nodded and answered the phone. "Doug."

"Where have you been?"

Carlotta's voice washed over him, warmth and light. The tunnel suddenly seemed to brighten. "Sorry."

"Where are you? You sound out of breath."

"I heard they closed the American River Canyons."

"Parts of them, not all of them. They've been working on this project to divert the river through the old dam. It's quite an undertaking...Let me repeat, where are you?"

"Where can you meet us?"

There was a pause as Carlotta sucked in breath. "Is the tunnel widening any?"

"It's been narrow."

"It should widen out into thirty-foot caves."

"Let's find out."

Carlotta said something that fuzzed out. "I can't hear you, do you copy?" Doug was just happy to hear her voice.

"I'm losing you," she repeated. "Meet me No-Hands Bridge, near the American River confluence. You should come out somewhere around either the quarry or the base of the old dam. If not, call me and I'll find you."

Doug choked back laughter. "Then what?"

"No-Hands...hitchhike...you there."

Then his phone was silent. He didn't need to look at the display to see that he no longer had a signal. The miracle was that he'd gotten reception underground.

"How far did she say?" Phil headed straight down the tunnel with Dooley trying to slow progress. Phil viciously forced him onward.

"Thirty-foot caverns and we're getting closer."

"He's been wounded badly," Dooley said. "Anything could happen to us. Nasty accident, cave-in, rising water, maybe a water snake."

"No water snakes here," Doug said. "You have a real name, tough guy?"

Dooley shrugged and smirked. "Shawn G. Smith. What does it matter now?"

"Who ordered the hit on Doug?"

"'Hit'? There was no hit. It was just a matter of resolving a problem with an ex-employee." Smith grinned.

"Not a hit, excuse me. How about contract killing?" Phil drew out the words. "Murder for hire? That appeal to you better, asshole?"

"We know you work for Cartwright," Doug said. "We know everything. Probably more than you can imagine."

"You can't imagine any of this in your plodding number-crunching mind. Because to you none of this adds up." Smith still managed to be taunting. "You think it should all balance out. Not too much in the debit column. Not too much in the credit column, because that's Puritan, Quaker, Shaker, whatever. Not too much money changing hands even though we still gamble on the Lotto. A currency goes up two pips against the dollar and you freak. Guess what, Doug…you are a part of it. You serve your financial masters too. You do their bidding. Your audits only make people play by the rules that are already rigged in favor of the house. You have no idea, no idea how it all fits together. Some homeowners report a loss on their home and you cry for them. You might as well be the financial advisor that feels good about charging a six percent commission to put his clients' money into a dumpy mutual fund. Or the boiler-room Wall Street thug that shoves his clients' money into a dead stock. It happens every day. And you, tough guy," he said, pointing at Phil. "Who's laws are you enforcing anyway? Ain't that America."

"You love your country?" Phil taunted right back.

"Love it. Greatest fucking country ever, and all founded on greed. The greedy banks loaned money they shouldn't have, packaged the loans and sold them to Wall Street, who bribed the ratings agencies to rate the debt high enough to sell off to pension funds, widows, and small villages in Norway. The mortgage brokers lied on applications, the appraisers boosted appraisals, the real estate agents pushed property that should have been out of reach. You know why? Because they wanted to make some money. They were greedy. That's the beauty of it. And do you know why people took on this debt in the first place? Greed. They were all going to become multi-millionaires, or priced out of the market, or whatever. It's a victimless crime, kids. The victims and the culprits are all the same. They said America was founded for religious freedom. That's a form of greed, right? By the way, how's that little señorita doing, from the church?"

"Peachy," Phil said. "You think killing an accountant for doing his job is a victimless crime? Fuck you, by the way. And I called for backup, in case you were wondering."

"I bet your boss just loved that." Smith chuckled.

"Yeah, especially the part where I text-messaged him and sent off a video of all this. You weren't the only one who got a signal, Doug."

Doug knew his incredulity was all over his face. "No wonder you weren't talking."

"No, I was recording for posterity."

"Oh shit." Doug shut his eyes briefly. "How long? Do they get to hear me doing my Bugs Bunny routine?"

"They get to hear Smith confessing," Phil drawled. "In part. Video recording time ran out. But it'll probably be enough to hang him."

Smith looked down at the handcuffs, at his feet. It appeared that his predicament finally sunk in.

Doug felt his mind and body expand as they emerged into a thirty-foot cavern. Sunlight shone through heavy brush at the end of the mine shaft just a few yards ahead. He remembered this. Robert Louis Stevenson stuff. The mud gave way to the river, and the river lapped at the cavern walls.

"There used to be rafts here," Doug said.

"If we find one, you get to row," Phil said.

Doug hacked at the dry manzanita and other brush with his bare arms and created an opening large enough to walk through. His feet splashed in the shallow but swiftly moving river. The bright sunshine outside hurt his eyes, and it took them a moment to adjust. Doug looked up at the huge sloping mountain face on both sides of the canyon stretching upward at least five hundred feet on each side. Directly in front of them lay huge slabs of concrete laid decades ago as the base for the now obsolete Auburn Dam project. One moment they were walking through the river—it came up to their ankles—the next, Phil's foot struck a heavy underwater impediment, and he stumbled. The phone dropped and Smith caught it. He laughed, turned until he winced with the strain of his movement in handcuffs, and flung the phone back down the tunnel. "I don't think anything got sent," he said, and yanked at the handcuffs to dislodge Phil, whose rocky footing made him clumsy.

Doug pivoted on the ball of his foot. He noticed Smith's eyes still watered. This time Doug clobbered him in the face, pounding him until a tooth broke and blood poured from his mouth. Doug balled his fist and aimed for the stomach, but missed and punched him in the groin. In complete pain, Smith sunk to his knees. He reached for Phil's ankles, and Phil was on him in a flurry of movement.

What happened next was hazy. There was a momentary gap in Doug's memory. The next thing Doug knew, Phil was unlocking the cuffs that bound him to Smith's corpse. Blood oozed from Smith's abdomen and shoulder.

"Did I do that?" Doug pointed at the blood trail from the abdomen.

Phil gave him a sick smile. "Let's not ask questions, okay? Not in the rabbit hole."

"Okay. We should go back for your phone."

"Let's not bother. There could be more of them, and I don't know about you, but I want out of here."

"The recording…"

"The signal went through."

Doug laughed as the tension went out of him. "Phil, you're a wild and crazy guy."

"Bet your ass, Alice."

Happy whitewater rafters still carried their overgrown rubber kiddie wading pools with the oarlocks to the water's edge at six o'clock. One or two college kids shouted upon seeing Phil and Doug stagger out of a cavern exit, wade through the river, and emerge waterlogged. The students pointed at the handcuff dangling from Phil's wrist. Doug knew he and Phil must look as if they'd tried to raft up the river and gotten bullwhipped.

"Hey." Doug waved at them. "Can you point us to No-Hands?"

Phil's voice was faint. "You've got two more hours of daylight, kids, stay safe."

The students, at a loss, gave them directions. Phil and Doug gazed at the gashes and trenches made by miners as the two men hiked for miles until they reached the base of an old concrete railroad bridge, now used only for equestrians and hikers.

The aquamarine Jetta waited on the shoulder of the highway, about one hundred yards above them in the canyon. A passing Placer County Sheriff's car honked at the Jetta. Exhausted and bedraggled, Doug and Phil reached Carlotta's car and threw open the car doors.

Carlotta looked straight past Phil and his blood-soaked shirt and instead scrutinized Doug with her luminous, sharp eyes as he shut the door and fastened his seatbelt. "I didn't know you'd be this wet."

Phil collapsed in the backseat. "Could you please take us to the nearest hospital?"

"Buckle up, Phil," Doug said, smiling at Carlotta.

"Kiss off, Doug." Phil pressed his hands hard against his wounded abdomen and closed his eyes.

Carlotta put the car in drive and aimed her wheels onto the river road. "Save the brotherly fighting for when we actually get to the hospital, guys." She handed Doug two cups of Starbucks coffee, one of which made its way to the backseat and into Phil's waiting hand. "I'll say one thing for you, Douglas Boyd. You know how to show a woman an exciting time."

CHAPTER 15

"Stock prices have reached what looks like a permanently high plateau."

—Irving Fisher (1867–1947), American Economist (and Skull & Bones member), just days before the stock market crash of 1929

Economic Calamity
Long Live Learning in the Land of the Free
August 1, 11:11 a.m.
By Martin Cheyne

I've been fired.
Ward Churchill can get away with saying the WTC victims deserved to die—saying it in the classroom, mind you—but I've been fired because of this blog.

Why was I fired? I am not entirely sure what the real reason is, but I suspect I was irritating the communist-fascists who are taking control of the country. I have been accused of a lot of things, but most people attack me by calling me a Commie or a Socialist because I despise the Federal Reserve System and the government-run Plunge Protection Team.

The truth is, I hate communism. I deplore fascism. I am a 100% pure believer in capitalism, liberty, and the idea that all men are created equal.

The truth is, all I want is for the government to stay the hell out of the markets. Government interference (bought and paid for by the "powers that be," the "men behind the curtain") created this mess.

In a free market, the banks would have never loaned the ridiculous money they loaned. They did because they knew the Feds would bail them out.

In a free market, people would only put their money in banks that lend prudently. They don't worry about it today because the Feds promise to return their money no matter what, through the FDIC.

In a free market, the invisible hand would have never allowed this mess to be created in the first place.

But, what do I know is this. Maybe I should have kissed ass a bit more and opened minds a lot less; then I would still have a job.

But, my loyal blog readers, I can't do that. I am going to blow the cover off this mess. I am going to expose the Communist Central Bankers and the true reasons for the PPT. More to come...

Trackback / Comment/ Blog This / Comments (89)

Office of the Assistant Dean, Economics Department, University of Nevada-Reno, August 1, 2:00 p.m.

"Do you understand al' that we've discussed, Mr. Cheyne?" The assistant dean, who looked ındistinguishable from anyone else in the administrative bureaucracy, folded her hands and gave Martin a disapproving look so exaggerated it was comical. "The Disciplinary Committee will review your case and contact you when a hearing date is set. In the meantime..."

"I've been writing this blog for four years." Martin no longer cared what the university thought. He accepted, Zen-like, his own arrogance in assuming that the rarefied bubble of academia would safeguard him from the retaliation Phil and Doug had experienced. If that smarmy-face Paul ever found out, God forbid.

Martin sat up straighter in the red leather chair. "I've made no secret of my views on the Federal Reserve, or on the government's monetary policies, and suddenly I'm the Don Imus of the academic world. And before you get your PC knickers in a twist, I think what Mr. Imus said was deplorable and in bad taste, but come on, he was hired to make outrageous, stupid, and tasteless commentary. They knew he was a loose cannon for years, and as long as advertisers didn't start pulling the almighty buck, everything was rosy."

"Mr. Cheyne—"

"Similarly, I am supposed to teach. To open up college students' minds. I am supposed to contribute to knowledge. I am supposed to help other human beings, future leaders, think critically, to question the status quo. In case you haven't noticed, the status quo is deplorable."

"Your presence at the university is a privilege, not a right." The assistant dean seemed less than convinced by his sentimental, Richard Dreyfuss-like speech about the pursuit of intellectual inquiry. "And your blog contains content that reflects poorly on the image of the university as a whole. You, as a teaching assistant and a graduate student, are a representative of this school."

"My blog is no more outrageous than any other TA's or even any professor's, except I don't have tenure," Martin said. He knew he was doomed, and he understood just how far he'd overreached in his zeal to change the world.

"You were warned—"

"I was never warned. Not once. Never got any letters, no one ever stopped by and asked me to tone it down." Martin raised his voice. "Not for something I do on my own time. No one ever said anything to me."

"You use the university computers and Internet—"

"I do so on my own time. And by the way, a number of highly respected professors from this school have commented on my blog. They get it. They see what I see. There's more going on than just whether or not I get a PhD, or whether a few alumni write nasty letters. Schools aren't infallible. Remember the Duke lacrosse players? The university didn't even count them innocent until proven guilty. And for God's sake, most of you people are so ignorant you think I'm a Marxist! That makes me a conformist by university standards."

The assistant dean shook her head and averted her face as though she'd just smelled something distasteful. "You harangue people with your radical views at every opportunity, Mr. Cheyne—"

"Radical! Since when is talking trash about the U.S. government radical or dangerous on American university campuses? Some people at the University of Michigan consider Ted Kaczynski and Timothy McVeigh, not to mention the 9-11 hijackers, 'proponents of civil disobedience'!"

"The committee will contact you in a few weeks," the assistant dean said, trying for a concerned tone. It made Martin bite his cheeks to keep from laughing. "I'm sorry that the situation has come to this. We would hate to lose you as a student."

Martin stood and edged his way toward the door. The chamomile tea and the sachets in her office made him nauseous. "We all might lose a lot more before this is over," he said as he closed the door behind him.

On the way out of the building, Martin paused to rearrange his box of books and his personal effects. He happened to look up at the wall of department benefactors. While normally the names of generous patrons failed to stir his interest, his intuition directed his eyes to several gold-plate names:

Deborah Crump
Tedson Enterprises
Richard Gauthier
Aaron Cartwright
Stewart Zwick
Ian Atkins
Perry McDonald

"All fans of our football team, are you?" Martin said out loud and paid no mind to the stares he received. "Academic standards, right. If I ever strike it rich, I'll donate a new wing to the campus hospital on the condition that they get all of your names off every damn donor wall on campus. I'll even throw in a new cancer research facility and a free-care community health clinic."

Sutter Auburn Faith Hospital Waiting Room, Auburn, 5:00 p.m.

"We'll let you know when you can see your brother," the emergency room doctor, whose name tag identified him as Dr. Emmerson, said. "You guys don't look a lot alike…"

"We get that a lot." Doug managed his most charming smile as he picked at the bandage on the arm he hadn't noticed got cut during the fight. Not from Smith or Dooley or whoever he was, but from the broken-off part of the tunnel wall when Smith threw him. Once he got in the hospital examining room and Phil disappeared into the E.R., Doug noticed his skin stung something fierce.

"Don't pick at it." Carlotta reached out and plucked his hand off it. Doug felt a bolt of energy go up his arm, and suddenly it ceased to be irritated.

Doug looked at Emmerson. "You guys have been great."

Emmerson nodded, curiosity in his eyes. "How did he get shot? Entry wound looked pretty serious."

"Guy attacked us," Doug said succinctly. "He's been stalking me."

"We are going to have to file a police report." Emmerson looked sympathetic. "You'll need evidence for that, and you can just ask me. Your brother's going to be laid up for at least three days. This isn't one of the city hospitals where they kick you out because they don't have the beds and the funding. Our chief surgeon would have a fit if your brother got released early. Heads would roll."

"Thanks," Doug said, grateful he didn't have to explain further.

Emmerson headed for the entry to the ER. "I'll send someone to get you and your wife as soon as your brother's out of surgery."

Moments later, Doug and Carlotta sat drinking weak coffee and eating chicken soup in the hospital cafeteria. In the cafeteria, the usual hospital odors of sickness and antiseptic were mercifully absent.

"Your brother?" Carlotta ventured after a lengthy period of silence.

"As close as any I could ever have." Doug kept reminding himself that he hadn't so much as gone on a first date with this woman, and he knew that shared danger often created a false or exaggerated bond. But he felt more natural with her, here, sharing a meal that epitomized institutionalism and comfort, than he ever had trying to impress some woman over an appletini or bottle of Châteauneuf du Pape at a trendy eatery. That had to count for something.

He realized she was prodding him to continue with her stare. "You probably know that, though. You probably know all about me."

She slurped a noodle. "I never think I know anyone just from their biographical data. I can read that you're an accountant, but that's not who you really are."

"No." The earth shifted as Doug made his admission. "It never was. I'm good with numbers and patterns, is all."

"So am I." She smiled. "So why, might you ask, am I with a small city paper?"

"It's not small-time. It's a major California publication, it's respectable." Did he just sound condescending? He hoped not, and he felt as if he'd crossed into first-date territory.

"It's not the *Washington Post*, but I've worked for the *Post*, and it's not the *New York Times*, even though I never want to live in New York. Not again."

"Thank God."

Carlotta blinked and smiled at Doug's forceful tone. Doug coughed and fished all the carrots from his soup, one at a time, the way he used to do when he was eight. "I mean, thank God, because they wrote this obvious puff piece on my…my former company and on Bull-Spears. Cock-stroking journalism. That's how Martin put it."

She burst out laughing.

Doug blushed. "I can't believe I just—"

"Don't worry, I have heard it all. Although that's a new one. I think I like Martin…your other brother."

Doug grinned. "Martin says we're *Two and a Half Men*, but I tell people we're sort of like the guy version of *Sex and the City*, minus the cosmos."

"And the shoe fetishes. You watch *Sex and the City*?"

"Oh, Paul's got a shoe fetish." Doug's throat shrank when he mentioned the show, as though he'd placed a metrosexual voodoo curse on himself. Paul's name came out as a creak.

"Phil told Webb about him. You feel betrayed."

"We all do," Doug said hoarsely. "I guess that's not fair exactly."

"Nothing's fair, not even love and war."

Doug nodded. "Martin will say he always knew Paul was an ass, but that was probably why we hung with him."

Carlotta nodded. "Sort of like going to the head cheerleader's house even though you know she's a bitch."

"Happened to you?"

She looked into her soup bowl. "Are these noodles or wet shoelaces?"

Doug knew an awkward sidestep when he saw one. He felt moronic, then righteously indignant. She needed him, after all, even if she'd saved him. She'd tailed him!

He pointed at her bulky purse. "What's that?"

"Flight attendant's case." She seemed accustomed to this question and smiled with faint amusement.

"You're not a flight attendant." He'd descended to sub-moronic level.

Her voice was gentle. "And you're not an accountant anymore. If you ever were."

"I..." Was this what it was like to have amnesia? To lose who you were? To forget who you had once been? He'd once been Doug Boyd. No. He still was. He was just a more conscious, more alive version of himself.

He wasn't going to do a header off the twentieth floor the way they did in Japan to restore his family's honor or company's honor or whatever honor. Hell, his mother had burned a bra. His father had set fire to half a Woolworth's because, supposedly, they funded the Vietnam War, exploited women and migrant workers, and discriminated against African-Americans.

This, then, was his act of civil disobedience, adding up the right numbers in a society that prided itself on fuzzy math and the bottom line. The numbers were unforgiving and neutral; that's what he liked about them. And there were people behind those numbers. The ancient Greeks, the Arabs, had invented numbers. Back then, if you added up the numbers on the abacus and the king didn't like it, you would probably be beheaded. The trouble today was that the king wasn't even in charge, the voodoo priests were.

"I know people, I've seen a lot, even here in Auburn," Carlotta said.

Doug finished his soup. "I want to apologize..."

"Please don't."

"I decided against it."

"Good." She moved the case about on the table. It was green with a yellow manufacturer's label sewn on the front. "You're a good man, Doug Boyd."

He needed air. The presence of her, spicy and sweet and whole and real, overwhelmed him. It was like being bathed in a mint julep.

"I'd better go see how Phil is doing. Are you…"

"I'm hanging around where the action is, and I have a story to write." She whipped her laptop out of her briefcase. "Seeing as how I saved your life twice, could I trouble you for a cup of coffee?"

Doug, detail-oriented, noted how she took it and felt goofily grateful when she smiled at him with sincere appreciation as she took the cup.

He turned back to look at her as her cell phone rang, jarring everyone in the cafeteria. She stowed her laptop away, left her coffee, and took her purse and laptop as she discreetly slipped into the outdoor courtyard where cigarette smoke already created a veil. She vanished into the gray.

Room 234 incorrectly had the name "Philip Boyd" on the door. Doug paid for Phil's treatment with the tiny cache he'd saved by not having a life. No need for insurance or anything that might alert anyone to Phil being alive, or require that his true name be given out. It was as depressing as most hospital rooms, but Phil looked quite a bit more chipper than most gunshot victims. He smiled at Doug. "Where'd she go?"

Doug played dumb to lighten the mood. "Who?"

"Don't 'who' me."

"Outside talking to her editor."

"So she's really a journalist."

Doug pulled a chair beside the bed, twirled it around with Fred Astaire flourish, and plopped on it with the metallic back of the chair abutting the steel bedrail. "Nah, she just wants my body."

Phil slapped his chest so hard he gasped and reached for the call button. "About damn time you woke up," he wheezed. He breathed from his stomach for a few moments, apparently decided he hadn't caused a hemorrhage, and draped his hand over Doug's shoulder. "About damn time!" He grinned so hard it most likely induced fresh pain, but Phil looked euphoric in a selfless, brotherly, back-slapping, "glad you'll get laid, man" sense.

"She just wants my notes," Doug said, feeling as gawky and geeky as in junior high. "For the article. I'm sure Webb can vouch for her, and he does, but—"

"But nothing." Phil leaned back and folded his hands behind his head, so as not to risk further trauma. "Helen said, oh, a few weeks ago, before Virginia, that you were slogging through the desert so long you were bound to hit an oasis."

"Helen said that?" Doug blushed, because Helen was usually wise about people, and he had an intuition that her influence had kept Phil from being hauled away in a body bag on countless occasions. "Well… she is the one who has custody of the brain."

Phil laughed. "That's not the good part. She predicted with her crystal ball that you'd probably get out your calculator and try to figure out what percentage of the oasis was a mirage…" Phil grinned. "And she said, quote, 'Tell him to bury the calculator in the sand and go stick his feet in the water.'"

"Hmm."

"She knows people. She's got a sixth sense."

Phil's smile turned to a frown, and Doug could tell how badly his friend missed his wife. He tried to lighten the mood again.

"Then it must have been offline when she met you, or you put something in her coffee."

"If I weren't afraid of starting up the bleeding again, I'd hit you."

They grinned at each other.

"Don't," Phil said, after a pause.

"What?"

"Start doubting her. Don't screw up like I did."

A moment of awkward silence passed before Doug spoke up again. "So…the docs say they want to keep you for a couple days."

Phil nodded. "I'm probably safest here. You and Barbara Walters—"

"I thought Lois Lane. The Margot Kidder Lois Lane. She was my childhood fantasy. That negligee she wore for Superman…"

"Whatever makes you fly. Anyway, you two should be safer for the moment now that our friend is gone."

"Maybe I can talk to Paul."

"Don't." Phil's mouth formed not just a line, but a barrier. "Don't you dare approach that bastard. Not until we figure out a strategy. He knows you too well."

"He knows the old Doug, who cowered in his house."

"The new Doug is still a kitten, and Paul will drown you. Don't go near him. Not until we can confront him together. He is deep in this thing, and with the right leverage we can get him to help us take down all the bad guys." Phil's smile turned devilish as he emphasized the word "all." "He won't be able to play big man then."

Doug didn't want to argue. "What would you do? I'm green at this."

"Not so green anymore." Phil was pensive. "While Marty crashes the Fed and Bull-Spears party way down south, you might go see what you can dig up at Arthur Whinney."

"Why would I go back there? I'm hardly welcome."

"You spent practically all your life there. You should be able to figure out a way."

Breaking and entering. Not that Doug, at this point, had any scruples against that, but… "I don't ever want to set foot in that sick pit of hell again."

"Then break into Bull-Spears," Phil said. "They've probably got more of the goods."

Doug couldn't think of a sane, logical counterargument, so he merely nodded.

Phil continued. "I'll give you a crash course on the way Fibbies do it. The man behind the curtain doesn't know what went down in the tunnels. So you and Carlotta can play Mulder and Scully under their radar and off their grid."

LeBrach and Associates, August 3, 3:00 p.m.

Sacramento Bee, A1, August 3, 2007
Bull-Spears puts out contract on whistleblower's life
By Carlotta McGinnis

AUBURN, C.A. – A former FBI agent thwarted an alleged contracted murder attempt of an accountant by a Bull-Spears employee during a camping trip two weeks ago in the Sierra Nevadas.

A casual men's camping weekend turned into a scene straight out of a John Grisham novel when former FBI agent Philip Schultz surprised what he thought was a bear in the woods.

The "bear" turned out to be Shawn G. Smith, the head of security for San Francisco-based investment bank Bull-Spears. Smith, who Schultz said was accompanied by at least one accomplice, allegedly intended to kill Douglas Boyd, 33, of San Jose, formerly an accountant for Arthur Whinney and Associates, which replaced the fallen accounting firm Arthur Andersen as one of the most powerful corporate accounting businesses in America. Unfortunately, according to Boyd, Arthur Whinney and Associates has followed in Arthur Andersen's footsteps.

At stake is the multibillion-dollar trade of buying CDOs, otherwise known as the business of bad debts. Schultz, based on hours of surveillance, believes Boyd, who he has known since college, is the target of a corporate-sponsored murder-for-hire plot.

Arthur Whinney and Associates, which could not be reached for comment, fired Boyd after he refused to submit a fake set of books that used an inflated valuation for two of Bull-Spears' most-advertised hedge funds. The holdings in the funds consist mainly of CDOs, which have been in crisis in recent months. When Boyd sought an independent valuation of the funds, he met with resistance and hostility. He was fired from the company, and now he lives in fear for his life.

Eyewitnesses at the California Club in Old Town Auburn Tuesday night witnessed Dooley threatening Boyd, who grew up in the area.

"There was a bad vibe about him," said bar patron Tony Stubbs, who witnessed the incident and came to Boyd's rescue. "He wouldn't leave this other dude alone. He was harassing him."

The harassment escalated to a confrontation in the Old Auburn Tunnels on Wednesday, during which Schultz was shot and Boyd sustained minor injuries while he took Schultz to safety. Auburn Faith Hospital said Schultz is expected to make a full recovery.

Smith pursued Schultz and Boyd into the tunnels around noon on Wednesday…

Continued on A7

Karina covered the *Sacramento Bee* with a file folder. Paul seemed too ego-absorbed these days to care about the deeds of mere mortals in the newspaper. If he did read the headlines, he would be selectively blind to everything but his own name. Yesterday there had been a huge puff piece about him.

A flashy sort of woman like that Joanne Huffman sauntered through the office. She looked as if someone had cloned Halle Berry. Karina picked up the phone, attempting to look busy. The woman gave her a complacent sneer.

Sisterhood of color, Karina thought. Yeah, right. To her, this woman was in all probability Paul's bimbo. To the woman, Karina was just another Hispanic secretary who can barely speak English. "Minorities aren't prejudiced, my ass," she thought.

"I'm here," the woman spoke slowly, as if to a five-year-old, "to see Paul LeBrach. My name is Zara Crystal."

Karina nodded with her best subservient smile and said in a perfect imitation of her mother's Guadalajara cadence, "Hold, please." She pressed the intercom and said, "Señor LeBrach, Za-ha-ra Cree-stal is here to see you."

Paul was out of his office before she finished speaking. He gave his guest that bedroom look that made Karina pity Patty LeBrach, who had never stood a chance. "It's lovely to meet you."

"A pleasure." Zara practically screwed him with her voice, and Karina had to purposely drop something off the desk so they wouldn't see her laugh, if they'd condescended to notice her. "My sister—Deborah, you know—she would be here, but she's tied up in D.C."

An image of Deborah Crystal, if that was her real name, bound and gagged for the delectation of some congressmen flashed through Karina's mind, and she almost giggled herself unconscious.

"Well, no slight intended to your sister, but I'm certainly not disappointed she sent you. So, what do you think of the capital of the Golden State?"

"Ah, sightseeing later. Business before pleasure." Zara dimpled.

"Well, since we're driving out to see that land your sister and her consortium are interested in, we can manage both." Paul gave a jaunty wave to Karina as he took Zara's elbow.

In and out. Kiss kiss, bang bang. Just Paul's style.

Karina was in Paul's office looking through the new client file as soon as she heard the door swing shut behind Zara's purple Prada heels.

She photocopied them all, then scanned each one and saved them all to a four-gigabyte memory stick. The one she particularly highlighted with Adobe Illustrator was a memo on Intacta Corporation's letterhead.

On Behalf of Deborah Crump, Chairperson
Intacta Corporation
Maclean, Virginia
July 2, 2007
Re: Counterproposal

Pursuant to LeBrach and Associates' e-mail of July 1, let me say that the defunct subdivision of Hidden Pines Place (which can be bulldozed, my friend Mike Clennahan says) and your Handover Enterprises (again, bulldozed) offer much more curb appeal than the properties you have mentioned thus far. Intacta Corporation has a consortium of private and government investors and advisors who can develop these properties into multi-use developments that will benefit the citizens of Sacramento and Auburn as well as the great state of California.

The details are far too extensive to discuss even over the phone, so either I or my representative, in the regrettable event I'm unable to travel to Sacramento personally, will happily meet with you to share this great vision that my company and its partners have conceived.

I look forward to working with you. Intacta offers many opportunities to our partners who see the potential of what we do.

Karina e-mailed all the files to Phil's private e-mail with the words, "I'm a concerned citizen who wants to help. These bastards have to be stopped." Then, she called the Auburn Faith Hospital. She was startled to find there was no Philip Schultz admitted, but once she explained the circumstances of his being admitted, the reception desk put her through to his room.

Auburn Faith Hospital, 5:00 p.m.

Even if Phil hadn't heard the doctor's suspicious voice in the corridor, he'd have still made his way, in a nurse's outfit and surgical mask he'd stolen yesterday while he was getting his physical therapy, to the staff-only areas where he could escape out a side entrance. Which he did. He probably had more medical bills to pay, but what was one more debt? If he survived this, he'd give the hospital a fucking endowment.

Then he'd buy a new car to replace the Volkswagen Passat he hotwired. It happened to belong to one of Phil's doctors, who could probably afford a new one, but it was the principle of the thing. Phil was the one who'd deceived them.

Karina's call had prompted thorny questions. Emmerson, the doctor who'd tended to him, had said confidentially, "Look, I knew that guy wasn't really your brother…people here are pretty cool if you just let them know what's going on. We've had a lot of Medicare and insurance fraud. But I'm sure if you tell them you're working for the Feds—"

"What?"

Doctor Emmerson, who smelled like peanuts (he said he was quitting smoking), showed Phil the morning edition of the *Sacramento Bee*. Carlotta McGinnis' article led the headlines and dwarfed even the latest Hollywood scandal, political faux pas, or Schwarzeneggerian mandate.

"Shit," Phil breathed.

"Is she married to that guy?" Emmerson wanted to know.

"No." Phil's teeth tightened, and he was grateful Helen wasn't around so he could throw her Dr. Phil advice in her face. "No, she isn't. Just another goddamn reporter out for a story."

"I hear you. We've gotten our share of that. But seeing how you knew about it…" Emmerson shuffled his feet in his doctor's shoes as if fire ants had suddenly crawled into them. "I can talk to the people here for you..." He left without Phil's assent.

The nurse who'd treated Phil had lambasted Doctor Emmerson as they headed to Phil's room. "—care what his noble motives were or that he was shot. It's medical fraud. And I called the FBI—they said he was involved in some kind of real estate scam, he was fired..."

As Phil called Doug from a prepaid cell phone he bought, he felt like a burglar who had discovered a murder victim. What are the ethics in that situation? Phil rubbed his eyes and ignored the persistent pain in his abdomen.

Doug answered, and Phil said, "Did you see the paper?"

"Paper? Oh, no. It got soaked by the neighbor's hose." Doug's tone of voice told Phil everything, including that Annette was listening. "I'll have to get one from Carlotta when we go out to San Jose."

"Good idea. Listen, I don't know what was going through her mind..."

"It doesn't matter. It's just a paper. The important thing is that you get home safe. Grandma is worried about your caving accident."

"Change of plans," Phil said. "I checked myself out of the hospital. I'm going to see our friend Paul."

"Remember what your doctor said? Nothing strenuous." Phil heard the are-you-nuts worry in Doug's voice.

"It's gone beyond that, and after what I've been through, Paul won't know what nuke hit him."

Phil heard the clarion call of a police siren behind him. Who said there was never a cop around? He glanced in his rearview mirror, but the black-and-white was in heavy pursuit of another felon. For the first time, Phil knew how criminals felt.

Martin's computer sailed out the window of the guest room like a sack of jewels dropped by the Pink Panther.

The man in the hula girl T-shirt landed a blow to Martin's left temple, causing linear thought to scatter before the pain. Another blow to Martin's nose.

"You and your friends couldn't leave well enough the fuck alone, could you? Mr. Professor? Well, I'm Earl Leeson. Your friends killed my brother, and I got honors in making you sorry your father ever humped your mother."

"Too late," Martin gasped as language returned. "I walked in on them having sex when I was six. Sorry."

Another blow to some vulnerable part of his body, and survival took over. Martin kicked out randomly, and by the grace of his guardian angel, made a solid connection. Leeson grunted, and Martin ran for the window, following his laptop through it.

CHAPTER 16

"Fascism should rightly be called corporatism, as it is the merger of state and corporate power"

—Benito Mussolini, Italian Dictator

Jekyll Island Resort and Club, August 4, 11:00 a.m.

Deborah Crump was the Martha Stewart of the financial world, although Wall Street grandes dames Abby Joseph Cohen and Muriel Siebert considered her a Jane-come-lately. Deborah Crump viewed them as pioneers, but come on, if they'd had her skin color, even light skin color, they'd still be kissing some white guy's ass. She was a personal friend of all the movers and shakers in politics and Hollywood. Deborah could also count on a senator's ear whenever Intacta Corporation needed some help in Washington. Frank Pearson may have been a powerful ally, but he didn't understand what it was to be a woman power player. Everyone had tsk-tsked over Martha Stewart, when all the men did the same thing behind boardroom doors. What the Plunge Protection Team was about to accomplish made insider trading trivial.

And she was here in the power circle, having come up from a sharecropper's shack in the Bottoms. At least that's what it said on her slightly exaggerated bio. Her grandmother on her mother's side had been a matriarch of the Creole elite of South Carolina, and no way in hell was she going to let "Little Debbie" get shackled to some illiterate boy and spend all her life scratching subsistence out of some cracker's overfarmed, leftover dirt. It was, after all, Deborah's mother's colossal error to marry just such an illiterate boy after all the advantages Deborah's Meemaw had given her daughter. Deborah's Meemaw always said you could never tell Deborah's mother anything, even after Deborah's father drank up the money from the crops, knocked around his wife, and then promptly sowed his seed in every woman he could get to with his beat-up, rusted pickup truck.

Deborah's Southern accent had carefully been schooled out of her by countless recitals of monologues delivered by Sidney Poitier and other Hollywood greats.

"Yo, Deborah," said Stewart Zwick as he loitered in the entrance to the stately Jekyll Island Resort and Club. He was one of those white guys that tried to pretend he was pretty fly. "You got enough clothes there, Queen of Sheba?"

Imbecile. She had only brought three suitcases plus her laptop, and the helicopter pilot hadn't even twitched when he looked at her belongings. No wonder Zwick was still single. Of course, she suspected he was closeted, one of the gay men who knew enough about fashion to match his socks and nothing else.

Deborah smiled with honey as she pulled her rain bonnet around her face. Thanks to the hurricane, Jekyll Island's small airport was shut down, so a whirlybird had made two trips to transport the group from the Jacksonville Airport. Secretary Pearson had taken Tedson, who kept his romance with Deborah discreet, and Zwick in that first flight. She'd gotten on civilly with Atkins and McDonald. McDonald in particular was a good old boy, but his demeanor was so earthy and outrageous that it quashed even a synapse of offense in her brain. He freely copped to the uncensored meaning of his company's innocuous name, LTL: "Ladies, Tits, and Legs," he said with a wink.

Deborah swooshed past Zwick. She desperately needed to freshen up before their two o'clock meeting in the notorious Federal Reserve Room. Only Frank would dare such an in-your-face move. The ignorant hotel staff and public at large would consider them just another group of business fat cats with pretensions of grandeur.

By Monday morning, she and her co-conspirators would be fatter, richer, and more powerful than Warren Buffett could ever dream. That maverick Bill Gates would be coming to them with his begging bowl outstretched. The Chinese and the Saudis could take a number, finally. Iraq would get rebuilt. She'd buy up the Hilton chain and ban that airhead heiress-cum-porn star from ever appearing in another magazine, on TV, on the Internet, anywhere in the public view. And she'd make her wear a burqa.

It wasn't all selfish or competitive. It would benefit the United States as well as the world. Another recession? Not in her damn lifetime. The future president would take care of everything, because he would owe her an enormous favor. This country would see some change. And she wouldn't forget the people from the bottoms, like her six sisters and brothers who'd never been out of the sticks, who still had dial-up Internet, for God's sake. None of them expected any better out of life. Her brother Leroy might have gotten to the NFL and made somewhat a success of his life, but that was a rarity. Deborah would swoop in and haul her abusive brother-in-law Johnnie to prison and resettle her sister Dymond and the kids on Park Avenue or in Malibu. Maybe the ocean would be better. They'd only seen the ocean on television.

Zara was the only other one who'd gotten out because, like Deborah, she hadn't had the spark smothered by her mother's martyred look and her father's brutality. Zara was a half-sister anyway, so she had more than her share of Meemaw's gumption, and Meemaw, too, had been an actress until she kicked the casting couch to the curb, so she liked Zara. Zara was probably turning to mush what few brains remained in the head of that two-bit real estate broker in Sacramento. Men. Even Pearson, happily married for probably the second time, gaped at Deborah and, most likely, rubbed his balls under the desk.

Deborah wasn't interested in their balls. She had Robert Tedson and her daughters, who would remember this day next year as the day their people took back the world. She'd already promised Robert she'd think about his marriage proposal and give him an answer when their takeover was a done deal. As men went, Tedson was a decent one, and he funded badly needed reforms, some of which she'd brought to his attention. Robert was the only man (other than James Earl Jones from a distance) who ever got past what he called her samurai armor. Her daughters genuinely adored him, so that sealed it. She had no real use for any other men beyond business.

"Kiss my Black ass, Stewart Zwick," she thought. "And whoever else stands in my way can get in line behind you."

LeBrach and Associates, August 3, 6:45 p.m.

Phil didn't need a gun to make the naked cocoa brunette knock the equally naked Paul to the floor. All he had to do was open the door to Paul's office. As his friend picked himself up off the floor, Phil noticed the beginnings of a spare tire, or at least tire treads, in Paul's abdominal region.

"Too many chicken wings, Paul? You're putting on the pounds." Phil was nonchalant as he stripped off his jacket and tossed it to the woman, who couldn't cover the wonder of nature that was her body fast enough.

"Fuck you, you FBI has-been," Paul spat.

"I wouldn't talk that way if I were you."

"Don't get all holier-than-Doug on me."

"You think you're a goddamn stud?" Phil caught a flash of Karina's black hair and knew she was savoring the thorough shellacking. "You think you're the goddamn Master of the Universe."

Paul smiled lazily. "I have the power."

"Not from where I sit."

"You sit on dick squat. No wife. Busted after all the years you spent treating the rest of us like we were beneath you."

Phil held up the memory stick. "Speaking of dick squat, this is about the size of—"

The woman interrupted. "You're wrong." At Phil's raised eyebrow, she said brashly, "Not you, and not about the…ah…anyway." She patted Phil's jacket and addressed Paul. "He's at least considerate. Bet he doesn't screw another woman while the secretary he's also screwing is sitting in the outer office." Scorn dripped from her mouth. "Debbie was right, boy. You were easy."

Phil stepped in momentarily, delaying Paul's further humiliation. "That'd be your sister, Deborah Crump, good friend of Aaron Cartwright, who tried to have my friend Doug murdered?"

The woman's lips opened in an ellipse. "How'd you know? We haven't been introduced. I'm Zara Crystal, by the way. You might have heard I was considered for the Diana Ross-esque role in *Dreamgirls*."

"You look just like your sister." Her name clicked in Phil's brain. "And my wife enjoyed that movie you did. She said it was unusually witty."

"Thank you. So we have a smart man who pays attention to his wife. Rare in my estimation."

"True." Phil waved the memory stick in front of Paul. "As for secretaries, yours did the screwing this time."

Paul, oblivious to his exposed body, leapt in primal rage at the door. "That bitch, that cunt, I'll..."

Phil and Zara formed a chain link and blocked Paul's path as Karina stole through the deserted office. At least Paul had calculated it would be deserted on a Friday with the exception of Karina. But he hadn't figured on the fury of a woman who'd been scorned, shot at, and scorned again.

"Karina's probably going to the FBI," Phil said, "and it's over for you, Paul. You probably don't even keep a gun around this place."

"I don't believe in guns," Paul squeaked. "That's your department, Philly."

"My gun could either rip your ass off or save it. You are goddamn lucky that, out of friendship, I'm giving you option number two. Because even if whoever is leading you around by the nose has all the power in the world, you'll go down anyway now that your former fans from your microlending scheme read the fine print on their agreements, and Milteer Capital called them harassing them to start paying off the debt sooner than they expected."

Paul knew enough about power structures to know that whoever was at the top of the Great Pyramid didn't care if he died of the Pharaoh's Curse. He also knew that good old honorable Phil was the only one who could possibly save him from moldering in a federal prison, or even worse, a state prison, and getting reamed up the behind in the shower for the rest of his life.

"What do you want me to do?" he said in surrender.

John Clarkson's Sacramento FBI Office, 7:30 p.m.

Carole Winkelman made John Clarkson consider yelling at her for the first time in all the years she'd worked there. He wanted to get home before his wife and his dog forgot what he looked like. It had been the worst goddamn week in his FBI career, especially with that story about Phil in the *Sacramento Bee*. He was very happy Phil survived, but he might have to kill him.

He hadn't gotten to his position without knowing when something smelled off, and Mike Clennahan reeked like a landfill. Phil had been stupid to enter into business with LeBrach, but he was still one of the best agents John Clarkson had ever commanded, and John decided to turn him loose. Too loose, apparently.

"What can I do for you, Carole?" He kept the friendly smile buttoned on.

"I know you want to throw something at me, but I'm hoping you'll hold off on your bullet pass," Carole said, referring to the pro football career he might have had until his then-sweetheart encouraged him to think about the recruiting offer the FBI made his senior year of college. His old man had been a twice-decorated Marine and a Detroit cop with no blemish, none, on his name. Serving the public was in John's blood.

"You got anything good to salvage this hellacious week, I'm listening."

"As if Phil protecting a corporate whistleblower wasn't enough good." Carole shook her head. "But if you need the cavalry to make sure the good guys win…" She stepped aside to allow a young Hispanic woman to enter. The woman plucked at a plastic bag she held, a bag that contained a memory stick. Under her arm she carried an expandable file. The file's fanned expansion nearly burst with all the documents.

"Assistant Special Agent in Charge John Clarkson," he said as he offered his hand. She shook it with a firmness that told him volumes about her backbone, however nervously her eyes danced.

"Philip Schultz's boss," she said.

"That's right."

She thrust the expandable folder and the memory stick into his hands with the confidence born of a righteous cause. "He made a mistake, but you have sacrificed a good man to politics, and I can prove it."

John didn't offer the usual cover-your-ass bullshit excuses. "And you are?"

"Karina Domingues. I work…worked…for Paul LeBrach, who is selling out his own country without knowing it, and would not care if he did." Unhesitating, she added, "I also slept with him, even though he's married."

She was probably gulled by a slick talker. John had had to bite his tongue in order to release Paul LeBrach, a little weasel if there ever was one. He flipped through the contents of the expandable file folder and whistled at them appreciatively. He turned to Carole. "I think we got enough to warrant bringing LeBrach in again."

"I would think so," Carole said with a prim nod that indicated she'd already conducted her own discovery of the evidence. "And to rehire Phil at double his salary."

"Where the hell is he, in the hospital?" John's question was directed at Karina.

"If I know Felipe," Karina said, blushing as John grinned at the Spanish rendering of the name, "he is convincing Paul to surrender." She stared at John directly. "You may want to question Paul's wife, who undoubtedly knows more than he would ever give her credit for."

"We'll do that. As soon as I call Quantico and Langley and yell at them. And I want that Clennahan in my office pronto, Carole. I want to know who in hell he's really working for, because I have the feeling we've all been manipulated, and someone's going to cry uncle before I'm done kicking ass."

Phil's voice stopped John in his reach for the phone. "I got that started for you, sir."

Karina and Carole whirled to see Phil march the actress Zara Crystal and a moderately repentant-looking Paul LeBrach into John's office. Paul shook his head at Karina, who gave him a sad, pitying smile that a woman in love gives to a man even though he's a complete S.O.B.

"Mr. LeBrach," John said, "I believe you are probably in a frame of mind to make a deal."

Paul's smile was weak. "That is what I'm best at."

Paul's Residence, American River, 8:00 p.m.

"Give the jerk credit," Patty LeBrach said to the two sexy male FBI agents and the moderately attractive token female colleague who spoke with a British accent, "he was anal about his private spaces." She giggled at her own unintended double entendre. "Oh sure, he said this safe held his *Playboy* collection, but I knew better."

She opened the safe with the memorized combination. She'd once been fairly good with numbers and could figure tips and bills in her head. She smiled at the two federal hunks and waved the woman toward the door. "Go ahead, search and seize all you want. The boys and I will be just fine here."

"I'm sure you will, Mrs. LeBrach." The woman spoke in a gracious, rip-your-throat-out polite way. "But Phil said that Paul was likely to keep his files away from you."

"Paul thought he kept a lot from me, but"—she played the maltreated wife to the hilt—"I always knew. I hoped he'd change someday. He could learn from Phil. That's a real man. Haven't you seen the papers? If his wife doesn't hop the next plane back here, someone else will snap him up, especially after that article."

Sacramento Street, Auburn, 9:30 p.m.

Carlotta faced Doug on the sidewalk of his grandmother's house. "I told them to hold back that article. As a favor to you and your friends. I was going to go with a brief story about a shootout in the tunnels, sources could not confirm, blah blah blah."

Doug folded his arms.

"For someone who's been walked on all his life until now, I'd expect a bit more sympathy." Carlotta stood straight and proud.

"What happened?" Doug felt obliged to give her the benefit of the doubt. He hadn't even told Webb Sutton about the article. Somehow in his ire, he'd held back that much.

"What always happens in the media. Remember the 2000 Election? Calling Florida for the Democratic candidate? Someone jumped the gun."

"That's a long way from—"

"It's a slippery slope that we tobogganed down decades ago, and we still have muck on our faces. If it bleeds, it leads. More gore, more sex, more disgrace. If two modern-day heroes can be called that."

A possibility lodged in Doug's mind. "Suppose instead of spiking your story someone got paid to run it so things would get a little messy? They nearly did for Phil. He just gave Paul the reduced-sentence immunity statue."

Carlotta looked as if she gave his outrageous theory more weight than it deserved. "You're a paranoiac, but I'm not surprised after what happened to Webb."

An even bigger gold nugget of possibility rattled around in his head. "Is he…what did they do?"

"You don't want to know, but physically he's fine. Headed to meet with your friend Martin."

Doug wasn't sure why she disarmed him after he had girded on his sword. The conviction in her compelling eyes, maybe. She'd saved his life twice without hesitation, and God knew she could be a target at any time.

"I'm a soft touch," he said aloud, and noticed they stood a heartbeat apart. She was a sexy woman in her flirty cream lace blouse that had hints of see-through without giving him a full visual body inspection. But he was most attracted to her toughness, intelligence, and determination, as well as the compassion she'd exhibited.

Carlotta smiled. "Thought so. I bet you cried when Bambi's mom died."

"I cried when Old Yeller got put down."

He believed her. He put his complete faith out into the world and tossed out his lonely sanity.

A high-beam flashlight trapped them both in its light. Doug froze until he heard Annette's voice and saw her warm-up-suited outline. "Doug? For heavens' sake, you can socialize inside the house. I'm not your mother."

Doug took the nonplussed Carlotta by the hand and walked her to his grandma's front porch. He made the introductions the way he had the time in high school when he'd brought Chrissie Bouchard to meet his family.

Annette took the full measure of Carlotta in about five seconds, then smiled. "It's chilly out for these old bones. Why don't you come in for tea, Carlotta? Lemon ginger? If you can stand to hang around with an old woman who likes the way you don't talk down to people in your writing. Not like those other reporters, who can barely string a verb and an object together."

"Lemon ginger tea would be lovely, Mrs. Nikolopoulos." Carlotta seemed to mean it.

"Call me Annette, dear. And I believe there are some cookies in the pantry, if Doug would look for them."

An hour later, Annette rose from her table as Carlotta and Doug made quick work of soaping and rinsing the teacups and the empty cookie plate. "I hope I'll see you again, Carlotta. Now, you young people don't need to end your evening,"—an old-fashioned cough—"and if you want to go out and have fun, you have my blessing. Just be safe. Don't worry me into the grave."

"Doug will be good," Carlotta said, straight-faced.

"That's what I'm afraid of." Annette radiated mischief as she waved herself out of the kitchen.

"What a grand woman," Carlotta said, and Doug felt her sincerity. "I hope she doesn't think we're, ah, doing anything improper…which I don't do on the second date anyway, and this isn't even a date."

"Okay. Carlotta, will you go out with me tonight?"

"I usually get a little more notice."

"That's what happens when you follow strange men to bars and save their asses."

Carlotta laughed. "So what are we doing?"

"Well, for starters…I'm not even attempting to be a good, upstanding citizen tonight."

"Oh, and what did you have in mind?"

Doug knew he had a keeper when he outlined his intentions and saw the conspiratorial look in her eyes.

Arthur Whinney and Associates, San Jose, August 4, 3:00 a.m.

"We could break in the old-fashioned way...we could hack into the database."

"Do you know how to do that?" Doug jerked a cliché black knit cap over his head.

Carlotta shook her head. "I bet they have security up the wazoo, encryption protocols, firewalls..."

"They change them every day. Made working there damned annoying. You were always an outsider."

Doug saw the sliver of smile in the Jetta's rearview mirror. "What?"

"Outsider. You always were." She meant it as a compliment. "You never belonged there."

"Yeah, that's how I know the side door alarm doesn't always go off when you open it."

"And you suggest we do that how?"

"Credit card. The lock's temperamental in sticky and muggy weather."

"Hallelujah for humidity."

They circled the block, parked the Jetta beside an apartment building, and made their way stealthily to the side door.

As Doug prophesied, the door gave way without protest or alarm. Carlotta shut it soundlessly behind them, and they found themselves in a darkened hallway that led to the elevators. Doug and Carlotta took the elevator to the Arthur Whinney offices.

"Not even a guard?" Carlotta moved through the ghostly cubicles, which reminded Doug of mausoleums, with the instincts of a born spy and safecracker. "Some guy dozing in the lobby behind his copy of *Field and Stream*?"

"There is one, and he does exactly that."

The credit card helped them gain entry to Richard Gauthier's office too. Apparently what Arthur Whinney did was sufficiently uninteresting to exclude the possibility that there ever might be a security breach, even in the manager's office.

Carlotta used a portable flashlight at low level to illuminate their search. Doug got them both sodas from Gauthier's private mini-fridge, and they drank as they reviewed the incriminating memos, notes, and statistics.

"Can we nail them with this?" Carlotta pored over some of Gauthier's convoluted language. "It all sounds shady, but I need a translator."

"That's why I'm here. Concentrate on anything from Cartwright, because he's the one who started me on this long, strange trip."

"Got it," Carlotta said as the taste of her low-calorie soda numbed the tiredness in her cells. Doug's breath smelled cloying. He felt the carpet under his hands like steel wool. He wanted to be out of here, especially when he read the e-mail printed out in front of his eyes. It was dated after they'd drummed him out of Arthur Whinney.

Dick—

Your boy is a problem. The squeaky link that can break the chain. We can handle the problem for you.

Aaron C.

The answering e-mail was much less mysterious:

Doug Boyd is a wimp and a nuisance. He may be harmless, but I don't want any questions haunting us. Go ahead. I'll check with the staff and send you his planned whereabouts. His luck will eventually run out.

Dick

Doug saw Carlotta's expression of tenderness as she took the memos from him. "Do we copy this stuff, or do we hope Gauthier doesn't come in on a Saturday?" She snapped pictures of the documents with her digital camera.

"Take them," Doug said. "Send them to Marty, post excerpts on his blog. After Monday, Arthur Whinney won't know whether to call a lawyer or cry for its mama."

"You hate this place."

"It's sucked the life out of people who worked here. It betrayed them. They deserve better."

Another high-beam flashlight seemed to blaze through the room, whiting out everything. Doug knew that this could not possibly be his grandma.

"Stop where you are," shouted the security guard from downstairs. "I'm calling the police."

Doug gathered up the documents, and he and Carlotta raced out of the office. Carlotta swapped her compact Nikon for an industrial-size camera. She popped the flash in the security guard's football-shaped face. "Smile, you just made the front page!"

While the security guard worked to react, Carlotta and Doug wore out their shoes on the way to the stairwell. The pounding beat of the guard's footsteps soon advanced on them. They reached the side door and were out into the night. They were free.

When Doug leaned over inside the Jetta to check that Carlotta was okay, he ended up with his lips on hers, and the exhilaration of the getaway made Carlotta return the kiss until the security guard's shouts spurred them to rush away. Bonnie and Clyde rode again.

CHAPTER 17

"Centralization of credit in the banks of the state, by means of a national bank with state capital and an exclusive monopoly."

—Fifth plank of the Communist Manifesto, 1848

Federal Reserve Room, August 4th, 1:00 p.m.

"Roll call vote," said Secretary of the Treasury Frank Pearson. "Deborah?"

"Agreed."

"Robert?"

"Agreed," said Robert Tedson, tapping his Montblanc pen on the long table. He, like Deborah, didn't bother to carry paraphernalia with the company logo.

"Stewart?"

"Agreed," Stewart Zwick said with a snigger as he brandished his Solid State Insurance mug. His snigger turned into a loud, tortured sniff.

"Perry?"

"Agreed, now let's get the Sam Hell out of here," mumbled Perry McDonald, jet-lagged and hung over. He stared into his LTL coffee mug. "I need to dunk my head in some ice and swallow a whole bottle of aspirin."

"Ian?"

"Agreed," the suave, Australian-born financier said, playing with a Lucite cube laser engraved with "Maroc International."

Secretary Frank Pearson continued the roll call vote for minutes that would never be taken. "Aaron?"

"Agreed," Aaron Cartwright said as he discreetly wiped the crust of sleepiness from his eyes. It was earlier in California, and he'd still be snoozing in his Frette sheets if he were home.

Richard Gauthier, invited to this meeting because of the "special services" Cartwright said he'd performed, slapped Cartwright awake and got a glare for his trouble. "Agreed," he said, confident.

"Very good," Pearson said. "So each of you, and the financial institutions you have partnered with or that you own, will get fifteen percent of the limited partnership. Mr. Gauthier, Arthur Whinney will receive ten percent for its services."

Richard Gauthier coughed convulsively as he did some mental tallying and realized he could retire to the Caribbean in a year if he felt like it.

"Paid by me, of course," Cartwright added, "as an increase in the retainer I pay Arthur Whinney."

Pearson curtailed whatever ass-kissing Gauthier might have been about to bestow on Cartwright. "In terms of the bad debts and devalued CDOs, according to the simple one-page document you signed…"

The unofficial members of the Plunge Protection Team Special Task Force (it excluded the chairman of the Fed, and the Chairman of the SEC—for obvious reasons) looked over the brief memos that would never be vetted by a legal department. Zwick sniffled again.

"We have to assume the onus of twenty percent of these bad debts?" Zwick sounded as if he'd just been told he'd bogied the eighteenth hole in the Masters.

"We've been handling these bad debts and washing them clean as a virgin whistle," Cartwright said. "The other major institutions can amply afford—"

Deborah interrupted. "And some of us have formed joint ventures. For example, Tedson Enterprises and Intacta."

Tedson had the perfect poker face despite the splotchy mole on his upper lip that he refused to have removed. "We have compatible interests."

Zwick and McDonald sniggered. Atkins shrugged.

A uniformed man from the hotel catering service entered the room and began serving lunch.

Pearson glossed over the innuendo in the men's eyes. "The CDOs our new partnership is buying will ensure our nation's prosperity in the long run. And clean the crap off your banks' balance sheets. Americans might all have to tighten their belts, although the people in this room won't feel the squeeze as much." Everyone smiled. "The value of the dollar will dip a bit according to our projections, but thanks to the global reach all of you enjoy, we may be able to manipulate the American dollar against the other major currencies, thus stimulating investment and economic growth. The Treasury will, by the next election, have much more latitude than it currently enjoys."

"Isn't all this going to come spiraling down?" Zwick's eyes darted about hyperactively. "Crashing, you know, like from a high?"

This time Deborah smirked, seeing the red rims of Zwick's eyes. Zwick inhaled loud and long and blew out red-flecked snot.

"The economics are sound," Pearson said.

"Stewart has a point," Deborah said. "When is the party over, and who pays the piper?"

"Us, and the public, much worse than you're pretending," McDonald said. "And if the public's hurtin', we'll be in agony. Besides, no way the president and the Congress will just let you rampage around like a rabid bull in an unlimited herd of fertile cows."

"Assuming the Treasury has that much Viagra," Deborah added.

Tedson smiled. "They will. A New Fair Deal can swing the election, sway the president, and sing the siren's song that the progressive politicians can only obey."

Perry peered at his lunch and scowled. "I said I wanted this pink, not alive." He beckoned the uniformed man over and thrust the platter of porterhouse steak into his serving hands. "Think you can manage to kill it first?"

The cell phone had recorded fifteen minutes of the meeting, but a good blogger always had a backup.

Martin Cheyne had borrowed a uniform from one of his newfound proletariat friends. The name tag read "Ashley Ellsworth, Ellerslie, Georgia." He could explain that Ashley, actually, could be a boy's or girl's name, but he hadn't yet thought how to explain the blouse.

Martin borrowed a Sony camcorder from one of the staff members, who had been recording the hurricane. When Martin returned with a fully pink but not conscious porterhouse steak, he cached the camera in the wine bucket that no one appeared to notice.

If these people were as arrogant as they smelled and sounded, he would have a gold mine to upload to the Internet. His laptop was out of commission, so he would have to wait to get to the mainland. The hurricane was moving down the coast. Already he could hear the scream of the winds decrease to a hoarse shriek. He remained outside the Federal Reserve Room listening to the casual discussion of the pillage and plunder of the nation by modern-day robber barons. They were insulated from the hurricane, but not from karma.

He would unleash the truth on the world. The water was still high, so he might have trouble leaving the island. But there was bound to be a computer with high-speed Internet access in someone's office that he could sneak into after the meeting had concluded. It would be quite a large video file…it could be on YouTube minutes after he posted it.

It would demolish faith in the government…what little faith strove to survive in the American consciousness.

Martin experienced a momentary crisis of conscience. So far, he had acted with absolute apostolic faith; he had believed that evil had to be exposed, no matter the cost. Once, he had defined Paul as evil. Now, outside of the comfort moral zone of academia, he wondered for just a moment if he were doing the right thing.

A powerful bear hug took over from indecision and held Martin captive. Leeson, his assailant from the altercation upstairs, hissed, "I'm going to choke the living shit out of you, and there's not a goddamn thing you can do about it."

A shotgun cracked, and a shell whizzed through the corridor outside the Federal Reserve Room. Martin heard the members of the PPT shout and shriek in terror.

Webb Sutton drawled from behind Martin and his assailant, "Oops. It's been years since I shot one of these. I'm usually used to putting holes in people with a keystroke. Still, old-fashioned ways work amazingly well. Except when I'm trying to figure them out. I might hit a few vital organs if I can't work the trigger properly. I think the safety's off."

The doors to the Federal Reserve Room flew open. Martin heard them, since the assailant had let his hold slacken and Martin could concentrate on sensory input from the outside world.

Secretary Pearson sounded scandalized. "Holding a waiter hostage? My God, someone contact hotel security."

"No need," Webb said. Martin heard the cock of the hammer. "I've got everything handled. And I'm so very grateful that happenstance has brought us face-to-face, Mr. Secretary, Mr. Cartwright. Would you care to comment on the conspiracy that's been hittin' the headlines?"

Leeson, evidently sensing he was about to be thrown under the bus—the federal prison bus—backed away from Martin and shouted, "Yeah, I'd like to comment. I was hired by Bull-Spears to take care of him." Aaron Cartwright frowned at Leeson.

Martin's vision had fuzzed out, but now it coalesced, and he saw Webb lower the shotgun. Webb approached Leeson and nodded at the hula girl stamped on his T-shirt. "Nice shirt."

"Eh, thanks."

"Whacking people for Bull-Spears obviously pays well."

"This man is not in my employ," Aaron Cartwright said.

Martin took the opportunity to zig and zag past the PPT members, who just stood as if they were spectators at a mixed martial arts event who fervently hoped not to get brain matter splattered on them. He rushed into the Federal Reserve Room, snatched the camcorder, and stopped the recording. His cell phone rang. He answered, jubilant at the signal.

"Martin, you're international news," Phil shouted.

Doug and a female voice cheered in the background.

"What, because of the hurricane?" Martin felt vigor return to his facial muscles. He'd never been so exhausted in his life.

"No, because assuming you've got the proof…" Doug began, with a snappy new confidence. "You can get it to your blog and Carlotta."

"Webb might not be happy to be undercut," Martin said as he walked out of the Federal Reserve Room with the phone and camcorder raised above his head like war trophies.

"Undercut out of what, a story?" Webb spoke, since the high-powered executives and the high-ranking Cabinet member seemed to have lost their collective persuasive powers. "My darling Carlotta would never do that."

"We're collaborating, Webb," Carlotta announced on the speakerphone that Martin had just activated.

"The hurricane's moving on, and it's headed inland to D.C.," Martin said, pumping his fist in the air. He switched on the camcorder and let fifty seconds of the PPT meeting play.

By now, everyone except Webb and Martin looked as if they were staring into their own open graves.

Doug's voice expanded through the corridor. "I assume that my friends and I have life insurance against retaliation from the FBI or hired corporate assassins?"

"Doug, you have no idea what you're playing with," Richard Gauthier said, his face inhumanly blue. "Why couldn't you have left well enough alone?"

"Is that a yes?" Phil's voice was strong as a redwood. "Because if it isn't, the Sacramento FBI may be breaking into your summer homes."

"You know what will happen when the public sees Marty's video," Webb said to the exposed cabal. "I hope one of you has Bill Clinton on speed dial. Now that man knows how to spin with charm. With the possible exception of Miz Crump, I don't think any of you have it. An' not everyone wants to divide the flag up and own a piece of it, an equal piece, an' be nannied the rest of our lives like Mr. Tedson would have us do. In fact, people all over the world are demandin' back their contributions to your cult."

"What do you want?" Secretary Pearson apparently knew he was sinking.

"The Federal Reserve annihilated and reformed," Martin said. "The PPT dissolved. Starting with your resignation, Mr. Secretary. I'm sure the president had no idea you were so dirty."

"And it's time for Bull-Spears to close its accounts, at least the fraudulent ones, and let investors roll them over into honest firms," Doug added. "Arthur Whinney can continue, provided all the management leaves."

"It's either that or complete disgrace and a scandal that will rip the country apart," Martin said. "And you all will be much, much worse off than you are now."

"Anything else?" The secretary asked with newfound confidence as he looked past Webb and Martin into the hallway beyond.

"Ye—" Martin stopped as four armed secret service officers rushed into the room. One tackled Webb, ripped the shotgun from his hands, and pinned him on the floor. The others stood on either side of Martin, who was helpless to defend himself.

"I think you two are missing a little something here." The secretary started circling the room and spoke casually. "You see, what you have just interrupted was official government business. There is nothing sneaky or underhanded here. This committee was formed by Executive Order. To provide financial stability to the markets." He paused to stare into Martin's eyes as he ripped the video camera from his hands and passed it to a secret service agent.

"What do you think would happen to the financial markets if we did not intervene? Banks would fail. Investors would lose everything. Capital markets would tumble, and the American way of life, the core of capitalism as we know it, would cease to exist."

Martin stared down at the floor, looking almost ashamed. "Not true," he said, quietly, and without much confidence. "America operated without a central bank for decades, mainly because the first two banks failed. Andrew Jackson stopped—"

"Would you shut up for just one minute? I don't think you are in a position to be interrupting, do you?" Pearson said through gritted teeth as the secret service agents tightened their grip on Martin.

"This isn't a scandal, there is no story here. This committee can, and will, do what it was assigned to do. You," Pearson shouted at Webb, "are a child pornographer. About to be fired, and, maybe, depending on your actions tomorrow, imprisoned. If you want to write your story, go ahead. We'll see what the public thinks of your credibility when we are done with you, if your story gets published at all. Oh, you may know Mr. Zwick?" He pointed at Zwick, who jumped and rubbed his nose furiously. "One of his holding companies owns your newspaper."

"And you?" He turned back to Martin. "You must be the blogger? The small-time untenured teaching assistant?"

"Instructor," Martin mumbled in response.

"You can write whatever you want. The five people who read your blog probably already think you are a nut job." Pearson began speaking faster.

"Mr. Schultz, ex-FBI, left in disgrace. Broke and alone, head of the Mortgage Fraud Task Force while the whole time engaging in mortgage fraud." Phil was silent on the other end of the speakerphone.

"And, Mr. Boyd, I've been updated on you. I've been told you are a church mouse. I know you will scurry off and hide." Pearson stopped circling. "Gentlemen," he said, addressing the secret service agents, "let them go. Give them a lift back to the airport, would you. We have a meeting to conclude here."

The dark-suited agents hustled Martin and Webb toward the door. Then Phil's voice came onto the speakerphone.

"Ms. Crump, you want to keep on screwing Mr. Tedson and pretending it's love, honey, but he only loves his 'progressive paradise.'"

"And don't gasp in outrage," Carlotta added. "Your little love nest on Catalina Island isn't a secret."

"The FBI file says you two are an item," Phil added.

"Abusing your powers again," Secretary Pearson said.

"I won't even touch that one, but just so you know, Ms. Crump, Mr. Tedson is screwing at least three other women, including your sister Zara. I've just put some names and photographs onto a PDF file and sent it to your office," Phil said. Martin could see the rage and betrayal in her face.

"Don't act surprised. Paul LeBrach and Zara Crystal are turning state's evidence."

Deborah glowered. "That bitch."

"And Ian—excuse me, Mr. Atkins." It was Carlotta's voice this time. "Remember the summer party you had in Dubai last year? The one hosted by your new twenty-two-year-old bride?" Ian sat up, alert. "Well,

Mr. Zwick and your wife, uh, let's just say 'hit it off.' I guess she wasn't too thrilled with the terms of her prenup." Zwick jumped again and shouted something undeterminable, shooting saliva everywhere.

Pearson ran for the phone and shut if off before any other accusations could be made. Martin called from the end of the hallway, "Have a good meeting!"

Martin knew they had lost some of their leverage, but their story would reach the far corners of the Internet. Someone would listen. And Martin had left behind a room of narcissists who, common interest or not, were above all competitors. The seeds of mistrust planted would cause them to tear each other apart. He could already hear angry bickering as the group sequestered themselves back in the room. Doug had plenty of evidence on Bull-Spears; Paul and Zara gave them enough to expose Deborah Crump's dealings through Intacta. And from the screams he could hear coming from the boardroom, he had no doubt that Crump would make Tedson pay a dear price for his betrayal. And, if he were a gambling man, he would bet that Atkins and Zwick would spend the rest of their lives engaged in fanatical and caustic competition with each other.

Webb, Martin, and two federal agents walked out the door of the hotel. Webb leaned towards Martin. "A man can be destroyed but not defeated," he whispered softly, quoting Hemingway's *The Old Man and the Sea*. "I can deal with the chaos at the *Post*, and with or without the video, this story is going to make Vesuvius look like a firecracker." The hurricane clouds were clearing outside. The sun emerged, and Martin waved hello. For once, a smile reigned in his heart, and he toasted it with an unclaimed glass of champagne on his way out the door.

PolitiChic
Is ANYONE reading Martin Cheyne?
August 4, 12:00 p.m.
By CheyneChick

The dude is running for his life from Fed hit men acting in a conspiracy that would shame Michael Moore. Mikey, on your best day of *TV Nation,* you couldn't expose this (or fabricate it, depending on who you believe).

It's like the plot of a Hollywood movie. And no one in the sane world, let alone the MSM, would ever deign to touch it, because Martin Cheyne is just a wacko.

Except if you read Webb Sutton from the *Washington Post* (I'm still not changing my name to WebbChick), or Carlotta McGinnis from the *Sacramento Bee,* of all places, or pretty much anyone from talk radio.

We need an immediate investigation into this. It's time for the Dems and the GOP to pull together and save the country. Starting with firing Secretary Pearson and bringing Bull-Spears before a Senate subcommittee. Then Corporate America can finally tremble.

"Is ANYONE reading Martin Cheyne?"
1200 Comments

CanadaOrBust, 12:34 p.m.

Our good old Canadian socialism never allows such a thing to happen. Our loonies aren't that valuable, eh?

Oh wait, the Canadian Parliament is debating a bill to relax the restrictions on foreign investments. It seems Tedson Enterprises has gotten a few of us 'Nucks out of the clutches of U.S. Homeland Insecurity.

Never mind. At least Molson and the Maple Leafs never let you down.

RockinInTheUSA, 12:36 p.m.

Those who are immediately screaming "bad, bad corporations" forget that it was WE THE PEOPLE who sought to make a quick buck by flipping real estate. (CheyneChick, shame on you for beating the endless hollow drum about Big Bad Business).

Martin Cheyne entertains me, but let's see some evidence here of wrongdoing. Mr. Cheyne should remember that without those evil, evil corporations, there would not be Starbucks on the campuses, no educational technology grants, no food courts... zip.

And I used to live in Canada. Health care sucks, even if your doctors are at least politer than ours. Oh, and I can get cheap prescriptions.

Warren C., 12:45 p.m.

I like Canada. Nicer, more civilized.

As for the proof of wrongdoing... we haven't gotten anything yet on Secretary Not-So-Frank Pearson, but someone just uploaded the dirt on Tedson Enterprises' so-called "progressive" agenda. This guy personally funds the most vicious activist groups, the ones that want to turn us all into those comatose humans in **The Matrix**. They can feed off us forever. Say bye-bye to your money AND your life AND your freedom. The worst part, folks, is that you gave it away. As we say in New Hampshire, "Live free or die!"

BBC World News
July 5th, 2007
American Greed and American Greatness

Across the pond in America, corporations and politicians have cooperated...to make themselves richer. Yet just like the colonists who revolted against King George III, a small, scrappy group of Yankees has tossed the tea into the harbour, digital-style...

CNN, Fox News, BBC World News, CNN Headline News, and other news channels weighed in on the controversy sparked by Martin's blog.

Secretary Pearson's office, of course, was unavailable for comment. A spokeswoman for Bull-Spears called the story "absurd," though sources reported the board of directors had already begun a search for a replacement for longtime Chairman and CEO Aaron Cartwright. Arthur Whinney and Associates stated that they were fully cooperating with the FBI and SEC investigation and delivered a statement about a "disgruntled ex-employee."

This media furor did not reach the Jekyll Island Resort and Club, since the hurricane kept the staff occupied. Some of the phone lines were down. The tycoons and financial magnates sequestered themselves in the Federal Reserve Room. Their cell phones worked, but by mutual agreement, each member of the PPT had turned off anything that might buzz, beep, play "Ode to Joy," or otherwise disrupt the proceedings.

EPILOGUE

NBS.com
Government Watch
July 3rd, 2008, 3:30 p.m. PST
by Martin Cheyne, PhD

Happy Fourth of July!

The Fed reform is taking longer than it should. However, the implosion of the fraud-racked Big-4 accounting firm Arthur Whinney and the collapse in the financial sector fueled by massive cross-short-selling (see September blog on the strange occurrences at the trading desks of the big investment banks where they engaged in massive short-selling of each other) has brought more public scrutiny to the goings on in this area.

The new Treasury secretary, William LeShell, seems to have a firm hand on the tiller of the Treasury, but reforming the Fed into a more comprehensive, responsive, and flexible fiscal solution will take years. So, our grandchildren will benefit. The major Democratic and Republican nominees have each outlined their own plans to reduce our national debt and ensure a healthy money supply. Even the chairman of the Federal Reserve has bowed to the will of the free markets.

This blogger was quite a conspiracy theorist before he became an on-air personality and commentator for NBS. However, Government Watch simply reports the facts. The bursting of the bubble has left us all in dire straits, but under new leadership, Intacta Corporation, LTL, and the rest of the major financial sector seem to be coming back off their twenty-year lows after the collapse of Wall Street titan Bull-Spears.

On a personal note, in response to all the comments who asked what my three college friends are doing now, they are all living the American Dream, or their own particular pockets of it. May you do the same.

I, for one, will continue to fight for what is right and good for America. I look forward to unleashing my new series of columns on the greatest threat we freemen face…The Bilderberg Group.

Barnes Farm, Outside of Blacksburg, Virginia, July 3, 6:30 p.m.

Helen, Megan, and Jason had settled around the dinner table with Helen's parents, Duncan and Barbara. Phil slapped an evening mosquito away and checked the PVC irrigation system in the strawberry fields. The scent of strawberries was innocent yet seductive. He felt like popping one in his mouth, but he figured he'd eat a real dinner. His father-in-law teased him about being a new man of the land, when Phil wasn't giving crime seminars on request at Quantico. His old contacts at the FBI were able to clear Webb of any wrongdoing related to the images on his computer. Phil had walked away from his house and filed bankruptcy. He could start clean. He would no longer be able to borrow money, but that was okay; he was determined never to do that again anyway. He'd sent money to and written recommendations for Karina and Paul's other ex-employees. He also consulted Paul's former microlending victims about their businesses. Will Thunder hadn't gotten around to fudging Paul's books, and he decided to make himself a star the old-fashioned way: on *American Idol.* He had even survived Simon Cowell's famous insults.

Helen shouted from the farmhouse that had stood proud and tall and sensibly gray since the 1830s, "Phil, Martin's being interviewed on NBS."

Phil raced to the house, not to watch Martin (Helen probably TiVoed the segment), but to embrace and kiss his wife. Helen had a smudge of mustard on her cheek, and he thought she looked perfect. Green paint from one of Jason's art projects adorned the other cheek.

"Your friends are famous," she said.

"Uh huh."

"And you're happy."

"Mm-hm."

"Even though Paul's in prison."

"Mm-hm."

"You're not even listening to me. Don't you feel sorry for Paul in prison, even with everything?"

"Sure I do." Phil kissed her. "He didn't hit the lottery like I did."

"And he isn't a hero like you." She kissed him back, and it tasted of new beginnings.

Visiting Area, Herlong Federal Corrections Institution, Herlong, California, July 3, 3:00 p.m.

Paul LeBrach looked better than Doug expected, considering that Paul hadn't gotten the sweetheart plea bargain and reduced sentence that the FBI had offered in exchange for his testimony. Martin, Doug, and Phil quashed that with their good-guy version of blackmail. Instead, the federal judge had sentenced him to two years and a $5,000 fine. He was facing state charges as well.

Paul may have been incarcerated and his broker's license taken away, but he made a fortune selling his story as a criminal to the right magazine. Hollywood was sniffing around the tale that Paul spun: how an average kid grew up to sell his soul and then redeem it. A bit of schadenfreude and a morality play, the producers said. Paul called it Enron Lite.

Doug wished he had come earlier in the day. His scheduled visit was nearly over. He'd indulged in his old habits of working out of necessity, and he needed to finish a tax return for the California Club. He was done working until July 5, and he only had this duty of friendship to attend to before he could go home. He had driven through the same Sierra Nevada scenery Paul had enjoyed last summer, and he knew that Paul could hardly be ignorant of the irony.

Across the iron table, Paul and Doug tried to think of things to say to each other.

"I haven't found God," Paul said. "I hate it when people say that shit. People in here, I mean."

"You're honest."

"For once in my life. That's what Patty says."

Doug gave Patty credit. She actually stuck by Paul, especially now that he needed her. She'd had her revenge, and the years of toxins had evaporated from her heart. She was now the forgiving wife who would play Tammy Wynette, or a disgraced politician's helpmeet.

"And you, Doug?" Paul, slick as a bird, shook off what he often called a "sensitive Lifetime TV moment." "Everything good out in the boonies? In the hometown? You and Phil. And Marty…" For once, Paul seemed to think better of his usual cheerful putdowns.

"Everything's good, Paul. I even managed to buy fireworks." Doug smiled and got up to leave.

He didn't hug Paul, even though he was sure that after a year in Fed custody with another year to go, unless he got paroled for good behavior, Paul missed the comfort of his friends and even his parents, who still supported him.

Doug and Paul made light, easy good-byes, and then Doug walked out of the federal penitentiary. He promised to return next week, and to testify on Paul's behalf at the parole hearing.

Forgiveness felt good.

Sacramento Street, Auburn, California, 6:00 p.m.

The house six doors down from Annette Nikolopoulos's residence echoed with Natalie Merchant's voice.

Carlotta spoke above the music. "Don't tell me you were at the office all that time."

Doug took in the sight of her as she sat in the now updated living room and finished her latest article on her laptop. She saved the document and abandoned her laptop on the antique coffee table they'd bought two months ago at an estate sale. Carlotta shifted her "pear belly," as she called her pregnant body, so that her foot wouldn't cramp, and she walked over to hug her husband.

"You weren't at work all that time." She leaned back and flirted with her eyes. "Were you?"

Doug smiled and kissed her. "I don't need to chase success outside anymore. It's all right here."

"Happy Independence Day, Doug."

AUTHOR'S NOTE

The housing bubble and the resulting credit crunch are issues that expose the very core of modern-day thinking. Both issues are the result of recklessness, greed, ignorance, and fraud all founded in the belief that wealth can be created by a clever method or scheme, and not by ingenuity, hard work, patience, and thrift.

It is easy to point the finger at the businesses and institutions that were directly involved: the Wall Street firms and the debt-rating agencies that packaged these very low-quality securities and sold them off as though they were high-quality securities; the banks that originally lent the money with virtually no diligence; the mortgage brokers that persuaded borrowers to overstate or misstate their financial resources; the real estate industry that blinded itself to the reality of the bubble as it formed; and the federal government for artificially keeping interest rates low and fueling the fire to keep the economy growing. These are the culprits pointed to in the media every day, and they certainly all deserve their share of the blame. But the true culprits are us, "We the People." We the people buy, using credit, things we cannot truly afford. We the people do this because we the people care more about having the trappings of success than we do about earning the trappings of success. We the people are tragically and unswervingly moving away from a culture that values substance and toward a culture that values style at any cost. We the people don't care how we get "stuff"...we only care that we get it. The condescending terms "rat race" and "wage-slave" have been used to describe someone who works for a living so many times by people I know personally, even by close relatives, I knew our economy, and possibly our society, was in serious trouble. Further, I knew a collapse was imminent.

I had my own Joseph Kennedy moment, when I realized people of modest means all around me had decided that they were entitled, for no reason other than ignorance and arrogance, to never have to work again. Even as the bubble pops and the signs of economic decline are all around, I had a college student ask me where to invest the thousand dollars she had saved so that she could avoid having to enter the "rat race." I believe the tragic sentiment has become ubiquitous.

The main purpose of writing this book was to entertain, to expose and explain some of the silliness that has taken place and maybe even laugh about it. But secondarily, I hope it piques some interest in the concepts of money creation as it applies to taxation—specifically the idea that inflation is, in fact, a tax on the public; the Federal Reserve and what purpose it truly serves in our society today; and the dangers of having big business and big government too closely aligned.

Finally, I encourage everyone to take more of an interest in both their own finances and the financial world around them. There are clear methods for valuing assets, including real estate, and we *can* identify when a bubble is being created. The warning sirens had been going for at least three years before the real estate bubble burst, but speculation and mob mentality took over, especially as our "trusted" professionals continued to tout the path that would make them the most money in the least time. The lessons from the bursting of the stock-market bubble just a few years ago were not learned. We are swarmed with advisors, from financial planners to stock brokers to real estate agents. All are there to make a living, and some are not knowledgeable or experienced in economics, business valuation, or complex financial issues, and some are simply unscrupulous. The collapse of this bubble has just started and will likely take years to fully deflate, but it has already caused economic damage that will last for years. We have only just now begun to feel the effects. The last line of defense and ultimate responsibility for your life and financial well being lies with you, and I advise you to act prudently and cautiously.

Thank you for reading, and I hope you enjoyed it.